Edgar & Ellen

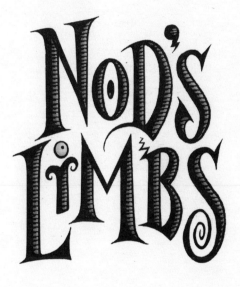

NOD'S LIMBS

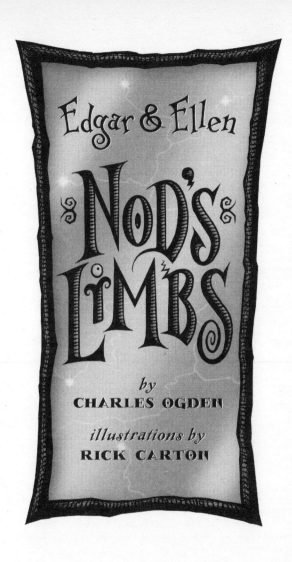

Edgar & Ellen

NOD'S LIMBS

by
CHARLES OGDEN

illustrations by
RICK CARTON

Simon and Schuster, London

Watch out for Edgar & Ellen in:

Rare Beasts
Tourist Trap
Under Town
Pet's Revenge
High Wire

First published in Great Britain by Simon & Schuster UK Ltd, 2006
A CBS company

Design by Star Farm Productions LLC
Text and illustrations copyright © by Star Farm Productions LLC, 2006

1 3 5 7 9 10 8 6 4 2

Simon & Schuster UK Ltd
Africa House
64–78 Kingsway
London WC2B 6AH

A CIP catalogue record for this book is available from the British Library

ISBN-10: 0 689 87543 6
ISBN-13: 9 780 6898 7543 4

Printed and bound in Great Britain by
The Bath Press

WWW.EDGARANDELLEN.COM

HERE IS MY DEDICATION—

I, Charles Ogden,
being of sound mind and body,
bequeath this book to my
personal inspirations for mischief:

To *Myron,* Imp the First,
I leave my last pack of poison,
and the unanswerable question
"For what is art, if not chaos?"

To *Uncle Johnny,*
I leave fish that can come out and play.

To *Cairo, Bain,* and *Van,* my Knights of the Brush,
I leave *Still Life with Mouldy Cabbage and Eggs* and
the last gallon of Black Plague.

To *Jack, Liam,* and *Katy,*
I leave Granddad's wooden teeth and
the heirloom thimbles.

Finally, to everyone with and without
words of encouragement along the way,
I leave this sentimental reflection:
None of it could have been done without you.

—CHARLES

WHO KNOWS WHAT MIGHT APPEAR?

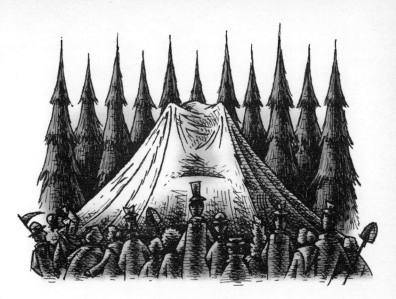

Nod's Lands

For the most part, Nod's Lands was a lovely place to live. It wasn't a big town, but it wasn't small either. It was, quite simply, an upstanding community of charming cottages and cheerful settlers, most of whom lived uneventful lives, making candles in the town's Waxworks.

Nestled as it was amid the lush Black Tree Forest and upon the banks of the Running River, Nod's Lands provided a comfortable, quiet place for its citizens to prosper. The days usually skipped along in a comforting sameness. But on this particular day, the

1

town was atwitter. Augustus Nod, the odd, reclusive man who had founded the town many years earlier, had written a proclamation:

All citizens are advised that a most exquisite and splendorous sight shall be revealed henceforth in the park of our founder, this May 8, 1792, at 3 o'clock in the afternoon.

All who come will be enthralled.

The citizens rarely saw the father of their town. He lived on the outskirts in a tall, grey house topped by a cupola ringed with spikes. Not even the postman dared approach the mansion.

"Do you suppose he'll be here?" whispered the baker Opal Buffington. She and the rest of the townspeople waited patiently in Founder's Park before a twenty-foot-tall object covered by a tarp.

"Can't be sure, can we?" replied Millard Matterhorn, the managerial manager for the Waxworks. "He hardly shows his face at the 'Works anymore."

At the edge of the park, Nod's Lands' corpulent

mayor, Thaddeus Knightleigh, paced, huffing and grousing.

"I can't *believe* Nod held this ridiculous event without consulting me. I'm only *mayor of the town. I* should know what's under that tarp!"

"Quite, sir," said his footman, Robbins.

"*I* build the landmarks around here," said the mayor. "The clock tower, Town Hall . . . not *one* covered bridge, but *seven*! These stately public works fill the populace with awe! And whose idea was it to paint cheery messages on the bridges?"

"Yours," said Robbins.

"Of course! I give daily inspiration to my citizens. All Nod has given us is his name, and that is quite *enough*."

"Right as ever, sir."

Gonggg. Gonggg. Gonggg.

The crowd's murmurings ceased as the clock tower struck three. As the last gong faded into the warm afternoon, Thaddeus shifted his feet uneasily.

"Where is he?" the mayor whispered to himself.

A tall figure stepped from behind the tarped object. Faces fell when the townspeople saw that it was not the mysterious Augustus, but instead Mr Hatfield Herringbottle, Esquire.

3

The gentleman cleared his throat.

"Good citizens of Nod's Lands! Our illustrious forefather was saddened that he could not join us today, but he has asked me, as his legal counsel, to host in his place the unveiling of a glorious monument for the eternal enjoyment of our town. Mr Smithy, if you please."

Town builder Silas Smithy came forward, and, with a *whoosh,* removed the tarp.

The crowd gasped. There loomed a shining statue of Augustus Nod, seated on an imposing throne – and it appeared to be made of pure gold.

The dour-faced monolith seemed the exact likeness of the man they knew, down to the spider-shaped birthmark above his left eyebrow. But something else was unmistakably amiss. *He had no limbs.* No arms. No legs. No ringed fingers or buckled shoes.

"Silas! Where are the limbs?" demanded Hatfield Herringbottle.

"I know not, Mr Herringbottle," said Silas Smithy, equally shocked. "Mr Nod just had me cast the pieces – I didn't put the thing together. But as sure as you were born, I made arms and legs for that statue. A thief must have *stolen* the golden limbs!"

"Mr Mayor," said Hatfield Herringbottle, "shall we form a search party?"

Thaddeus Knightleigh sized up the limbless statue and stifled a laugh. "Oh, I rather like it this way, don't you?"

But when he saw the concerned faces of his citizens, the mayor assumed a more serious expression. "Oh, very well. We shall fan out and search for these arms and legs ourselves. Perhaps they've only been misplaced." Thaddeus couldn't suppress a chuckle. "Hurry though! Before people start to call us Nod's *Limbs*."

1. Woe and Despair

"*Nod's bods!*" cried Edgar, throwing down his shovel. "We can't dig all this ourselves. We'll never reach the balm spring!"

His twin sister, Ellen, who had long since tossed her shovel aside, was clawing the dirt with her bare hands.

"We must . . . keep digging . . . or Pet . . . dies."

Edgar turned to look at the one-eyed hairball sitting on a nearby pile of rock. A hazy film coated its yellow eye, and its hair, though greasy and tangled as ever, now showed strands of grey. A poisonous bite from Ellen's carnivorous plant, Morella, and the subsequent destruction of the remaining balm (the mysterious, earthy goop Pet needed to survive) had left the creature hovering near death. The only cure lay in finding the source of the balm, which was beneath layers and layers of dirt.

"Sorry, Pet," said Edgar, plopping down beside the ailing creature. "This is all our fault."

Ellen glanced back at her brother. "We can't quit," she muttered. "We never quit."

But in the faint light of the lantern, Ellen could see the torn fingernails, scrapes, and blisters that told of their vain effort so far: Despite hours of digging, the twins had managed only a six-foot deep hole. Before the cave-in, the tunnel had dropped at least thirty feet.

"Bite your tongue, Sister." Edgar sighed. "No quitting. Just better planning."

"Planning?"

"Yes!" Edgar sat up a little. "Time to take advantage of our strategic strengths."

Ellen faced her brother and crossed her arms. "Shall we recap our *strategic strengths,* Brother? Hmm. Let's see. First, we plotted to collapse the Knightlorian Hotel and ended up securing its eternal purple existence."

"A minor setback."

"Then, we blew up Augustus Nod's laboratory and burned his journal to ashes."

"Words, words, words."

"And if memory serves," Ellen remarked, pointing to the mountain of dirt, "*I* caused this little cave-in."

"Now, Ellen, the ground was already unstable when you stomped your foot."

"And then when that crazy circus blew into town," Ellen continued, leaning into her sibling, "*you* got us suckered out of our own house!"

"It was a lousy sham," growled Edgar.

"Oh! Let's don't forget that we betrayed Heimertz and Dahlia and they've been imprisoned in a gorilla cage for life!"

The ever-smiling Ronan Heimertz, the former caretaker of the twins' house and grounds, had lived in a shed in the backyard. For years he had been the only person the twins feared, and they were relieved when his circus family had carted him and his girlfriend away on charges of attempted murder. Edgar and Ellen had discovered too late that Heimertz was innocent – the one person protecting both them and Pet.

At the mention of their loyal groundskeeper, Pet slipped off its perch and slunk dolefully towards the twins.

"We've spent years scheming against that vile Stephanie Knightleigh and her crooked family . . . and in the end, *they're* going to get the last laugh!"

Edgar stood up and took a deep breath. "So we regroup. We go back up to our house—"

"*Their* house, Edgar," Ellen interrupted. "The Knightleighs own it, remember? And by this time tomorrow, Eugenia Smithy and her crew will be swinging a wrecking ball at it. That's where our *strengths* have got us." Ellen plopped down on a pile of earth and scowled. Pet snuggled against her, and Ellen reached down to stroke its thinning hair. She winced as a few strands fell away but didn't say anything.

Edgar stared for a long moment at the rubble. Then he narrowed his eyes and cracked his knuckles.

"Don't say it, Brother. Don't you dare . . ."

"I have a plan, Sister."

"I knew you were going to say that."

2. Hugs and Kisses

"Operation: Jail Bail, ready for delivery."

Ellen sat at the large writing desk in the second-floor map room, placing a stamp on the letter she had just written.

"A rather clever scheme on such short notice," said Edgar. Out of pure habit, he tossed Pet in the

10

air, then remembered too late the patient's delicate state. He caught the creature as gingerly as he could. "Heh, sorry there, Pet. But this two-pronged plan will give us time and muscle, the two things we need to unearth the balm spring and get you healthy."

Pet gamely waved a few hairs in encouragement, but then winced as if it had strained something.

Ellen read her letter aloud to Edgar:

> *Dear Heimertz (Ronan, that is — not any of you other Heimertzes who may be reading this),*
>
> *Sorry we got you in trouble with your family — especially the part when they chained you up and threw you in the cage. We thought you'd like to know that Edgar and I have a new home improvement project, and we are really digging into it with gusto. Also the Knightleighs are coming over soon for a big party, and I bet they're really going to bring the house down. Well, we hope your restraints aren't too tight. You sure know how to pick them, don't you?*
>
> *Hugs and kisses,*
> *Ellen*

"Hugs and kisses?" Edgar sneered. *"Blech."*

"It has to sound natural," said Ellen. "If someone is screening his mail, they can't suspect anything."

Pet nodded its eyeball.

"If you say so," said Edgar with a shrug, then gave one of the many map-room globes a spin. "So how do we send mail to a travelling circus?"

"They were heading west when they left town, right?" said Ellen. She consulted a tattered map on the wall marked NOD'S LANDS AND ENVIRONS, 1799. "Here's Nod's Limbs . . . and the next town west is . . . hmm."

On the outside of the envelope, she wrote:

> *To Ronan Heimertz*
> *In custody of the Heimertz Family Circus*
> *Greater Peaseblossom, or other points west*
> *(Please forward. Don't make us come after you.)*

As Ellen heated a glob of red wax to seal the envelope, Edgar produced a metal sliver no thicker than a pine needle from his satchel: a lock pick, his favourite escapist's tool. He placed it on the envelope, and Ellen dripped the wax onto it. She then stamped the wax with a seal, thus securing the little pick to the letter even while concealing it.

"Now for the second stage of our plan, Brother," said Ellen.

Edgar twirled a spark-plug wrench with his nimble fingers.

"To the Smithy & Sons Construction yard!"

"Let's hope it buys us time," said Ellen, and as the twins set out, they sang:

> *The seconds mock – tick, tock, tick, tock—*
> *So goes the heartless beating clock.*
> *Tick away till Knightleighs knock*
> *Our dwelling down to rubbled rock.*
> *Can Heimertz free us from this fate?*
> *Oh, if only time would wait!*
> *But never does the tock abate,*
> *Ticking towards Pet's deathly date.*
> *Somehow, some way we must defend*
> *Our home, our friend from dreary end.*

3. The Waxworks Beckons

After their visit to the Smithy & Sons construction yard, the twins took an alternate route home to throw potential snoops and sneaks off their tail.

Edgar grinned as he wiped olive paste off his footie pyjamas.

"When Eugenia turns the key on her bulldozer tomorrow, she'll discover that olive paste does wonders for an ignition system," he said as they neared the old Waxworks. "Why can't every scheme go so smoothly, eh, Pet?" He gently lifted Pet out from his satchel, and placed it on his shoulder. The creature made a small noise, but Edgar couldn't tell if it was a snigger or a cough.

Ellen didn't reply; she had stopped in midstride and was pointing to the abandoned factory.

The grounds around the dilapidated building had, until recently, been host to the garish colours and boisterous sounds of the Heimertz Family Circus. But the carnival had left town after the big top's collapse, and neither Edgar nor Ellen had anticipated finding anything but darkness and quiet around the old factory.

Instead a fleet of unmarked white trucks clustered at the entrance to the Waxworks and a large crowd peered through the factory windows. Searing lights shone through the windows and the cracks in the walls.

"It can't be the circus, can it?" asked Edgar. "They wouldn't return so soon after what happened."

"Even if they did," said Ellen, "that showboating Heimertz family would sooner travel on broken pogo sticks than in plain white trucks. Something else is going on."

"Less talking, more stalking," said Edgar, already slipping through the grass towards the building.

In its heyday the Waxworks had been a majestic building bustling with hardworking citizens making candles from dawn to dinnertime. But when Edgar and Ellen had previously explored the factory, they had seen no hint of its former glory. All that remained were decaying worktables; rusty candle-dipping contraptions; cobwebbed cogs and pulleys; and enormous vats of cooled, caked, crusty wax.

Edgar, Ellen, and Pet slipped past a handful of familiar locals: Executive Business Executive Marvin Matterhorn, Hotel Motel owners Mr and Mrs Elines, Buffy (proprietress of Buffy's Muffins), Sirs Malvolio and Geoffrey of the Renaissance re-enacting Gallant Paintsmen, and several other of the siblings' former prank victims.

All of them jockeyed for position in front of the windows, eyes fixed on whatever was going on inside.

The twins ducked under a tape barrier marked DO NOT ENTER and sidestepped Nathan Ruby, rookie for the local yard maintenance squad, Lawn and Order, who was busy gulping down a chocolate muffin.

Another dodge or two brought the twins to a hiding spot behind an old, crusty vat.

"Brother, look!"

A handsome man with perfectly tousled hair raced across the factory floor on roller skates. He kept looking behind him at a pair of eight-foot-tall metal robots on wheels chasing him. Despite his too-thick make-up, the man's features were immediately recognizable.

"Edgar," hissed Ellen. "It's, it's—"
"Blake Glide!"

4. Disquiet on the Set

Krshh-krshh-krshh-krshh.

Blake Glide skated as fast as his legs could go. The machines gained on him, their sharp pincers clacking with menace.

"Rarrrr!" hollered the robots through speakers on their heads. "Rarrr! Rarrr!"

"Submit now to . . . the Rollerbots!" called their leader.

"Never!" shouted Blake Glide. He *krshh*ed to the far side and reached the enormous, ten-foot vats marked WAX DIP. He backed against a vat as the Rollerbots drew closer.

"You've rolled your last, Earth Man!" burbled the lead monster through his tinny speaker.

Blake Glide turned a steely eye on his foes.

"That's what you think, you tanking tower of titan – er, titanic tank of – uh . . ."

"Cut!"

Famous film director Otto Ottoman threw his

megaphone on the floor and stomped towards his star. Every member of his crew sighed and stepped away from their cameras and microphone booms.

"It's *towering tank of titanium!*" screamed the director. "How many times are we going to do this scene? Listen, B. G., the Rollerbots need to go to the bathroom, and that will take *two hours* in the costume department."

Edgar whispered to his sister, "I thought we'd scared that no-talent hack so badly he was never coming back here."

Blake Glide had once visited Nod's Limbs as part of the mayor's tourism initiative, but had left abruptly when he discovered the town was populated by man-eating aliens (or so the twins had led him to believe).

Blake Glide hung his head. "I'm sorry, Double O. I just can't concentrate. It's—"

"Don't tell me," snapped Otto Ottoman. "This town, this town, *this town!*" He jerked his head at the gaggle of spectators peeking through every factory window. "B. G., ever since you were cast in *Revenge of the Rollerbots*, you've been complaining about shooting in Ned's Limbs . . ."

"*Nod's* Limbs," corrected Blake Glide in a hushed voice. He glanced fearfully at the legion of onlookers.

"You don't know this place, Otto. But I do. And I should never have come back—"

"Look, it's not my fault your dinner theatre investment went belly-up," said Otto Ottoman sternly. "Now *your* big-shot paycheck means *I* have to shoot on a budget smaller than *Attack of the Slurms*! You know, the studio wanted Dashiell Cragg from the beginning. I hear he's still available . . ."

"Cragg?" said Blake Glide. "You *wouldn't*. He's no actor . . . He's a chin dimple!"

"I *would*. They'll have my carcass if I waste any more time or money."

"But this place isn't right. Weird things happen here. Last time? They tried to . . . *eat me*."

"Blake, baby, I love your intensity. Keep that energy!" The director clapped his star on the back and sat down in his chair. "Someone oil Mr Glide's skates!"

"No one ever believes me," muttered the star. But behind him two pyjama-clad shadows stifled a snigger, and one of them whispered, "*We* believe you, old buddy."

"Did you hear that?" Blake Glide whipped his head around.

"Places, everyone!" the director bellowed, and everyone, even the reluctant star, complied.

For the first time the twins noticed that the cast and crew of *Rollerbots* were not the only occupants of the Waxworks. On the edge of the set, behind a barrier of velvet ropes and a sign reading VERY VIP SEATING, the twins spotted the beefy body of Mayor Knightleigh and his wife, Judith, flanked by their two children: Ellen's archnemesis, Stephanie, and her younger brother, Miles. As always, Stephanie wore a purple dress that complemented her perfect red curls; Miles, however, wore a foam hat shaped into a rough likeness of Blake Glide and clutched a pennant that read: NO. 1 GLIDEHEAD.

"Oh great. Princess Warts-for-Brains is here," said Ellen.

"Come on," said Edgar, crawling towards a golf cart marked FEATURE FILM DIRECTORS ONLY.

"What are you doing? We've got to get back to the caves," whispered Ellen.

"Oh, just one teensy prank? It's *Blake Glide*. What do you think, Pet?"

Pet nodded furiously, though it pained it to do so.

"Okay, okay, don't sprain your moustache," said Ellen. "I suppose he does deserve a proper welcome. Here, use this brick for the accelerator."

Blake Glide skated back into position. A woman with a clapboard stepped in front of the camera and barked, "*Rollerbots*. Scene fifty-six. Take twelve."

She snapped the board with a crack, and Otto Ottoman cried, "Action!"

Blake Glide *krshh-krshh-krssh*ed across the floor again, wearing a convincing look of horror. The Rollerbots followed.

Edgar turned the ignition key on the golf cart and lined up the steering wheel.

"I christen thee the SS *Mayhem*," he said, patting the dashboard.

"Long may you sail," said Ellen, dropping the brick on the accelerator.

Thus did "one teensy prank" set off an extraordinary course of events that would change everything in Nod's Limbs forever.

5. Glide and Seek

The golf cart careened through the set, barrelling across the director's chair, the assistant director's chair, the assistant assistant's chair, and finally, the Very VIP Seating. Cast and crew dove out of the way, and a thunderstruck Otto Ottoman buried his head in his hands.

"It's possessed by aliens!" screeched Blake Glide. "It'll kill us all!"

Stephanie pulled her brother onto a scaffold as their mother clambered to safety atop the soda machine. Their father dove for cover under a card table. Unfortunately his girth knocked out the legs of the flimsy table, and it collapsed, propped up by the mayor's belly.

The cart hit this homemade ramp and – with an agonized *"Oooof!"* from Mayor Knightleigh – flew through the air. It sailed across the room and landed just short of Blake Glide. The force of the landing tipped the floorboard like a seesaw and catapulted the terrified movie star across the factory.

"Talk about *sailing*!" said Ellen.

"Extra points for distance," said Edgar.

Even Pet managed an excited hop on Edgar's shoulder.

Screaming like a howler monkey, Blake Glide crashed through a door marked A. NOD, PROPRIETOR.

"My star!" cried Otto Ottoman.

"My hero!" cried Miles Knightleigh.

"My stomach!" cried Mayor Knightleigh.

Miles was the first through the broken door, followed by a camera crew and one dismayed director. The pack of curious Nod's Limbsians who had been huddled outside the windows now pushed inside to see the calamity for themselves. The movie star had flown headfirst through an oil painting on the opposing wall. It was a portrait of Augustus Nod, and Blake Glide's thrashing legs protruded from Nod's mouth like a forked tongue.

"Quick," called Otto Ottoman. "Call Dashiell Cragg!"

Miles grabbed his idol by the skates and pulled. "Talk to me, Mr Glide! Don't go towards the light!"

"*Gormph!*" responded Blake Glide. Several townspeople joined Miles in dragging the movie star from the hole. He fell to the ground, moaning through a mouthful of canvas.

Mayor Knightleigh hastened into the crowded office. "What kind of two-bit Tinseltown operation are you trying to pawn off on us, Ottoman? I should

have you run in for attempted mayorcide!"

The twins peered in from the doorway.

"Nothing like the wail of an action hero to brighten up the day," said Edgar. Pet bristled in agreement.

"Don't you mean 'flail'?" asked Ellen, grinning.

"How about 'jail'?" yelled Stephanie Knightleigh behind them. "I just *knew* I'd find you menaces lurking around here. And now you're *busted* for the last time—"

"GOLD!" cried Blake Glide.

Silence fell as the action star hobbled to his feet and reached through the ripped painting. He pulled out a small ingot of sculpted gold. The crowd gasped audibly, for every Nod's Limbsian recognized what it was: a tiny replica of the limbless statue of Nod that sat in Founder's Park. This figurine, however, was decidedly *limbed*.

"Wonder of wonders," said Buffy. "So *that's* what it was supposed to look like."

"What else is in there?" asked Marvin Matterhorn. "More gold?"

Blake Glide was already rooting around inside the wall, but Miles examined the painting's ornate frame.

"Hey, it swings out," he said. "It's a secret vault, just like the ones at our house, Dad!"

Mayor Knightleigh chuckled nervously, but no one seemed to notice. Instead Otto Ottoman pushed his star away from the hole long enough to swing the painting out. Just as Miles had said, a large compartment lay within, like a hidden safe. The lighting crew turned the spotlights on its contents: a porcelain ink pot, a spiny quill, a wax mould, wax copies of the statue, and a pile of yellowed papers.

The paper on top of the stack bore an elaborate

stamp made from gold leaf that read: WILL AND TES-
TAMENT. The onlookers gasped.

Blake Glide, Mayor Knightleigh, Otto Ottoman,
and a few others reached for the papers all at once.
But before their fingers could touch anything, a
ringing voice froze them in place.

"Do not touch that document!" cried a frail old
man. He prodded through the crowd with a silver-
tipped walking cane until at last he stood before the
vault. He buttoned his suit jacket and straightened
his crisp necktie.

"Be this Augustus Nod's, or be it not," began the
man, "a final testament of any kind is a sacred thing.
This is a matter for the law, and none other."

"I played Louie 'the Law' Lindman in *Legal
Weapon*," boasted Blake Glide, his hand extended.
"So I'm sure I'm qualified to—"

"Hands to yourself, Mr Glide!" warned the old
man. "So says the senior partner of the law firm
Herringbottle, Pratt, and Filbert. I am Lyman
Herringbottle, and my great-great-great-great-great-
great-great-grandfather wrote this will at the behest
of Augustus Nod himself. Should this sheaf of paper
prove authentic, it may very well be the single most
important document in Nod's Limbs' history."

6. The Reading of the Will

"Mr Herringbottle, I assure you," said Mayor Knightleigh, "this couldn't possibly be the *real* will of Augustus Nod. Everybody knows he went insane and disappeared. He never left a will."

"Not that anyone found," Lyman Herringbottle corrected. He lifted the paper gingerly, and his eyes sparkled. "Herringbottle family legend has long told of the lost will and what would happen if it were ever recovered."

"What . . . what *would* happen?" asked the mayor. His face had gone pale.

"That, good sir . . . ," began Lyman Herringbottle. He removed his red handkerchief from his breast pocket and dusted off the imposing wooden chair behind the desk, then hiked his trouser legs and sat down. ". . . is a singular tale, indeed."

The old man withdrew an unlit pipe from his jacket and clenched it in his teeth. He carefully examined the yellow paper. "Yes, yes, the seals are genuine!"

Several people in the crowd gasped.

"My ancestor, Hatfield Herringbottle, was Nod's Limbs' first lawyer, and one of Augustus Nod's few confidants," Lyman Herringbottle said grandly. "Oh, the tales whispered down from generation to generation in the Herringbottle households! They tell of a Nod descending into madness, a Nod who wrote the most curious of last wishes, a Nod with a . . . *golden* secret."

"More gold?" asked Blake Glide, and everyone in the room seemed to tense.

"Sadly," said the lawyer, "Nod disappeared before entrusting his final testament to the hands of his lawyer. For all Hatfield knew, Nod had taken the will with him wherever he had gone. To find it after all this time . . . Well, we are all witness to history this day. I ask you: Shall I now give this document the public reading it has been deprived of for two hundred years?"

"No need for that—" began Mayor Knightleigh, but he was drowned out by a loud "YES" from the crowd. The townspeople and movie crew pressed closer as the lawyer carefully untied the string that bound the papers.

With great care and deliberation, Lyman Herringbottle placed a pair of reading glasses on the bridge of his nose and squinted. He licked his lips and pursed them several times before he began to read.

"October 13, 1802," he began. "My dearest idiots—"

"Now really!" cried Mayor Knightleigh. "Must we hear the ravings of this kook? He squandered his fortune on crazy schemes, and went as bonkers as a bedbug by the end! What's the point of entertaining this further?"

The movie crew, and even a few Nod's Limbsians, turned and gave the mayor the most gusty "shh!" he had ever received. He deflated as Herringbottle cleared his throat and continued.

> *My dearest idiots of Nod's Lands, or Limbs, or*
> *any which whatever you are,*
>
> *I am dead and you are not. Well done!*
> *Whatever will you do for an encore?*
>
> *If things have gone according to plan, you*
> *are now gathered in the sylvan glade of*
> *Founder's Park, and my legal counsel, the*
> *estimable Hatfield Herringbottle, is reading*
> *this aloud to all who care to hear it. Speak up,*
> *Herringbottle, they cannot hear you in back!*

"Yes! Speak up, Herringbottle!" shouted Marvin Matterhorn. "We can't hear you in back!"

"Oh, yes, excuse me," said Lyman Herringbottle, reading on slightly louder.

> *A will is often an old man's chance to divide up his possessions among his loved ones, choosing who will get, say, Granddad's wooden teeth and who the heirloom thimbles. Of course, I have no loved ones, surrounded as I am by such dolts and cattleprods as the people of this hapless hamlet. Sheep, the lot of you! Not a unique thought in any of your pumpkin heads! Following blindly that blackguard mayor of yours—*

"Uh, does he say who gets the little statue?" Blake Glide interrupted. "Because if he doesn't mention it, I *am* the finder . . ."

Lyman Herringbottle harrumphed as he scanned the pages. "He does seem to go on at length about his fellow citizens . . . Oh my! Shameful language! . . . I don't even know what that . . . Ah, here, it picks up a bit on page four."

Perhaps I have been wrong, and there is one with the intellect and backbone I seek. But he (or she) will have to prove himself (or herself). Can I discover this from beyond the mortal coil? Yes. Bless me, I can.

I propose a contest. Find the golden limbs.

Oh, I know well where they lie, for it was I who took them. I! Why should a whole and complete statue of Nod be bequeathed to the very town that took so much from the living Nod, leaving him incomplete, less than himself? Thus I reasoned, and the night before the limbs were to be joined to my statue, I hid them. Knowledge of their location shall die with me; I have left only six little verses, and they are rigidly tight-lipped on the matter. These verses — one of which you shall find in this very document — are riddles, clues, and mental puzzlings to vex and confound you, yes, but also to guide you.

Whosoever finds these limbs has earned my approval, dead though I may be. The statue

*belongs to the town as ever, but, Successful
Hunter, the limbs are yours, as are each and
every one of my possessions, from gold coin to
coniferous fir.*

*If you citizens of Nod's Limbs are as dense
and dim as I suspect, you will earn all you
deserve – naught but misery! I'll wager my
weight in candlewax that greed and betrayal
will tear you apart before you find a thing!
Still, perhaps . . . perhaps . . . one of you is
clever enough to carry on in my name. Good
fortune. Or no fortune.*

*Yours nevermore,
Augustus Nod*

"My, oh my," whispered Buffy.

"Mine, all mine," murmured Otto Ottoman.

"So that includes the little statue?" asked Blake
Glide.

7. The First Clue

Murmurs spread through the crowd.

"What a waste of time," called Mayor Knightleigh over the buzz. "Everyone knows the old scoundrel squandered his fortunes and died penniless – there were no 'gold coins or coniferous firs' left! What point would there be in winning his possessions now?"

"Well, that's not true," whispered Edgar to his sister. "There are lots of firs on our property, and we know Nod owned that."

"Shh, Brother," said Ellen. "Apparently *they* don't know that!"

"Daddy, you're forgetting the limbs!" said Stephanie. "Whoever finds them, keeps them!"

The mayor peered disapprovingly at his daughter, but others were already nodding in agreement.

"Those limbs would be quite valuable," said Marvin Matterhorn. "Think of the businesses that could be launched and mercilessly franchised!"

"Or the number of shiny, candy-apple tractor mowers we can add to our fleet!" said Lawn and Order's Chief Strongbowe.

"Gramercy!" exclaimed Sir Malvolio. "Golden victory shall restore the Gallant Paintsmen to former glory! To the riddle, man! Hence!"

"Right you are, right you are," said Lyman Herringbottle, turning the pages of the will.

"Well?" cried Otto Ottoman. "Don't keep it to yourself. Read it out loud!"

"Yes, yes, I was getting to that," said Lyman Herringbottle. "No need to be rude. See here – he's written it out on this last page. It reads:

The stolen limbs you hope to find—
The secret, then: to read my mind.
My golden effigy holds the key
That will begin the mystery.
So peer thee inward, where I think
You will find the missing link.

The room was quiet for a moment until Blake Glide moaned and threw his arms in the air.

"Oh, it's hopeless! Impossible to solve. The gold is lost forever!"

"What's an 'f and g,' Stephie?" asked Miles, pulling on his sister's sleeve.

"Not 'f and g,' Miles," said Stephanie. "'Effigy.' It's another word for something that looks like someone, like a doll . . . or a statue."

"A *golden* statue," said Nathan Ruby.

"By Jupiter, he's right!" exclaimed Marvin Matterhorn. "Nod's golden statue in Founder's Park. Ingenious!"

"Now that's just fun," said Fire Chief Gully Lugwood. "A treasure hunt is going to be a big hit with my kids, I can tell you."

"It'll be a hit with the whole town!" said Buffy. "Why, I'll bet we'll all have a hoot of a time solving this thing *together*."

Several of his fellow citizens nodded in agreement, though the film crew, the Knightleighs, and the twins expressed varying degrees of disgust.

"Hey, where's B. G.?" asked Otto Ottoman. His eyes darted in every direction, but Blake Glide had vanished. Just then, tyres squealed outside as a car pulled away in a hurry.

"Scoundrel!" said Sir Malvolio. "He's on the hunt!"

8. Lost and Founder

The cluster of cars outside the Waxworks dispersed like the sparks off a firework.

"Let's make this an orderly procession!" called Police Chief Gomez. "Keep your peepers open for those pedestrians!"

"Let me through!" yelled Mayor Knightleigh out the window of his limousine. "The mayor goes to the front of any line!"

A stream of cars rolled onto the street, including a van full of Rollerbot parts and buckets of make-up. The driver and his front-seat passenger, two of the movie crew, were arguing about hidden meanings in the riddle, and didn't hear the murmurs of two stowaways in back.

"Looks like we're the only ones who know Nod didn't die *totally* penniless, despite what Knightleigh thinks," said Ellen.

"Sister, if we find the limbs, we get everything, including his house. *Our* house," said Edgar. "Knightleigh may own the deed – but it'll be worthless!"

"And with the gold, we'll have enough money to buy a steam shovel. We'll save Pet *and* our house in one fell swoop!" Ellen pulled Pet from the satchel and held aloft the little lump. "Rest easy, Pet. There's just a simple battle of brains between us and these treasure hunters."

Pet tapped Ellen's forehead with a lock of hair.

"A war of wits," said Edgar, "and everyone else is unarmed."

The van pulled up to a stop. The twins tucked Pet into Edgar's satchel and ducked out the back. On the trim green lawn of Founder's Park, the imposing statue of limbless Nod gazed down with reproach at the people hurrying towards him.

Blake Glide stood by the statue, hands in his pockets and whistling with unconvincing innocence. The bronze nameplate in the base, which read NOD: FOUNDER OF NOD'S LIMBS, 1742—? had been wrenched off the front and thrown on the grass.

"What's happened to our statue?" cried Chief Strongbowe.

"It was like that when I got here, I swear," said Blake Glide.

"Public property defaced!" cried Mayor Knightleigh as he hustled onto the grounds. "This treasure hunt has gone from farce to civic nuisance."

Marvin Matterhorn ran to the statue and examined the space where the nameplate had been.

"There's a little compartment here! Just like the nook behind the oil painting," he said. "But I don't feel anything inside. It's empty."

"Of course it is," said the mayor. "I'm telling you this whole business is a hoax! There's no clue in this statue!"

Disappointed murmurs rippled from the crowd.

"I suppose you're right, Mr Mayor," said Fire Chief Gully Lugwood. "We shouldn't have got our hopes up to find some old clue—"

"Unless *he* has it," said Otto Ottoman, pointing at Glide. "You were here first, B. G. You didn't pocket the clue on these good folks now, did you?"

Blake Glide's jaw dropped and he clutched his chest. "Double O! I'm shocked! You don't really think—"

The Nod's Limbsians were just as appalled.

"That . . . that wouldn't be fair!"

"Movie stars would never be dishonest. Would they?"

"If we can't trust a famous person, who *can* we trust?"

But the members of the film crew – seemingly not

ready to trust a movie star – set upon Blake Glide.

"I didn't steal anything!" he protested, as the crew turned out his pockets. Expensive moisturizers, an empty money clip, and a variety of breath mints fell to the ground – but no gold.

During the distraction, Edgar and Ellen tiptoed up to the statue's base and gazed into the dark recess.

"They didn't examine the statue very closely," said Ellen. "Sloppy work."

"Typical townies. No doubt they missed something," said Edgar, fishing a flashlight from his satchel. "Let's shed a little light on things."

The light revealed a small compartment chiselled into the granite base, the perfect place to store a clue. Aside from dust, however, the nook was bare. Edgar and Ellen exchanged puzzled glances.

At last, the search of Blake Glide's pockets, wallet, and socks came up empty for stashed clues.

The mayor waved his arms. "Upstanding citizens, can't you see the chaos this treasure hunt is already causing in our town? First there's the, er, disfigurement of this fine statue. And the way many of you drove over here . . . well, twenty-five miles per hour *indeed*. Now unwarranted pocket searches? We can't afford further disquiet. By the authority vested in me

by the mayor – who is me – I am officially shutting down this nonsense."

But none of the upstanding citizens seemed to hear. They milled about the statue, mumbling to themselves and rubbing their chins in thought.

Stephanie Knightleigh walked behind the twins and hissed in their ears. "Enjoy your last night in your snug little beds," she said. "If I had my way, you'd be chained to them when the wrecking ball hits tomorrow."

Edgar reached into the satchel and pulled out a pipe wrench. He smacked it in the palm of his hand. Stephanie sneered.

"You don't have the guts," she said, turning her back on the twins. She walked back towards the family limo.

"Brother, what were you planning to do with that?" asked Ellen. "A wrench attack would have been so . . . *Knightleigh* of you."

"This isn't for her," said Edgar. "I have an idea. We just need this crowd to clear out."

"ATTENNNNNTION-TION-TION!" The announcement echoed so loudly that the treasure hunters stopped talking and covered their ears. Red-faced Mayor Knightleigh stood by his limousine with a bullhorn in his hands. The volume, it seemed, had been turned all the way up. "THE HUNT IS OVER-ER-ER. THERE IS NOTHING-ING-ING TO SEE HERE-ERE-ERE. THERE IS NO!-O!-O! GOLD!-OLD!-OLD! NOW SKEDADDLE-ADDLE-ADDLE!"

9. Gold-Brained

The would-be hunters shuffled away from the statue. The mayor, returning to normal colour, patted the disappointed citizens on their backs as they went.

"Now, now," he said. "What on earth would anyone do with a golden limb anyway? And goodness, it's almost eight thirty. Bedtime! Tomorrow this will all seem so silly."

The Nod's Limbsians filed out of the park, followed by the film crew. ("Man, the things these small town yokels do for fun.") The twins returned to the foot of the statue.

"Now we strike," whispered Edgar. "Remember what the riddle said about the statue?"

"Sure," said Ellen. "The riddle is inside. And

none of these simpletons looked for a secret compartment in the statue itself – *Watch out*!" Ellen pulled her brother behind a bush as Chief Strongbowe shone his flashlight through the park to ensure the last of the stragglers was headed home.

"Yes, a secret compartment – but not just anywhere," said Edgar. "Remember the exact words: 'So peer thee inward, where I think/You will find the missing link.' *Peer where I think*, Sister!"

Ellen nodded. "'The secret then; to read my mind.' It's in his head!"

Edgar and Ellen scaled the statue and examined the figure's head, using Edgar's flashlight. Edgar gently tapped the chin, the nose, and the ears with his pipe wrench.

"A very delicate process, Sister. Only a well-trained ear can pick out details like the thickness of the metal . . . the flaws in the structure . . . the hollow spots within – *Hey!*"

Ellen yanked the wrench away.

"No mystery, Edgar. It's in his head!" she said, and she gave the golden forehead a mighty whack.

Gong!

The golden head rang like a church bell. The twins slapped their hands over their ears.

As the echoes waned to a dull hum, the twins heard a soft clattering sound. Nod's eyes had fallen back inside his head, and now the statue stared out with eerie, empty sockets.

Edgar shone the light into the right eye and peered in. "We were right! A riddle, carved into the back of his head! We've done it, Sister!"

"Read it to me," said Ellen, seizing charcoal and paper from the satchel. "Quick!"

Edgar moved the light to and fro and began to read:

> *Always telling, never talking.*
> *Always running, never walking.*
> *But on her limbs she bears a clue*
> *She will not yield to show to you.*

"Okay, did you get that?" he asked.

"Got it!" said a voice from below. The twins looked down to see a woman writing in a spiral notebook. She stood next to a man with a camera around his neck. "Fancy sleuthing, you two! Can't wait for our readers to get a load of this!"

Before the twins could react, a flash blinded them, just long enough for Nancy Weedle, star reporter of the *Nod's Limbs Gazette*, and photographer Snap Watson to hurry out of the park, taking the story of the century with them.

10. Demolition Day

The twins slumped on their beds while an exhausted Pet dozed in the satchel.

"Come sunrise, the whole town will get the second riddle in their morning paper," said Ellen. "We need to solve it *now*."

"It's obvious, right? 'Always running, never walking.' It's the Running River."

"Of course. But where, Brother? It's nothing but a long, muddy stream. The riddle mentions limbs. Are they the other little creeks that flow into this one?"

"Perhaps, or the banks of the beach. What is that 'Always telling, never talking' business?"

"A reference to a babbling brook? Maybe the Running River wasn't always such a quiet trickle."

"If so, Nod might have tied the clue around a brick and sunk it into the riverbed."

The twins debated methods of dredging the river until their eyelids grew heavy and they fell asleep.

In the early hours of dawn, a low rumble echoed through their house. It was the sound of approaching machinery.

Edgar opened one eye. "No. *No!*"

Ellen leaped to the window. "Bulldozers! Dump trucks! A *wrecking ball*! Why didn't the olive paste work?"

Down below, a woman in coveralls and a hard hat strode up to the house and plunked a metal pail onto the front steps. An oily green slop sloshed onto the ground.

"Hey, twins! You misplaced your snack!"

"Blasted Eugenia Smithy!" Ellen snarled. "Impossible to fool."

"Edgar! Ellen! Out of the house!" Eugenia called. "Today is doomsday for your domicile!"

"Failure most bitter!" cried Edgar.

But his sister was already halfway down the stairs. Edgar hurried after her.

"What are you going to do?" he asked.

"Our best weapon now," Ellen said, "is greed."

The twins stepped out to meet the construction forewoman face-to-face. Instead of sneering or scowling or baring her nails, as she was often wont to do, Ellen looked calm.

"I'm surprised you're at work today, Eugenia," said Ellen.

"I doubt you're surprised by much, Ellen," said Eugenia. Several other construction workers approached cautiously. Eugenia spoke to them over her shoulder. "These are the ones. Be careful, like I told you. They won't go quietly."

"Oh, of course we will," said Ellen. "We don't have time to dawdle around here. We've got to find the *gold* before the rest of the town does."

"Gold?" asked one of the workers.

"You didn't hear about the treasure hunt? It was in all the papers. Nod's will has been found, and it's riddled with riddles. They point the way to the missing *solid gold* limbs of Nod's statue. Whoever finds them gets to keep them."

The workers eyed one another to see if anyone was buying the story.

"Nice bluff," said Eugenia. "I expected an attack of poison arrow frogs, or Hungarian biting flies maybe. But a distraction tactic, that's new—"

"'Always telling, never talking,'" began Edgar. "'Always running, never walking.'"

"'But on her limbs she bears a clue she will not yield to show to you,'" Ellen finished.

"What was that?" asked a bushy-moustached worker.

"The next riddle in the hunt," said Ellen. "I wish we could figure it out, but it's just so hard."

The man stroked his moustache. "Well, see . . . 'always running, never walking.' That . . . that's the Running River, I reckon."

Eugenia glowered. "Doggone it, Steve—"

"Okay, but what about the rest of it?" asked a thick-necked man. "What kind of limbs does a river have?"

"I guess that just means the banks," said Steve. "Hey, what about the beach? That's where *I'd* bury treasure if I had some to bury."

Edgar, Ellen, and the other workers all agreed that was a brilliant idea, and congratulated Steve for his quick thinking. Despite Eugenia's protests, the group took a quick vote and determined that the house demolition could wait another few hours while they searched the beach. Edgar produced an old shovel and presented it to the team.

"This should make quick work of all that sand," he said. The men grabbed it and made for the river, whooping.

The twins followed, leaving Eugenia Smithy alone on the front stoop. As they ran they sang:

The search is on! The treasures call
Somewhere beneath the sandy sprawl.
So do put down that wrecking ball—
You've got a beach to comb!
The shrewdest only shall behold
Scads of riches, wealth untold.
(Plus if you're on the hunt for gold,
You can't tear down our home!)

11. Down by the River

When Edgar and Ellen arrived at the Running River, however, their high spirits plummeted.

It seemed every citizen of Nod's Limbs had read the riddle in the morning paper and had come to the same conclusion. Treasure hunters clogged the beach, and many others paced the riverbank on both sides. The high school football team examined the north bank by crawling along in a sort of practise-drill exercise while the residents of the Nod's Limbs Retirement Community scoured the beach with metal detectors. Blake Glide and the movie crew could be seen burrowing with film canisters as Sirs Malvolio and Geoffrey used paint trays to scoop sand

and pan it for gold. Children with plastic shovels and buckets scampered everywhere, picking up random scraps of trash and taking them to Janitor Clunch, who held a sign that read: IF IT ISN'T A CLUE, IT'S LITTER.

"What a way to spend a Saturday!" said Betty LaFete.

"Such an educational game!" gushed schoolteacher Suzette Croquet. "Riddles to tickle my little students' minds!"

"I'm gonna find that gold, you betcha!" said little Timmy Poshi. Miss Croquet smiled and patted him on the head.

Ellen groaned. "What sickening displays of civic teamwork."

"Sister, we have to clear this place out so we can search in private," said Edgar. "If only I had some Hungarian biting flies . . ."

"No time," said Ellen. "Start digging, before one of these simpletons finds our golden ticket!"

The twins plunged their own shovels into the sand, just like the others around them.

As the horde of hunters grew, Principal Mulberry of Nod's Limbs Grammar School climbed a stepladder and spoke through a megaphone. The townspeople politely stopped their digging to listen.

"Greetings, fellow treasure hunters!" she cried to hails of cheering. "I'm really happy with the town-wide participation we're seeing. Now to keep the proceedings from getting disorderly, how about we add a dose of our classic Nod's Limbs *cooperation*!"

More cheers from the masses. The twins redoubled their shovelling while everyone else was preoccupied.

Principal Mulberry cleared her throat. "That's super, everyone! Well, the PTA and I thought that the best way to give everyone a chance to play this game was to divide ourselves into teams!" She smiled and nodded at the rousing applause. "Let's crack this nut together!"

With Principal Mulberry presiding over the process, several groups took shape. The football team and the marching band joined together to become Team Gridiron. A cluster of women from the retirement centre became the Silver Lining Ladies, and the Cairo Avenue shopkeepers dubbed themselves the Bottom-Dollar League. The Teacher-Janitor Alliance pledged a tight union ("Wise minds! Clean schools! Golden future!"), while Sir Malvolio and Chief Strongbowe merged the Gallant Paintsmen and Lawn and Order to forge the Gauntlet.

Groups of school-age children were divided evenly into teams. Miles Knightleigh had donned the pirate hat he won at the Heimertz Family Circus, and suggested his group be called the No-Quarter Pirates. His teammates endorsed the idea, and with cries of "Yarr!" and "Yo ho, ho!" they brandished sticks in the air like cutlasses. (Upon further reflection, however, they decided "no quarter", which means "no mercy", might give other hunters the wrong impression, so they opted for the much more considerate *Some*-Quarter Pirates.)

At last Principal Mulberry made the teams official

by recording them all on her clipboard. Then the hunt began anew – after a countdown and a whistle to "give things a proper beginning".

Meanwhile the twins had stopped their aimless digging to observe the spectacle.

Ellen leaned on her shovel and pulled a pigtail. "We're missing something," she said at last. "Everyone in this town came to the river because the clue seemed so easy. But it would be just like Nod to lead people astray."

"Good point, Sister," said Edgar. "If these dimwits think this is the place, then it *can't* be right."

So as Mayor Knightleigh pulled up in his limo ("Great buttered biscuits! Can't a mayor sleep in on a Saturday without his town going berserk?"), the twins retreated from the cheery bustle to review the riddle.

"'Always running, never walking,'" said Ellen. "What else runs all the time?"

"Your mouth," said Edgar.

"'Always telling, never *talking*,'" said Ellen, smooshing her brother's face into the dirt.

Edgar laughed and wiped his face. "Okay, okay. What's always running? Refrigerators. Respirators. Hotels. Clocks. Sewage treatment plants."

"Great, but none of those things can speak," mused Ellen.

"*Telling* and *talking* aren't necessarily the same thing," said Edgar. "When you sneak up behind me, I can *tell* you're there from the stench."

"Can you *tell* what I'm going to do next?" Ellen balled up her fist for another sisterly pummel, but froze midstrike. Her wide eyes grew even wider.

Edgar peeked out from behind his arms.

"Brother," said Ellen. "I have the answer."

"Well, it's about time, Sister!"

Ellen smirked. "Exactly."

12. The Wisdom of the Pirates

Mayor Knightleigh realized his attempts to shoo everyone back to their homes were futile. The formation of the teams had brought organization and energy to the search as teammates cheered one another on, conferred on best locations to dig, and took shifts to stay fresh. The hunt was now an unstoppable force, and the mayor could do nothing but fume in the back of his limo.

"Disorder, disorder, disorder!" he raved.

Before long the entire length of each riverbank was pockmarked with holes, but no second clue had been found. Treasure hunters leaned on their shovels in exhaustion.

"I have scoop blisters," whined Timmy Poshi.

"I have sand between my perfectly straight teeth!" wailed Blake Glide. *"Where is that clue?"*

That's when the Some-Quarter Pirates trooped up to Principal Mulberry and asked to use her megaphone.

"Um, yo ho ho, everyone," said Calvin Hucklebee in a meek voice. "The Some-Quarter Pirates, we, uh . . . uh, we had, well, an idea."

"Don't be shy, little fella!" said Chief Strongbowe. "Pipe right up!"

"Well, we looked at the clue again, and it seemed to some of us that, well, there are other kinds of things that run," said Calvin Hucklebee. "First, Donald Bogginer said that the air conditioner in his house is always running, which made Burl Turkle think of how his watch always runs too. And then I was like, 'Hey, can you tell time on that, 'cause, like, I only use digital—'"

"What's your point?" shouted Blake Glide.

Miles Knightleigh leaned into the megaphone.

"Avast, mateys, the next clue be at the clock tower!"

"Miles!" roared Mayor Knightleigh as he wriggled out of his limo. But the crowd's noise drowned him out.

"Hey!" cried Nathan Ruby. "The tykes are right! Clocks are always *running,* and they always *tell* time."

"Well met, small rogues!" cheered Sir Malvolio.

"Nifty!" shouted Sir Geoffrey.

"The clock tower was around in Nod's day," Janitor Clunch concluded. "That must be the answer!"

Chief Strongbowe pointed down Florence Boulevard.

"To the clock tower! And don't trample the petunia beds!"

13. Tooth by Tooth

The Some-Quarter Pirates were escorted to a place of honour at the front of the throng, and the children led the parade, swinging and swashing their pretend cutlasses. Blake Glide, Otto Ottoman, and the movie crew joined in, though they looked rather annoyed, and a grumbling mayor brought up the rear. On the way, the hunters chatted about how obvious the riddle now seemed.

"'But on her limbs she bears a clue she will not yield to show to you,'" recited Marvin Matterhorn. "That's a reference to the clock's hands, you see? The next clue must be written on them. Elementary, really."

The Nod's Limbs clock tower – commissioned by Mayor Thaddeus Knightleigh himself – had stood at the edge of town for more than 200 years. As the crowd approached, its heavy black hands were swinging upwards towards the noon hour.

The pirates threw open the door at the foot of the tower and led the parade up a narrow, spiralling staircase. Above them, sunlight streamed through the translucent clock face, onto the guts of the clock-works, alternately casting them in warm light and cold shadows.

A girl in striped footie pyjamas appeared on the staircase ahead of them, blocking the way.

"Sorry, folks, nothing to see here," she said. "The clock tower is being fumigated for an infestation of cuckoo wasps. You better clear out before clouds of noxious gas cause a sudden outbreak of death."

Many in the crowd groaned in disappointment.

"What rotten timing," said Chief Strongbowe. "Well, folks, safety first."

"Are you crazy?" cried Blake Glide from several flights down. "Why would you believe the weird girl in the pyjamas?"

"Now, now," said Principal Mulberry. "Here in Nod's Limbs we don't judge others by their sleep-wear."

"Look!" yelled Otto Ottoman. "There's another one!"

Indeed a boy in matching striped pyjamas could be seen in the clockworks, clinging to the tooth of a gear that was rotating slowly upwards. The townspeople weren't sure what he was up to, but it certainly looked nothing like fumigation. The moviemakers in the mob surged forward, propelling the Nod's Limbsians with them. Ellen found herself shoved aside as the treasure hunters rushed to a land-ing near the top of the clock's face.

If the face had been transparent, the hunters would have had an excellent view of Nod's Limbs from their lofty perch. But the only thing visible through the giant opaque plate was the shadow of the clock's hands, which were drawing very near to twelve o'clock.

The cog from which Edgar now dangled was propelling the minute hand – and Edgar – closer to the numeral "12." Blake Glide elbowed his way to the fore, and leaned over the rail.

"What is that little gremlin doing?" Blake Glide asked.

The cogs continued their slow turn. A half-minute more and Edgar's hands would be crushed between the teeth of the gears. He risked a glance at the clock face behind him.

There, just below the twelve, a small window no bigger than a thumb was cut into the face. When the clock struck twelve, the window would reveal the back of the hour hand. Edgar was perfectly placed to see it—

"Yow!" hollered Edgar, as Stephanie landed on his fingers. She had lashed one sleeve of her lavender sweater to a cog-driving shaft above Edgar and swung across to the gear. "Get off!"

"Oh, excuse me," said Stephanie, digging her heel into Edgar's knuckles.

Tock. Tock. Tock.

The gear continued to climb, the tocks echoing through the tower. Edgar bit his tongue, ignoring the pain in his fingers while Stephanie steadied herself: The two squinted into the window. They could

just see the back of the hour hand, where an inscription was carved.

"Somebody better have a pencil!" Stephanie shouted. She read out the words she saw.

> *Well done! But it's neither here nor there.*
> *For next an owl's hut needs repair;*
> *Then seek a white raven, tangled in knots—*
> *Only my heir can connect the dots.*

"Perfect, Miss Knightleigh. I've got it!" said Nancy Weedle, writing in her notebook.

The teeth of the two gears began to close on Edgar's fingers, and Stephanie tried to swing back to the landing.

"Oh, no, you're taking me with you!" shouted Edgar, and he grabbed her foot just before the gears bit down on him. Stephanie yelped as the two swayed in midair, suspended only by her sweater.

"Mr Glide! Mr Glide!" cried Miles. "You can save them, just like you saved the nuclear acorn in *Squirrelman*!"

Blake Glide trembled as he looked down the dizzyingly high tower.

"Well, you know, that was a little different, since

I had sap blasters, and, uh, the insurance on my cheekbones doesn't kick in until next week, so . . ."

"Leggo! Leggo!" cried Stephanie, kicking her legs. "We're going to *faaaaaa* . . ."

The crowd shrieked as Stephanie's sweater ripped, and the two children plummeted towards the ground, ten storeys below.

Whump.

Edgar slowly opened his eyes.

"'Whump'?" he said. "I expected 'splat.'"

"Not when the Volunteer Firefighter's Brigade is on the case," said Fire Chief Gully Lugwood. He and several firefighters held the canvas tarp they used to catch jumpers from burning buildings. (Of course, this was actually the first time they'd ever been able to use the tarp, since Nod's Limbsians always practised proper fire safety rules and exited burning buildings from the designated fire escapes.) Gully Lugwood was ecstatic. "We weren't the first to catch the clue, but luckily, we caught you!"

Ellen raced down the stairs ahead of the crowd.

"Brother, you're still in one piece!" she said, giving him a relieved punch in the arm. She glanced at a dazed Stephanie, who was rubbing her head. "Drat. So is she."

14. Unsportsman-like Conduct

The Nod's Limbsians filed out of the clock tower, buzzing about the next riddle, but amid the speculations, some grumblings too could be heard.

"I think those children were trying to find that clue *without* the rest of us," said Arthur Poshi. "Flabbergasting!"

"*Children* wouldn't do such a thing," said Buffy. "Then again, Blake Glide himself snuck ahead of everyone to get the first clue, didn't he?"

"Do you get the feeling that not everyone is playing fair?" asked Betty LaFete.

Several people around them muttered and nodded.

"Did anyone stop to ask what we do when we *find* the limbs?" asked Marvin Matterhorn. "Are we going to sell them, and then split the money evenly? Give every team a gold finger or toe?"

The crowd seemed stumped by the idea. Finally, wax museum curator and custodian Ernest Hirschfeld spoke up. "Probably best to donate the limbs to the museum. That'd be the only fair thing . . ."

"You'd certainly benefit from that," said Marvin Matterhorn. "Tell me, Ernie, do you think that's what Blake Glide plans to do if he finds them first?"

Disagreements erupted from the group, and Principal Mulberry clapped her hands to silence the growing disquiet.

"Now, now, everyone," she called. "Where have all our happy faces gone? This riddle seems a little bit tougher, and we're going to need our very best teamwork to find the answer. We in the Teacher-Janitor Alliance have an idea about how to proceed next."

The principal outlined a plan for the teams to divide and explore an element of the clue. The words "owl" and "raven" seemed to point to the Nod's Limbs Zoo (even though the only birds on display were pigeons and chickadees), so the Silver Lining Ladies and the men of the Gauntlet would check that area first. To follow the clue about needing repairs, the Crosstown Contract Bridge Club and the Some-Quarter Pirates would check Greasy Billy's Gas Station and Mr Chung's Cuckoo Clock Hospital. Several other teams were dispatched to shoe stores, Junior Nature Scout meeting dens, and the canoe dock to investigate "knots".

References to a "hut" were perplexing, since no one could recall such a structure in Nod's Limbs, but Team Gridiron volunteered to check the shopping mall. There, the food court boasted a Hamburger Hut *and* a Taco Hut – plus, there was the Kwik-Foto Hut in the parking lot and, for what it was worth, Sal's Fine China Hutch across the street. The Library Card League and the remaining teams were dispatched to seek reference to birds in town history and lore.

Blake Glide and the rest of the movie crew broke into teams of two or three, and left before Principal Mulberry could finish outlining her strategy.

"Great plan, everyone! Let's meet at the town hall after dinner to go over our findings," said Principal Mulberry. "And remember: All for one and one for everybody!"

The teams tromped off to their assigned locations – though this time, Marvin Matterhorn, Arthur Poshi, and a few other Nod's Limbsians held back from the big groups. All of them had their excuses ("Paperwork piling up in the office," or "Hedges getting a little unruly"), but, curiously, not one of them left in the direction of his or her office or home.

15. Homophones Are Where the Heart Is

As the twins walked home through the forest, Ellen destroyed all the mushrooms in her path with punishing kicks.

"We're playing Nod's game," she said. "He's got us bumbling around just like the other goofballs in town."

Edgar strolled along with his head down and his hands clasped behind his back. He nodded slightly.

"We've got to get ahead of them, Brother," Ellen fumed. "We've got to break this next riddle before the rest of town does and take them *out* of the hunt. One thing's for sure, it's not at the zoo, because that's too easy – *Are you even listening to me?*"

Edgar looked up, startled. "Zoo, sure. Um, what were you saying?"

"Do you want to find those limbs or don't you? Concentrate, Edgar!"

Edgar stopped walking. "Wait. This . . . this may be nothing. Or maybe not. Where Nod is concerned, who knows?"

Ellen plopped onto a fallen pine and tugged a pigtail. "Let's hear it – even a half-wit's hunch will be better than anything those Nod's Limbsians come up with. I mean, zoos didn't even *exist* when Nod was alive. Imbeciles."

"Well, when Stephanie was reading the riddle, I got a look at it too. I noticed something that she didn't mention."

Ellen arched an eyebrow. "Go on."

"There were a couple of misspellings that, I don't know, just didn't feel very *Nod*. The first line read, 'Well done! But it's neither here nor there,'" said Edgar. "But *here* was spelled *h-e-a-r*, and *there* was *t-h-e-i-r*."

"Fairly common mistakes," said Ellen.

"Then the last line: *'Only my heir can connect the dots.' Heir* was spelled *a-i-r*."

Ellen snorted and mashed another toadstool into the dirt. "Okay. That's a little fishy."

"That's what I'm trying to tell you. Nod was a mad genius, right? He wouldn't make a careless mistake in his riddle unless he did it on purpose. To tell us something."

"Feh," muttered Ellen. She stood up and paced the thick brush and bramble of the Black Tree Forest. Then she turned and faced her brother.

"Hobophones," she said.

"What?" said Edgar.

"*Hobophones*. Words that sound the same but are spelled differently. Like *where* and *wear*. Or *Nod* and *gnawed*." She mimicked a fierce chewing motion. "What would Nod be trying to tell us by using hobophones?"

"I think you mean *homophone*," said Edgar.

"Whatever. But it *must* mean something," said Ellen. "I just can't figure it out – yet. I do know this: only *we* have this part of the clue."

"And Stephanie," Edgar pointed out. "She saw it too."

"Watch me tremble in my footies," said Ellen. "She probably didn't even notice the misspellings. And everyone else is following the wrong lead!"

16. Feed a Fever

When Edgar and Ellen put their minds to a problem, any number of things could happen. They might slip marsh-thistle spines into each other's bed sheets, or launch Pet from the broken bidet in the third-floor bathroom. Such activities often inspired their best ideas.

Today, however, they retreated to their own

corners to think – Ellen to the ninth-floor ballroom (which had a comforting clutter left behind by Judith Stainsworth-Knightleigh's home decoration failure) and Edgar to the parlour on the seventh floor, where he tootled half-heartedly on his out-of-tune pipe organ.

As the afternoon dragged by, Edgar gave up his absentminded music making, and climbed to the attic-above-the-attic for a change of scenery. There he aimed the twins' massive telescope at the town below to see how the other treasure hunters were faring.

Moments later he raced to the ballroom.

"Come on, Sister! You won't want to miss this!"

Ellen followed her brother down two floors to the den, where Pet nestled on the couch. They had left the hairball there to enjoy its favourite pastime – watching nature documentaries on the old black-and-white TV set. But the show had ended hours ago, and because Pet no longer had the energy to change the channel, the little creature sat slumped miserably against a throw pillow watching *Antique Belt Buckle Showcase*.

"I got a look at something in the telescope. Something fun," said Edgar as he turned the dial to the Nod's Limbs Public Access Channel. Reporter Natalie Nickerson stood in the foreground. Behind her a mob of angry Nod's Limbsians accosted Blake Glide, who cowered from their shouts and shaking fists.

". . . which is why," Natalie Nickerson was saying, "these citizens are accusing movie megastar Blake Glide of foul play in the treasure-hunt craze that's sweeping town. Here's Ethel Elines, owner of the Hotel Motel. Mrs Elines, can you tell our viewers what happened?"

Natalie pulled frail-looking Mrs Elines by her elbow into the frame of the camera.

"Well, dear, it isn't my place to say a bad word about anyone, you understand," the old woman said. "But that handsome young man over there was actually digging out the bottom of our chicken coop. I believe he was even using my husband's shovel. Now our chickens are homeless and confused. What am I going to do?"

"There you have it, viewers," said Natalie Nickerson. "Blake Glide: coop raider, shovel thief. But he isn't the only one falling victim to gold fever. Our whole town seems gripped in its, uh, grip. Reports are coming in of shops closing unexpectedly, wandering bands of trowel-toting treasure hunters stopping traffic and crowding malls – and multiple incidents of neighbours digging in one another's yards *without permission*."

A red-faced Chief Strongbowe leaned in and grabbed Natalie Nickerson's microphone. "Crushed pachysandra! Uprooted azaleas! Ravaged rhododendrons! My crack squad of gardeners won't stand for landscaping chaos. Lawn and Order will prevail!" He handed the microphone back to Natalie. "Ma'am."

"Madness," said the reporter. "Even my crew has abandoned their posts to go for the gold. I'm operating my own camera for this report! Now back to you in the studio, Barbara . . . Barbara? Are you there?"

Ellen turned off the TV. "Sweet little Nod's Limbs," she said. "Not so sweet these days, eh, Brother?"

"Nod predicted they'd dissolve into a greedy frenzy," said Edgar.

"While they're *dissolving*, we'll be solving." Ellen spread a piece of paper on the floor on which she had written the riddle.

Well done! But it's neither hear nor their.
For next an owl's hut needs repair;
Then seek a white raven, tangled in knots—
Only my air can connect the dots.

"Everyone else is only looking on the surface," said Ellen. "They see this bit about ravens and owls, and they think of zoos and chicken coops. But Nod's too clever to be so straightforward. Something is hiding here. Two phrases stand out to me: *needs repair* and *tangled in knots*."

"He's telling us something is broken," said Edgar. "We need to fix something. Or undo something."

"Or *unscramble* something," Ellen said.

Edgar sucked in a breath. "You mean . . . The thing that needs to be repaired isn't a *real* hut . . . it's the words themselves: *an owl's hut!*"

"Exactly. And there's no hog-tied bird anywhere in Nod's Limbs. It's the phrase *a white raven* we need to untangle!"

Edgar whooped and kicked his legs in the air. Even Pet seemed to bounce with joy. "Sister, that's brilliant! This is the closest I've ever come to wanting to hug you!"

"Thanks for resisting," said Ellen. "Now let's split up and do some unscrambling. You take the owl, I'll take the raven."

The twins sprawled on their bellies on the floor of the den with nubby pencils and scraps of paper, and began to rearrange the letters of the riddle.

It was simple enough to piece together gibberish phrases, but coming up with something that actually made sense proved more difficult. Edgar wrote and rewrote nonsense on the chance he would stumble across something. After what seemed like hours of scratching and erasing and half-mumbled cursing, he made his first discovery. The words "an owl's hut" could be reordered to spell "low haunts".

"What could be lower or more haunting than our basement?" he asked.

"No," his sister said. "Keep trying."

Edgar growled and hunched back over his sheet.

He muddled through a few more attempts (with Ellen rejecting "tuna howls", "Sultan Who", and his favourite: "oh walnuts") before arriving at two very promising leads.

"What do you think of 'town's haul' or 'south lawn'?" asked Edgar.

Ellen sat up. "Maybe it means both! The town's haul would be the golden limbs – and they're hiding in a south lawn somewhere."

"Did log cabins even *have* lawns in those days? Maybe he means Founder's Park," said Edgar. "Is that what your clue unscrambles to? It must!"

Ellen scowled. "I wish it would, but it's more stubborn than *you* are. So far 'a white raven' only gives us 'heavier want', 'naïve wreath', 'have tinware', and, um . . . 'variant whee'."

"Simple!" said Edgar, clapping his hands. "*Have tinware*. It's buried in a tin box in the southern half of Founder's Park. Grab a shovel, Sister, and let's get digging!"

"What about the homophone clue?"

"I don't know. Maybe there's a sign in Founder's Park we have to see first. It might point to the exact spot to dig."

"Hmm. It's worth a shot. What do you think,

Pet?" Ellen glanced at Pet, but its eye had shut and its tuft of hair lay flat.

"Ellen, we've got to hurry. Pet doesn't have long. We just need to dangle a golden pinkie or two in front of Eugenia's crew, and they'll get the spring dug out in no time. But first we need to find the limbs."

17. Sounds Like Victory

But the twins found that they were far from the first to search Founder's Park.

A hundred freshly dug holes dotted the lawn – south *and* north. Dozens of senior citizens with metal detectors (Team Golden Oldies) scoured the turf, listening for the faintest *ping* from their machines. After one white-haired gentleman in shorts and knee-high argyles heard such a beep, he flung down his detector and began digging.

"Ding-doggity!" he yelled. "Another bottlecap! When did the litterbugs take over our town?"

His teammates muttered curses without looking up from their work. The twins surveyed the scene in dismay.

"Did they unscramble the clue, too?" asked Ellen.

"I don't think so," said Edgar. "I think this town is really starting to lose it. They're just digging randomly now. Either way, they've already churned up the entire south lawn."

Ellen sat on the ground and groaned. "There's nothing buried here. Nothing! We're going to lose Pet . . . our house . . . everything!"

"No, no," said Edgar. "We were on the right track. I can feel it! Maybe 'have tinware' wasn't the right unscrambling – maybe there's another phrase we missed."

He took their paper scraps from his satchel and laid them out in front of him. As Team Golden Oldies

filed out of the park for dinner, Ellen joined her brother in poring over the jumble of letters.

"Bah! Fidgety little letters, getting all tangled up with one another."

But Edgar was obsessed. He scrawled on every inch of the paper, looking for every variation of the words.

"Good gravy, Sister, you've missed the most obvious one! *Whereat Ivan*! We just need to find this Ivan fellow and . . . Oh, wait. What about . . . Let's see, move the *H* . . . need this *A* . . . and another *A*, and . . . could it be? . . . YES!"

Edgar kissed the sheet of paper and did a celebratory cartwheel that landed him in one of the Golden Oldies' holes. He popped his head out of the pit and held out the paper for his sister to see. She peered at the list of words he had written, and at the bottom – right beneath "Ethan waiver" – she saw the words "weather vain!!!!"

"Wrong again, Edgar," said Ellen. "Weather *vane* is spelled *v-a-n-e* . . ." She gasped. "Homophones," she said. Now it was her turn to cartwheel. "The town's haul is in a weather vane! You're not as dumb as everyone says you are, Brother."

"I try," said Edgar, hopping out of the hole. "One problem, though. There must be hundreds of weather vanes around this town. Where do we begin?"

Ellen sat on the edge of the hole and thought about this a moment.

"It's not a haul we're after," she said. "It's a *hall*. As in—"

"Town Hall's weather vane!"

18. Sparring on the Spire

Nod's Limbs' stately Town Hall – another monument built during the Thaddeus Knightleigh era – loomed over Founder's Park directly to the east. In summer months, the building's dome enveloped Nod's statue in shadow from dawn to midmorning. Two hundred years ago, Thaddeus would regularly arrive at his office early just to enjoy the sight, which was, despite all his great public works, the only way he had ever been able to overshadow Augustus Nod in his lifetime.

Like all good town halls, a tall spire topped the domed roof, and, in turn, an ornate bronze weather vane topped the spire. And while most weather vanes depict a proud rooster – or perhaps a whale in coastal towns – Nod's Limbs' vane honoured an entirely different creature: a bee, the humble insect whose wax had fuelled the success of Nod's candle-making empire. After years of exposure to rain and snow, the glistening bronze bee had tarnished to a seasick green.

Edgar and Ellen sized up the leafy ivy that climbed to the roof.

"Exceedingly simple," said Edgar. "We climb up the ivy, you boost me onto the dome, I crawl up to the spire and check the weather vane."

"I boost you?" asked Ellen. "How about *you* boost *me*? It was my idea that cracked this whole thing wide open!"

"Your idea?" said Edgar. "Okay, smarty, last one to the top does the boosting."

The twins scrambled up the building, stepping on each other's fingers and jabbing at each other's eyes. Ellen reached the roof first (by head-butting her brother at the last second), and she sprawled atop the dome with a contented sigh.

"Ah, that was fun," she said.

She pulled Edgar up and the two took in the vista of the river and the seven covered bridges. When viewed from either end of town, the bridges bore jolly messages, one word per rooftop. Looking from the east end, they hailed, WELCOME FRIEND TO NOD'S

LIMBS. STAY AWHILE, and from the west, COME BACK
SOON FRIEND AND TAKE CARE. From Town Hall's
vantage point in the middle of town, the messages
didn't make much sense when looking either direction; nevertheless, Edgar and Ellen knew those big,
cheerful words by heart.

"Remember our carefree days when our only
worries were how we were going to repaint the
bridge messages?" Edgar asked.

"Ah, yes," recalled Ellen in a faraway voice. "GO
AWAY NOW FOOL OR GET SCARRED."

"Who could forget FLEE MORTALS IT'S NOD'S
LIMBS' ZOMBIE FEAST?" Edgar sighed. "Don't worry,
Sister. We'll be back to our old ways soon, once our
home is no longer threatened by Knightleighs. We
just need to finish this hunt once and for all."

"Going up," said Ellen, waiting for her boost up
the side of the dome. But then the twins heard a
scraping, scrambling sound from the other side.

"Someone else is on the roof," whispered Ellen.

"Another treasure hunter?" asked Edgar softly.

Ellen held a finger to her lips, and they tiptoed
around the perimeter. On the other side they encoun-
tered the one thing worse than a treasure hunter.

"You!" cried Ellen.

"You!" cried Stephanie Knightleigh.

Stephanie wore lavender mountain climber's boots and a bike helmet, and she held a rope that had been lassoed around the weather vane.

"Following us, eh, Knightleigh?" said Edgar. "Figures you would let our brains do all the work."

"I would never follow you," said Stephanie. "I couldn't stand being downwind."

"You noticed the misspellings too, then? And kept it to yourself?" said Ellen. "Sneaky, sneaky."

"Withheld information? Me? *Never*," she said with mock surprise. "I just assumed Nod was an idiot."

With that, she tightened her grip on the rope and sprang.

"She's going for the vane!" said Edgar, but Ellen was already in motion. As Stephanie scaled the dome, pulling herself up with the rope, Ellen caught the trailing rope behind her and followed. Stephanie saw her pursuer and raised her mountaineer's boot.

"Spikes!" yelled Ellen. She dodged the boot and managed to grab Stephanie's leg. Halfway up the side of the dome, the girls found themselves locked in an aerial wrestling match. They flailed, kicked, and shoved until the taut rope began to sway, sending them tumbling around the side of the dome like some sort of deadly maypole dance. As the two girls pitched back and forth, Edgar clambered past them on the rope, using their arms and legs as rungs.

"Get back here!" called Stephanie, grabbing at Edgar's arm. Edgar's leg caught in the rope, and the trio whomped and wailed at one another, trying to break free.

Suddenly a metallic squeak stopped them cold.

"That wasn't—" began Edgar.

"It was," yelped Ellen. The metal spire supporting the weather vane gave another sickening groan. They felt the rope twitch, and with a long *creeeeeeeeeeeak*, the spire bent nearly in half. The three combatants swung out over the side of the roof like fish on a hook. Beneath their toes, Edgar, Ellen, and Stephanie could see the steps of Town Hall waiting to catch them, a full four storeys below.

Hardly daring to breathe they swayed back and forth with the steadfast rhythm of a clock pendulum, but the spire had stopped bending.

"Oh walnuts," said Edgar.

"Gnaw, Edgar," said Ellen. "Gnaw yourself out of these knots. Get the limbs and save Pet. If I've got to go, I can't think of a better person to go down with than the Purple Princess."

"Would you stop being so dramatic?" said Stephanie. "Besides, your body would totally break my fall."

But before Edgar could sink his teeth into the rope, he saw movement below.

"Oh no," he said. "I forgot! Principal Mulberry – she said everyone should meet—"

"At Town Hall after dinner!" said Ellen. "They'll find our clue!"

Indeed, clusters of Nod's Limbsians, having just polished off their dinners, were now trickling into the plaza in front of Town Hall.

"Maybe they won't notice us," said Ellen. "Everyone just act natural."

"Are you kidding?" said Stephanie. "I'm not cracking my head open for some dumb hunt. *Hellllp!*"

It was Fire Chief Gully Lugwood himself who climbed the fire engine ladder to cut them down.

"Well, you aren't white ravens, but you're certainly tangled in knots," he laughed. Then he got a closer look at his rescuees. "Oh. It's *you* two again. And . . . Miss Knightleigh! What on Earth . . . ?"

He gasped, then fixed them with an accusing glare. "You youngsters wouldn't be after another clue, would you?"

He was met with silence. He looked past the

three and saw the tarnished bee. Then Gully Lug-wood gave a curt nod to his crew below.

"I'm going to need a blowtorch," he called. "I think there's a lot more than three trespassing kids up here."

19. Face the Maestro

When Edgar and Ellen and Stephanie touched down at last, few citizens paid them any mind. All eyes were on the sheared-off weather vane being lowered to the ground after them.

"Curse you, Stephanie," said Ellen. "Thanks to you, the whole town gets the next clue *again*."

Stephanie didn't reply – she was watching her mother and father stride through the crowd.

"Daddy! Mother!" she called.

Judith Stainsworth-Knightleigh came close and replied in a low voice. "We distinctly told you to *avoid* attention. What do you call all of this?"

"The twins—" began Stephanie, but her mother cut her off with a wave of disgust. Her father looked as green as the weather vane.

The rest of the townspeople and scattered movie

crew gathered around as the Volunteer Firefighter's Brigade fiddled with the vane. At last Gully Lugwood uttered a triumphant "Aha!" as his penknife slipped inside a latch on the bronze bee's abdomen. The bee opened like a book, revealing a poem etched on its insides.

The fire chief read in silence for a moment, but after shouts from the crowd ("Share! Share!" and "Surely, it's your civic duty to read it to all!" and so on), he cleared his throat and read aloud:

> *Now face the maestro, though it may howl.*
> *Foot it four furlongs and bring ye your trowel.*
> *Horseshoe hermit king and blue,*
> *As sixteen sees four, so must you too.*

Not long ago, the treasure hunters would have speculated aloud, sharing their ideas about the riddle's solution. Now, only silence followed the reading of the clue.

Edgar and Ellen crouched low and whispered to each other.

"Face the maestro – is that Nod?" asked Edgar.

"Well, his statue is right across the street. It seems obvious, doesn't it?" said Ellen.

"Which can mean only one thing," said Edgar. "*That* isn't the answer."

Despite Edgar's assertion, most townsfolk lined up between Town Hall and the statue, facing due west as the riddle seemed to suggest. Remnants of the teams huddled together for hushed conferences. The twins strained to hear the whispered words.

"The maestro, the hermit king – it all points to Nod's statue. Is there another riddle hidden there?"

"No, no, it clearly said to walk four furlongs *past* the statue, and to bring a trowel. The next clue is buried!"

"Fine. What's a furlong?"

20. Mutiny

"Well, there's nothing about a horseshoe hermit king in here," said Ellen, slamming shut a book titled *Mane and Tail*. She and Edgar had returned to their house, but had come up with little more than theories for the solution to the clue.

They had looked in all kinds of books in their library, the biggest help coming from the dictionary's entry for "maestro": "a master, especially one who conducts an orchestra or teaches music." So far, though, the only musical footnote in town history was Willy Ach's All-Kazoo Barbershop Quartet, which had been a townwide rage in the early 1900s. Aside from that, nothing.

At one point Pet tried to get Ellen's attention by tickling her ear with a frizzled tendril, but Ellen was too absorbed in her research to notice. Eventually the creature leaned too far and rolled off Ellen's shoulder onto its own eyeball. After that, it napped fitfully on the dictionary stand. The twins were soon asleep as well.

As morning light spilled through the grimy windows, a familiar *twang-thump* sound came from downstairs, and the twins snapped awake.

"That was one of our traps!" said Edgar.

"The Wilhelm Screamer, from the sound of it," said Ellen. "Let's go!"

As the twins ran down the stairs, they found exactly what they had expected on the second-floor landing: a stuffed crocodile head, snout down, dangling from a set of ropes. The old beast had fallen from the ceiling and swallowed an intruder, whose sneakers jutted from the toothy maw.

"Thought you could sneak up on us, eh, Stephanie?" said Ellen. "Well, now you're gator fodder!"

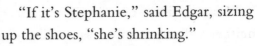

"If it's Stephanie," said Edgar, sizing up the shoes, "she's shrinking."

"At ease, Wilhelm," said Ellen, hoisting the crocodile on creaky pulleys back into the air. Wilhelm spat out a quavering young pirate.

"Miles, what are you doing here?" cried the twins.

The boy straightened his feathered hat.

"I thought you might, um, be able to help me solve the clue," he said nervously.

"What's wrong with your little pirate buddies? Why aren't *they* helping you?" Edgar looked suspicious.

"They made me walk the plank," said Miles. "Calvin Hucklebee made himself captain of the Some-Quarter Pirates since he solved the first clue – or he says he solved it, at least. But I'm the one who knows everything about pirates."

"What do you need from us, Miles? Make it quick," said Ellen.

"I had an idea, but Calvin wouldn't listen, and neither will my family," said Miles. "I remember reading something in an old pirate comic about the word *maestro*. It was issue 77, or maybe 78, of 'Captain Bloodgut of the Barbary Coast', but last year my mom threw all my comics away—"

"We don't have any comics, Miles," said Ellen.

"That's okay. Stephanie told me once you had a really big room full of maps. Maps are what I need."

"Maps," said Ellen. "Sure. Knock yourself out. But" – she blocked his way – "you have to tell us everything you find out."

Miles nodded. Ellen started to lead the way to the map room when Edgar grabbed her elbow and pulled her aside.

"Are you out of your lumpy skull?" he hissed. "Why are you letting him use our resources?"

Ellen only sucked her teeth.

"He's one of *them*," continued Edgar. "If he discovers something – and that's a big *if* – he'll blab it to everyone. And in case you've forgotten, *he's a Knightleigh!*"

Ellen spun on her brother and whispered, "First of all, we haven't had a bright idea all night. In case *you've* forgotten, we're racing against time. I'd team up with a dirty sock if it would help save Pet. And second of all . . ."

Ellen's voice trailed off. The twins had an unspoken agreement never to mention the frightful days when Ellen had been under a personality-altering trance and had unwittingly attended a particularly cruel slumber party at Stephanie's. The other girls had behaved unspeakably to Ellen, and the only one who didn't make fun of her – the only one who had shown her any kindness – had been Miles Knightleigh.

"It's just, well, Miles isn't so bad," said Ellen at last. Edgar goggled, but kept his mouth shut.

21. A Bad Day For Mr Frimmel

Miles pored over rolls of yellowed paper, unfurling each map carefully and examining it.

"What exactly are you looking for?" asked Edgar. "A way out of this town?"

"No, silly," said Miles. "I know where that is. No, it's something Captain Bloodgut said when the Corsican She-Devil attacked his ship."

"Do tell," said Edgar.

"Well, when the Corsican She-Devil appeared out of nowhere off the starboard bow of the *Squawking Parrot*, Captain Bloodgut said something about a 'malevolent maestro' bringing her there. And I just had a hunch . . ."

"Comics," said Edgar, rolling his eyes. "What *can't* they teach us?" He slid out of his chair and left to go watch TV, mumbling that he'd found more interesting things when plucking nose hairs.

Pet lay in Ellen's lap, shivering. Ellen regarded Miles sceptically as he unfurled another map (OVERLAND TRADE ROUTES FOR NORTHERN NOVA SCOTIA) and quickly rolled it back up.

"Why does your cat have only one eye?" asked Miles.

"It lost a fight with a giant sloth," said Ellen.

"Neat," he said. "Hey, did you hear what happened last night? Everybody walked west for four furlongs – turns out that's half a mile – and then they were at 1604 West Florence Boulevard. You know, Mr Frimmel's store? The Clarinet Emporium? Well, everybody saw the sixteen and the four, just like the riddle, and it made them a little nutsy and they tore up Mr Frimmel's store! They didn't find anything, but I knew they wouldn't. People have been digging up and down the street all night. They're like crazy dogs. Or squirrels. Squirrels dig holes too sometimes. I've seen it – Ooh! Ooh! I found it! I found it!" cried Miles, leaning over a map of the Mediterranean Sea. "'Maestro' means—"

"Forget it," said Edgar, slouching into the room. "The limbs have been found. We've lost."

22. The Mayor Victorious

The twins wanted Pet to rest at home, but the creature wouldn't let Edgar close his satchel without being tucked inside. The twins and Miles ran all the way to Nassau Way, where it seemed everyone in town had gathered outside a long, low building. Two hundred years ago, this old building had been the Nod's Limbs Livery Stable, where citizens rented horses and carriages of the finest quality. Today it was still a stable, though its only regular inhabitants were cranky old Mr Bundersen, the stable master, and cranky old Gertie, the mare who pulled the hayride wagons each Falling for Fall Festival.

Mayor Knightleigh stood outside of the stables next to a cartful of golden arms and legs. He basked in the glory of the TV camera lights as he spoke into Natalie Nickerson's microphone.

"So then I realized Nod wasn't referring to *himself* as the maestro, he was referring to my late ancestor, Thaddeus Knightleigh, who of course lived down this street in stately Knightleigh Manor. So when you face northeast from town hall and walk a half-mile towards the manor, you arrive here at the stables!"

Miles fumbled with the handful of maps he had brought with him. "Aw, gee, I was so sure I was right," he said glumly.

The mayor continued. "When I saw the stable, I said to myself, 'Mr Mayor, you may be a clever and handsome man, as well as a great civic leader, but what about the rest of the clue?' You will be relieved to know I had an answer for myself. I said, 'Self, this is where the *horseshoes* were, the very ones used by Nod, the *hermit king,* on his horse whose name, legend has it, was Old *Blue*.'"

"I thought it was Clip-Clop," said Ernest Hirschfeld.

"No, no. Definitely *Old Blue*. Lo and behold when I looked in the fourth aisle, inside the sixteenth stable, what did I find behind a loose board but these very precious limbs, thus ending our hunt and making me the legitimate owner of all Nod's possessions, which I can assure you, was only these limbs."

The mayor beamed, but he seemed to be the only one excited about the news. A few citizens (and at least one major motion picture star) wept openly.

"You will all be happy to hear that, through the good will of me, I am donating these limbs to the Nod's Limbs Museum of Wax. Now, I know they're not strictly wax, but it will be nice to see them on display and remember what fun we had looking for them and how generous I am. Bob!"

Bob, the mayor's intern, stepped forward.

"Cart these keepsakes to the museum, Bob!" said the mayor. "As for the rest of you, go on home and get back to your normal, non-gold-hunting lives. Bye-bye, now!"

The crowd began to wander away.

"I can't believe Knightleigh outsmarted us," said Edgar, clenching his fists. He turned on Miles. "You were sent to throw us off track, weren't you?"

"I wasn't! I did it on my own!" said Miles. "Um, that's not what I mean. I mean I was on the right track, I just know it!"

"It just doesn't seem fair," said Miss Croquet. "He already has so much."

"Museum? Ha! If I didn't win them, I don't want to *look* at them," said Marvin Matterhorn. "My family is boycotting the Museum of Wax from now on."

"Come, Sir Geoffrey," said a saddened Sir Malvolio. "Hence! I am mistempered by our defeat in this folly for gold—"

"I know that gold!" blurted Sir Geoffrey, pointing at the limbs. "That's our paint, Malvolio! *Mead Gold*!"

The senior Gallant Paintsman cast a glance at the cart, tilted his head curiously, and then moved in for a closer look.

Mayor Knightleigh stepped in front of Sir Malvolio and held up his hand. "Move along now, *sirs*. Surely a garage somewhere needs a fresh coat of paint."

"Beg pardon, my lord." Sir Malvolio pushed past the mayor, "But methinks Sir Geoffrey speaks true!"

"Darn tootin' I speak true!" Sir Geoffrey raced to the cart and picked up one of the legs. "I had Mead Gold in my hair for weeks after that crazy girl in pyjamas flipped out on Mrs Stainsworth-Knightleigh's show!"

The mayor stormed after Sir Geoffrey. "Drop my leg, painter!"

Upon hearing the commotion, the townspeople began to gather again.

"Doesn't weigh much for pure gold!" Sir Geoffrey tossed an arm to Sir Malvolio.

Heidi Birchbeer grabbed the other arm from the cart and scratched it with a fingernail. Gold paint flecks fell to the ground. "The – the limbs aren't gold! This *is* paint!"

"Great hog!" Lyman Herringbottle held the final limb aloft. "This leg is wood!"

"Nod buried wooden limbs?" asked Betty LaFete. "This was all a hoax?"

"A hoax indeed, madam," said Mr Herringbottle, "but not by Nod. This paint is new."

"Aye. Whilst the quality of our paint is legendary," boasted Sir Malvolio, "it has been to market nary a decade!"

"That's right!" shouted Sir Geoffrey, shaking an arm at the mayor. "Someone here has planted *fake limbs*!"

The mayor looked stunned.

"You – you mean, I've been *had*?" he asked. "That, well, that seems unsporting, don't you think? I shall launch a full investigation to ferret out the guilty party, but until such time, perhaps we should post-pone the search—"

"The hunt is back on!" shouted Chief Strongbowe.

The townspeople's sorrowful faces turned jubilant.

"We can still find the *real* gold limbs!"

"But who planted the fake ones?"

Neighbours eyed one another warily, but one thing was for sure: *Someone* was not playing fair. The citizens of Nod's Limbs rushed away as quickly as they had gathered, desperate to find the next clue.

Edgar leaped in the air.

"I knew it! I knew that melon-headed mayor could never outwit us!" he shouted. "Now what do we do?"

"Batten down your hatches and follow me!" said Miles.

23. That's a Fair Wind A-Blowing

"Are you sure about this?" asked Edgar. They had returned to Town Hall with the old maps Miles had carried from the twins' house. Edgar glanced around, checking for spies.

"I'm double-triple sure," said Miles. "I *knew* I knew what Captain Bloodgut meant! Pirates in the old days, they had names for each of the winds. That way, when the wind blew, they wouldn't say something boring, like, 'The wind's coming from the south.' They would say something much more awesome, like, ''Tis a cruel sirocco blowin' trouble our way, an' no mistake.'"

Miles smoothed a map on the ground. The map depicted the coastline of the Mediterranean Sea as well as curving lines and arrows showing channels, reefs, common wind conditions, and other notations for the savvy sailor.

In the lower right the map bore the customary compass pointing the way to north, south, east, and west. Just as Miles had said, each point of the compass had a word written beside it naming a wind. To the south, 'sirocco'; to the southeast, 'marin'; to the north, 'mistral'; to the west, 'zephyros'; and to the northwest—

"Maestro!" cried the twins together.

"Miles, you're a black-hearted, red-bearded, hook-handed genius!" said Ellen.

"And don't ye be fergettin' it," said Miles. *"Arrr."*

He unfurled another parchment, this one the old map of Nod's Lands that had been tacked to the wall of the map room. "Okay, so we just look on this map and see what's four furlongs northwest of Town Hall."

But it wasn't quite that easy. The map didn't have a scale, and furthermore, that quadrant of the map showed nothing but forest.

"We better get exploring," said Edgar.

"But we can't waste our time walking all over town," Ellen protested, snatching the map.

"I've got an idea," said Miles, taking off his shoe.

"Not all over town, Sister. Just northwest," said Edgar.

"No, really, I think I've got it," said Miles.

"Ah, yes, good thing northwest is only a quarter of the whole town," Ellen replied. "Miles, put your shoe back on."

Miles sighed and grabbed the map from Ellen.

"Hey!" she exclaimed as Miles spread his shoelace across the parchment.

"I bet it's here," he said, pointing. "My shoelace says so."

"Oh, well, why didn't we ask the shoelace in the first place?" snapped Edgar.

"No, look. See?" said Miles. "I used my shoelace to measure the distance between Town Hall and the corner of Florence and Fifth – Mr Frimmel's store. That was four furlongs, right? So I use that same length to go from Town Hall towards the maestro . . ."

The end of the shoelace fell right at the base of Nod's Limbs historic Crabby Apple Tree.

"We could have done that," Ellen snorted, wagging a footie in the air. "But we don't care much for shoelaces."

24. The Root of the Problem

The three headed across the river towards Cairo Avenue and the Crabby Apple Tree.

"Where do you suppose we start?" Edgar asked as they walked. "I don't see a horseshoe factory or a hermit king's house. I guess we case it now, and come back at night for further exploration."

Ellen scanned the street in both directions. Cairo Avenue was lined on both sides with pretty Victorian houses in pastel blues and yellows. Manicured lawns and evenly trimmed hedges acted as a buffer between the homes and bustling Cairo Avenue. Just ahead of them, a spindly crabapple tree grew in the middle of the street.

The Crabby Apple Tree was said to be where Nod first tied his horse when he arrived in the desolate forest that was to become Nod's Limbs. The tree was so beloved that future generations preferred to split traffic *around* it rather than cut it down. Edgar stared at the tree and chewed his lip. All of a sudden, he hollered, "Criminy! The Crabby Apple Tree, Sister! Don't you see? Horseshoe! Hermit! King! Blue! Those are all kinds of *crabs*!"

"*Shh!*" hissed Ellen. "I mean, that's brilliant, but still – *shh*!"

"We're the best!" Miles whisper-yelled.

"It all makes sense!" said Edgar. "'As sixteen sees four' – four is sixteen's square *root*!"

"Yay!" said Miles. "What's a square root?"

"Who cares?" said Ellen. "Come nightfall, it's time to dig!"

"So the scent's hot again, is it, kids?" said a voice behind the hedges. Don Pickens stood up holding a pair of hedge clippers. "I'll help you dig. We won't have to tell anyone else about it."

"Tell anyone else what?" said a man in the next yard over.

"Crud," said the twins.

"Oh no you don't, Johnson!" cried Don Pickens to his neighbour. "You just want the gold for yourself!"

The bickering gathered the attention of motorists and other neighbours. As the word "gold" floated over Cairo Avenue in the middle of a sunny Sunday afternoon, restraint and cordiality melted like a double-decker ice cream cone in a hothouse.

The twins and Miles watched helplessly as hordes of citizens attacked the dirt around the Crabby Apple Tree. With no more to go on than "it's in the roots," treasure hunters grabbed shovels and hoes from nearby gardens and burrowed holes on all sides of the trunk, flinging clods of dirt into one another's faces. Soon the ground was as pocked as a rotten sponge. At last Mr Pickens heard a *thunk* under his spade, and the frenzy stopped.

There was no concealing the find. The townspeople tensed with anticipation as Mr Pickens unearthed a rusty metal box. It was so corroded that the lid fell off when he touched it. He gingerly pulled an old scrap of paper from inside and was forced to read it aloud:

> *There and back and there again.*
> *To find the limbs, now seek Nod's friend.*

The riddle's perched above the floor,
By one, then two, then three, then four.

Sated by the new riddle, the hopeful hunters quickly retreated, each off to crack the riddle on his or her own.

After the twins and Miles – the last to leave – trudged away, a cool maestro blew over Cairo Avenue. With most of its roots exposed to the sky, the beloved Crabby Apple Tree swayed in the breeze, toppled, and split in two.

25. The Blackest Hour

Since Miles was expected home for dinner, the twins returned to their house alone. Pet rode on Ellen's shoulder until a slight breeze blew a clump of the creature's hair onto the road. After that they put Pet in Edgar's satchel. Edgar kicked the dirt as they walked along.

"Sister . . . are we wasting our time with the hunt? Would we have been better off down in the cavern, digging out the spring?"

"No telling how far we could have got," said

Ellen. "Meanwhile Pet gets worse and worse . . . and our doomed house . . ."

They walked in silence for some time. At last Edgar said something so unexpected it made Ellen grimace.

"I wonder where our parents are," he said.

In all the years since their parents had disappeared, leaving a note saying they had gone on extended holiday, neither Edgar nor Ellen had ever actually wondered out loud about them.

Ellen took a long time to respond. "Do you think things would have turned out . . . differently if they were here now?"

"*Differently*, sure," said Edgar. "It's *better* that I wonder about."

Ellen grunted. "Look what having parents did for Stephanie. I want Heimertz back. He cared about Pet . . . and us."

"If anybody could have dug out the spring, it was him. And who would dare knock down this house with a caretaker like *that* protecting it?" Edgar paused. "But I don't think he's coming back, Sister."

"I guess he never got our note," said Ellen, dropping her head into her hands. "Now there's no one to help us but *us*." After a moment she looked up again. "I'd give up everything to save Pet."

Edgar nodded. "But what's the better way to do it? Solve a madman's riddle or go back to shovelling out the balm?"

"If we go back to the caves, we'd need to devise a way of digging faster," said Ellen. "Some method of moving large amounts of earth."

"Sort of like the way those townies tore into the Crabby Apple Tree," said Edgar. "We need an army of people like that."

Ellen pulled her pigtails. "Yes . . . yes. An army like that. How do you suppose we could convince a large number of people to come to our house and dig in a frantic frenzy?"

"Oh no – no more riddles," said Edgar.

"Oh *yes* – we just need a riddle of our own," said Ellen. "We have to convince the Nod's Limbsians that *the golden limbs are buried at our house*."

Edgar smiled a crooked smile. "I see, I see. If

they thought Nod's treasure was hidden, say, *in our cavern* . . . right beneath the cave-in . . . Why, they would shovel themselves crazy to get to the bottom, wouldn't they?"

"That they would, Brother!" said Ellen. "We just need to plant a fake riddle that points to our house, and the locals will come flocking with their shovels. We'll uncover the balm in hours, not days!"

"Which means we need to solve this *Nod's friend* thing first, so we can plant *our* riddle in its place," said Edgar.

Pet nuzzled Edgar's hand.

"Hang onto your follicles, Pet," he said. "We're going to save you yet!" And the rest of the way home, the twins sang:

> *Make them think the gold is under*
> *This grey house and they'll come plunder,*
> *Tear the very ground asunder—*
> *That greedy, grasping group.*
> *Digging, digging, ever deeper,*
> *'Midst the crawlies and the creepers,*
> *Find a secret spring and keep our*
> *Pet off Death's front stoop.*

26. In the Blink of an Eye

"Nod's friend . . . Nod's friend." Edgar paced back and forth. "Nod didn't have any friends! He was a miserable old codger who died lonely and poor!"

The twins had turned their den into a sort of war room with reference books piled everywhere, maps covering the walls, and Natalie Nickerson blathering away on the TV, keeping them informed of breakthroughs (or the lack thereof) in the outside world. After some debate they had decided that the line "seek Nod's friend" could have but a single meaning. While the old hermit seemed to have no friends in the human realm, his journal made it clear that he did have one trusted companion: a certain fuzzy, one-eyed hairball seated before them. The twins had tried to extract information from Pet about Nod, his habits, his acquaintances, and had even given the creature a pencil so it could make some of the doodles it used to communicate.

But Pet was too weak to write legibly, and it had grown frustrated and crabby. It seemed to lose more hair every time it moved, and it finally let the pencil fall and closed its eye tight. Now it lay in a bundle of rags the twins had piled together as a little nest.

"Looking worse than ever," sighed Ellen.

"Which?" asked Edgar glumly. "Pet? Or our chances of finding the limbs?"

"Both," said Ellen. "At least with the other clues I had some idea of where to begin. Now, our only lead may go from dead *end* . . . to *dead*."

At this, Pet's eye popped open. The creature gazed at Ellen and quivered.

"Uh, the *deadline* you mean . . . for solving the clue . . ." Edgar elbowed his sister in the ribs.

"Right, of course," said Ellen. "Ugh, I just *wish* Nod's journal hadn't gone up in flames."

"If only I'd read the passages more carefully," said Edgar. "But we were just interested in the balm and Pet. And there wasn't much in there, either. Mostly scientific jargon."

"Still, I don't recall any mention of him having dinner guests, sending fruit baskets, or mailing out holiday cards," said Ellen.

"Or he didn't write about it, if he did," said Edgar. "I mean, the only *friend* of Nod's that we know of is—"

"Pet. I know. But Pet can't tell us anything, Brother."

Pet blinked.

"There's got to be a way!" said Edgar. "A way to communicate. *Something*."

"Look at it, Edgar! It can barely blink—" Ellen stopped. "Wait! That's it!"

"What?"

"Pet." Ellen dropped her head down, so it was level with the hairball. "We're going to ask you some yes or no questions. Do you think you can blink the answers? Once for yes, twice for no."

Pet blinked, albeit slowly.

"Okay, Edgar, what should we ask it? We should try to make this quick – I think even blinking takes its toll."

"Pet, did Nod have any friends besides you?" asked Edgar.

Pet blinked twice.

"That's what I thought! So, where do we go from there?"

"Maybe we're getting too caught up on the 'Nod's friend' bit. There *are* three other lines to the clue."

"True, but the fact that the next clue is 'perched above the floor' doesn't give us a whole lot to go on."

Both the twins were pacing now, trying to think of the right question to ask.

"Okay, what do we know?" said Ellen. "Nod was

a hermit. He didn't have anybody in his life . . ."

Pet shifted as much as it was able, but the twins didn't notice.

"And he died penniless, except for this house—"

Pet shuddered so hard, it fell out of its nest. This got the twins' attention.

"What? What is it, Pet?"

Pet blinked twice.

"No? What do you mean?"

Pet's eye closed and stayed that way. It could do nothing more.

"Wait, Ellen, what was the last thing you just said?"

"That Nod died penniless."

Pet blinked. Twice.

"Nod *wasn't* penniless when he died?"

Pet blinked twice, and looked expectantly from one twin to the other.

Ellen pulled a pigtail. "Nod was rich when he died?"

One blink.

"Very rich?"

This time, Pet blinked four times, just for emphasis.

Edgar frowned. "So Herringbeetle was wrong. What does it matter anyway?"

"You dunderhead – don't you see? Everyone thought Nod was penniless, because he lived alone in the woods and didn't leave a will. If Nod *was* wealthy when he died, where did it all go? Money, possessions, land – it had to go into *someone's* hands. What if whoever has it, is this 'friend' in the riddle?"

"But where are we going to look? We're already on one treasure hunt – I don't fancy starting another one with even fewer clues."

"What about a safe bet?" said Ellen, grinning. "And when I say 'safe', I mean it literally." She pointed to a map of Nod's Limbs – the corner of Florence and Sydney. Though few modern landmarks existed on the 200-year-old map, there was one in particular that had stood the test of time: the Nod's Limbs Bank.

"Safety deposit boxes, Brother," said Ellen. "The little vaults in banks where people keep their most cherished secrets locked away. Maybe Nod left some clues there for us to find."

27. Break-In

"Typical," said Edgar. "Nod's Limbsians make breaking and entering no fun at all."

It was a little after midnight, and he and Ellen were crouched outside the bank beside an unlocked basement window. Ellen swung it open as Edgar put his crowbar back into his satchel with a disappointed sigh. The twins crawled into the room, where private lockboxes lined every wall.

"At least I'll get a little practise with my lock pick," said Edgar, lighting up the room with a flash-

light. "We sent my best one to Heimertz, but I have a hand-sharpened hairpin I've been itching to try."

Ellen nudged her brother and pointed to a big sign on the wall:

FORGET YOUR KEY? NO PROBLEM! USE MINE.
(DON'T FORGET TO PUT IT BACK!)
—BECKY FAFF, PRESIDENT, NOD'S LIMBS BANK

A nail next to the sign held a single key on a colourful lariat.

"This town is so *infuriating*," Edgar groaned. "It's like we're living inside a sugar cube."

"Come on, they're all alphabetical, so this shouldn't take long," said Ellen. She grabbed the key. "If there's no Nod, we scram."

"I can't believe we haven't discovered this room before now," said Edgar, eyeing the rows upon rows of lockboxes. "Some of these date back to the 1700s – centuries worth of skeletons in closets, all at our disposal!"

"Look, here are the *N*s," said Ellen. She and Edgar started reading names off the labels.

"Needermeyer . . . Neferhausen . . . Nickerson . . . Nopworst . . . No, I don't see a Nod."

"Blast!" cried Ellen. "I felt *so sure* we'd find something here."

Ellen leaned her head against the boxes in frustration.

"Come on, Ellen, we're wasting time."

"But I just know there's something we're missing!" She looked at the boxes in front of her, trying to think of what to do next, when one of the names caught her eye.

"Edgar! Look!"

The way the boxes were shelved, the *K*s fell directly above the *N*s. Edgar followed Ellen's gaze and gasped.

"A. Nod Knightleigh."

28. Keep Your Enemies Close

"It — it can't be Augustus, right?" Ellen finally asked. "He wasn't actually a *Knightleigh*, was he?"

Ellen put the master key in the lock, and gave it a turn. The mechanism resisted at first, as if two centuries of dust had jammed the inner workings. But with a gritty, grinding sound, the lock clicked. The twins held their breath as Ellen slid the box open.

Just then they heard someone fumbling with the door. The twins froze – they were in the middle of the room with nowhere to hide. Becky Faff was obviously a trusting soul, but even she would probably be suspicious to find the twins alone in the dark, breaking into a Knightleigh's lockbox.

The door swung open. The twins could see a silhouette of a person, but it didn't look quite tall enough to be the bank manager. In fact, it bore a resemblance to—

"*Stephanie!*" cried Ellen.

"What? Who's there?" Stephanie Knightleigh looked around frantically as Edgar shone his flashlight at her.

At first it looked like she was dressed in all black, down to her black boots and black gloves, and a black ski mask pulled up to her brow, but then the twins realized that the colour was actually a deep eggplant. When Stephanie saw the twins, she dropped the duffel bag she was carrying.

"You two!"

"Felon!" said Edgar. "We caught you *red-handed*, Stephanie! You broke into the bank!"

"*I'm* the felon?" said Stephanie, regaining her composure. "You broke in first! I've caught you

117

with your hand in someone's lockbox! Just wait till I tell my father!"

"Just wait till we tell the whole town!" Ellen shot back. She grabbed Stephanie's mask off her head. "This doesn't look like deposit apparel."

Stephanie glared at the twins, and the twins glared right back, and no one said anything for several seconds. Finally Stephanie broke the silence.

"Okay, so we both had the same idea," said Stephanie, "Now what'd you find?"

"Like we're going to tell *you*," Ellen spat.

"You tell me, or I have you arrested." Stephanie whipped out her purple cell phone.

"You're bluffing!" Ellen hissed. "You'd be in just as much trouble as—"

"As what? *You* two?" Stephanie asked with smirk. "Tell me, whose father is the most powerful man in town?"

Ellen scowled, but Edgar touched her elbow. "She's right. We don't have much of a choice. Nobody would believe us over a Knightleigh." He leaned into her ear and whispered, "And we can always sabotage her after we get out of here."

"Fine. We'll" – Ellen choked a little – "compromise."

Stephanie grabbed her mask back from Ellen. "Okay, rules. One: While we're in this bank, we truce – no stealing, no smuggling, no dupes. Agreed?"

The twins nodded, though Ellen's face still looked like she'd eaten a bushel of lemons.

"Two: We share *all* information, and can use it as we please."

The twins consented.

"And three: We don't tell *anyone* what we find here."

"Done," said Ellen. "Now will you let us get back to spying? You're about as stealthy as a garbage truck."

"And you smell like one. Now, what have we got?"

Ellen reluctantly stepped out of the way, and Stephanie saw the name on the lockbox.

"That's Knightleigh property! As a descendent, whatever's in that box belongs to me!"

"Ah, ah, ah," said Ellen. "Share all information, remember?"

29. The Lockbox

Whether the twins and Stephanie expected to find rolls of bank notes, another miniature golden statue, or even further clues to the hunt, they were all disappointed. The sole contents of the lockbox were a small stack of unopened letters and a heart-shaped locket.

Stephanie reached for the locket, but Ellen grabbed it first and opened it. Inside were two inked drawings. They were very old, the kind drawn in the days when no one smiled for portraits. A man and a woman gazed up at them. Even though neither of them smiled, they made a handsome couple.

The man was clean shaven, with wavy dark hair and an aquiline nose. The woman also had dark features, but for her large, light eyes. Despite her beauty there was a distinct sadness about those eyes.

"Who's the guy?" asked Ellen. "Nod?"

"Doesn't look much like the statue," said Edgar.

"So who do you think it is?"

Stephanie snatched up the locket.

"Don't you dare pocket that," warned Ellen.

"I wasn't going to," Stephanie retorted. "Everyone knows that you always put an inscription on a locket. See?" She pulled a gold chain out from beneath her collar. On it was a K-shaped locket with the inscription:

To Stephanie,

The sun shines more brightly when you're a Knightleigh.

Love,
Mother and Daddy

Ellen rolled her eyes.

"Now, let's see," Stephanie examined the back of the old locket. "Yes, look: 'To my sweet Agatha, with all my love, Pierre.'"

"Putrid," said Edgar.

Stephanie didn't say anything. She had started to look a little uncomfortable.

Edgar turned his attention to the letters. "Hey, these are addressed to Augustus," he said, sifting through them. "But they're all returned to sender. Mrs Pierre Knightleigh. These must be portraits of Pierre Knightleigh and his wife, Agatha."

"So *A* stands for Agatha, not Augustus," said Ellen. "But why the 'Nod'? Unless—"

"No! It can't be!" shouted Stephanie. Edgar dropped some of the letters at the outburst.

"What's the matter with you?" asked Ellen.

Stephanie clutched her ancestor's locket so tightly her knuckles turned white.

"Pierre Knightleigh was the son of Thaddeus Knightleigh, Nod's Limbs' first mayor."

"So?"

"So, as every Knightleigh knows, Pierre married Babette Croquet, and they had a son, Haggis Knightleigh—"

"They named their kid after sheep guts?" asked Ellen.

"Apparently it was fashionable at the time," huffed Stephanie. "Look, the important thing is, *Pierre and Babette* continued the Knightleigh lineage. He was never married to any *Agatha*!"

"I still don't see what the big deal is," said Edgar as he opened the top letter. He perused the contents and let out a long, low whistle.

"What does it say?" asked Ellen and Stephanie in unison.

"You're not going to believe this," said Edgar, and he began to read aloud:

To my dearest father—

I am writing for the last time. You yet refuse

to answer my letters, and no one has heard from or seen you in months. It is of the utmost importance that you show yourself, or at least make known your existence.

Since Thaddeus' death and burial in the Knightleigh tomb, his widow has been calling for an inquiry into your own whereabouts. Father, she wants to declare you dead! I do not believe that you are—in my heart, I know that you are alive somewhere, though whether you have departed our fair town forever I cannot fathom.

Still, you must be aware of the consequences of your absence. Without a legal will bequeathing all your many possessions, the widow Knightleigh will insist that I, as your only child, inherit everything— not just your monetary wealth, but the Waxworks, the acres of forest, the house, and <u>what lies beneath the house,</u> will all pass to my husband—and thus the rest of the Knightleigh family.

I love Pierre, but his mother is not to be trusted. She is cruel and possessive, and she wields a power over Pierre that I cannot break. I am afraid of what corruption might arise should the Life Balm come into her hands. And what of dear Pilosoculus? She would stuff its little eyeball and display it on her mantle like some kind of trophy!

I cannot prevent this if you do not come forward. I grow weaker by the day, and I do not know how much longer I will survive the sickness inside. I know you feel I have betrayed you by marrying the son of your enemy, but still am I committed to protecting you and the secret of the balm, for the good of all.

Please, papa, forgive me. I miss you, and love you,

Your Agatha

Edgar folded the letter and stuck it back in its envelope.

"So Nod had a daughter," he said.

"And since she married Thaddeus' son, all the Nod wealth passed to the Knightleighs," said Ellen. She and Edgar both looked at Stephanie, who had taken several steps backwards into the darkness. Her skin was ashen.

"I – I didn't know," she said, almost to herself. "Why didn't Daddy tell me?"

A thought struck Ellen.

"Your father! He was the only one insisting that Nod died penniless. But he knew! He knew that if no one ever found a will, the Knightleighs could keep Nod's money forever!"

"But now there *is* a will," said Edgar, "and it clearly states that all of Nod's possessions go to the person who solves the hunt. It's not just the limbs anymore . . ."

"It's everything," said Stephanie bitterly. The shock in her eyes had turned to fiery anger, but when she spoke, her voice was like ice cracking. "You're loving this, aren't you? Someone finds the golden limbs, and lucky ducky gets the Knightleigh fortune to boot, all because of a stupid technicality."

125

She threw the locket back in the box and slammed it shut. "You think you'll be the ones? I can promise you this: No one will get a single penny from us, limbs or no limbs!"

30. Back to the Dart Board

The twins went straight home after leaving the bank. Pet was still curled up in its nest in the den. Patches of its hair had whitened even while the twins were away, and it didn't wake as they entered.

"The Knightleighs are about to lose everything," said Edgar. "Even better, they're going to lose it to *us.*"

"But no one can find out about this, not until we have the limbs in our possession," said Ellen. "Can you imagine how crazy people would get if they knew the extent of the inheritance?"

"We just have to solve this clue first," said Edgar. He pulled it out again and looked at it for the hundredth time. "I just don't get it. There's something we're missing. Ellen – stay focused, will you?"

Ellen had picked up some darts and begun tossing them at the old map of Nod's Limbs on the wall.

She ignored her brother as she pulled the darts out of the map and threw them again.

"Something we're missing . . ." she muttered.

Thwack.

"Something so simple . . ."

Thwack.

"We've overlooked it completely . . ."

Thwack. Ellen looked at the dart she had just thrown. It had landed on one of the covered bridges. The centre one.

The Cairo Avenue bridge.

"Brother! Brother, I think I've got it!" she yelped, running to the map. Edgar looked up from his doodlings, startled.

"What is it?"

"Look!" Ellen grabbed his pencil and wrote, from west to east, on the bridges' roofs, "Welcome Friend to Nod's Limbs. Stay Awhile," and from east to west, "Come Back Soon Friend and Take Care."

"The middle bridge . . . ," Edgar gasped.

There were two words written on the roof of the Cairo Avenue bridge: "Nod's Friend."

31. Stephanie Says So

After fleeing the bank in anger, Stephanie Knight-leigh had roamed the town for some time muttering to herself. When she finally arrived home, it was almost two in the morning, and her mother was waiting by the door.

"Where have you been, young lady?" Judith Stainsworth-Knightleigh demanded. "Your father and I have been worried sick. We need you at full strength if you're going to help us solve this hunt. Sleepyheads do us no good. Isn't that right, dear?"

The mayor grumbled from a nearby armchair, where he had fallen asleep in his gargantuan pyjamas and fuzzy slippers.

"Mmm, quite right. Stephanie, what's the meaning of this late-night activity?"

Normally Stephanie would rue such upbraiding from her parents, but tonight she didn't care. Tonight she wanted answers.

"Does the name Agatha mean anything to either of you?" she asked.

"Agatha?" said Mayor Knightleigh. "No, no, I don't think so." But his voice wavered ever so slightly.

Judith's eyes narrowed at her daughter.

"What are you talking about, Stephanie?" she asked.

"I think you know, Mother," Stephanie replied. "Agatha *Nod* Knightleigh, first wife to Pierre Knightleigh. Just how big *was* our family fortune after Thaddeus died?"

"How did you – *where* did you—" spluttered the mayor.

"It doesn't matter. I want the truth."

"You want the truth?" said Judith in a dead voice. "Fine. The truth is this: There never was a Knightleigh fortune. Thaddeus drove the family finances into the ground, so when Pierre and Agatha fell in love, he was more than happy to marry them off, thinking she'd eventually inherit all of Nod's wealth."

"But that hateful old buzzard loathed us Knightleighs so much, he disowned his own daughter!" snorted the mayor.

"Yes, he thought he had cut us off for good," said Judith. "But then he disappeared and left no will. By default, Agatha ended up with her father's fortune after all. She died shortly after that, leaving Pierre a rich, rich man."

"But Nod *did* leave a will," said Stephanie.

"We never knew about it!" cried the mayor. "Of all the rotten luck! Why did this happen during *my* reign? And my plan was so brilliant—"

"What plan?" snapped Stephanie.

"Er, well, I thought that, well, if *I* were to find the golden limbs, then we'd finally own Nod's inheritance fair and square."

"*You* planted the fake limbs," said Stephanie. "Of course you did. Daddy, if you had just told me, I would have helped – I would have made sure it went off without a hitch! Now your townspeople are crazier than ever!"

"Don't talk to your father that way," said Judith. "What could *you* have done? Besides, no one else knows the history. *If* someone manages to find the limbs, they'll have no idea the true wealth they're entitled to."

"As a matter of fact, two other people know all about it," said Stephanie.

"*What?*" shouted her mother and father at once.

"Those twins were with me when I discovered everything. They'll keep quiet for now – it's not in their interest to blab until the hunt's over – but you can bet that their big mouths won't stop talking after that."

131

"Would – would anyone believe them?" asked the mayor. His eyes darted back and forth.

"Don't you see? It wouldn't matter," said Stephanie. "I've never seen the town like this. All it will take is the suggestion. We didn't have to look very hard to find Agatha's story. There are probably other records like this in Herringbottle's files that back it up, and our greedy townspeople won't stop until they find them."

"It – it can't be," said Judith. "There are no records."

"Are you absolutely sure, Mother? Are you willing to bet our whole fortune on it? Our credibility? You haven't been all that popular since the *Better Homes Than Yours* fiasco – what would you do if you were further disgraced?"

"Stephanie! That's enough!" But Judith's voice shook. She reached into the pocket of her robe and removed a monogrammed handkerchief to dab her eyes.

Stephanie hesitated. She had never seen her mother cry before.

"You can't let it happen, Stephanie!" wailed her father. "You can't let them take everything away! What will we do? What will we do?"

"I just wanted to be a good hostess. It's all I ever wanted. That and fabulous shoes," Judith blubbered.

Stephanie looked at her parents, awestruck. They had always been in control, and now, when things really mattered, they could barely form coherent sentences.

Stephanie stood as tall as she could and put her hands on her hips.

"Mother. Daddy. No one is going to break this family. Especially not two vagabonds who don't even *have* shoes. I have a plan."

Stephanie explained her scheme to her parents, who nodded weakly as their tears dried. Shortly afterwards she left the house again, and neither the mayor nor Judith protested.

However, Stephanie had not noticed her little brother sitting at the top of the stairs. Miles sighed mournfully; never had the boy looked so disappointed.

32. Ye Olde Switcheroo

"We have to make it sound like one of the regular clues," said Edgar. He hovered over Ellen's shoulder as she tried to compose the false clue they would plant at the bridge. "But it's got to be easy enough to be figured out quickly. We need to get everyone in town over here and digging."

"And it will go much faster without you breathing down my neck," said Ellen.

Edgar glanced back at Pet, who still lay unconscious in its nest, breathing shallowly. The creature looked as flat as a deflated balloon.

When Ellen was finally satisfied with her handiwork, the twins had one more detail to attend to.

"We're about to invite hordes of prying eyes into our house," Edgar said. "The last thing they need to see is the one-eyed mystery wig."

"You're right," said Ellen. "But where can we hide Pet?"

Edgar looked out the window and felt a pang of guilt as his eyes fell on their old caretaker's dilapidated shack.

"We can hide Pet in Heimertz's shed," he said. "No one would look for gold in that rickety old thing."

Once Pet had been safely tucked into an open accordion case, the twins ran all the way to the Cairo Avenue bridge. When they looked up at the ceiling – as "perched above the floor" seemed to indicate – they saw only the rafters, supported by thick beams that spanned the bridge.

Edgar walked the length of the bridge. "'By one, then two, then three, then four.' Here! The fourth beam! Could it be that simple?"

In a hole in the top of the fourth timber, the twins found a small, folded piece of parchment.

"This is it!" said Edgar. "Let's see what it says . . ."

"Later, Edgar," said Ellen. "We still have a lot to do before dawn."

The twins replaced the parchment with their homemade clue, then dashed back towards their house. But instead of turning up the nameless lane, they crossed onto the property of the Knightlorian Hotel next door.

The lobby was quiet, with one security guard fast asleep behind the front desk. From past ventures into the Knightlorian, the twins knew that the room assignments were kept in a file cabinet. Unfortunately the guard's chair was smack-dab in front of it.

Ellen crept up beside the guard. His feet were kicked up on the desk, and his hands were folded across his chest. He snored pleasantly.

"Here, hold his feet," said Ellen.

"Are you crazy? He'll wake up."

"No, he won't. There are light sleepers, heavy sleepers . . ." Ellen pointed to a small puddle on the floor. "And then there are drool sleepers. Move him."

Edgar frowned, then gently lifted the guard's legs off the desk, struggling under their weight.

The guard groaned and recrossed his arms.

"Don't drop them!" whispered Ellen.

"You . . . try . . . lifting . . . tree trunks . . ." grunted Edgar. He tugged on the legs, and the chair rolled aside.

"Okay, let's see," said Ellen as she perused the files in the cabinet. "Looks like the whole cast and film crew are staying here."

"Just find what we're looking for!" Sweat started dripping from Edgar's brow. "I can't hold these much longer . . ."

"Here, I've got it. Room 1013. Let's go."

Just then, Edgar's fingers slipped, and he dropped the security guard's legs. They hit the floor with a giant *thud*. The guard sprang to his feet.

"Wha – who's there?" he cried, looking around. But he was all alone, and as he settled back into his chair to resume his nap, he failed to notice the elevator's pointer going higher and higher, until it stopped on the tenth floor.

When the twins reached room 1013, the Presidential Suite registered to Blake Glide, Edgar pulled a tourist map of Nod's Limbs from his satchel. He spread it out on the floor.

WELCOME FRIEND TO NOD'S LIMBS STAY AWHILE was handwritten across one side of the bridges' roofs, and COME BACK SOON FRIEND AND TAKE CARE, was written on the other. The twins had drawn a circle and stars around the Cairo Avenue bridge, along with the words, "Be sure to visit this beautiful, historic site!"

"Too obvious?" asked Ellen.

"You can't be too careful with this mental lightweight," Edgar replied.

The twins slid the map under the door and returned to the elevators.

"With any luck, hordes of hunters will soon be banging on our door, demanding to dig up our foundations!" said Edgar.

33. Bamboozled

The sun was rising over the eastern hills as the twins ran back to their house to work on the clue they'd found at the bridge. But first, they ducked into Heimertz's shed to check on Pet.

The creature slumbered in the accordion-case nest and did not stir when Ellen stroked its hair.

"Time to save Pet," said Edgar. He unfolded the clue and read it aloud:

You think you're clever, you've followed the clues,
Well, won't you be shocked when you hear the news,
This whole hunt was fake! I hope you don't mind,
But there never were any gold limbs to find!
Ha ha!

The twins were silent for several minutes.

"It – it can't be," said Ellen. "The whole thing was one big wild goose chase? Why would Nod go through all the trouble?"

"We know that he hated pretty much everybody in town," said Edgar thoughtfully. "One last joke from the grave?"

"I can't believe we've been pranked by a guy

who's been dead for 200 years!" said Ellen. "It's . . .
it's . . ."

"Impressive," finished Edgar. "We should try
something like that when we get old and crusty."

"Edgar, this isn't funny! The will's a sham! Without the limbs, how will we get our house back?"

Ellen patted Pet on top of its closed eyeball.

"I'm sorry, Pet," she whispered. "We did our
best. But your old pal pulled our legs from beyond
the grave."

"Ellen, there's still our fake clue at the bridge,"
said Edgar. "No one else knows the hunt's not real.
People will still flock here with their buckets and
picks and shovels. We may not be able to save our
house, but at least we can still save Pet."

34. The Hobo and the Pirate

Later that morning, a peculiar figure could be seen
walking towards the Cairo Avenue bridge. He wore
baggy trousers and a polka-dot shirt, and had long,
straggly brown hair. His Coke-bottle glasses made
his eyeballs look three times larger than normal, and
he walked with a cane.

People passing in their cars paid him little notice, until Miles Knightleigh ran by on his fake peg leg.

Something about the man's walk made Miles pause – Miles lifted up his eye patch for a better look, and saw a large, bronze ring on the man's hand. It had a bulging bicep embossed on it – the ring every die-hard fan would recognize as the prize for winning a Best Muscles award from the AAA – the Action Actors' Academy.

"Mr Glide! Mr Glide!" shouted Miles. "Where are you going? Can I come, too? Why are you dressed like that?"

"Quiet!" said Blake Glide. He glanced around for eavesdroppers. "No one's supposed to know it's me."

"Got it," squealed Miles, snapping his eye patch back into place. "Are we undercover? Incog-neato? Awesome! I can be undercover too, see? *Arrr!*"

"Yes, yes, that's swell. Now if you want to come, hush up!" said Blake Glide.

"Okeydokey," Miles whispered. And the two continued up Cairo Avenue, the short, clownish man and the tiny pirate.

"This is just like when you went undercover as a garden gnome in *The Slurminator*! You sure showed those giant pus-sucking larva!"

"Why, thank you. It's always important to really try to embody a character, to get inside its head and say, 'Hey, what would a real garden gnome do in this situation.' Uh, but that's beside the point," said Blake Glide. "We've got to stay focused here."

"Focused. Right. Totally focused," said Miles. But focusing was hard since he practically had to run to keep up with the movie star and the peg leg kept slipping out of place.

As they approached the river, they passed Stephanie's best friend Cassidy Kingfisher, who was on her way to Knightleigh Manor. Cassidy looked sceptically at the oddly dressed man, but recognized the young pirate.

"Miles, what are you doing?" she asked, pulling him aside. "And who is that creep?"

"Mr Glide and I are undercover," Miles

whispered. "I don't know where we're going, but we're getting there fast!"

"Undercover?" said Cassidy. "Why would you be – Ooh, are you following a clue? I'll bet you are, aren't you?"

"Mr Glide would probably want me to say no," Miles said.

"Aha! Thanks, Miles!" Cassidy shouted, running off.

"No problem!" Miles called back.

Blake Glide had kept walking, hoping Miles would be sidetracked enough to forget about him. What he did not know was that, next to the mayor himself, Cassidy Kingfisher had the biggest mouth in all of Nod's Limbs. As she ran towards Knightleigh Manor to tell Stephanie the big news, she let slip to everyone she met along the way that Blake Glide had figured out the fifth clue and was, even now, striding up Cairo Avenue towards the river.

35. Shall We Gather at the River?

By the time Blake Glide and Miles reached the Cairo Avenue bridge, a crowd had collected behind them. The action star sighed heavily as he realized his attempt to go incognito had failed.

"B. G.! You figured out the clue, and you didn't tell me?" Otto Ottoman pushed his way through the throngs. "I'm hurt, Blake, baby. It hurts me, right here it hurts me." The director tapped his chest.

"You were going to fire me!" cried Blake Glide.

"That doesn't mean I don't love and respect you," Otto Ottoman replied.

The rest of the Nod's Limbsians were getting impatient.

"Where's the clue? What's the answer?" came shouts from the crowd.

Just then, the mayoral limo pulled up and the mayor, Judith, Stephanie, and Cassidy jumped out of the car.

"What is the meaning of this?" asked the mayor, bulldozing through his citizens. "I didn't call a town meeting or a press conference, and I know it's not Love Our Bridges Day, because that's next month!"

"The clue! The clue!" shouted the Nod's Limbsians. "Blake Glide has the answer to the clue!"

"Does he now," said the mayor. He glanced at Stephanie, who nodded ever so slightly, then turned back to Blake Glide. "Well, then, congratulations,

Mr Glide! Your intellect truly matches your acting ability!"

"For once, the mayor speaks the truth," said Edgar. He and Ellen had been hiding beneath the bridge, waiting patiently for Blake Glide to pick up on their blatant hint.

"So, *Nod's friend* is the bridge that bears the words," the mayor continued, putting his arm around the movie star. "You are a credit to the acting community! Well, sir, go get that clue!"

"Uh, right," said Blake Glide, and, with all of Nod's Limbs watching breathlessly, he stepped onto the bridge.

Blake Glide poked around for a while, but he didn't really know where to look and didn't find anything resembling a clue. Ellen was about to march up to him and point out the hiding spot when Stephanie called out, "Um, maybe it's in one of those beams up there, Mr Glide."

"The beams! Yes!" cried the townspeople. "But which one?"

"I would, uh, try the fourth one," said Stephanie.

"At least she's serving some kind of purpose," said Ellen, but Edgar looked troubled.

"She seems to have all the answers, Sister," he

said. "I'm glad we got to the clue when we did. A few hours more and we might have been too late."

"Yeah, too late to learn there wasn't any gold to begin with," Ellen muttered.

"How do we get up there?" asked Blake Glide.

"Never fear, we've got ladders!" came a voice from the crowd. Fire Chief Gully Lugwood stepped forward with the rest of the firefighters, a couple of whom carried retractable ladders. "We always travel with them, in case of an EKR – Emergency Kitten Rescue!"

The firefighters set up their ladders on the fourth beam.

"Can I climb up to get it?" asked little Timmy Poshi.

"I think you're too small, son," his father replied, "but as neighbourhood watch commander, I'd be happy to—"

"Very noble, sir," said Police Chief Gomez, shoving his way onto the bridge, "but this is a matter for the authorities, and I should probably—"

"Now wait just a doggone second, Gomez," said Gully Lugwood. "These are my ladders, I know how to climb them best—"

"But I was the one who figured out the clue!"

Blake Glide protested. "I should be the one to get it. Plus I do all my own stunts!"

"Now, now," said the mayor. "In the case of a stalemate, the mayor always casts the deciding vote, and I've decided that *I* should be the one to get that clue—"

The townspeople surged onto the bridge as everyone sought a chance to retrieve the clue.

"Oh, for cripes," said Ellen. "This is ridiculous. Will one of them just get it already? Pet is *dying*."

"Not even you and I argue this much," said Edgar, shaking his head.

36. My Kingdom For a Clue

Finally Stephanie scooted past all the bickerers and climbed the ladder herself. Everyone fell silent, except for Blake Glide, who whined, "Not fair. *I'm* the famous movie star."

Stephanie reached the beam and promptly found the small hole where the twins had hidden their clue. She pulled out the piece of paper.

"Got it!" she shouted triumphantly, descending the ladder.

Once on the ground, Stephanie unfolded the paper.
"Shall I read it out loud?" she asked.

"Yes! Yes!" cried the Nod's Limbsians impatiently.

"Okay, here we go." Stephanie looked down
smugly at the clue, but her face paled as she read it
over. "Wait," she said, almost to herself, "this isn't
right . . ."

"Oh, give it here, then," said Blake Glide, snatching the clue from her hand. "Let a professional actor
give it a proper reading."

He cleared his throat and in a booming voice, read
out:

Cluck like a chicken and squeak like a mouse,
It's time to head to the towering house!
Slip down the stairs to the cavern below,
Follow the arrows, they show where to go.

"Towering house?" said Mr Poshi. "The tall grey
eyesore by the hotel?"

"It must be!" called Suzette Croquet.

"At last!" said Blake Glide. " A clue I can understand."

The mob needed no further prompting, and made
for the twins' house, looking more like a buffalo

147

stampede than an orderly Nod's Limbsian parade.

Edgar and Ellen, however, stayed put.

"Did you see Stephanie?" said Edgar.

"I know," said Ellen. "She looked shocked."

"It's almost like she expected the clue to be something else," said Edgar. "Plus, she knew right where to look . . ."

With the crowd now cleared, the twins saw Stephanie, at the other end of the bridge, her brow still furrowed in puzzlement. She looked up to see the twins staring back at her. Then she snarled, and her fingers curled into trembling fists.

"You planted that clue!" Stephanie and Ellen yelled at the same time. They strode towards each other, fury in their eyes.

"The hunt hasn't ended at all!" shouted Ellen. "Of course! You just wanted everyone to *think* it was a hoax, so no one would challenge your family's ill-gotten wealth!"

"You put that clue in the rafter," Stephanie seethed. "Why? Why send everyone to your own house? What are you up to?"

"Where's the real clue, Stephanie? Where is it?" Ellen dove at her nemesis. "You rotten, vomitous, scum-skinned toad!"

"I found it first, you greasy pipe-cleaner!" Stephanie jumped out of the way just in time.

Ellen came at her again, and this time, Stephanie wasn't so lucky. Ellen bowled her over, and the two girls rolled across the bridge, pulling hair and scratching skin.

"Ouch!"

"Quit it!"

"Get off me!"

"Had enough, cream puff?"

Edgar, who until this point had cheered on his sister but had wisely chosen to sit out the fight, noticed something slip out of Stephanie's pocket. It was a small metal tube. Edgar snatched it up, and out fell a scroll of paper tied with a golden thread.

"Sister! Sister! I've got it! I've got the clue— *Oomph!*" Stephanie had managed to untangle herself from Ellen and grabbed Edgar's knees, toppling him.

"Give me that!" she screamed, lunging at the clue, but Edgar tossed it over to Ellen.

"Sister, catch!"

"Ha! Monkey-in-the-Middle! You're familiar with monkeys, right, Steph? Your family's full of them."

"I'm . . . never . . . the monkey!" Stephanie shrieked, so forcefully it startled even Ellen. Stephanie charged

towards her, but Ellen just threw the clue back to Edgar.

Maybe it was because she was so excited, or maybe she didn't remember where she was standing, or maybe she just didn't know her own strength, but Ellen threw the piece of paper just a little too hard, and it sailed right past Edgar and out a bridge window.

"Now look what you've done!" cried Stephanie. She and the twins raced to the window, but, despite the Running River's snail-paced current, they could see no hint of the clue. It had sunk, or dissolved, or simply been swept away.

"I can't believe it," Stephanie murmured and buried her head in her hands.

"What do you care?" asked Edgar. "You wanted the hunt to end anyway. Now it has. For good."

Stephanie looked up, clenching her teeth. "I wanted to *win*."

37. Setting Sail

"Uh, Stephie? Stephie, can I talk to you?" Miles had appeared at the end of the bridge.

"What do you want, Miles?" barked Stephanie.

"Um, this landed on the riverbank." Miles held up the piece of paper. The gold thread had fallen off, but the twins and Stephanie knew instantly what it was.

They ran at the boy, but Stephanie got there first. She grabbed the paper with one hand and unsheathed Miles's wooden pirate sword with the other.

"Stay back," she yelled, swinging the sword to keep the twins at bay as she scanned the clue. "Back! I'm warning you – no! No! It can't be!" Stephanie clutched the note and fled, pirate sword in hand.

"Miles!" Edgar said. "I thought we were allies! How could you give the clue to *her*?"

"She's my sister," said Miles. "She'd beat me up if I gave it to you."

"But – but—" Ellen stammered. Her lip was dripping blood and her footie pyjamas were even dirtier than usual from her tussle with Stephanie. "Oh, never mind. Come on, Edgar, we've got to follow her."

"I remember what it says," said Miles quietly.

"What?" Both the twins stopped abruptly.

Miles recited:

From where I stand, I look down on you all
Your egos so big, your virtues so small.

'Mad' some have called me, and in the same manner,
I call you all fools from my roost in my manor.

"*My manor?*" cried Edgar. "He means his – I mean, *our* – house!"

"Oh no," said Ellen. "We sent everyone there – The whole town is already at our house! We've got to get back there!"

"But where to look?" said Edgar. "The clue didn't mention any specifics. It could be anywhere in the whole house."

"What's a . . . a *Bordox*?" asked Miles.

"Not now, Miles," said Ellen.

"I think it's important. See, I had to give Stephie the riddle, because she's my sister. But she's being really mean – er, meaner than usual – so I didn't give her *everything*."

"What do you mean?" asked Edgar.

Miles held up a torn fragment of paper.

"I tore off the last lines. They tell you where to look."

"Great Bluebeard's ghost!" exclaimed Edgar, plucking the paper from Miles' hands. "It's not *Bordox*—"

Edgar showed Ellen the scrap:

From Burgundy to Bordeaux,
The world's in your grip,
Now sail on past Port
For one final trip.

"I've seen some of these words before," said Edgar.

"Of course you have," said Ellen. "Bordeaux, Burgundy – They're places. France, I think."

"Not just that. I've seen them in . . . in our house somewhere."

The twins thought for a minute, until both Edgar and Ellen shouted, "The wine casks!"

> *Oh, what fools we've been! What folly*
> *Not to guess Nod's grand finale!*
> *The seat of all his melancholy,*
> *His home, of course. That fox!*
> *Hurry! Hurry! The crusading*
> *Hunters are by now invading,*
> *Hear the rasping, jarring, grating,*
> *Shovels mine the rocks.*

38. An Ancient Double-Cross

In some homes of a certain age, enormous oak barrels in the cellar are remnants of a long-ago era of extravagance. In those days the filthy-rich kept an abundance of wines and brandies and other luxuries to shower on guests (and themselves) as a sign of status. But for most of the twins' lives, the sturdy casks in their subbasement provided not status, but crevices to hide in and perches to pounce from.

Recently they had discovered that one of the casks did not hold liquid at all, but a secret set of stairs. This barrel was actually a hidden door to a passageway that led to the cavern beneath their house – and to the balm spring.

Edgar called after Ellen as the twins ran back to their house.

"But, Sister," he panted, "we inspected all the casks after we found the secret passage. Every one was empty."

"Well, we must have missed something," Ellen replied, "because the wine casks *have* to be the answer to the riddle – holy smokes, look at this!"

The gold-hungry mob had wrenched the twins' front door from its hinges. When the twins reached the subbasement, they could hear the frantic *schik-schick-shick* of hundreds of shovels at work in the cavern below.

"Move your keister, Matterhorn!" called a muffled voice. "That's my dirt mound!"

"Get your pickaxe out of my pile, Poshi!"

"I never did like your butterberry muffins, Buffy!"

Edgar and Ellen's plan had worked perfectly: The treasure hunters had followed the twin's arrows (some cut from plywood, some hammered out of tin, some chalked onto the floor), which had led them down the stairs to the balm pit.

"The greedy devils," said Ellen. "They'll reach the spring in no time. Pet will be saved!"

"Hurry, let's check the casks for those limbs," said Edgar.

The wide, round faces of the casks rose twice as tall as the twins themselves. Each bore a sign identifying the wine within: BORDEAUX, BURGUNDY, PORT.

"Nod mentions all of them but this one," Ellen said, stopping before the rightmost cask, which read AMONTILLADO.

"That's it!" said Edgar. "You sailed *past* Port, Sister!"

Edgar threw open the door and entered the belly of the barrel.

Even in the dim lights of the subbasement, it was clear that the wine cask held only cold, dank air.

"Empty," said Edgar. "The hunt's a bust."

"Give me your flashlight," said Ellen.

"Sister, it's over," said Edgar.

"Give it to me!"

Edgar rooted the flashlight out of his satchel and handed it to his sister. Ellen shone the light over every inch of the interior, as if waving it like a magic wand might conjure up some golden limbs.

It did not. But just before turning off the light, she noticed something else hidden in the dust.

A mildewed envelope.

"No!" groaned Edgar. "No more riddles! We solved all six, Nod! We beat you, you old coot!"

Ellen picked it up gently as if the crisp, decayed paper might disintegrate altogether.

"Brother, I don't think this is a clue. Look."

The front of the envelope, in words so faded the twins could barely read them, was addressed TO MY OLD FRIEND AND COLLEAGUE, THE ESTIMABLE AUGUSTUS NOD.

Ellen pulled out a handwritten letter. The beam of the flashlight revealed faint words:

Dearest Augustus,

Well, well, well. What have we here in this old barrel? I can't say I am surprised to find the so-called "stolen limbs" stowed away in <u>your</u> home. Unlike our fellow citizens, I have never believed the simple stories of their theft. Vindication! What were you planning for them, I wonder? No matter. They're mine, now. It seems Providence favours the "dull-witted laggard" you sacked from the Waxworks, eh, Augie? Take that to your grave!

Signed most sincerely,

Thaddeus

P.S. Vote Knightleigh!

"Swindled!" cried Ellen. "You can't even trust a *dead* Knightleigh."

Edgar threw the note on the ground and stamped on it. "Thaddeus, you loathsome pustule! You rotten sack of louse larva—"

Edgar's string of curses was cut short by a scream from the cavern below.

39. Bone-a-Petit

"I – I was just digging, and my shovel struck something." Betty LaFete had turned as grey as an overcast day. "And then I saw a foot! I thought – I thought it might be one of the limbs – but then I realized, it wasn't a *gold* foot at all – it was a *bone* foot!"

Diggers crowded around for a look. Sure enough, the bones of a foot protruded from the dirt, and a little farther up, they could see a few skeletal fingers.

Edgar and Ellen pushed through, hoping that someone had unearthed the spring. They spied the foot and sagged in disappointment.

"Rats," said Ellen. "It's only Nod."

The twins had already found these bones on an earlier adventure, when a dirt collapse had nearly killed them.

"Nod? Did you say *Nod*?" cried Betty LaFete. "Have I dug up our town founder? Am I cursed?"

"The clothes look old enough," said Ernest Hirschfeld, examining a nearly disintegrated velvet waistcoat. "Could it be that Augustus Nod buried himself with his treasure?"

"Who cares? I smell gold!" shouted Marvin Matterhorn, throwing his shovel back into the ground.

"Rest-thee-well, gentle sir," said Sir Malvolio, bowing respectfully to the skeleton. Then he jammed his spade into the earth with a gleeful snort.

The rest of the Nod's Limbsians followed suit, abandoning the remnants of the town founder without another moment's thought. They worked steadily, delving deeper and deeper into the dirt. As they toiled, their flashlights dimmed and darkened one by one – but even this couldn't slow them, and they made crude torches to light their way. In flickering firelight, they burrowed ever on.

"They're going to make it!" whispered Ellen at last. "Our plan worked!"

"It all comes down to good scheming," said Edgar.

Just then, Calvin Hucklebee's shovel broke through to an open space.

"I found it! I found it!" he shouted. His older brother nudged him in the ribs. "Oh, I mean, nope, didn't find anything."

But it was too late. The treasure hunters attacked the dirt wall with their shovels, digging until the chamber beyond revealed itself. Stale air drifted out, and the townspeople covered their noses. For all their ardour, nobody dared venture into the cave. They hesitated on the edge of the opening, no one daring enough to step inside.

No one, that is, except Edgar and Ellen.

The twins pushed to the front and peered into the darkness.

"This is it," whispered Ellen.

"*Our* treasure," breathed Edgar.

The twins were about to plunge in, when out of the blackness came a low but distinct *skitch . . . skitch...skitch*.

Something was in there.

Something *alive*.

40. Greatest Show Unearthed

Everyone heard it. No one moved.

Hundreds of pairs of eyes gazed at the black hole, and then they could just make out a stir in the shadows.

Skitch . . . skitch . . . skitch . . .

A bent form caught the glow of the torchlight.

Snarled heaps of dark, grimy hair covered the creature from top to bottom, seeming to bristle and writhe. The onlookers stumbled backwards over one another, speechless with dread.

Skitch . . . skitch . . .

Slowly, the thing shambled closer.

A musty gust from the grotto rustled the beast's tangled hair, exposing a wide, yellowish eye.

"Brother" – Ellen dug her nails into Edgar's hand – "It's . . . it's . . . a giant *Pet*."

Blake Glide finally broke the silence.

"GAAAAA! A FLESH-EATING SLURM!"

The action star fled, knocking aside all in his way.

When they saw their hero run, the entire lot of treasure hunters dropped their buckets, shovels, and torches and scrambled after him.

"Our greed has loosed a demon!" howled Buffy.

"Why couldn't I have been content with a life of lawn care?" wailed Chief Strongbowe.

"I don't want to be a pirate anymore!" cried Calvin Hucklebee.

Only the twins remained, though they dared not approach the creature. Then, two pale, spindly arms reached out from beneath the veil of hair.

163

"Arms?" cried Edgar. "This is no Pet!"

The creature drew closer. The black pupil of its eye expanded and contracted like a beating heart.

Edgar ransacked the contents of his satchel for anything that might keep the beast at bay: his claw hammer, his wrench – *anything*. At the bottom he found an old bicycle pump and aggressively pumped the handle.

"Don't make me use this, fiend!" he growled.

Ellen struck an absurd kung-fu pose.

"I have a black belt in eye poking, Cyclops," she said, as she snaked two fingers in the air and hissed.

The creature stepped through the threshold of its lair, stretched to an astounding height, and howled. The twins grimaced and covered their ears as the wail echoed through the cave. The thing lurched forward and snatched the twins up, pressing them against its coarse, rank hair. The twins squirmed and kicked, but could not break free.

"Put us down!" cried Ellen. "I'm warning you!"

"Don't underestimate us, you festering – *oof!*" The grip tightened and expelled the remaining air in Edgar's lungs.

With the twins helpless in its hold, the pillar of hair bellowed again; but the cry softened into a hyena-like cackle, and settled finally into deep, rich, *human* laughter.

"GLORY BE, I'M FREE!"

The hairy mound spun in a mad circle, laughing and hopping with Edgar and Ellen in tow. "Children! Sweet, sweet children! The most beautiful things I have ever seen!"

"Who are you calling *sweet*?" Edgar snapped.

"Beautiful?" Ellen snarled. "You dare!"

The shaggy figure dropped Edgar and Ellen to the ground and danced a rickety jig. In the light of the half dozen torches abandoned by the treasure hunters, the twins saw that the dreaded "slurm" was not a flesh-eating monster at all, but a man – an old but lively man in serious need of a bath and haircut.

"Who are you?" asked Ellen.

"Who am I? Who *am* I? Hmm." The old man stopped spinning. With long, ragged fingernails he pulled aside his filthy mane like curtains in a haunted mansion and revealed a second eye, bright and full of life.

"Last time someone addressed me – mind you, that was some time ago" – A magnificently crooked smile spread across his face – "I believe they called me . . . *Augustus*. Yes, that's it. Augustus."

"Augustus?" the twins repeated in unison.

"Augustus Nod. Pleasure to make your acquaintance."

41. Say Good Knightleigh

"Nod?" Edgar blinked.

"Nod's *Limbs* Nod?" Ellen tilted her head and squinted.

"Nod's *Lands* Nod," corrected Augustus. He coughed. "Some harebrained jesters renamed my municipality after the disappearance of my statue's limbs—"

"Forget about disappearing limbs!" shouted Ellen. "What about the reappearing *you*?"

"It's not possible," said Edgar. "You'd be more than 200 years old. . . . We – we found your skeleton!"

"Skeleton? Well, it's not mine, I can assure you," said Nod. "You need not believe it for it to be true. How I survived I will never reveal, but—"

"Balm!" exclaimed Edgar. "Can it be? Is it powerful enough to keep you alive all this time?"

"You know of my Life Balm?" asked Nod. "Alas,

it is as I feared. My imprisonment left too many details unguarded in my laboratory. It stands to reason such secrets could never lay undiscov – NO TORCHES!"

The old man sprang at Edgar, who had picked up a torch and approached the musty tomb.

"Don't worry. We know all about the balm's explosive properties. You mentioned it in that journal of yours – and I have firsthand experience to back it up." Edgar wedged the torch in a crevice, a safe distance from the threshold.

"My private works – *you* young ones have read them?"

"Yes," said Ellen. "It was about as exciting as reading the ingredients on a tube of toothpaste."

"*Toothpaste*? Now who would use a paste made from *teeth*?" asked Nod.

Ellen grabbed two metal buckets and rushed into the chamber. "As much fun as it is hanging around an unstable cave, chewing the fat with a 200-year-old relic, we're on a mission."

The twins ventured into Nod's prison. They saw little in the flickering light, but they could hear something ahead . . .

Gurgle, gurgle. Blip, blip, bloop.

Something cool splashed Ellen's cheek. She wiped it away, but her skin continued to tingle. "Balm . . ."

Their eyes adjusted to the dim light, and they found themselves in a grotto about the size of a doctor's waiting room. The only furnishings were an itchy-looking mattress made of Nod's own hair and a few stones that had been crudely chiselled into the shapes of tops and building blocks. In the middle was a pool of gooey liquid that bubbled forth from the earth.

"We really did it, Ellen. We found the spring."

Nod shuffled in behind them.

"Astounding, is it not? For thousands of years, man has searched for a spring of eternal life. Deluded seekers had naught to guide them but myths, shadows of hope to the desperately mortal. But I found it."

"Could it actually bring you back from death?" asked Ellen. "Even if you got hit by a train or something?"

A familiar voice spoke from the grotto's entrance. "We could certainly test that theory, Ellen."

Stephanie Knightleigh stepped in from the tunnel.

"Good instincts, sweetheart," said Mayor Knightleigh, following her.

"I told you the twins were behind all this, Daddy."

Judith Stainsworth-Knightleigh appeared beside her husband, holding a torch. "And it is high time we put all this dirty business behind *us*."

The Knightleigh family stepped into the chamber. Gone was the brash smile worn by the jovial, crowd-pleasing mayor. Gone was the jolly man who had headed so many silly parades and ridiculous festivals. Instead Mayor Knightleigh's eyes had become piercing black bullets, and his lip curled more than Stephanie's hair.

"You are trespassing on my property," he said, picking up a pickaxe. "And in my town, trespassers are prosecuted to the fullest extent of the law."

169

42. Remains of the Dead

"I would recognize that triple chin anywhere!" said Augustus Nod. "You, sir, must be the slimy seed of none other than that gluttonous scoundrel, Thaddeus Knightleigh!"

"Hey!" yelled Stephanie "Whoever, or whatever, you are – You are in the presence of power!"

"I am in the presence of criminals!" Nod spat. "Thaddeus Knightleigh was a fiend so wretched that any descendent of his must be equally as crooked!"

"Spot on, old-timer," said Edgar.

"We can vouch for that," agreed Ellen.

"Now see here! No one speaks about my great-great-great-great-great-great-grandfather Thaddeus that way! Or about *me*!" roared Mayor Knightleigh. "I don't know who you are or what you are doing down here . . ."

Judith Stainsworth-Knightleigh stepped next to her husband. "But the laws of our town clearly forbid the habitation of transients within our borders. No soup kitchens, no shelters, no homeless. It's bad for tourism."

"You morons," said Edgar. "Do you have any

idea who this man is?" He pulled two handfuls of Nod's long, dirty hair away from the old man's face. "Doesn't he look a little familiar?"

Mayor Knightleigh grabbed the torch and held it closer to the man before him; the light bathed Nod's face and the mayor peered carefully at him. Suddenly he stumbled back.

"N-n-n-not possible!"

"Stand your ground, you—" began Judith, but she choked as recognition dawned on her too. "Oh my heavens!"

"A ghost!" shrieked the mayor.

Only Stephanie stood firm. "Daddy, he smells too gross to be a ghost." She examined the gnarled old man in front of her. "But you do look an awful lot like the statue of Augustus Nod."

"Indeed, for I am he!" Nod answered.

"But how—?" Stephanie began, then glanced at the twins. She shrugged. "You know, I should be shocked. Yet somehow, when it involves you two freaks, I find that few things genuinely surprise me anymore. Whoever you are, old man, I don't have time for this."

"But the limbs – we just wanted the limbs – the limbs were all," the mayor babbled.

"Look no farther. *Here* are Nod's limbs!" quacked Nod, kicking out his skinny arms and legs. The mayor shuddered.

"Why are *you* looking for them?" asked Edgar. "It was *your* ancestor who took the golden limbs."

"WHAT?" cried Stephanie.

"Yes, so he did," said Nod. "That blathering nincompoop Thaddeus intruded upon my house, looking for the rumoured 'secret ingredient' that made Waxworks candles burn so bright. Before he could uncover such mysteries, he stumbled upon my golden limbs – the luck of an idiot! He stole them from me, as sure as crabapples are tart. But the simpering backstabber wasn't content with that, no! He returned later, still bent on finding my candle secrets. This time he managed to come upon me in my laboratory. Couldn't stop gloating about the limbs, could he? That is, until he caused the explosion that trapped me underground—" Nod stopped. "There's a skeleton down here, you say?"

"Right over there," said Ellen, pointing back to the pile of bones that stuck out of the ground.

"Woo hoo ha ha!" Nod laughed. "Who'd have guessed? All these long years I have cursed Thaddeus for his treachery, and it turns out he went and got himself buried under the rubble of the explosion *he* caused!"

"You mean," began Ellen, "you mean that skeleton is *Thaddeus Knightleigh?*"

"I'd bet my life on it," said Nod. "And I have a lot of life to bet!"

"That's a lie. Thaddeus is buried in his tomb," said Stephanie, kneeling beside the skeleton. But when she looked among the bones, she noticed a signet ring with a familiar crest.

"Daddy – Daddy, it's the Knightleigh crest!" she cried. "This *is* Thaddeus!"

43. Burying the Truth

"Nod . . . two hundred years old if he's a day . . . *the* Nod . . ." Mayor Knightleigh stammered while Judith Stainsworth-Knightleigh wrung her hands.

The twins slipped back into the grotto. Stephanie watched them fill buckets with balm as she mused to herself.

"If Nod's 'will' spelled disaster for us, what will his *existence* mean to the Knightleigh legacy?" She yanked the flickering torch from her mother's white knuckles and moved closer to Nod.

"Stephanie!" shouted Ellen. "Don't!"

"Keep that fire back!" Edgar yelled.

"Listen, mister, I don't care how you managed to stay alive all this time. I don't care why you're here and what you want. The little treasure hunt you left for us? It caused quite a stir."

"Young lady," Nod said calmly, "no matter your agenda, I can assure you, that torch will cause a great deal more than a stir."

"You think you can trick me, old fool?" said Stephanie. "If that skeleton is Thaddeus, I bet *you* murdered *him*! He learned about your twisted under-ground experiments and tried to stop you—"

"ENOUGH!" Nod thundered. "You insolent, iniquitous, treacherous frogspawn!"

"Frogspawn," said Ellen. *"Nice."*

"Your beastly ancestor brought fire to the balm spring and triggered a devastating explosion," Nod continued.

Stephanie smiled. "Is that so?"

"Oops," Edgar said.

"Too much information, Nod," added Ellen.

"But that's what happened, dear twins," Nod replied. "He was waving that blasted torch of his as he boasted and accidentally lit a glob of balm . . ."

Stephanie pointed her torch at the balm-filled buckets. "Balm? This stuff?"

"Stephanie, do you really think you'd fare better than old Thaddeus?" asked Ellen.

"Of course. You're talking to the under-twelve champion of the Spring Is Sprung Sprint. Daddy, Mother – why don't the two of you go back upstairs?"

The mayor and his wife did not need a second prompting. They clattered back up the tunnel into the cavern.

Ellen stepped in front of Nod. "Listen, Stephanie. You think I'm despicable and I think you're . . . well, frogspawn pretty much covers it. But what you're about to do . . . It would be *murder*."

"Technically? Not." Stephanie pointed the torch at Nod. "The way I figure, whatever kept him alive all these years will do the same for you. You'll be kicking and screaming down here for centuries." She paused. "I can live with that."

Stephanie Knightleigh dropped the torch into a bucket.

The last thing the twins saw were Stephanie's auburn curls dashing into the blackness of the tunnel, followed by a blinding flash.

And then everything went black.

44. A Touching Farewell

KABOOM!

The explosion came from underneath the mansion. On the twins' front lawn, the crowd of treasure hunters screamed as the earth quaked beneath them, knocking many to the ground. The house before them swayed ominously and creaked like a redwood in a windstorm.

"Revenge of the slurms!" cried Blake Glide, his award-winning biceps wrapped tightly about Janitor Clunch. "Nowhere to run! Nowhere to hide! The slurm army shall wreak their vengeance!"

"The whole town will be sucked into the abyss for its greed!" cried Mrs Elines. "Forgive my selfishness! I only wanted to use the gold to build some luxurious whirlpool suites in my humble motel!"

"The shame!" wailed Buffy. "How could I abandon the noble taste of scones for the bitter, cold tang of gold?"

"Wait, where is our mayor?" called Principal Mulberry. "Did he get out of the building? *Where is our mayor?*"

"*There!*"

The crowd erupted in jubilation as Mayor Knightleigh and Judith barrelled out the front door of the creaking mansion followed closely by Stephanie. Clouds of dust and ash belched from the door and windows, and chunks of slate and rock broke off the swaying house, peppering the Knightleighs as they escaped.

"Sweet cream of corn!" exclaimed Principal Mulberry. "Our mayoral family is alive!"

"Any slurm bites?" asked Blake Glide. "Check for slurm bites, people! That's how they multiply!"

Mayor Knightleigh glanced at his daughter, cleared his throat, and drew his gut up into his chest. Back in the sunlight, he quickly forgot his fears.

"My fellow Nod's Limbsians, it seems our treasure hunt has come to an unfortunate end. Sadly, there was an unexpected cave-in below. The limbs — and the horrible creature guarding them — have been claimed by the earth. The golden treasure shall be recovered nevermore."

45. Return to Sender

The blast had hurled Edgar and Ellen against the opposite wall, and they strained to get their bearings in the blackness. Rock and rubble poured into the tunnel, sealing the grotto's exit.

"My head," groaned Edgar.

"My ears," whined Ellen.

"I think I hurt my bottom," said a meek voice between them.

"Miles?" cried the twins.

Miles Knightleigh clicked on a penlight and held it under his pudgy, eye-patched face. "Arrr."

"Where did you come from?" Ellen demanded.

"I was here the whole time."

"You were?" Edgar asked. "We didn't see you."

"Oh, I'm used to that," said Miles. "I snuck down here to help you."

"Stop your chitchat and get to digging!" barked Nod.

Just then a chunk of cave fell loose from the ceiling between Miles and the twins, followed by a flood of pebbles and dust. They could hear a creak in a nearby wall, followed by a crack and the sound of cascading rock.

"This cavern couldn't withstand a second explosion," Nod said. "It is about to come down upon us."

"Your sister condemned us to die down here, Miles!" yelled Edgar.

"So that little purple troll is your sister, eh, boy?" cried Nod. "At least this cavern will claim another Knightleigh before I perish."

"As Knightleighs go," said Ellen, "this one's all right."

"Aw, thanks, El-*aaaigh*!" Miles caught a gob of earth in his mouth. Another chunk of the ceiling gave way, and Ellen hugged the remaining bucket of balm as boulders fell over the mouth of the spring.

KRAAAAK-OOOOOM!

"Dig for it!" cried Edgar. "Get to the surface!"

"It's no use," said Nod. "We would need the strength of a hundred men, and we are but four – three too young and one too old. This shall be our tomb."

A rupture raced up the nearest wall and across the ceiling. The twins and Miles screamed in terror as a river of dirt and silt poured down from above. But even in the dim penlight, Edgar noticed something emerging from the crack in the wall. It looked at first like thick, fleshy worms. And then he realized what they were.

"I know those fingers!"

A slab of earth toppled out of the wall like a ten-ton domino.

THOOOOM!

A behemoth of a man wriggled out and dropped before them. He had hands the size of boulders, legs the girth of two oak trees, and a gleaming smile that seemed wider than his head.

The twins raced into his waiting embrace and hugged their rescuer with all their might.

"HEIMERTZ!"

KRAAAAK-KOOOOOM!

With a single sweep of his mighty arm, Heimertz gathered the twins, Nod, and Miles, and shoved them into the channel he had come through. The passage felt narrow as a gopher hole, but it was enough room for the five of them to crawl up to the floor of the grand cavern.

But the cavern too had felt the effects of the blast. Sheets of earth dropped from the walls and stone rained from above.

"We'll never make it!" Nod cried.

As they dashed for the stairs, the cavern collapsed, burying the lab, the tunnels, and the balm spring beneath tons of earth.

46. Everyone Still Loves a Parade

" . . . And so let this tragic day linger long in our memories," said Mayor Knightleigh, "well into next week, after which we can all forget about such glum and grisly matters and kick off our seventh annual March of the Mini-Mayors parade!"

Sniffles and sobs faded momentarily at the mention of the word "parade". The mayor noticed the change in mood.

"Yes, my flock! Parades . . . plural! Lots of them!" Mayor Knightleigh's voice boomed. "Parades! Festivals! We shall never again dwell upon the gold bug that threatened to burrow into our very hearts! Golden limbs? Bah!"

Calvin Hucklebee approached the mayor with his pirate hat in his hands. "Where is Miles, Mr Mayor?" he asked. "I sort of owe him an apology."

"Miles . . ." Stephanie said, snapping her head towards the house. "He wasn't – he couldn't have been in the . . . No, he *must* be around here somewhere."

"Yes," Judith whispered to her daughter. "Where is that boy? I put him in your charge."

Stephanie rounded on her mother. "You expect

me to crush our mortal enemies *and* watch my little brother?"

Glass crashed behind her, and the citizens turned to the tall, narrow house that now leaned cruelly in the darkening sky.

"A structure like that can't take the strain of all that swaying—" Eugenia Smithy began.

"GREAT GALLOPING GALILEO!" cried Marvin Matterhorn. "It's coming down!"

Indeed the walls began to buckle, casting down a hailstorm of broken stones.

Stephanie had waited forever for this moment. She had endured a lifetime of rivalry and one-upmanship, an eternity of aggravating pranks and calculated sabotage conceived in the dark halls of this house. And while everyone around her gasped in alarm at the sickening sounds of the structure twisting in its socket, Stephanie smiled.

At least, she smiled until five dusty figures ran out the front door.

A pirate, a giant, a walking mound of hair, and lastly – side by side as Stephanie always saw them in her nightmares – two pale twins in striped footie pyjamas.

47. Up and Crumbling

Miles, Nod, Heimertz, Edgar, and Ellen raced out of the house just as the cupola slid off the top, like the upper tiers of a melting wedding cake. The cupola spun as it fell. The wrought iron spikes of the roof, which had pointed skyward for more than two hundred years, now sliced towards earth at astonishing speed.

"She's breaking apart!" shouted Nod. "Stand clear!"

The spikes speared the dirt right behind them as they dove for cover behind Heimertz's shed. The cupola shattered, showering them with splintered wood and glass.

The house swayed one last time, then split open, like a pirate galleon dashed on a rocky coastline. With a tumultuous shouting sound like the voice of a thousand waters, the mighty walls rushed asunder. The house launched its guts – furniture, globes, organ pipes, suits of armour – onto the lawn.

Then the dank earth closed sullenly and silently over the foundation of the towering house at the end of the nameless lane.

The twins peered out from behind the shed with

mouths agape and lips quavering – even Nod seemed stunned. It was Miles who finally spoke up.

"Wow," he said softly.

The twins turned to Heimertz. He was panting heavily, and though his smile never drooped, his head and arms looked painfully bruised and bloodied.

Ellen stared up at him. "How . . . ?"

Heimertz took Ellen's letter from his pocket and shook it gently. Edgar held out his palm as his favourite lock pick tumbled from the creased paper and into his grip. Then the caretaker's smile slid off his face, and he slumped to the ground with a groan.

"Heimertz!" cried the twins.

"Ronan!" shouted a woman behind them.

Madame Dahlia, mistress of the Heimertz Family Circus' Botanical Beastiary, emerged from the shed and propped the fallen man's head on her shoulder.

"Ronan, we escape from one jail together," she said softly. "Do not now escape somewhere else I cannot follow."

Heimertz opened his eyes and softly patted her cheek. A half-hearted grin wavered on his face.

"Thank the stars!" Madame Dahlia said as she dabbed at Heimertz's wounds. "I will nurse my darling back to health. He will live. I fear another may not, however. Our littlest friend . . . is having the death look." Madame Dahlia took out a bundle of rags from the folds of her skirt and handed it to Edgar. He unwrapped the bundle carefully; a tuft of hair lay within.

Pet was now entirely white, and it looked up mournfully at the twins with a grey eye, its pupil ringed in red. The twins gasped.

"Unless some miracle you have planned, this is your Pet's ending hour," whispered Madame Dahlia as Pet's eye closed.

48. Pet's Cemetery

"Pilosoculus!" Nod exclaimed before the twins could respond. "Why, you look terrible, old chap! Young lady, let's save the rascal, shall we?"

"Yes, definitely!" said Ellen, holding out the bucket of balm she had rescued from the cave-in. "You're not done yet, Pet!"

Edgar gingerly laid Pet in the bucket, and the creature sunk below the surface of the white balm.

"Is — is that what's supposed to happen?" asked Edgar.

"Watch closely, my boy," Nod replied.

The small group huddled around the bucket gazing into it as if it were a crystal ball. Even Miles dared not speak.

The townsfolk had watched the collapse from a safe distance, but now they drew nearer the destruction and the curious band of survivors in its midst.

Still, nothing stirred in the bucket. At last an orb the size of an orange floated to the surface of the goop: an eyeball.

Closed.

"No," whispered Ellen. "Pet!"

"But we made it in time!" said Edgar.

"Pilos," murmured Nod. "Would you please . . . quit . . . *teasing*!"

At this, Pet opened its eye wide. It leaped out of the gloop and into Ellen's arms. Miraculously the colour was already rapidly returning to its hair, and its eye gleamed yellow as ever.

"For Poe's sake, Pet, you're going to pay for that one!" said Edgar, but his smile stretched so impossibly high up his face it looked as if it might fly off his cheeks. The twins swung the creature around and around and tousled its hair until it was again back to its black, matted snarls.

Pet's eye – so cloudy and dull moments ago – now sparkled at the old horseplay, until it caught sight of Nod. Nod gazed back at it, tears in his eyes.

"Pilos – all these years I thought that surely you were dead, for your lifesource was bound with me. It was my fault, my petty feud with a petty man that put you in danger. I am sorry I abandoned you, old friend." Nod stopped, choking on the last few words.

Pet merely blinked and sprang into the old man's shaggy beard. Nod hugged the creature and tousled its tendrils.

"Good to see you again, you rotten old pile of whiskers," he said.

49. The Awakening

"Miles!" cried Stephanie. "You were in there? How? Are you okay?"

Miles didn't respond. He turned his back on his sister and plopped onto the ground, arms folded.

By now the townsfolk had finally drawn close enough to get a good look.

"Mama?" asked Penny Pickens. "Who's that big bundle of hair?"

The old man wheeled about and faced the crowd. He placed Pet on his shoulder and bellowed.

"Quit gawking like fish on a plate and say good day! These gape-jawed expressions are no way to greet your town founder!"

The crowd gasped.

"Founder? Nod? Ridiculous."

"That's impossible!"

"Hey, his limbs aren't gold!"

"Oh, I am he, all right. Augustus Nod! And these two heroic children have released me from two

centuries of internment within the presence of –
well, some natural compounds that suspend death
beyond all natural law! For two maddeningly solitary centuries I was held captive underground by the
greedy design of Thaddeus Knightleigh!"

Lyman Herringbottle stepped out from the crowd,
pushed his spectacles up the bridge of his narrow
nose and studied the hairy man. "Most curious . . ."

Nod pointed a long, bony finger at the Knightleigh family. The mayor, Judith, and Stephanie had
receded behind the townspeople and continued to
slink slowly towards the limousine.

"Knightleigh cretins!" Nod bellowed. "Go no
farther!"

The citizens of Nod's Limbs looked anxiously at
the howling old man, then at their mayor and his
family, and then back to their accuser.

"He's clearly mad . . . right?" stammered the
mayor. "No one could believe such a claim . . .
Could you?"

"Silence! Your townsfolk shall know of your
treachery! And you shall pay a price for this wickedness." Nod seemed to tower over the crowd now.
"The mayoral torch passed from generation to corrupt
generation in your family is hereby extinguished!"

"YOU CAN'T DO THAT!" screamed Stephanie. "I'M THE NEXT MAYOR!"

"You wouldn't make a very good mayor, Stephie."
Miles dropped his pirate hat and eye patch in the
dirt. "You tried to explode this man. And Edgar and
Ellen." He swallowed hard. "And me."

"Miles! I had no idea you were even there!"

Cries of astonishment rose from the crowd.

Meanwhile, Lyman Herringbottle removed his
spectacles, wiped them clean, and put them back on.
He squinted and tugged a wiry tuft of Nod's beard.
"Similar jawline . . ."

"You don't deserve to be mayor, Stephie," said
Miles. "Not ever." He looked up at his mother and
father. "And you don't either, Dad."

The few citizens who stood near the Knightleighs
now took a step back.

"Is't true, my mayor?" asked Sir Malvolio. "Didst
thou try to . . . *harm* these poor children . . . and this
o'er-bewhiskered gent?"

The buzz of the crowd grew louder, and the
mayor stumbled towards them with his arms open.

"Friends . . . neighbours . . . Nod's Limbsians . . . ,"
he called. "I . . . I . . . of course I didn't try to harm
these beautiful children!"

"Liar!" cried Ellen. "You set off the explosion that destroyed everything we own!"

"But we lived to tell your dirty tale," said Edgar.

"Why did you let Stephie try to kill us?" asked Miles.

Mayor Knightleigh whipped around and pointed his fat finger directly at Stephanie. "It was *her* idea!"

"DADDY!"

"She lit the fire that caused the explosion!" The mayor looked desperately to his wife. "Isn't that so, dear! Tell them! We wanted nothing to do with such madness!"

Judith looked at her daughter coldly. "I tried to raise her properly. Wrote, and then read her all the right books, sent her to all the appropriate seminars . . . but it seems—"

"JUST LIKE THE SCOUNDREL, THAD-DEUS KNIGHTLEIGH!" boomed Nod. "You would say anything to save yourselves! But this day you shall be undone by your own greed and deceit!"

"Fascinating!" Lyman Herringbottle, finished with his inspection of Nod, giggled and shook his head. He addressed the townspeople, who were frozen and fixed on the startling revelations about their mayor and his family. "Ladies and gentlemen of the town of Nod's Limbs, as strange as it may be, this man is indeed our town founder."

"I couldn't agree more," said Nod with a grunt.

"Look here above his left eyebrow – you've all seen it on the statue," said Lyman Herringbottle. "Here it is: the birthmark, shaped like a spider. Nigh-indisputable evidence!"

Not a murmur or cough could be heard from the transfixed crowd.

"I cannot explain how he has endured for two hundred years," continued Lyman Herringbottle. "I know little of the laws of nature. I do, however, know the laws of the land. And since this is indeed the man himself, I can only follow the basic dictates of my profession: Augustus Nod, in light of your unexpected re-emergence, you are officially restored ownership of all your assets and estates."

"We know where his money went!" said Edgar. "It was wrongfully inherited by—"

"I know full well who inherited Nod's wealth," said Lyman Herringbottle, fixing the Knightleighs with a stern gaze. "I have been doing a little exploring among our records at Herringbottle, Pratt, and Filbert, and they have proven to be exactingly complete. I'm afraid the Knightleigh family will find itself parted from a significant sum of cash and land holdings by this time tomorrow."

"Did you hear that, villains?" Nod asked. "No? Well, let me state it plainly then: GET OFF MY LAND, KNIGHTLEIGH FLOTSAM!"

Nod's eyes bulged beneath his shaking mound of hair. Some in the crowd began to boo the mayoral family.

The mayor, his wife, and Stephanie ran to the limousine at full speed. Before she ducked inside, Stephanie turned and yelled.

"We'll be back on top again," she cried. "Just like that hairy fossil over there, a Knightleigh *never says die!*"

The limo peeled down the road towards Knightleigh Manor.

"Forgotten again." Miles sighed. "Good."

50. You Can't Go Home Again

Having spent days in a spiralling cyclone of greed and madness only to then be witnesses of wanton destruction, attempted murder, and mayoral disgrace, the good people of Nod's Limbs had little energy left to muse over the miraculous reappearance of a two-hundred-year-old man.

"I'm pooped," confessed Mrs Elines as she walked away with her husband.

"Me, too, lovebird. I could use a good nap."

Blake Glide walked off towards the Knightlorian. "I sure would have preferred real gold over a really old guy," admitted the movie star. "I'll be completely broke after this flop of a movie comes out."

"I think this means we'll need to nominate some candidates to replace Knightleigh," said Becky Faff. "You know, Mr Glide, I'm betting you'd make one heck of a mayor . . ."

"You think so? Well, I did play a police commissioner in *Lethally Handsome II: When Looks Kill*. Yeah, I think politics come pretty naturally to me . . ."

"Bah! Two hundred years and you people are still sheep," said Nod. "Who ever heard of an actor running for *office*?"

"Better go fire up old Annabelle, rookie," Chief Strongbowe said to Nathan Ruby. "Time to restore some much missed Lawn and Order to Nod's Limbs."

"Come, good knight." Sir Malvolio clapped a

hand on Sir Geoffrey's shoulder. "Our fair bridges need a fresh coat of Soothsayer Scarlet."

"That's the really bright red paint, right?"

Sir Malvolio rolled his eyes as the two men alighted their saddles and galloped east.

As Augustus Nod and Lyman Herringbottle discussed the legal ramifications of the town founder's return, the rest of the townspeople dispersed with surprisingly little fanfare, mumbling things such as: "Gold is where the heart is", "The only golden rule is kindness", and "Buck yourself up! Tonight is meatloaf night!"

Edgar and Ellen sat together on the lone step left intact at the base of their former home. They could see Miles kicking pebbles down the lane, and Dahlia tending Heimertz, but they didn't have the energy to console friends at the moment. Ellen traced her finger along the word "Schadenfreude", which was etched across broken stones in the rubble.

A healthy Pet bounced buoyantly amid the wreckage. Then it dove into the ruins and emerged with one of Edgar's slingshots between its shiny, black tendrils. It playfully wagged it at the twins, but neither cracked a smile.

"Thanks, Pet," muttered Edgar.

"Yeah, Pet." Ellen let out a huge sigh. "I mean I'm glad you're going to be all right and all. I really am. But . . . our house . . ."

"Where will we live now?"

The twins looked like wilted weeds.

"Why so glum, ragamuffins?" Nod asked lightly as he shuffled over to them.

"Everything we had . . ." Edgar gestured at the junk-covered lawn.

"Everything we own . . ." Ellen lifted the torn canvas of her favourite work of art: an oil painting of mouldy cabbage and eggs.

"Own?" said Nod. "Why do you lament over matters of ownership? You are sitting on my property!"

The twins stood up. "Are you saying you want us to go?"

"Oh, sweet children," said Nod. "*Of course* I want you to go. I'm a hermit! Can't stand people. Not a one of them. Leopard can't change his spots, you know."

The twins stood in dumbfounded silence.

"Well, off with you, then," said Nod, and he turned to pick through the rubble.

"You evil, evil, dust mop of a man," murmured Ellen.

Pet leaped into the old man's arms. Nod chortled and grabbed the creature by the scruff. "Ho! No, my little beast, *you're* not going anywhere. We shall live as friends again!"

There was nothing for the twins to do but shuffle off, away from the only place they had ever called home. They glanced back once. Pet wiggled a tendril, but Nod did not notice. He was still chattering away, now admiring the Knightlorian, where purple banners on the rooftop waved in the late afternoon wind.

51. The Final Riddle

Edgar and Ellen wandered aimlessly down Ricketts Road.

"Where – where should we go, Sister? If the Gadget Graveyard were still around we could build a shelter there—"

"But it's not around, is it? And besides, this is all Nod's property now, and he seems about as interested in sharing it as Knightleigh was."

"How about the forest? We could, er, camp for a while. Or we could live in the sewers."

"Of all Fate's wicked twists!" shouted Ellen. "When we said we'd give up everything to save Pet, I didn't think we'd actually have to give up *everything*! If we had just found those limbs!"

"Sister," said Edgar, cracking his knuckles. "What *do* you suppose Thaddeus did with the golden limbs? I mean, they've got to be out there somewhere – if we could find them, we'd have enough money to do whatever we want! We could leave Nod's Limbs for good!"

"Edgar, for all we know he melted them down to make golden water bowls for his poodles. They could be *anywhere*. And I've had enough of riddles for a lifetime."

"You're right, you're right," said Edgar. The twins continued walking silently in no particular direction.

"Still, something else is bothering me," he said after a long while.

"What's that?"

"If Thaddeus has been buried in the caves for all these years, what's in his tomb?"

52. Out on the Limbs

For two centuries the ornate mausoleum of Thaddeus Knightleigh stood just inside the gates of the town cemetery, providing a substantial monument to Nod's Limbs' first mayor.

"There's no mayor in here," said Edgar, looking at the name carved above the door. "Just Nod's Limbs' dirtiest secret."

As homes for the dead are provided with only modest security measures in a town like Nod's Limbs, Edgar's trusty crowbar had little difficulty cracking open the front door. Beyond lay a dark and stifling chamber.

The twins crept into the crypt, where a large sarcophagus rested atop a marble slab. On the sides

were etched several scenes of a barrel-chested man –
presumably Thaddeus Knightleigh – building a brick
wall, saving children from a burning building, and,
in one bizarre instance, wearing armour and slaying
a dragon.

"I'm going to take a wild guess and say he designed
this himself," said Edgar. "Especially the part over
here where angels are feeding him grapes."

Beneath the angels was an inscription:

REST THEE WELL, SWEET THADDEUS.
LONG MAY YOU MAYOR IN THE HEAVENS.

"Somehow," Ellen whispered, "I don't think the
heavens are where old Thaddeus has been mayoring."

Edgar pushed the lid of the sarcophagus. It budged
slightly.

"Help me with this!"

Ellen wedged the crowbar under the lid and
heaved. With the twins' combined efforts, they were
able to slide the heavy slab aside by about a foot.

The twins looked wide-eyed over the lip of the
sarcophagus. In the beam of Edgar's flashlight, they
saw not bones, but limbs.

Four limbs.

Golden limbs.

The sound of clapping made them turn. There, in the doorway, stood Augustus Nod. And though it was difficult to detect amid the man's bushy hair, the fuzzy form of Pet protruded from an area that was probably the man's shoulder.

"You found the limbs, pups," he said. "You solved the puzzle."

"They're ours to keep!" said Edgar. "The will said so—"

"But I'm not dead, am I?" said Nod. "A will's not much more than inky parchment as long as a man is breathing."

"How did you even know the limbs were here?" Ellen demanded.

"Thaddeus always did have a flair for the dramatic. I had a hunch. This was the most . . . *theatrical* place he could conceive of, at least until he figured out what to do with them. A pity! He never had the chance, did he?"

"You're going to send us packing then, I suppose," said Edgar.

"Children," Nod said sternly, "I have been in deep consultation with my private councilor." He jerked his thumb towards Pet. "I am reminded that I once despised this town because none was worthy to be my heir. None had the gumption, the intellect, the *independent spirit*. But you two have proved me wrong."

"What are you saying?" asked Edgar.

"I've decided I may be able to extend an offer. Strictly for services rendered, you understand. But I'm going to need some assistance making my new home livable."

"Your home?"

"Yes. The so-called Knightlorian Hotel is standing on my land, and, as such, is *mine*. They got the basics right – tall and skinny, good bones – but they've almost ruined it with purple flags and neat rows of petunias. Would you be available to help set things straight?"

"Would we?" asked Edgar.

"I *do* have some decorating experience," said Ellen.

And thus the three humans and a Pet stepped merrily from the dusty mausoleum, each twin dragging a golden arm and leg and singing:

> *The seconds cheer: hoo-ray hoo-ray!*
> *As blackest hours melt away,*
> *And second chances rule the day—*
> *Let's turn that Knightleigh eyesore grey!*
> *Our house may be naught but debris,*

But Pet is saved and Heimertz, free,
With Nod returned in jubilee—
How strange – we've found a family.
Away the future winds and wends,
And only time may tell the end.

But when they reached the Knightlorian, they did not notice a limousine idling at the nearby cemetery gate. The back window rolled down and Stephanie Knightleigh peered out, her cheeks as red as her curls.

"So you figured out the final riddle first, did you? Well, that's okay," she murmured to herself. She looked down in her lap at a crusty bucket filled with white gloop. "Because a Knightleigh never says die."

. . . It Ends

With an eye for the macabre and a near-unlimited budget, Edgar and Ellen began remodelling the former Knightlorian Hotel into a suitable new home. Edgar cleverly mixed hundreds of gallons of paint he had purchased from the Gallant Painstmen into a new, tar-like hue he dubbed Black Plague, and set Miles Knightleigh – a regular visitor now – upon the task of painting every wall inside the building.

"All by myself?" Miles had asked.

"Of course not!" Edgar replied. "You're a full-fledged captain of the high seas now, Scurvybeard. Recruit a pirate crew and put them to work!"

"Aye, aye, Edgar!"

Ellen and Dahlia set about rehabilitating the plants they had recovered from the destroyed greenhouse, including Ellen's dear, snapping Morella. Though many plants had been reduced to tatters, the effects of a collapsing house proved to be no match for Edgar's experimental "growth serums".

They picked among the rubble of the old house to salvage what they could. A particularly surprising find was the old telescope from their former attic-above-the-attic, which had miraculously survived the fall.

As they worked amid the debris, they took solace at a welcome sight: occasional visits from townsfolk, who heaved busted muffin-mixers or mangled mannequins or rusty rotary engines into the ruins. The town junkyard – Edgar and Ellen's hallowed Gadget Graveyard – seemed to be making a comeback.

Heimertz relocated his rickety shed to the foot of the Knightlorian. Now sporting a wonderfully menacing scar on his cheek, he resumed his aimless caretaking of the grounds with Madame Dahlia by his side.

In a matter of weeks, the determined twins, Miles, Pet, Heimertz, Dahlia, and the increasingly mischievous Augustus Nod managed to convert the hotel into (the twins had to admit) an even better version of the original tower mansion.

Instead of a dumbwaiter, Pet now coasted about the house at its leisure in an exceptionally fast elevator. Rather than spy at the town through slats of the attic-above-the-attic, the twins now found the views from each floor's balconies to be uniquely inspiring to their prank planning. And the saunas, hot tubs, and whirlpools throughout the interior made excellent homes for all of Ellen's and Dahlia's plants (Morella and the burly Gustav guarded the front gates with snapping jaws and flailing fronds).

One cool, autumn night the twins sat atop the penthouse balcony, forced yet *again* to listen to Nod's ridiculously childish laughter as he heaved water balloons at Nod's Limbsians walking below.

"Weeee! Ha, ha!" Nod leaped up and down like a chimpanzee. After another successful water bombing campaign, he picked up Pet and tossed it playfully. "Did you see that, Pilos? A perfect strike!" The old man shouted to the street below. "You're a little wet behind the ears, Matterhorn! Hoo, hoo!"

Edgar tossed a grape into Ellen's open mouth.

"The possibilities are limitless now, Sister," said Edgar. "What shall we do first?"

"I seem to recall an old blueprint of yours, Brother . . . something about a windmill and giant pile of manure?" said Ellen. "Operation: Blowstink?"

"Yes," said Edgar. "Let's start small for now."

THE END

(SNiff SNiff)

BOOK 1

Edgar & Ellen: Rare Beasts

Edgar and Ellen dream BIG when it comes to pranks. After they learn that exotic animals are worth tons of money, the twins devise a get-rich-quick scheme that sends Nod's Limbs into a frenzy!

BOOK 2

Edgar & Ellen: Tourist Trap

Mayor Knightleigh wants to turn little Nod's Limbs into a premiere holiday destination. But Edgar and Ellen have a plan to give the too-sweet townspeople all the attention they deserve!

BOOK 3

Edgar & Ellen: Under Town

Someone is causing a lot of trouble in town, but it isn't Edgar and Ellen! To catch this new mischievous miscreant, the twins must scour the sewers and uncover someone's dirty secret.

Enjoy Edgar & Ellen?
Add to the adventure at
www.edgarandellen.com!

Enter the Wonderfully Wicked World of Edgar & Ellen! Become a reporter for the *Nod's Limbs Gazette* and use your byline to share the horrible truth! Write your own mischievous tales starring Edgar & Ellen! Watch the cartoon or play the diabolically great games!

Experience
www.edgarandellen.com

KILLING THE EMPERORS

The outrageous Baroness Troutbeck, Mistress of St Martha's, has another cultural battle to win against the British Establishment: this time, against the horror of modern art, as demonstrated by the likes of Tracey Emin and Damien Hirst. But shortly after she enthusiastically announces the war to her close friends, Baroness Troutbeck is kidnapped. Panic spreads throughout the London art world when they realise that nine more victims are missing. Could the perpetrator be a traditionalist with a grudge against contemporary art? Baroness Troutbeck's sidekick Robert Amiss and other loyal friends must work with Scotland Yard to find her. But can they reach her in time?

KILLING THE EMPERORS

KILLING THE EMPERORS

by

Ruth Dudley Edwards

Magna Large Print Books
Long Preston, North Yorkshire,
BD23 4ND, England.

British Library Cataloguing in Publication Data.

Dudley Edwards, Ruth
    Killing the emperors.

        A catalogue record of this book is
        available from the British Library

        ISBN   978-0-7505-3944-9

First published in Great Britain by Allison & Busby in 2012

Cover illustration © Christine Goodwin by arrangement with
Arcangel Images Ltd.

Published in Large Print 2014 by arrangement with
Allison & Busby Limited

Magna Large Print is an imprint of Library Magna Books Ltd.

Printed and bound in Great Britain by
T.J. (International) Ltd., Cornwall, PL28 8RW

014978607

To Robert, friend and ally, who passed on to me the excellent advice that – since there's usually nothing to laugh at – one should learn to laugh at nothing.

'Nothing that you will learn in the course of your studies will be of the slightest possible use to you in after life – save only this – that if you work hard and intelligently you should be able to detect *when a man is talking rot*, and that, in my view, is the main, if not the sole, purpose of education.'

–John Alexander Smith, Waynflete Professor of Moral and Metaphysical Philosophy, Oxford, 1914

Dramatis personae

I've indicated old friends and in which book and number in the series they first appeared:

1 – *Corridors of Death (CoD)*
2 – *The St Valentine's Day Murders (TSVDM)*
3 – *The English School of Murder (TESoM)*
5 – *Matricide at St Martha's (MaSM)*
10 – *Carnage on the Committee (CotC)*

Robert Amiss, ex-civil servant and holder of a variety of jobs who was the main character in this series until in *MaSM* Troutbeck turned him into a sidekick *(CoD)*

Charlie Briggs, hedge-fundie with more money than sense

Sarah Byrne, competent constable

Myles Cavendish, ex-SAS (Special Air Service of the British Army), Baroness Troutbeck's favourite and occasionally live-in lover *(MaSM)*

Martin Conroy, employed by Inland Revenue, ex-SAS reserve

Mary Lou Dinsmore, African-American ex-lover of Troutbeck, academic-turned-BBC-arts-presenter, now married to Ellis Pooley *(MaSM)*

Adam Eichberg, celebrity auctioneer

Sir Henry Fortune, careerist curator and senior lover of Jason Pringle

Chester Herblock, opportunistic American art consultant

Anastasia Holliday, Australian performance artist on the make

Horace, currently resting parrot *(CotC)*

Marilyn Falucci Lamont, billionairess American socialite and art collector

Jim Milton, Commander at Scotland Yard who often has a tough time; long-time friend of Amiss's *(CoD)*

Vernon Morrison, lazy constable

Plutarch, horrible cat *(TESoM)*

Ellis Pooley, earnest Old Etonian Detective Inspector, right-hand man of Jim Milton, close friend of Amiss and husband of Mary Lou Dinsmore *(TSVDM)*

Jason Pringle, amoral art dealer and senior lover of Sir Henry Fortune

Mike Rogers, ex-SAS colleague of Myles Cavendish

Rachel Simon, Amiss's on-off girlfriend and now wife; diplomat-turned-teacher *(TSVDM)*

Oleg Sarkovsky, dodgy Russian oligarch obsessed with status

Sir Nicholas Serota, Director of the Tate galleries and sadly – like all the artists in this book other than Holliday – not a figment of my imagination

Jake Thorogood, corrupted art critic

Baroness (Ida 'Jack') Troutbeck, Mistress of St Martha's, self-indulgent, happy reactionary *(MaSM)*

Gavin Truss, 'if-you-think-it's-art-it's-art'

head of an art college

Hortense Wilde, priggish ideological art historian

Anyone called **Zeka** – nasty Albanian contract killer

Once upon a time there lived a vain Emperor who was obsessed with dressing elegantly and showing his clothes off to his people.

Word of his refined habits spread over his kingdom and attracted two scoundrels to the palace. 'We are two very good tailors,' they said, 'and after many years of research we can weave a cloth so light and fine that it looks invisible to anyone who is too stupid and incompetent to appreciate its quality.'

The chief of the guards sent for the court chamberlain, who notified the prime minister, who ran to the Emperor with the incredible news. The Emperor received the scoundrels, who told him that the cloth would not only be invisible, but would be woven in wonderful colours and patterns created especially for him. Delighted to know that as well as having an extraordinary suit, he would discover which of his subjects were ignorant and incompetent, he gave them a bag of gold and had them equipped with a loom, silk, and gold thread. After a few days he called the old and wise prime minister, revered for his common sense, and instructed him to find out how the work was proceeding.

'We're almost finished, but we need a lot more gold thread,' the scoundrels told the prime minister. 'Here, Excellency! Admire the colours, feel the softness!' The old man bent over the loom and tried to see the fabric that was not there and felt cold sweat on his forehead.

'I can't see anything,' he thought. 'If I see nothing, that means I'm stupid or incompetent and I'll be fired.' So he praised the fabric and reported favourably to the Emperor.

When the scoundrels met the Emperor to measure him for his suit, they showed him the imaginary fabric. 'Look at the colours and feel how fine it is.' Of course the Emperor did not see any colours and could not feel any cloth between his fingers and he almost panicked. But when he realised that no one could know that he couldn't see the fabric and realise he was stupid and incompetent, he recovered.

Finally, the scoundrels brought him the invisible suit. He took off his clothes, put it on and looked in a mirror. The Emperor was embarrassed but since none of his bystanders were, he felt relieved. 'Yes, this is beautiful and it looks very good on me,' he said.

'Your Majesty,' requested the prime minister, 'the people have heard about this extraordinary fabric and want to see you in your new suit.' The Emperor was doubtful, but then he realised that only the ignorant and incompetent would think he was naked.

The ceremonial parade was formed. A group of dignitaries walked at the very front of the procession and anxiously scrutinised the faces of the people in the street. All the people had gathered in the main square, pushing and shoving to get a better look. Applause welcomed the regal procession. Worried that they couldn't see the clothes, and fearful of admitting their stupidity and incompetence, the crowd began to make laudatory comments. 'Look at the Emperor's new clothes. They're beautiful!' 'What a marvellous train.' 'And the colours! The colours of that beautiful fabric! I've never seen anything like it in my life!'

However, a child, who had no job to protect and could see only what his eyes showed him, ran up to the carriage and cried, 'The Emperor hasn't anything on.'

'Fool!' his father shouted, running after him. 'Don't talk nonsense!' He grabbed his child and hustled him away. But the boy's remark, which had been heard by the bystanders, was repeated over and over again until everyone cried: 'The boy is right! The Emperor is naked! It's true!'

The Emperor could not admit that he knew the people were right and thought it better to maintain the illusion that anyone who couldn't see his clothes was either stupid or incompetent. And he walked more proudly than ever, with his noblemen holding high the train that wasn't there at all.

–Hans Christian Andersen, 'The Emperor's New Clothes'

Prologue

March 2012

'Yes, Sarge. Right away, Sarge,' said Constable Vernon Morrison. He switched off his radio crossly and gave it a two-fingered salute. 'More bollocks,' he said to Constable Sarah Byrne. 'Now he says we're to do a detour via the South Bank to see if any troublesome lowlifes need picking up. And we're to check anywhere they might be hiding and up to no good.' His fingers went up again. 'Well, I bloody don't want to. And I won't. We've patrolled up and down and around every blasted road within a radius of half-a-mile of effin' Waterloo Station till my legs are droppin' off. I'm totally knackered.'

'But, Vernon...'

'Don't you "but Vernon" me. I'm freezin'. I don't need no stroll by the effin' river: I need a sausage sandwich and a mug of tea.'

He made a poor shot at mimicking a pedantic voice: '"The reputation of London is at stake, Morrison! We cannot have tourists bothered by aggressive beggars, Morrison! Move them on, Morrison! Move them on!' What planet's he on? What tourists in their

21

right minds are going to be hangin' round by the river this time of night in this weather?'

Byrne adopted the cheery tone that usually worked when her three-year-old was whining. 'Tell you what, Vernon, why don't we head for that cab shelter near the Embankment? They'll have good sausages. And if we get there via the South Bank, everyone will be happy. It won't take any longer to get there that way and we won't have to fib to Sarge.'

This had the hoped-for magical effect. 'You're right, Sarah. Those boys do a good sausage sandwich. OK, we can go that route, but you need to know I'm not goin' into any holes and corners. There's more of them around here than the Sarge has braincells. And this time of night, they'll be pongin' to high heaven.'

Cleverer, more ambitious and more conscientious than her older colleague, Byrne had brought humouring him to a fine art. Within a couple of minutes Morrison was plodding along uncomplainingly by her side on the way to the South Bank while deep in reminiscences about how he had built up the model railway that so annoyed his wife. He was so interested in what he was saying that he made no protest when she occasionally shone her torch into the shadows.

As they reached the side of the National Theatre, a chill wind dissipated his good humour. 'Why are we botherin', Sarah? All decent people will have gone home by now. Who cares what's happenin' in the dark corners? The only ones there will be the pissers, the pissed, and the passed out.' He snorted appreciatively at his wit. 'Come on. Speed up and head for Embankment Bridge.'

Not for the first time, Sarah wondered what use this fat slob was to anyone and why he thought the tax payer should subsidise his laziness. But he was the experienced officer and she was the rookie and she realised she could no longer keep him on the path of duty even if she used the desperate expedient of asking him if he was planning to buy any more rolling stock in the near future. Morrison quickened his pace as they swung into the South Bank. They reached the undercroft where skateboarders leapt and twisted and skidded and fell off all day and she flashed her torch.

'There's no one there, Sarah. Even those nutters don't risk life and limb here in the middle of a winter night.'

'I thought I heard someone calling.'

'I bloody didn't. And even if I did, I wouldn't care. Come on. My sausages call.'

Looking back guiltily, she saw a dishevelled figure emerging from the gloom and beckoning vigorously. 'Hang on, Vernon. There's a bloke wants a word.' She stood her ground and Morrison stopped reluctantly.

'Bloody wino,' he said, as the gaunt, bearded man caught up with them.

He looked at Morrison resentfully. 'I may be a bloody wino,' he said, in an accent more educated than Morrison's, 'but I'm not blind. And I'm not stupid. There's someone hanging in there and you should be seeing if you can save him.'

'Oh, for fuck's sake! You're seein' things.' Morrison adopted his most patronising tone. 'It may have escaped you – it being dark and all – and you havin' had a few, if the smell of whisky is anything to go by – but that whole underground bit is covered from top to bottom with graffiti of people doin' all sorts of things. Probably includin' hanging. Them sort of images are all the rage these days. It's called modern art.'

'I'm not seeing things. Someone's hanging in the corner at the back on the left. He's all in black so I wouldn't have noticed him only it was the best place to sleep. And he's hanging from too far up for me to reach.'

'You'd better be right about this,' said Morrison. 'Wouldn't do you no good to waste police time.'

'What's your name, sir?' asked Byrne, to Morrison's disgust.

'George. Glad to see someone with manners.'

'Could you show us, please?' The undercroft was quite well lit, but the corner at which George pointed was very dark and she needed her torch. A grumbling 'it stinks' indicated that Morrison was following. George stopped; she followed the line of his pointing finger and shone the light up a wall at something long, dangling, and black. A snort came from behind. 'You know what that is?' said Morrison. 'That's another one of them so-called graffiti-paintings by that vandal Banksy. You see them black balloons? He's famous for balloons.'

As the beam of Byrne's torch moved up and down, Morrison shouted triumphantly, 'Look at that placard. I'm right. It even says "Banksy". In big letters.'

Uncertainly, Sarah went up close to the figure and touched it. Feeling cloth, she tugged, and the light fabric tumbled to the ground. 'Vernon, you dickhead,' she yelled. 'I don't care if it says "Leonardo da fucking Vinci" on it. It's a real man with a noose around his neck. Don't you think we should find out if he's dead?'

Chapter One

January 2012

'I used to want to kill the talentless so-called artists,' said Baroness Troutbeck, 'but now I want instead to fill the tumbrils with the critics, the dealers, the curators, and all the rest of the charlatans and dunderheads peddling trash in the name of contemporary art.'

She paused for a moment, tugged absent-mindedly on the massive rope of jet that stood out starkly against her voluminous red kaftan, reached for her glass, and had another sip. 'Not forgetting, of course, all those who wrecked the art colleges and chucked out into the world generations proud to be untutored and unskilled. The gullible little wretches were convinced that you could be an artist without being able to paint, draw or sculpt. Or for that matter know anything at all about painting, drawing, or sculpture. Or beauty.'

She took another sip, nodded approvingly, settled herself more comfortably in her vast green leather armchair and beamed at her friends. 'These martinis really are excellent, don't you think? Sometimes it's a bit of a

chore being chairman of ffeatherstonehaugh's, but if it means you have somewhere you can rely on getting decent food
and drink it's worth putting in the effort.'

'I still prefer vodka martinis, Jack,' said
Mary Lou Denslow.

'You really must grow out of your filthy
American habits, Mary Lou. Vodka is for
people without taste buds. Which of course
sadly all Americans are. Martinis are to gin
as Roman Catholicism is to the Pope.' She
frowned. 'Well, to Roman Catholic popes,
that is. These days there's no guarantee that
a pope will necessarily be a Catholic. I expect that in the interests of inclusiveness
there will be a call for the next one to be a
Wiccan single lesbian mother on benefits.
Perhaps I should offer myself as a compromise candidate.' She took yet another
sip, smacked her lips appreciatively, and
smiled seraphically. 'Now apropos the gin,
it's absolutely vital that you choose either ...'

'Oh, shut up, Jack,' said Mary Lou. 'Get
back to business. Why are you allowing the
artists to live? What happened to your plan
to have Damien Hirst pickled in formaldehyde and called *The Physical Impossibility of
Producing Art If You've No Fucking Talent?*'

'I dithered a bit about this. I was tempted
by the alternative of having him cut in half,
dangling the bits from a gibbet, and calling
the result *Hanged for a Calf?*'

Ellis Pooley raised an enquiring eyebrow. 'You're losing me, Jack. I've heard of Damien Hirst and know he made money out of a dead shark, but that's about it. Where does a calf come into it?'

'What sheltered lives you must lead at Scotland Yard.'

'For God's sake, Ellis,' broke in Robert Amiss. 'How can you be married to Mary Lou...'

'The thinking man's crumpet,' beamed the baroness.

'Stop stealing old jokes, Jack,' said Mary Lou. 'That one dates from the seventies.'

'The old ones are the best, Mary Lou. Like Joan Bakewell, the prototype! Dreadful leftie and had an affair with that ghastly pseud Harold Pinter, but so very fanciable. Even now.'

'As I was saying,' said Amiss, 'how, Ellis, can you be married to the culture industry's iconic broadcaster and not know anything about art?'

'I know quite a bit about art,' said Pooley indignantly. 'Decent art, that is. I just ignore most modern art because I'm too busy to waste my time looking at rubbish.'

'Can't argue with that,' said the baroness. 'Mary Lou, you're paid to comment on crap. Explain Hirst to your husband.'

Mary Lou sighed. 'If I must. Ellis, you know about the YBAs.'

'No.'

'Oh, stop it, Ellis,' said Amiss. 'I know you're a fogey but now you're sounding like an octogenarian judge.'

Mary Lou patted her husband's hand. 'The Young British Artists, hon. Hirst and Tracey Emin and so on. The ones who made BritArt big business over the last couple of decades.'

'Oh, them! Yes, of course. Emin's that dreadful woman who made a fortune from her filthy bed.'

'That's the one, darling. Complete with empty vodka bottles, condoms, tampons and much else you'd rather not think about before dinner.'

'Or even afterwards,' said Pooley.

'The egregious Tracey specialises in what you might call the cartography of the knicker stain,' said the baroness grimly. 'They were presenting that sort of trash as art in a hundred art colleges years ago, but Emin was so noisy and shameless she attracted attention. And, of course, the vandals of the art world took her up. They like them loud and disgusting. It's *épater les bourgeois* all over again. Only this time it's the smug, well-heeled, liberal establishment doing the épatering.'

'Emin's a fame whore, Ellis,' said Mary Lou patiently. 'And very successful at it. She sells her horrid pointless installations and crude drawings by providing a complementary narrative of confessional and self-revelatory bullshit. She's also been smart about becoming pals with existing celebrities, and aspiring celebrities flock to be photographed with her. She became a Conservative supporter just as it appeared inevitable they'd be getting into government and the prime minister is so keen to seem cool that he declared himself a fan and asked her to provide Number 10, Downing Street, with an artwork to give it a bit of "edge".'

Pooley groaned.

'I read about that,' said Amiss. 'A neon sign flashing *More Passion* in scruffy handwriting, wasn't it?'

'Yep.'

'I'd have preferred it if it said *Smaller Government*,' said the baroness gloomily. 'Or *Lower Taxes*. Or *Fiscal Continence*. Or *Why don't you meddling little Napoleons just piss off and leave me alone?*'

Mary Lou laughed. 'You probably have the same politics as she does. These days she seems passionate mostly about tax rates. She threatened to leave the country when the fifty percent higher rate came in.'

There was a long sigh from Pooley. He leant forward and picked up his glass. 'It's enough to drive even me to drink. Don't tell me *More Passion* was paid for from our taxes?'

'No, hon. It was a gift that's been arbitrarily valued by the media at a quarter of a million, thus enabling artistic luvvies to cry that Tracey is a true patriot. Mind you, she produces plenty of neon signs, and having one in a prominent position in Number 10 should at least treble their value. Probably helped her become Professor of Drawing at the Royal Academy.'

'Can she draw?' asked a depressed Pooley.

'A bit. Not well. It doesn't matter. She's on her way to becoming Dame Tracey. Or even Lady Emin.'

The baroness winced. 'We've already got enough vulgarians in the Lords. Mind you, I suppose she deserves credit for exercising some decorum in her Downing Street choice. I remember two of her earlier neons that asked respectively *Is Anal Sex Legal?* and *Is Legal Sex Anal?* Now those would certainly have been edgy, especially when the PM was entertaining ayatollahs.'

She sighed. 'Mind you, they didn't even have the virtue of originality. In the seventies, another pretentious but more talented git called Bruce Nauman produced a neon light that said *Run From Fear / Fun From Rear*. However, I digress. Let's get back to Hirst, who was the leader of that particular artistic pack. He knew how to fleece credulous halfwits. He first hit the headlines when his piece involving maggots and flies feeding off the head of a dead cow wowed Charles Saatchi.'

'I know about Saatchi too,' said Pooley. 'A

plutocratic adman who made another big fortune out of dreadful art.'

'He's married to Nigella Lawson,' said the baroness. 'Yum, yum. That's Nigella. Not her food.' She paused. 'Well, the food's not bad, but compared to Nigella's sumptuous...'

'Stop drooling, Jack,' said Mary Lou. 'Saatchi offered Hirst a £50,000 commission to do whatever he darned well liked and the result was a shark in formaldehyde in a giant glass tank (or vitrine, as the cognoscenti call it) called *The Physical Impossibility of Death in the Mind of Someone Living.*'

'Hence my *The Physical Impossibility of Producing Art if You've No Fucking Talent,*' beamed the baroness. 'But tell Ellis what happened to the unfortunate shark.'

'It rotted, a fin fell off and the liquid went murky. Someone said instead of watching a tiger shark hunting for dinner it was like entering Norman Bates's fruit cellar and finding Mother embalmed in her chair. Adding bleach made it worse. After cleaning up it was still disgustingly green and wrinkled.'

'I don't suppose there's any chance Saatchi threw it out?' enquired Pooley.

Amiss and the baroness guffawed in unison.

'Don't be daft, hon,' said Mary Lou. 'We're talking about the asylum that's contemporary art. The Saatchi curators skinned it and stretched the skin over a fibreglass mould.

The poor thing sure didn't look good. But that didn't stop fuckwits clamouring to possess it. Sir Nicholas Serota...'

'Who?'

The baroness erupted. 'You know perfectly well who he is, Ellis. He's the bloody nincompoop who will be first into my tumbril. He runs an empire of galleries including that storehouse of junk known as Tate Modern. Tat Modern more like.'

Pooley spoke slowly. 'What ... happened ... to ... the ... wretched ... shark?'

'I feel we're on a postmodern journey,' said Amiss. 'We could call it *Cherchez le Cadaver.*' He saw Pooley's face. 'Sorry.'

Mary Lou patted Pooley's hand again. 'Saatchi enlisted an American international celebrity dealer called Larry Gagosian, hon, and he rang around the usual suspects. Allegedly Serota offered two million bucks...'

'Of taxpayers' money,' snorted the baroness.

'...but it wasn't enough.'

'There are celebrity dealers?' asked Pooley.

'There are celebrity hairdressers,' said Amiss. 'Celebrity cake-makers. For all I know there are celebrity undertakers. Of course there are celebrity dealers.'

'The Gagosian dude isn't known as "Go-Go" for no reason,' continued Mary Lou. 'He flogged what remained of the shark to the American billionaire art collector...'

'... celebrity art collector,' put in Amiss.

'...Steve Cohen for somewhere around eight million bucks.'

Pooley looked stunned. 'There's more,' said Mary Lou. 'Hirst seems to have suffered from scruples, so he obligingly spent a few thou on a job-lot of sharks and replaced Cohen's later that year, had another stuffed, gave it some fancy conceptual bullshit name and sold it to a Korean Museum for four million.'

'Scruples my fanny,' said the baroness. 'He made Cohen pay the costs of the replacement.'

'I didn't know that.'

'The only surprise is that he didn't charge the shark.' She gazed at Pooley's shocked expression with grim satisfaction. 'Oh, and incidentally, Charles Saatchi, asked some years later if refurbishing Hirst's shark robbed it of its meaning as art, replied "Completely". Needless to say he said that when he no longer owned it.' She gesticulated at the crystal jug. 'Pour some more martinis, Robert. Ellis needs sustenance to bolster his strength so as to cope with the calf.'

'Oh, yep,' said Mary Lou. 'The calf. You'd better do this, Jack. You're more up to speed on this than me.'

The baroness waited until Amiss had refilled her glass. 'Right. Now pay attention, Ellis. Our hero split a cow and a calf from nose to tail...' She paused. 'Silly me. Of course he didn't. Hirst doesn't do anything much himself other than marketing. He has an atelier, where his assistants do the actual work. Apparently at one time he had as many as a hundred.' She snorted. 'I try to maintain my sense of humour about all this, but when I hear some halfwit explaining that Hirst is merely following in the footsteps of Rembrandt, who had a stable of students and helpers, sometimes I want to explode. Rembrandt was a genius, he taught the gifted young how to emulate him and he would let them paint less important bits of some of his pictures and occasionally their copies of his work got passed off as his. But to mention him in the same breath as bloody Hirst is blasphemy.'

'True, Jack, but calm down,' said Mary Lou. 'Get on with the story.'

'He had a dead cow and calf split, exhibited each of the four halves in a separate chic vitrine and called the result *Mother and Child, Divided*. It won the Turner Prize, which, as you will know, is named after an innovative painter of genius and is awarded annually to whatever bluffer has caught the eye of the knaves and fools who dominate the contemporary art world.' She took an invigorating swallow. 'Particularly the eye of the said Sir Nicholas Serota – or Sclerota, as I prefer to call him – who's been the prize's guiding genius.

'So anyway, my cunning plan was to string up Hirst, split his cadaver and call the result *Hanged for a Calf?* Note the question mark after "calf". Arguing about the significance of that could keep imbecilic critics happy for years.' She shook her head. 'But then I thought leaving his corpse unadorned would represent a lost opportunity. As you know, I am a thorough woman. This would be a perfect opportunity to display a wide range of his...' As she always did when preparing to favour her listeners with her Churchillian French, the baroness paused, set her lips in an exaggerated moue and enunciated painstakingly, *'oeuvres id-i-o-tique de plagiaire.'*

'So he's a plagiarist as well as talentless?' asked Pooley.

'Let's say his detractors point out that there's nothing he's done that someone else didn't do first. A bloke called Ernie Saunders had a preserved shark – which he'd actually caught himself – on the wall of his shop in Shoreditch in 1989, two years before young Damien even placed the order for his dead fish. It was exhibited in 2003 in a gallery run by the Stuckists under the title *A Dead Shark Isn't Art.'*

'Stuckists?'

'The Stuckists have a quaint old-fashioned view that artists should be able to draw and paint, and rightly dismiss conceptual art as

36

pretentious, specious, nihilistic rubbish. The name is courtesy of Tracey Emin herself, who once shrieked "Stuck! Stuck! Stuck!" at an artistic boyfriend whose painting was insufficiently avant-garde for her taste.'

'Did anyone buy Saunders's shark?'

'Of course not. He offered it for a bargain million quid, pointing out that would save the buyer of his pickled shark more than five mill compared to what he described as "the Damien Hirst copy", but there were no takers.'

'Hirst was a brand by then, hon,' explained Mary Lou. 'As far as the art establishment was concerned, he had a monopoly on dead fish and animals.'

The baroness emitted another snort. 'Even though a bloke called John LeKay, whom he was very close to for a while, had exhibited animal carcasses years before Hirst produced his cattle. And lent him a science catalogue showing a cow bisected lengthways which inspired *Mother and Child, Divided*.'

She leant forward and shook her finger at Pooley. 'Then there was the sculpture, *Hymn*, a hugely enlarged version of a torso from his son's anatomy set, which bore a startling resemblance to *Yin and Yang*, an anatomical torso exhibited a few years earlier by LeKay. Hirst had a bit of a setback here. Out of the million he got for *Hymn*, he had to cough up quite a bit because the toy manufacturer and the toy designer had complained about breach of copyright.

'Now, Ellis, are you still paying attention?'

'Yes, ma'am.'

'You must remember Hirst flogging a skull covered with diamonds.'

'Now you mention it, I do. Nasty-looking, vulgar thing.'

'During the time he was most friendly with Hirst, poor old John LeKay had constructed skulls made of soap and wax and adorned them with artificial diamonds and Swarovski crystals. He sold them for around a thousand quid. Hirst had a skull made out of platinum, had someone stick about fifteen million quid's worth of diamonds on it, called it *For the Love of God* and demanded fifty mill. Didn't quite get all of that. It ended up with a consortium that included him. But don't worry about Damien. The lad's a multi-multi-multi-millionaire. Unlike John LeKay.

'Which leads me neatly to the multi-coloured spots.'

'Which you will daub all over his body,' said Mary Lou.

'Certainly not. Which I will have daubed by an assistant. I'm not one for unnecessary physical labour, as you know.'

'I'd be surprised if Hirst was the first artist to paint spots,' said Pooley.

'You mean to have spots painted in his name,' added Amiss.

38

'And you'd both be right. Yes, it's an old idea and yes, he wasn't any good at it. Indeed he described the few spots he painted himself as "shite". But his industrious assistants produced many hundreds of spot canvases, which have earned their employer millions.'

'At least he's honest,' said Amiss.

'Candid would be a better word, Robert. But I will admit Damien can sometimes be almost endearing. He once explained that the best spot painting "you could have by me" would be one painted by his assistant Rachel. And when an interviewer pointed out to him that other artists claimed he had stolen their ideas, Hirst's response was: "Fuck 'em all!" Why *should* he care? There's no copyright on ideas.'

'Has the art establishment ever shown any signs of worry about all this?' asked Amiss.

'Worry?' said the baroness in her best Lady Bracknell voice. 'Worry? This month that ghastly Gasgosian creature stuffed the eleven galleries he's got dotted around smart bits of the world with a global exhibition called *The Complete Spot Paintings of Damien Hirst, 1986-2011*. All the small, medium, and big spots your little heart could desire.' She emitted a heavy sigh.

'While you're at it, don't forget about Tate Britain,' said Mary Lou.

The baroness took an enormous silk handkerchief from the recesses of her kaftan, mopped her brow theatrically, breathed deeply a few times and had a draught of Martini. 'I will be calm. Yes, Tate Britain!' She breathed deeply again. 'You and I might think that since this lucky museum owns a magnificent collection of British art since 1500, it might show us the best of it. But Sclerota's in charge of that too. Last time I was there, pre-twentieth-century art was restricted to a few rooms. Modern tat was rampant.' There was another heavy sigh. 'I suppose we should be grateful that Sclerota didn't insist that in this year of the Olympics, as the world focuses on London, Tat Britain should be cluttered up for five months with an enormous Damien Hirst retrospective. No. Reason has prevailed. It's Tat Modern that's hosting his rubbish. Mind you, it's having to have its floor reinforced at great expense because huge vitrines of formaldehyde and assorted animal carcasses weigh a lot.'

'You're looking baffled, Robert,' said Mary Lou.

'I just don't understand why people are taken in.'

'Having hailed the talentless as talents in the first place, their reputations are at stake. How can all these critics and curators who've hailed Hirst as a genius fess up?'

'Besides, if dealers and collectors were to admit the emperors were naked,' said the baroness, 'they'd lose their own shirts.' She sniggered. 'Did you hear that story about the arch-luvvie, the play director Sir Trevor Nunn? Apparently, he bought one of Hirst's spin paintings...'

'What are they?' asked Pooley, wearily. 'And whom did he nick the idea from?'

'You dribble paint onto a revolving surface and see what happens. Artists – including, inevitably, John LeKay – have been doing this for decades. Hirst added motors to speed up his assistants' production line. Eventually Nunn met Hirst at a party and told him he had one of his spin paintings. Hirst asked the title and the price. Now Nunn had bought this before Hirst's prices went stratospheric, so he'd paid a mere twenty-seven thousand quid. A delighted Hirst then confided that this painting was the work of his two-year-old son, with some help from a ten-year-old pal. Nunn got over his disappointment when he later sold the thing for nearly fifty thou.'

'They're all mad,' said Pooley.

'It's a madness that's made a lot of them rich. Take the case of the journalist, A.A. Gill. In 2007, he asked Christie's to auction a painting of Joseph Stalin for which he'd originally paid two hundred. When they refused, on the grounds that they didn't deal in Hitler or Stalin, the cunning sod asked if they'd sell Stalin by Hirst or Warhol and they said they certainly would. Sadly, Warhol was dead, so Gill had to make do with his mate Hirst, who agreed to paint a red nose on Stalin and signed it. It went for a hundred-and-forty-thousand.'

'I'm speechless,' said Pooley.

'Just as well,' said the baroness. 'Less competition for me.'

'We've wandered a long way from your method of disposing of Hirst, Jack,' said Amiss. 'Will he have diamonds stuck to his head?'

'Certainly not. Unlike Hirst, I'm not made of money. But I'll have his orifices stuffed with cigarette butts.'

'Why cigarette butts?' asked Pooley.

'He's flogged cabinets full of them.'

'I thought he flogged cabinets full of pills,' said Amiss.

The baroness clicked her tongue. 'He did indeed. As – again - had been done before him. Hirst and many of his contemporaries claim to be original in their use of commonplace objects, when they're just providing variations on what Marcel Duchamp thought of nearly a century ago. They burble these days about being in the vanguard of transgressive art...'

'What's that?' asked Pooley.

'Art that pushes the boundaries and has the knickers of the bourgeoisie in a right old twist. I've nothing against that myself. I sometimes fancy a bit of transgression. However, the point is that all this was done by the Dadaists after the first war and Marcel Duchamp, whom one might term the Dada of them all, had most of the ideas that the YBAs pass off as their own. Take the Hirst Stalin. One of Duchamp's japes was to paint a moustache and goatee on a reproduction of the Mona Lisa and exhibit it. It was Duchamp who announced that objects he called "readymades" were art.' She paused. 'Well, him being a frog, he called them "*objets trou-vés*". He kicked off with a bicycle wheel and a bottle rack. Then came the urinal.

'Stop looking so depressed, Ellis. It gets worse. Duchamp bought a urinal from an ironworks called Mott, called it *Fountain*, signed it R. Mutt and tried to exhibit it. It was rejected, but later became the icon of conceptual art, since Duchamp's message was that anything he said was art, was art. "I declare myself an artist, and so anything I say is art is art" became an immutable law. Actually, Duchamp was making a case for artistic freedom and he was also making a joke, but the law of unintended consequences gives us Hirst and his chums and an art establishment bowing down before them.'

'Like the Israelites worshipping the Golden Calf,' suggested Pooley.

'Funny you should mention that. Hirst gold-plated a calf's hooves and horns, called it *The Golden Calf*, and flogged it for nine mill.'

Pooley groaned.

'Fill us in on the cigarette butts,' requested Amiss.

'Hirst branched out into butts. Standing butts and lying-down butts carefully arranged by his loyal workforce. Some of the cabinets were edged in gold to appeal to Arabs. They went for hundreds of thousands of smackers.'

Amiss sighed. 'The older I get, the more it's borne upon me that there's one born every minute.'

'In the case of Mr Hirst,' guffawed the baroness, 'he also believes that you should never give a sucker an even break. Especially if the sucker is rich. In that regard he does have a touch of genius. He's an alchemist: he takes base metal and turns it into gold.'

'Well at least what you've been planning is pretty original, Jack. I don't think even Hirst has come up with snuff installations before now,' said Amiss.

Mary Lou laughed. 'Jack, didn't you once suggest suffocating Jeff Koons in a giant plastic inflatable penis and sticking him outside some museum?'

'I most certainly did. I settled on Washington's Museum of Crime and Punishment as the location.' The baroness looked pensive. 'But I could never decide on quite the right

44

title for the work. Obviously, I thought of *Dick*, but I'd reserved *Dickhead* for my creation combining real bits of that Quinn bloke who won fame with the sculpture of his head made from his frozen blood.' She glanced at Pooley. 'Come on, Ellis. You're off-duty. Stop looking down your nose like a Reverend Mother who's discovered the novices having an orgy in the cloister, and choose a so-called artist to rub out.'

'It would have to be the ghastly Emin.'

'Predictable, but nonetheless a good choice. We would be well rid of her maudlin narcissistic ramblings about her gynae-cological workings. How would you dispose of her?'

'Wrap her up in her unmade bed and roll it down a cliff?'

'That's a bit unimaginative by your stan-dards, Ellis,' said Amiss. 'What's the point of reading all those crime novels if you end up with such a pedestrian method of murder? Think Edgar Wallace.'

Pooley took a small sip of his martini and concentrated hard. 'OK. Poison her pud-ding with the cholera bacterium and claim she caught it because of her insanitary habits.'

'But what would you call this work of art?' asked Amiss.

The brooding silence that followed was broken by the baroness. 'I have it. Crown

45

her with a neon light flashing *Just Deserts*. And not with a double s.'

'I'm getting into the spirit of this,' said Amiss. 'Can we create a giant Campbell's can full of soup and drown Andy Warhol in it? And yes, yes, I know he's dead but we could exhume him.'

'And call it *You Say Tomato and I Say Die?*' suggested Mary Lou.

'Tempting though it would be to settle scores with any number of dead frauds,' said the baroness, 'I'm a busy woman and there simply isn't enough time. We have to stick to the living.'

'Can we get back to why you've concluded that artists are the wrong targets?' asked Mary Lou. 'You've strayed a long way from where you started.'

'I know you interrogate people for a living these days, Mary Lou, but it would be a shame were this to prevent us from dallying a while in conversational byways.'

'At the rate we're going,' said Mary Lou, 'we'll never even get a glimpse of the highway.'

The baroness looked at her watch. 'Wait till we've eaten. Now where the hell is Rachel? Ring her, Robert, and tell her to hurry up. If she's not here in five minutes we'll go in to dinner without her. I'm damned if I'm going to put the artichoke and goat's cheese soufflé in jeopardy. It's taken three arguments with

46

the chef to get it quite right. The fellow's congenitally unsound on the chilli issue.'

As Amiss headed for the door with his phone at the ready, she shouted after him: 'Tell her it's an emergency: the martini jug is empty.'

Disaster was averted when Amiss's wife arrived in the bar just in time, accepted with equanimity that the baroness considered her tube train breaking down an inadequate excuse for missing martinis, and the soufflé and all that followed were such a success that even the baroness could find no fault. The marrowbone stew with herb dumplings had caused her so much ecstasy she had been moved to charge into the kitchen to congratulate everyone. In the interstices of criticising her guests for insufficiently attending to their food and wine, she listened with surprising attentiveness to Rachel's account of what life was like as a probationary teacher in a London comprehensive.

By ten p.m. the five friends had settled in the gallery and had resolved the inevitable arguments with the baroness about whether, what, and how much they wanted to drink ('You're a crowd of blasted puritans'). Pooley and Rachel were drinking decaffeinated coffee ('Wimps! The whole point of coffee is caffeine. I'll have a double espresso.') and nothing else ('Typical!'). Mary Lou and Amiss had mollified their hostess by each ordering an Americano, agreeing to help her do justice to the decanter of port, and showing some interest in her impassioned explanation as to why the traditional Portuguese manner of treading grapes was immeasurably superior to anything a machine could do. After a few minutes, Pooley leant forward and said, 'Jack, I hate to interrupt, but I can't stay long. If there's anything else you want to tell us about, you should get on with it. I've an early start tomorrow and murderers to locate.'

Reluctantly, the baroness turned her attention away from the delights of the Douro River Valley. 'I was seeking to alert you to the destruction of art, of course. Pay attention.'

Amiss yawned. 'You're always banging on about the destruction of something.'

'What do you expect, when the Western world is going to hell?' She reached again for her glass. 'Do I not spend my life selflessly battling with the forces of anarchy?'

'You're usually leading the forces of anarchy.'

'Only on battlegrounds of my choosing,' she said stiffly. 'When it's a necessary means of getting my way. And anyway, I never defend intellectual or moral anarchy.'

'I've heard you defend blackmail and intimidation,' remarked Rachel.

'If they're my ends, they justify my means.'

Pooley was getting irritated. 'Can we cut

the philosophical niceties, Jack. I'm a simple policeman. Get to it. What's up?'

'We have fought the culture wars together, my friends,' she said, waving her glass of port for emphasis. 'But we cannot rest. The forces of darkness still reign. They must be overthrown. This time it's the Satanic army of the art world that must be destroyed.'

Mary Lou looked apprehensive. 'Haven't you won enough cultural battles to justify hanging up your sword, Jack?'

'Absolutely,' said Amiss heartily. 'When you come to think of it, you've been pretty comprehensive and successful.'

The baroness threw him a contemptuous look. 'You're mistaken if you think such blatant flattery will get you off the hook, Robert. I don't indulge in false modesty...'

'You can say that again,' said Mary Lou.

'Darling, please don't interrupt her,' said Pooley. 'It only slows everything up.'

'...so I recognise that I have had some small success in routing the evil forces of political correctness at St Martha's and Paddington University.' And, of course, there was the Knapper-Warburton. But I cannot rest upon my laurels. There's much more to be done.'

She leant forward confidingly. 'Now, I recognise that I cannot fight and win global cultural wars. Mine have to be small canvases. Like Jane Austen's. I am not Tolstoy.'

'You're a bit more like him than Jane

Austen, if I may say so,' said Amiss. 'At least in your appetites.'

She ignored him. 'So the small canvas this time is related to art. And once more I need help.'

'What kind of help?' asked Rachel.

'Stop looking so apprehensive. I'm not going to kidnap Robert. Now pay attention and I'll tell you what we have to do.'

Chapter Two

February 2012

His phone rang mid-morning. Since the caller sounded like a frantic skylark, Robert Amiss realised it had to be Petunia Stamp, the college secretary of St Martha's. Trying without much success to make sense of the cacophony of twitters, he gathered that she was upset. He pictured the fluttering little creature – pink alice band slightly askew and chest heaving underneath some frightful knitwear appliquéd with kittens or butterflies – and wondered yet again how Baroness Troutbeck – who suffered fools appallingly – could stand her. And vice-versa.

'Take it slowly, Miss Stamp. Is something the matter?'

'It's the Mistress, Mr Amiss. The Mistress. Where, oh where, is the Mistress?'

Patient questioning elicited the information that the baroness had been expected back in Cambridge the previous night but had not turned up. Since she often arrived early in the morning, no one had worried until she failed to surface at the monthly council meeting. 'A council meeting, Mr Amiss! She missed a council meeting! You know she would never miss a council meeting. And no message. No message. And she's not answering her phone. Something terrible must have happened to her. What will we do? Should I send for the police?'

'Leave it with me for the moment, Miss Stamp. If anything's happened to her, it would probably be here rather than in Cambridge. I'll investigate and get back to you. And don't worry. You know she's the toughest of tough old birds.'

Interpreting Miss Stamp's silence as an indication that she didn't know whether to be comforted by this undoubted truth or horrified by his *lèse-majesté*, he said goodbye in what he hoped was a manly reassuring voice and rang off.

'Sorry to have got your PA to rout you out of a meeting, Mary Lou, but it's urgent.'

'I was interviewing a grumpy poet for tonight's programme and was glad to have

51

an excuse to get rid of the asshole. What's up? You sound agitated.'

'It's contagious. Miss Stamp's been on the phone in a right old state because she can't find Jack. And I admit to being worried. She didn't turn up for this morning's council meeting. And they can't get hold of her.'

'Hell, I'm worried! That never happened during my time at St Martha's. Never ever.'

Amiss got up and began to pace. 'That's what's troubling me. Jack's reliability and punctuality are positively aggressive.'

'Are you thinking what I'm thinking?'

'Car crash?'

'Precisely. The way she drives it's a miracle she's never had one.'

'But if she was in hospital she'd have had ID and St Martha's would know by now.'

'Unless Myles was down as next of kin. And they wouldn't have been able to find him. Isn't he still in Iraq?'

'Last time I heard. But she wouldn't have named Myles. He's away too much.'

'Supposing...?'

'Really bad crash and a fire?'

'Yep.'

'Oh, God, Mary Lou. Of course it's possible. What'll we do?'

'I'll get Ellis to put someone on to it. It shouldn't take long. It would have to have been an accident on the North Circular or the M11.'

'Unless she went by a scenic route?'

'With a motorway available on which to do a ton?'

'Sorry. Dumb idea.'

'But then of course there's the other horrible possibilities.'

'Heart attack? Stroke? Burglars?'

'That sort of thing. I'll ask Ellis to send someone round to her flat and will be back to you as soon as I hear anything that counts as news.'

'You're supposed to be a crime writer,' Amiss said to himself crossly. 'Think of a benign reason why she's disappeared.' He thought of the baroness's propensity for pursuing even unlikely potential conquests – male and female – as well as of her greed for all the good things of life, but then he thought of her sense of duty and her fierce loyalty to St Martha's. He made a vain attempt to get back to work, but finding himself looking as blankly at the screen as it looked at him, he decided to engage in displacement activity. With Radio 4 talking at him of all manner of political and cultural controversies which he could hardly take in, he attacked the kitchen belligerently and tidied up everything in the flat he could find to tidy. Resisting the temptation to bother Ellis Pooley, he forced himself to sit down at the computer, pay bills, and answer emails. He rang Miss Stamp again, found her frantic, failed to steady her, went out for a walk, phone in hand, made an unnecessary visit to the supermarket to buy unnecessary food and went home and tried to interest himself in Sky News. But Middle Eastern tensions, domestic rows about public expenditure cuts, and a hurricane threatening American cities failed to do the trick. 'I've been so worried,' he told his wife when she got home, 'that I thought of taking my mind off Jack by giving Plutarch a bath.'

Rachel looked at the fat feline sprawled across the rug. 'That would have been a suicide mission.'

'I know. I know. That's why I never bathe her. But it would certainly have distracted me.'

'Phone Ellis.'

'I don't want to seem to be fussing. He'll be doing what he can. Mary Lou would have called if there was news.'

'Oh, for heaven's sake, Robert. Impossible person though Jack is, we're all very fond of her and you and Ellis have been through so many wars together that you're blood brothers. Phone him. Now!'

'He's virtually certain that she can't have had a crash on the way to Cambridge,' Amiss reported. 'There were only half a dozen during the relevant period and everyone involved has been identified.'

'Has he had her flat checked?'

'Yes. A neighbour had a key. Nothing suspicious. And her car's gone. He was flummoxed and wondering whether to get her reported as a missing person.'

'She wouldn't like that if she'd simply gone AWOL.'

'But she wouldn't have gone AWOL when she was due at that meeting. It wasn't as if it was even just routine. She'd mentioned to me there was a row brewing about something or other which she had to resolve. She was trying to decide whether the appropriate tactic was conciliation or repression. You know Jack. She was looking forward to it.'

'So he'd better have her reported as a missing person, then.'

'That's what I told him. No choice.'

'How are you?'

'Miserable. Scared. Edgy.' He gave a bleak laugh. 'Like Tracey Emin. Come on, wife. Take me out for a walk and a drink and try to get my mind onto something other than that the most likely explanation is that Jack Troutbeck's dead.'

It was after eight o'clock the next morning. Amiss had given Rachel breakfast and had walked her to the tube, assuring her unconvincingly that he would call on his innate male ability to compartmentalise, avoid tormenting himself about Jack, and get some work done. Having instructed himself to hold off until nine from ringing Pooley, he looked at newspapers online and found himself reading the same paragraphs over and over again and checking his watch every few minutes. At half past eight, when the phone rang, he jumped up so energetically that he knocked over his coffee and the dregs spread over his keyboard. He paid no attention but grabbed the receiver. Plutarch, ever alert to the main chance, seized the opportunity to leap on his chair and curl herself into a contented marmalade circle.

'It's Ellis. No news, I'm afraid.'

'I'm sort of relieved.'

'I know what you mean.'

'What are the theories?'

'We haven't got any. We're still searching for the car. And no one here's much interested. I've got someone going through all the routine procedures with the help of her secretary: photographs, credit card details, habits, places she frequents and so on. We got hair from her London bathroom so we'll have her DNA soon. But there's no sense of urgency about this. My colleagues think academics and peers are all dotty anyway, so she's just some old bird who's wandered off somewhere on a whim. Maybe with amnesia.'

'I thought of that. But it wouldn't explain why she didn't answer her phone.'

'It's a very long shot when you know her.

But if you don't... Anyway, Jim'll be back from his Interpol meeting tomorrow and he'll take it seriously. Until then there isn't much I can do.'

'OK,' said Amiss, trying to conceal the fear in his voice.

'*Courage, mon vieux*,' said Pooley. 'Think of what she's come alive out of in the past. Nine lives and all that.'

'She's used most of those up,' said Amiss gloomily.

The phone rang an hour later. Having dried his keyboard and tried vainly to make it work, Amiss had been out to the computer shop and was back in business.

'Don't let me interrupt if you're writing.'

'Oh, for heaven's sake, Mary Lou.' As he stood up and began pacing, Plutarch again took possession of his chair. 'Surely you've learnt by now that most writers are desperate for distraction. By this time most mornings, I've managed to postpone starting a new chapter by answering emails that could have waited for hours and reading several newspapers on the net on the spurious grounds that I need to stay in touch with reality. If you hadn't called I might have been driven to iron a shirt.'

She didn't respond.

'And, of course, I'm worried sick about Jack.'

'That's why I rang. So am I. And I keep thinking about that dinner at ffeather-stonehaugh's. She was so right. I feel a bit ashamed. I agreed with her but I haven't done anything since to challenge the pernicious orthodoxy she's complaining about and, of all of us, I'm the gal who should.'

'But then you want to keep your job, don't you?'

'Yeah. Same old excuse everyone uses. You toe the line or you're identified as a heretic. And we all know nothing good happens to heretics. Ellis had a bit of a go at me on the way home that night for not standing up to the thought police and speaking my mind. You know when he gets priggish?'

'Don't I just!'

'He went on about the courage of one's convictions and that sort of thing. So I asked him when he last bit his tongue when a superior officer told him to do something he thought stupid or wrong – as opposed to actually immoral, which Ellis would die rather than countenance.'

'Don't tell me. That same day?'

'The day before, it turned out. Honesty is one of my guy's many saving graces.'

Amiss paced on. 'There isn't much we can do anyway, is there? Jack was calling us to arms, but the enemy is widely dispersed and we seem to lack either weapons or troops.'

'I guess we could do a bit of chipping away

here or there when we get a chance. I can try to get more of a voice in arts programmes for the good guys. And if you decide to do a novel about that world, maybe you can make a difference.'

'Hah! Do you know how many copies the first one sold? Or what my advance was on this one? And before you ask, I'd have to be a few drinks in before I'd be able to bring myself to tell you. If I didn't do some journalism we'd be in complete penury. I'm relying on Rachel to hurry up and become one of those super-teachers who're brought in to turn around sink schools and are rewarded with six-figure salaries and titles.'

'Don't they have to work hundreds of hours a week?'

'She'll cope.'

'Might you seriously have a go at the art world?'

'If Jack comes back. This morning, not being able to write, I've been reading up on some of what she was going on about. Here's something from an open letter the Stuckists wrote to the benighted Serota some years back. It was a sensible, civil criticism of postmodernism.'

'Oh, holy shit,' groaned Mary Lou. 'Post-bloody-modernism rears its horrible head again. That's the incomprehensible fashionable gibberish that drove me out of academia. I hate meeting it in my new line of work. What's it supposed to mean in this context?'

'Search me. It seems to embrace all the skill-free stuff that can be done by people who couldn't paint a house or sculpt a ball out of plasticine. You know, the stuff Jack was moaning about. Along with pointless performance art, people being videoed picking their noses and all that kind of thing.'

'Postmodern almost always means waste of space and trashing of the admirable.'

'The Stuckists's view. They suggested to Serota that postmodernism ... hang on a second, I was just reading it.'

He leant across Plutarch, who snarled and extended a claw.

'That postmodernism was "a cool, slick marketing machine where the cleverness and cynicism of an art which is about nothing but itself, eviscerates emotion, content and belief." The Brit artist, they went on, seemed uninterested in vision or insight, merely in maintaining "his or her media kudos in the art brat pack."'

Amiss resumed pacing. 'They sent this to Serota for comment along with a manifesto called *Remodernism*, which called for a new spirituality in art, culture, and society to replace postmodernism's spiritual bankruptcy. Mind you, it admittedly was full of heresies like the proposition that art that has to be in a gallery to be art isn't art.'

'And Serota's response?'

'That they wouldn't be surprised to learn that he had no comment on the letter or the manifesto.'

'What a contemptuous shit! Well, that really puts him on my hate list.'

'Mine too. Then they had an exhibition of paintings in Liverpool that – from what I've seen on the net – included plenty of interesting and talented stuff. They offered the Tate a hundred-and-sixty paintings allegedly worth £500,000. The donation was turned down ... hang on ... I have to navigate around Plutarch to find the primary source.'

Cautiously, he once more leant across the cat, who took noisy umbrage. 'Bloody animal. You'd think the mouse I was clicking on was a real one being wrenched from her slavering mouth. I've only just evaded serious injury.

'Anyway, the offer was rejected by Serota, who told them portentously that Tate curators and Trustees felt the work lacked sufficient quality "in terms of accomplishment, innovation or originality of thought to warrant preservation in perpetuity in the national collection." The bugger didn't mention any conflict of interest, like that the curators and Trustees were likely to have taken a dim view that many of the exhibits satirised Serota and the bloody Tate.'

'If he'd any sense of humour he'd have accepted and displayed their most famous image of him, called *Sir Nicholas Serota Makes an Acquisition*. It shows him smiling maniacally behind a large pair of red knickers on a washing line, asking himself: "Is it a genuine Emin (£10,000) or a worthless fake?"'

'Were the knickers clean?'

'Yes.'

'So I guess they couldn't be authentic.'

'What a pro you are, Mary Lou. You always get to the heart of the matter. Or, on this occasion, the gusset.'

Rachel came through the door late that afternoon just as Amiss was coming off the phone. 'Any news?'

He nodded. 'Not about Jack. But there are two more mysterious disappearances that could conceivably be related if your imagination is active enough, since Jack actually was trashing their reputations over dinner last month. They're an art dealer and a museum big shot.'

'What? Who? Charles Saatchi and Sir Nicholas Serota?'

'No. Jason Pringle and Sir Henry Fortune. I seem to remember Jack said they were dreadful, corrupt old queens.'

He paused and scratched his head. 'Well, if the manager of Pringle's gallery is right, they're now missing, dreadful, corrupt old queens.'

'Any details?'

'No. Ellis will be in touch when he's talked to Jim. It's just more waiting. Be a pal and take my mind off it. Distract me. How was your day? Did you do what we talked about last night?'

'It was grim. Grim, grim, grim. And only incidentally because I was worried about Jack.' He saw her expression and led her to the armchair. She squealed, 'No, Robert, I can't sit on that till I've changed. She's been moulting all over it.' Rachel glared at Plutarch, who was oblivious, for after an ill-tempered period of exile, she had regained possession of Amiss's typing chair.

Amiss looked guiltily at the protective covering that Plutarch had earlier succeeded in dragging aside. 'Sorry. I didn't notice she'd done that. I'll sort it out while you change and I'll get you a drink. White wine?'

'The way today's gone, I feel more like cyanide. But not for me. For some of my colleagues.'

By the time Rachel emerged from the bedroom in T-shirt and jeans and minus make-up, Amiss had managed to remove the worst of the fur, had ejected Plutarch into the garden where she was stalking small vulnerable creatures, some particularly soothing Mozart was playing softly in the background, and the ice-bucket held a decent Sancerre. Rachel sat down and managed a wan smile as she accepted a glass.

'What was the worst of today, darling? Did another one bite you?'

'No. It was violence-free and I actually had a few classes where the majority paid some attention. It was colleagues who sapped my spirit.'

'Go on. Tell all.'

'I can't find any way of stopping that blasted feline-worshipper...'

'The RE teacher?'

'Yes. Maureen. Not that there's either much religion or much education in what the silly cow offers the kids. It's all about peace and love and inclusiveness and celebrating each other's festivals and avoiding anything that might offend anyone, which seems to mean mentioning anything to do with Christianity, which being the majority religion, is apparently inherently offensive to minorities.'

'Judaism's OK, then?'

'Don't be absurd. Judaism's always worse with people like Maureen. She's got the kids doing a project about suffering Palestinians in Gaza. It seems to involve quite a lot of work with felt hearts and pebbles. She went on about it at some length and all I can say is that she doesn't seem to have what one might call a nuanced view of what's going on in the Middle East. In fact her take on it would probably go down great down the local mosque.'

'You didn't mention...?'

'Being Jewish? I certainly did not. I'm trying to avoid her, not start another row. She was the one I fell out with in my first week because I got cross when she told me there was nothing more important to teach children than that man-made climate change was about to destroy the planet. Do you remember? I said it wasn't proven that it was man-made, that frightening children didn't seem to me to be a good idea, and that really I thought we'd be better off making them literate and numerate? I thought she'd have a stroke.

'Unfortunately, our shared experience as cat-owners brought her back to speaking to me today. She insisted on showing me a dozen photos of her little treasures and expressing her disappointment that I haven't yet shown her one of dear Plutarch. Why I was ever fool enough to admit I lived with a cat I can't imagine. In future, I intend to be a denier.'

'You couldn't just mention that Plutarch is a vile step-cat thrust upon you through no fault of your own?'

'That would seem disloyal. After all, when I accepted you for better or worse I knew what that entailed in the cat department.'

As if on cue, a screech came from the

next-door garden.

'Get away, you horrible animal. Leave that bird alone. Oh, no! You murdering beast!'

Amiss and Rachel looked at each other and shrugged.

'Another one bites the dust,' said Amiss wearily. 'Go on.'

'That wasn't the worst of today. It was the art that got me depressed.'

'Art?'

'I'd been thinking about what Jack had said about that night, so I asked my best class what they knew about art and artists. Do you know, there wasn't one of them that had ever been to a gallery. And I drew complete blanks with Michelangelo, Leonardo da Vinci, Turner and any other obvious candidates I tried on them.'

'Did they know there were such things as artists?'

'A couple of them had seen religious pictures in church. That was about it.'

'You mean they hadn't even heard of Damien Hirst.'

'No. But three of the girls had seen Tracey Emin on the telly talking about her abortion and thought she was great.'

'Oh, dear.'

'So at the staff meeting after school I said I felt they weren't being much exposed to beauty and asked if it would be possible to take them to the National Gallery some afternoon. My God, you'd have thought I'd suggested a brothel. And a brothel three hundred miles away on an ice-floe full of expiring polar bears at that.'

'First, the deputy head began to explain how many staff would have to be with me by way of back-up. He droned on about risk assessments. Of course I knew there was a lot of bureaucracy involved in the simplest school trips, but this was beyond belief. We'd have to be prepared for all kinds of weather, transport-related problems, pre-dictable hazards, accidents, misbehaviour in the gallery, paedophile security guards, and God knows what else. We'd have to have at least three people in attendance with first-aid qualifications and there would have to be a precise breakdown of responsibilities.'

She rubbed her forehead wearily. 'Hon-estly, these kids are fifteen, not five. I was tempted to – but didn't – point out that they're mostly roaming the streets on a Saturday night getting drunk and laid and that broad daylight in Trafalgar Square was probably pretty safe by comparison.'

There came an ear-splitting yowl and the sound of something heavy crashing against the kitchen door. 'Tom from down the road trying to impose his authority yet again, I'd guess,' said Amiss as he got up to investi-gate. 'He's pretty good at hot pursuit.'

Rachel lay back and closed her eyes as

Amiss went into the garden, broke up the fight, chased the tom away, and threw a furious Plutarch into the kitchen. 'When will you grasp that you shouldn't take on something half your age and twice as fit, you stupid creature?'

There was a yowl as he investigated a bloody ear. A louder one as he cleaned it with antiseptic was accompanied by an expletive from Amiss. By the time Plutarch had been calmed down, fed and watered and had accompanied Amiss back to the living room, Rachel had been rejuvenated by a refreshing nap. She looked with distaste as the cat made a beeline for the back of the sofa, leapt to the top, and hung out of it. 'I haven't asked you for ages, Robert, but I don't suppose there's any chance Plutarch's owner is likely to get out of jail soon, is there?'

'He's not even up for parole in the foreseeable future. Unless they change the law drastically, I'm afraid Plutarch is a life sentence. Of course, that's her life, not yours.'

'I always hoped that Jack would take her on.'

'It came up in conversation recently. She said she'd love to have her back at St Martha's for a holiday, but that sadly she'd made too many enemies. Apparently peeing in the piano was such a bad breach of etiquette that even Jack was powerless in the face of public opinion.'

'You tread on my dreams,' said Rachel. He gave her a hug. 'It's OK,' she said. 'It's OK.'

'Anyway she can't have more than ten years left, darling, and she's much better than she was. It's ages since she climbed the curtains or managed to open the fridge.'

'When you say better, you mean slightly less athletic.'

'And a bit mellower. For instance, she hardly ever bites and the scratches are positively gentle.' Rachel looked at the new plaster on the back of his hand. 'Special circumstances this evening. You'd be angry if you'd had your ear chewed by a tomcat.'

'I expect I would. All right. Forget I mentioned it. It was a moment of weakness.'

'So back to your art expedition.'

'Ah, yes. The doomed art expedition. "What's the point anyway?" asked the head of English. "It'll be wasted on them. They don't care about art."

'I was opening my mouth to suggest that this might be related to no one having ever bothered to show them any, when Maureen pointed out that it would be offensive to Muslim students to show them figurative art. I pointed out that only the most conservative of Islamic clerics regarded that as sinful, and she said it would be culturally insensitive to run the risk. Another colleague asked why I should choose somewhere as passé as the National Gallery? Surely the kids deserved to see something more relevant to their lives? What could the Renaissance mean to them? And yes, she suggested Tate Modern. And she's the deputy head of history.

'I said I thought they could do with a little more sense of the past, and there was silence. It was becoming clear that the consensus was that I am a pathetic, naïve nuisance. Then the head gave me his full attention and said, "Rachel, of course it's excellent to see a newcomer with such enthusiasm. And, yes, the world would be a better place if we could move beyond the curriculum. But we must be realistic. These children will do well to scrape a few exams and get low-grade jobs. I don't think we should give them ideas beyond what is likely to be their station. My advice to you is to teach to the test. Yes, that's what the job is all about. Teach to the test. Teach to the test."'

Amiss got up, sat on the arm of her chair, and put his arm around her. 'Do you feel like quitting?'

'No, I feel like fighting. But on a ground of my own choosing. No one can make much of a difference at my level without support from the top. I need to keep my head down, pass my probation period, and find myself a job in a school run by people who encourage aspiration and achievement.'

The phone rang and Amiss rushed to it. 'Ellis. Yes ... Of course there must be a con-

nection ... It's much too much of a coincidence. Idiots... OK, I'll do that... Yes, of
course... Straightaway.'

'Ellis still can't persuade anyone that there
could be a link,' he told Rachel. 'He reckons
if I tip off the press anonymously and get
them speculating, it might help. Let me just
hunt out my cloak and my dagger while I
think of some way of leaking that doesn't
make me seem like a complete nutter.'

Chapter Three

Around the time Miss Stamp had first been
twittering at Amiss, Jack Troutbeck had
woken up in an unaccustomed state of be-
fuddlement. Instead of hurling herself out
of bed to attack the day, she opened her eyes
slowly, but since she was in pitch darkness,
that didn't help. She could remember getting into her car in London to drive to
Cambridge and then an arm coming from
behind her with something that smelt sweet.
'Bloody hell,' she said to herself. 'Chloro-
form! How quaint.'

Sitting up, she flailed around looking for a
lamp or a light switch: finding neither, she
threw back her head and bellowed, 'Where
the hell am I? Someone put on the light.'

Someone obliged almost immediately, and neon lighting flooded the room. A few seconds later it went off again, then on again, giving the baroness no time to see anything except that she was in a small, plain room. After a couple of minutes of flickering, she shouted irritably, 'Stop doing that, for Christ's sake.'

'Feerst say please,' ordered a disembodied, guttural voice.

The baroness started. 'Who and where the hell are you?' The lights continued to flicker. 'I said stop doing that,' she yelled.

'I say you feerst say please, Laidee Troutbeck.'

'So you did. Please stop doing that whoever you are.' The lights stopped flickering.

'You thanking me.'

'That's pushing it,' she snarled.

'You thanking me or light go on off again. In o-maj.'

'In what?'

'O-maj. Martin Creed.'

'Martin Bloody Creed? Turner Prize.' The baroness groaned. 'I remember. He won with *The Lights Going On and Off*, didn't he? Now would you kindly explain what has brought about this elaborate practical joke?'

'I explain later. Maybe.' As the lights began to flicker again, the baroness muttered 'Thank you,' with a bad grace, and they stayed on.

'Now why am I here and who are you?'

'You prisoner. No escape or you want crazy Albanian kill you. They look to you, they listen you all time, all day, all night. Have knives. Machine guns.'

The baroness looked around her, observed that there was a CCTV camera and that the only window appeared to be covered with corrugated iron, tested one door that led to a windowless bathroom and another which was firmly locked. She guessed she was in a portacabin.

'I see. And who is my genial host?'

'You know who I am, Laidee Troutbeck.'

'It's Oleg, isn't it?'

'I Sarkovsky.'

'Oleg, I know we parted brass rags...'

'What means this?'

'I know we had a row, but is that a sufficient reason to kidnap and imprison me? And, indeed, to address me so formally.'

'Situation formal. You discover later. Now, you wait.'

'For what?'

'It is secret.' He sniggered. 'You say much. Now I say. I deep also. And busy man. I go. Goodbye.'

The baroness's rant to her friends about the iniquities of Sir Henry Fortune and Jason Pringle had included the information that Fortune was regarded by the deferential art world as a person of such eminence that even Sir Nicholas Serota himself could not have looked down on him. True, he had never been in charge of a major art collection, but he made sure everyone knew that his record in running fashionable museums abroad was second to none. He had managed to get himself appointed to curate several major exhibitions in British museums and also served as an international artistic adviser to a variety of galleries and arts councils with the occasional visiting professorship thrown in. An invaluable committee man who could be relied upon to know who would be the winners in any internecine fighting in the art world, his complete lack of artistic integrity served him well. The baroness had actually remarked that whatever you thought of bloody Sclerota, he seemed genuinely to believe his own noxious propaganda, while Fortune would have his own granny cleft in twain and exhibited in formaldehyde if that won him another cushy job.

Sir Henry was very thick with Pringle, with whom he'd been an item since they were students at the Courtauld Institute. It was reputed that it was Pringle who first gave him the nickname 'Bubbles', which he hated but which stuck, even now that his red curls had long departed. Although it was common gossip that Pringle's insatiable appetite for redheads and Fortune's less frequent mooning after darkish teenage hunks occasionally caused massive rows in which there was much accusation and counter-accusation about gingers and rent-boys, their partner-ship seemed rock solid. As unkind people said, they had too much in common ever to split, particularly their shared view of art as a means to promote Fortune and Pringle. It was no accident that Fortune frequently acquired for one or other of his museums a work by a young artist whom Pringle was promoting – a guaranteed method of putting prices through the roof. When he was in London, Fortune stayed with Pringle in his Kensington penthouse and, loyally, they talked each other up at launches and art fairs. Pringle might have lacked the Midas touch of Charles Saatchi, but he was rich. He gave disproportionate but not exclusive attention to those he fancied and had a keen and cynical eye for artistic trends.

The police had been told that although both men were to speak on Thursday night at the opening of an exhibition in Pringle's gallery of works by his latest wunderkind, neither had shown up and both were un-reachable by phone. Mid-morning on Friday, leaving Serafina, the intern, in charge, Allegra, the gallery manager, had gone to Pringle's apartment and had rung the doorbell, but though she had brought with her the spare key her boss kept in the office, she was too scared of what she might actually find to put the key in the lock. When she consulted the hall porter, he told her it was more than his job was worth to leave his post. 'If you want my advice, Miss, though don't quote me, you should call the cops.'

When she got back to the gallery Allegra nervously called 999, but she was hesitant and slightly incoherent, and initially she was dismissed as a bit of posh totty who was getting worked up about nothing.

After midday, there was a near-hysterical call from the head of an art college. Where was Sir Henry Fortune? He was supposed to be giving the awards to the prize pupils and making a speech, but staff, students, parents and notables had already been waiting half an hour and there had been no word. If Allegra didn't know where to find him, what was to be done?

Allegra couldn't help the lunch-date stood up by Pringle either, but the two calls had stiffened her spine, and after consultation with Serafina, who was even posher than she was and much more confident, she rang 999 and made a fuss.

By late afternoon, the spare key had been picked up and by half past six Pooley had a report. There was no one in Pringle's apartment and no sign of anything untoward. Two suitcases in the spare room with Fortune's name tags had been unpacked and his clothes were neatly hung-up and put away. A half-drunk bottle of champagne in the fridge suggested they might have had a quick stiffener before leaving for the gallery, even if there were no glasses to be seen. The porter recalled them leaving and said he assumed that, as usual, they would be hailing a black cab. He also unbent sufficiently to mention that Pringle's cleaner had been upset this afternoon that he had neglected to leave her wages on the kitchen table.

The police were sufficiently impressed by the grandeur of Pringle's apartment and by his friend's knighthood to spread the story around when they got back to the Yard. Pooley had been making so much fuss about the baroness that he was one of the first officers to hear from the missing persons unit that another nob – indeed two nobs – had disappeared. However, his attempts to suggest any link had fallen on unreceptive ears.

He and Amiss were disappointed that the newspapers and news channels he had called had shown little interest. However, the evening newspaper ran with a small story by its arts correspondent speculating on why Fortune and Pringle were not to be found. Had those indefatigable patrons of the arts been deflected from the gallery because they were in hot pursuit of some startling new talent with which to engender shock and awe in the art world?

The police called the wunderkind whose big event had been marred by his mentors' absence to enquire if he'd any useful information. It took his assistant some time to fetch him, for they were immersed in the difficult process of making a video showing his struggles to make a video, and at the time of the call, the artist was standing on his head in the nude, trying to keep a banana wedged in his bum while balancing a basket of tropical fruit on his feet. He had given up on trying to hold a pineapple in his mouth, for even with some judicious surgery, the fruit had proved wholly uncooperative. When the phone rang, he had just got his teeth around a large plum. It hurt a bit because of the lacerations caused by the pineapple, but he'd got a good grip on it.

He was furious at having to take the call, but he hid his disgruntlement, bemoaned his inability to help, and instead expressed his gratitude for all that these two inspirational legends of the art world had done for him and people like him. He did not mention that he thought Pringle treated him like a whore.

Back at work, he resumed his earlier position with some difficulty, the assistant jammed the banana and plum back into position, balanced the basket on his feet, and covered the entire ensemble with imitation snow flakes. The theme was climate change but the artist was becoming desperate at his inability to think of a knock-out title. For the moment they were running with 'Climate Carmen' (after Carmen Miranda). Then he had a moment of inspiration. He spat out the plum. 'Not a banana,' he cried. 'What was I thinking of? Buy a feather. Now.'

His assistant looked at him in bewilderment.

'A feather?'

'A feather.'

'What kind of feather?'

'Oh, for fuck's sake,' cried the wunderkind as he tumbled to the foot He sat up and ran his fingers through his plentiful red curls. 'A feather from a cock. And make sure it's a big one.'

'From a cock?'

'Yes, you idiot. A cock. Like in hen. I've just realised this work is to be called "Cocktail Climate". We'll substitute the feather for the banana.'

The assistant's weariness and irritation left him in an instant. 'Oh ... My ... God!' he said. 'That's perfect. You'll be a dead cert for the Turner.'

The media got good and interested on Friday evening, when Jake Thorogood's editor, who had been expecting copy from him all day for his Saturday art column, eventually tracked down his current squeeze and found she hadn't been able to get hold of him since Friday morning. They had been having a leisurely breakfast when Thorogood answered the doorbell. He had stuck his head into the kitchen and said he'd be back in a moment but he had never returned. She thought she'd heard a car driving off, but couldn't be sure. What she was sure of was that Thorogood wasn't given to leaving the house in February clad only in a nightshirt and silk dressing gown.

Thorogood worked for a major liberal newspaper, was an able intellectualiser of modish opinions, was often photographed sharing a joke with art-world celebrities, and was therefore one of the media's own. Even the tabloids were interested, for they quickly discovered that Thorogood, Fortune, and Pringle had together made the reputation of Anastasia Holliday, the leggy blonde who had recently made abject art the talk of the town with her inventive ways of using her bodily fluids and her unselfconscious Australian coarseness. Attempts by journalists to get hold of Holliday drew a blank, and it was not long before she had also been added to the missing persons file. No one had seen her since her brief attendance at the event at Pringle's gallery at which he and Fortune had been no-shows.

Grave articles in the fashionable press about all that was owed to these icons of artistic experimentation had as their counterpoint pages of photographs in the tabloids of work the subs particularly despised as confidence tricks. As Amiss observed to Rachel, one mightn't think much of the popular press, but when it came to seeing that talentless rubbish was talentless rubbish, the lowliest hack was likely to show better judgement than the panjandrums of the art establishment. He recalled the baroness referring to Thorogood as the Judas Iscariot of art criticism, her contention being that he knew what was good and beautiful but didn't have the balls or integrity to stay loyal to it.

The art world, the press, and the police were now as one in believing that some lunatic had a grudge against contemporary art. Was there somewhere some more traditional artist running amok? A stern finger of suspicion was pointed at the Stuckists, a few of whom were pulled in for questioning. The disappearance of the baroness confused the picture and therefore she was mostly ignored. Hysteria went up a notch when Dr Hortense Wilde's husband said she'd gone out to the garden centre first thing Saturday morning and hadn't been seen since.

'Dear God,' said Amiss, when Pooley rang him. 'I know her. Ghastly woman.'

'How do you know her?'

'Met her at the in-laws with Jack the other week. Complicated story.'

'We need a council of war, Robert. You

seem to know a lot about these people. Jim's back from Paris. I'll find out how he's fixed and get back to you.'

'Now Hortense Wilde's gone missing,' Amiss told Rachel when she got home.

'You're kidding.' She shuddered. 'That was a really appalling evening.'

'It sure was.'

The evening had started well. Apart from that brief period when her daughter's wedding had caused Dr Simon to turn into an hysterical seeker after perfection, Amiss was very happy with Rachel's clever, warm-hearted parents. The baroness clearly liked the house, which was sprawling, comfortable, and bookish. She enthused about their garden and approved their brand of gin. She and Martin Simon turned out to have a common interest in military history, from which they moved on to great war paintings and art in general. As Amiss fetched the baroness another drink, the doorbell rang. 'Hannah will get that,' said Simon. 'It's just our new neighbours. They moved in today and we thought it would be kind to offer them dinner. They seem pleasant enough.'

Hortense Wilde was long and thin with a face so elongated that she reminded the baroness of a Modigliani. Over drinks, there were polite questions about where she and her rather crumpled husband had moved from and why. The baroness, on her best behaviour, had affected interest even though she wasn't the centre of attention. The trouble started over dinner when Hortense asked Amiss what he did. 'Er, I've had quite a few jobs,' he said, 'but most recently, I've been writing a bit.'

'What do you write?'

'I do some journalism, but mainly I'm trying to concentrate on novels. Crime novels.'

'And are you published?'

'Yes. My first came out a few months ago and I'm finishing the second.'

She laughed tinnily. 'I'm afraid I won't have read you. I don't go in for popular fiction. Is it all sex and sadism?'

'No, it isn't,' said the baroness, who had suddenly lost interest in the conversation going on to her left. 'Robert doesn't write penny dreadfuls. He writes entertainingly for intelligent people.'

'I'm sure he does,' said Wilde. 'But I'm afraid I'm more interested in serious issues.'

'Here's a serious issue then,' said the baroness, who was already spoiling for a fight and thought she might have spotted a promising foe. 'Why is the art world peddling so much crap these days? Robert and I were in Tat Modern today and it was crammed full of rubbish. Now admittedly, that's to be expected from the gormless artistic elite. But Martin told me a story just now about how far this disease has spread. Go on, Martin.'

Martin Simon, always a man to avoid any kind of confrontation, looked nervously at her. 'Oh, I don't know, Jack. Hortense mightn't be interested.'

'Any sane person should be interested. Nay outraged. Go on. Go on. If you don't, I'll have to give her a mangled version of it.'

'Very well,' he said meekly. 'Jack was expressing an interest in contemporary art earlier, Hortense, so I told her about visiting the new National Museum of Art in Cardiff when I was there on business last week. I was particularly taken by the work of a distinguished eighteenth-century painter called Richard Wilson. However, part of one of his interesting landscapes was obscured by a huge pile of small cardboard boxes – six and a half thousand to be exact, as this was a reaction to the local council's plan to build six and a half thousand new houses. They were bird boxes, as the Welsh title meant something like "Birds of a feather flock together". What amused me was that they came in flat packs and had to be assembled by the museum staff.'

'It seems perfectly valid to me,' said Hortense Wilde.

'How can it?' asked the baroness. 'It's a waste of money. It requires no talent, no skill. It's utterly pointless. Surely you can see that?'

'I think perhaps I see more than you do, Jack. I'm an art historian.'

Amiss saw his parents-in-law exchanging a grimace of embarrassment. The baroness, on the other hand, wore an expression closely resembling that of Plutarch preparing to stalk a tasty victim. 'How interesting,' she said silkily. 'There are a lot of you about these days. Would I have read anything of yours?'

'I don't write for the general public.' She repeated the tinny laugh. 'I'm afraid the discourse in which I engage is above most people's heads.'

'I'll never understand academics who think they should be paid just to talk to each other,' snapped the baroness. 'Shouldn't your job be to make the obscure limpid and the profound accessible and generally help the ordinary person appreciate a great picture? Like Walter Pater or Kenneth Clark did?'

Wilde laughed again. 'I don't think either of those men left anything worth passing on to a modern generation.'

'They introduced many to truth and beauty.'

'Oh, really, Jack.' Wilde raised her hands. 'Truth!' she said, as two fingers on each hand made air quotes. 'Beauty!' she said, and repeated the gesture. 'These are really passé concepts. I am pleased to have played my part in ejecting this reactionary poison from the artistic consciousness. We have moved on from a belief in the socially constructed to an understanding of the inevitability of cultural relativism. But you wouldn't understand that unless you move in intellectual circles,' she added, with a kindly smile. 'The analysis of trauma and the psychosexual in the field of postmodern feminist theory, for instance...'

The baroness groaned loudly. 'Oh, God,' she said. 'Spare me that PC pseudy claptrap.'

'Jack is nothing if not forthright, Hortense,' interjected Hannah Simon brightly. 'She is also the Mistress of St Martha's in Cambridge, so she does move in intellectual circles. But I think it would be best if you two agreed to differ and we talked about something else.' She turned to Wilde's husband. 'We were having such a fascinating conversation about Hampstead, Gervase, that I didn't have time to discover what you do.'

'I'm an educational theorist.'

'An academic?'

'Yes.'

'Which side are you on?' asked the baroness.

'Sorry?'

'Which side are you on? Traditional or progressive?'

'Progressive, of course.'

Hortense Wilde looked at the baroness

with ill-concealed dislike. 'Gervase has been a seminal force in helping to lead teachers away from notions of imparting knowledge rather than facilitating children to find out for themselves in their learning zone what interests them.'

'Oh, dear God,' said the baroness. 'So I've him to thank for so dumbing down schooling that at St Martha's we have to provide remedial teaching for semi-literate undergraduates.'

'Now, now, Jack,' said Martin Simon. 'I know you have strong opinions, but we don't want a falling-out.'

Amiss gave way to temptation. 'Really, Jack, I think you should hold back on this one. My wife's a teacher,' he said to the Wildes. 'Darling, why don't you tell Gervase and Hortense what life is like in your school.'

'There were pools of blood on the carpet,' Amiss told Pooley. 'So naturally the following day Jack rang up without a care in the world to rejoice about having had so much fun. I mentioned that it was a bit difficult for the Simons to have their neighbours roughed up, and that while they thought they were terrible pills, they had reeled when she accused them of being Marxist throwbacks who leeched off the taxpayer while destroying the twin bedrocks of society and culture.'

'Good old Jack.'

'Indeed. She was thrilled to know she'd been so pithy. And Rachel hadn't been much better. Anyway, that's Hortense.'

'Robert?'

'Yes, Ellis.'

'Has it occurred to you that since all these people have almost certainly been kidnapped by the same person, they are therefore presumably imprisoned together?'

'Dear God,' said Amiss. 'I know this is a terrible thing to think, let alone say, but wouldn't you love to be a fly on the wall?'

Chapter Four

The baroness had once idly pronounced in a House of Lords debate that everyone should be forced at school to learn vast tracts of poetry by heart lest someday they might find themselves in solitary confinement and need to ward off madness. She now had a chance to test her hypothesis. While she had always claimed to be as happy in her own company as she was joyous in her own skin, by that she meant happy reading, writing, or generally being busy without anyone else around. This prison, however, did not run to books, paper, radio, parrot, or any diversions whatsoever.

Although only soap had been provided, she

had managed to stretch her ablutions out to about fifteen minutes, after which she had looked for food and drink and found that all that was there was water that had to be drunk from the tap. She was starving, and thought of demanding food, but then concluded that since Sarkovsky was torturing her for his own reasons, she would not give him the satisfaction of showing she minded.

Not being of a meditative or spiritual disposition, she found sitting on a narrow bed contemplating white walls completely boring, so she marched up and down reciting. She began defiantly with Kipling's *If*, and was relieved that she could remember all four verses. She shouted loudest the lines:

'If you can force your heart and nerve and sinew / To serve your turn long after they are gone, / And so hold on when there is nothing in you / Except the Will which says to them: "Hold on!"'

There was Marvell. She was delighted to find she still remembered 'To his coy mistress', and made much of 'Let us roll all our strength, and all / Our sweetness, up into one ball: / And tear our pleasures with rough strife / Through the iron gates of life'. With Keats, she triumphed again with 'On Looking into Chapman's Homer', making it right through from 'Much have I travell'd in the realms of gold' to 'He stared at the Pacific – and all his men / Look'd at each other with a wild surmise – / Silent, upon a peak in Darien' and doing a creditable imitation of stout Cortez.

She then fell into uncharacteristic melancholy during Byron's 'Youth and Age': 'There's not a joy the world can give like that it takes away, / When the glow of early thought declines in feeling's dull decay', and had to flog herself to get to its dismal end, but she then cheered herself up by remembering Byron had died at thirty-six and therefore didn't know what he was talking about. She raised her spirits further with Hilaire Belloc's 'Tarantella', 'Do you remember an Inn, / Miranda?', and John Betjeman's 'A Subaltern's Love-Song', and when describing Miss Joan Hunter Dunn's exploits with a tennis racket, fell silent in happy recollection of a very satisfactory fling with a doubles partner in her sixth form. That triggered off an equally satisfying memory of what she had got up to with a mixed doubles partner in the local tennis club.

She was contemplating making a shot at 'The Rubaiyat of Omar Khayyam', when she looked at the camera and decided on an experiment. Fetching the towel from the bathroom, she pushed her chair over to the corner, climbed onto it and covered the camera. Within a couple of seconds the lights began to flicker on and off again. She removed the towel: they stayed on. Sighing, she accepted she was under close scrutiny and climbed down. She had declaimed, 'Awake! For morning in the Bowl of Night / Has flung the stone that puts the stars to flight', when she had a better idea. Damn them, if they were spying on her, they might as well suffer too.

The baroness loved singing, and she had the lungs and the diaphragm for it, but she knew that when she broke into song in the presence of friends they would clap their hands to their ears and beg her to stop. She was a realist, so she pretended but didn't believe that the problem was that they were tone deaf rather than that she couldn't hold a tune.

She considered her repertoire and decided that what circumstances required were Puccini arias. She always refused to go to operas unless they were performed in the original, but her own linguistic skills were so lacking that she had the greatest difficulty in learning any lines in a foreign language, so all she could offer were short extracts. Her rendition of the noisiest bits of *Nessun Dorma* were followed by a goodly chunk of *Si, mi chiamano Mimi*, but it took the high spot of Madame Butterfly's misguided belief that Lieutenant Pinkerton would be back soon to provoke a reaction. The lights went on and off, the baroness went on singing, total darkness descended, but she reprised the passage over and over again until interrupted.

'I'll give you food if you stop singing,' said a voice in an accent that she recognised from her occasional encounters with Sarkovsky's bodyguards.

A deal was struck after five minutes of negotiation and with a clear understanding that the boss would not be told that she was being fed. The lights went on for long enough to allow the baroness to shut herself in the bathroom. After a few minutes, she heard a door open and close: the lights went on and she rushed out and grabbed the plate of food on the floor. She couldn't remember when she had last enjoyed anything as much as the goat's cheese and corn bread. She thought of her last angry meal with Sarkovsky and wished that she had taken heed of Kai Lung's wise words: 'Better a dish of husks to the accompaniment of a muted lute than to be satiated with stewed shark's fin and rich spiced wine of which the cost is frequently mentioned by the provider.' When she had finished, she lay down on the uncomfortable bed and hoped that her friends would be quick about tracking her down.

Wherever she was.

Some of her friends were trying to do just that. The council of war was held at the Pooley flat that evening. Mary Lou was stuck at work and Rachel had gone to see her parents. 'It's not that I wouldn't postpone if I could be of any use, Robert,' she'd said, 'but I can't see that I've anything to contribute. Whereas you Three Musketeers have form. Good luck.'

Amiss, Pooley, and Milton sat round the kitchen table, ate takeaway pizza and drank red wine. The mood was gloomy. 'Now that Jim's back and all these others are missing,' said Pooley, 'Jack's disappearance is no longer being dismissed lightly.'

'It's got to be Oleg Sarkovsky who's behind this,' said Amiss.

'I agree,' said Pooley. 'But I got nowhere when I suggested it to the AC.'

'Oleg Sarkovsky?' asked Milton. 'Isn't he some dodgy Russian oligarch? What's he got to do with this? Hasn't she got enemies closer to home?'

'Well, of course she's got enemies, Jim,' said Amiss, pushing his almost untouched plate away. 'We're talking about Jack. But Sarkovsky's the only serious one who comes to mind at the moment. Although I don't like Sir Nicholas Serota and I doubt if he liked what she said about him in the culture debate in the House of Lords last week, he has a thick skin and plenty more pressing enemies than Jack Troutbeck. Besides, even Jack never suggested he was a criminal. Well, except culturally.'

'So tell me about this Sarkovsky.'

'You begin, Ellis.'

'We had dinner with Jack some weeks back, when you were away. She was rather worked up about the iniquities of the contemporary art world.'

'In other words,' said Amiss, 'she did a lot of ranting.'

'Eventually, it turned out that this new obsession had been inspired by her relationship with Sarkovsky.'

'Her relationship? What sort of relationship?' asked a startled Milton. 'I thought she and Myles were still an item.'

'Well, yes, when she isn't off having dalliances. Or him off adventuring in the Middle East. Which is where he is at the moment.'

'She described Sarkovsky as her walker,' said Pooley. He paused and considered. 'No, she said she was *his* walker, but then modified it to trophy.'

'As in trophy wives?' asked Milton.

'No and yes,' said Amiss. 'In such matters apparently he likes tall blondes half his age with big chests. He swaps a wife from time to time when she reaches what he considers her sell-by date. But being uneducated and sensitive about it, he was attracted by the idea of an intellectual trophy. Brain-candy, I guess. He met Jack at some social gathering where she was holding forth about the wonders of Western civilisation and presumably thought her the answer to an ignoramus's prayer.'

'What with Jack being a baroness and the head of a Cambridge college, she enhanced his status just by being seen with him. But he also wanted her to educate him about culture.'

Milton was bewildered. 'Why would she do that? Isn't she too busy to be a tutor?'

'The bait was luxury, Jim. Extreme luxury. You know our Jack's a sybarite. She loves travelling in extreme comfort. And staying in the best suites in the most expensive hotels. She said we'd get the idea if we thought of a tutor on the Grand Tour with a rich, vulgar, and doltish spendthrift. They went to Venice on the Orient Express so she could introduce him to Byzantine art and architecture as well as to the Renaissance.'

'And by private plane to Rome so she could teach him some classical history,' contributed Pooley.

'And cruised around the Greek islands in his yacht so she could tell him about the origins of democracy and recite Byron at him.'

'I can see the appeal of all that,' said Milton. 'Do you want any more of that pizza, Robert?'

'No, no. Have it. What an appetite you've got tonight.'

'I'm busy.' Milton reached across and cleared Amiss's plate. 'I live alone. I forget to buy anything. I get hungry. Married blokes have wives to force them to eat, I seem to remember. Divorced ones don't.'

'It's not quite that simple, Jim. Ellis and I don't exactly have wives wearing pinnies and cooking up a storm. I imagine we can both see the attractions of a fully-staffed yacht as well as the next man. And according to Jack it was opulent in the extreme. She said rather apologetically that Sarkovsky was in the second eleven on Planet Oligarch, seeing as how – unlike Roman Abramovich, of whom he was madly jealous – he didn't own a football team and has only one yacht, which shamingly doesn't double as an aircraft carrier or have an escape capsule. It does, of course, have the obligatory helicopter pad – a convenience she took to. And she waxed pretty eloquent about the virtues of the butler and the chef on duty on board, as well as their equivalents in Sarkovsky's various houses.'

'Was he paying her as well?'

'No. Just picking up all the tabs. But she had hopes of extracting a tidy donation from him for St Martha's.'

'So for heaven's sake, what was the problem? It sounds like a mutually satisfactory arrangement. Why would he want to kidnap her?'

'They were falling out rather often, particularly about conceptual art, which other billionaires were buying in truckloads and which she consistently ridiculed. She got the impression that he was furious that Abramovich's girlfriend had set up a centre for contemporary art in Moscow and that he was harbouring similar ambitions to do the same in St Petersburg, where he was born. So to make sure he stayed on the artistic straight and narrow she missed no opportunity to beat him up any time he said a kind word about what she thought was crap. You know how tactless she can be.'

'I certainly do,' said Milton.

'And although she was firmly of the view that she was successfully pretending she enjoyed his company, she despised him and it showed. If you think – as she does – that apart from low cunning he has no intellect, it's hard to disguise. I heard her on the phone once berating him for tastelessness and generally taking the piss out of him about everything from his baldness to his struggles with English, for which he seemed to have no aptitude whatsoever. I don't think he's a man who would take that well.'

'If people got violent with Jack every time she was tactless,' observed Milton, 'she'd have been dead and buried a long time ago.'

'Most people aren't Oleg Sarkovsky. Tell him, Ellis.'

'Jack asked me to find out how dodgy he was, but then refused to take what I found out seriously enough.'

'He's a real villain, you mean?'

'As I said to Jack, Russian oligarchs made billions through ruthlessly taking advantage of the chaos that followed the collapse of the Soviet Union. Depending on their point of view, you could call them entrepreneurs or you could call them bandits. Sarkovsky was never going to be Robin Hood. The trouble is he turned out to be more like the Sheriff of Nottingham.'

'Didn't he usually lose out to Robin?' asked Amiss.

'I mean in the sense of robbing the poor for the good of the rich. And showing no mercy. Sarkovsky was notoriously corrupt as well as rough with his business competitors. Some of them ended up dead.'

'What did Jack say to this?'

'That Russia in the early nineties resembled the Wild West, and one can't judge it by the standards of Little-Moreton-on-the Marsh. So I added that the word was he's a bit of a psycho. And won't brook criticism. A journalist who was on his trail ended up dead.'

'Did she listen to that?'

'Up to a point. She listened, but then she asked how that murder could be pinned on Sarkovsky considering Putin has journalists rubbed out as often as he shoots bears. To which I said that it couldn't, but there were very good grounds for suspicion. Also, his most recent ex-wife is on the record accusing him of beating her up.'

'Jack's reaction to that?'

'She asked if the ex-wife's accusations had netted her an extra few tens of millions in the divorce settlement. And wanted more evidence about the deaths he's alleged to have ordered. She was procrastinating, if you ask me.'

Amiss shrugged. 'There was a golden pot at the end of the rainbow for St Martha's, and that's always Jack's top priority.'

'Doesn't she mind where it comes from?' asked Milton.

'No. She long ago said fundraising was prostitution and you didn't demand that your clients had good-conduct medals. Just as long as they didn't give one the metaphorical clap.'

'So she ignored your advice?'

'Not completely,' said Amiss. 'I rang her just before she went with him to Marrakesh and she admitted being slightly perturbed. Myles had called her from Iraq to say he'd heard a few bad things about him from some old SAS-hand.'

'But that didn't make her cancel the trip.'

'No. "I think this might be make-or-break weekend", she said. "But for now I must fly. Like Chambers Dictionary, I'm Morocco bound."'

Milton sighed and reached for the last piece

of pizza. 'And what happened in Morocco?'

Amiss took another mouthful of red wine. 'She called me on Saturday evening to explain that every prospect pleased and only Sarkovsky was vile. On the plus side, she was in the Churchill suite in La Mamounia, had seen some fine Islamic architecture, been massaged with all manner of fabulous unguents in the spa, had eaten outside in a balmy breeze, and when she rang she was sitting on her private terrace, smoking a superb cigar, drinking a fine brandy, and gazing at the enormous garden which Winston Churchill pronounced the loveliest place in the world.'

'And the minus side?'

'The food was disappointing and she couldn't get it into Sarkovsy's thick head that Islamic art and architecture were worthy of admiration. Relations were already strained when he had a call that put him in a terrible mood. He'd a few by then and he fessed up. Turned out he'd an art adviser he'd been keeping secret from Jack because, as he put it, he didn't think she was very fresh about art and he'd secretly spent a few hundred million behind her back on Hirsts and Emins and Koons and the rest of the usual suspects. Still, she'd been troubling him with her negative comments about conceptual art so he'd had an independent evaluation of the art he'd bought through the said adviser. He'd just been told his collection had gone down drastically in value.'

'She didn't sympathise, I suppose?'

'She sure didn't. She told him it served him right. That had he bought art of intrinsic value of the kind she had been trying to educate him to appreciate, he would have a collection of which he could be proud, but that by going for the trophy shock-and-awe art recommended by people without taste or scruple, he had landed himself with a load of dross which would probably be worth nothing in ten years' time. And serve him right. If he had any sense, she said, he should sell the lot now.'

'That didn't go down well?'

'It didn't. He threw a tantrum and stormed off. She retired to her magnificent suite to commune with the ghost of Churchill.'

'And what did Churchill recommend?'

'More brandy. But she was sufficiently rattled to ask me to locate Ellis and find out if he'd learnt anything more about Sarkovsky. She had a feeling that he might be having business problems.' He gestured at Pooley. 'Over to you, Ellis.'

'He was indeed having business problems. I met her a couple of days after she got back to tell her to drop Sarkovsky, but she said he didn't appear at all on Sunday and had sulked all the way back to London on Monday, so that in effect they'd dropped each other. She then admitted she might be tempted if he relented and repeated an earlier offer to take her on an adventure tour up the Amazon, so I gave the unexpurgated story. There were good reasons to think he'd had a business partner blown up just because he wanted one hundred percent of the company.'

'He wasn't just getting his retaliation in first in the manner of Russian crooks?' asked Milton.

'My sources didn't think so. They're not very judgemental in Russia, but apparently they were a bit shocked because he and the business partner had been friends from childhood.'

'So how did he get away with it?'

'Bribery.'

'And the journalist who allegedly was murdered?'

'Was a young investigative reporter from the local paper who was concerned about medical supplies bound for local hospitals being hijacked on an industrial scale and diverted into the black market.'

'The link with Sarkovsky?'

'Apparently she had evidence his trucking company was involved. But once again, the police dropped the case before any charges could be brought.'

'And the wife?'

'Turns out she was backed up by the first

ex-wife, who said he used to get violent when he didn't get his own way and once nearly strangled her. But, mysteriously, they both withdrew their evidence after their dogs were shot. That was the evidence that worked with Jack. "He had his ex-wives' dogs shot!" she cried. "That's it. No one who would have dogs shot deserves the benefit of the doubt. Why, he might strangle Horace if he said something rude to him. I don't mind taking risks for the sake of St Martha's, but I'm damned if I'm going to have my parrot put in jeopardy."'

Milton laughed. 'How very Jack. But I still don't really get it, Robert. Surely if Sarkovsky was crazy and wanted to get rid of her he'd have done what Russians do and ordered a drive-by shooting or poisoning with ricin or something. He's hardly got her locked in a cellar while he decides what to do with her. I also don't get it about the others. Where do they come into it? Why would he have it in for them as well? Aren't they the art establishment Jack despises?'

'I don't understand either. Except that he's a psycho.'

'OK,' said Milton. 'I'll start enquiries.'

'Enquiries? Shouldn't you be breaking down the doors of Sarkovsky's houses with battering rams and giving him the third degree?'

'This is London, Robert. Not Moscow. We

wouldn't get search warrants on the basis that he and Jack had a row in Marrakesh several weeks ago and that he's got a dodgy reputation. Anyway, we're not keen in the Met to make enemies of incredibly rich people who can afford top-of-the-range lawyers. But I'll talk to the AC asap.'

'Do you think you'll get anywhere with him, Jim?' asked Pooley.

'Very likely not. But the Commissioner's away so I've no choice.'

'You'd better hurry up before Sarkovsky nabs the next one,' said Amiss.

'You don't think he's finished?'

'He's a thorough sort of bloke from all I've heard. If I were you, I'd be warning all the curators and dealers and artists and wankers in London to batten down the hatches and hide under their beds.'

Milton's phone rang. 'Yes ... shit! ... yes ... yes ... yes ... why do you think it's connected? ... yes ... yes ... yes ... Try to find out if there's a connection with Oleg Sarkovsky... Oleg Sarkovsky. A London-based Russian billionaire... OK.'

He disconnected. 'We need to go back to the Yard, Ellis. An American art consultant and one of his clients have gone missing from his London hotel for a few days. Even the AC's taking it seriously now.'

Chapter Five

'What the hell's an art consultant?' asked Milton, as they sped back to the Yard.

'Give me a minute.' Pooley speed-dialled Mary Lou. 'What the hell's an art consultant, darling? Some American bloke called Chester Herblock's gone missing and that's his jobtitle ... yes ... yes ... yes ... yes ... OK...Thanks... No, no, but I think Sarkovsky's behind it... I don't know... Could be a very late night... Me too... Bye.

'Mary Lou says art consultants are top-of-the-range advisers hired by the rich and ignorant to make them appear discriminating. They choose the art; you pay the bill; they get a big commission. The more you pay, the bigger the commission. She's heard of Herblock. He's a mega-rich celebrity art consultant. It's a grand name for an art adviser.'

'So he could be the person who advised Sarkovsky to buy the stuff Jack loathed,' said Milton. 'OK, Ellis. Take charge. I have to go and report to the AC. Hell, I wish the Commissioner wasn't away. The AC will inevitably find our theory about Sarkovsky fanciful.'

Pooley had just finished reading the reports of the disappearance of Herblock and the woman with whom he'd been staying at the Dorchester when he was told that no one could find Gavin Truss, the head of the Central London School of Art, who hadn't been seen anywhere since leaving his office for the preview party at Pringle's gallery. Pooley knew who he was. He'd seen the baroness demolish him on *Newsnight*

The confrontation had arisen because of the baroness's allegation in her Lords speech that – because of the cancer of conceptualism – art schools had long since ceased teaching their students anything worth a damn and should be denied as much as a penny of taxpayers' money. Gavin Truss – who had spent a quarter of a century teaching the subject and for a decade had been head of the Central London School of Art – was small and superior, with a manner and tone that – rather like the baroness – denoted his utter certainty in the rectitude of his opinions. Having had a few of her more trenchant remarks quoted at him, he sat back in his chair, tugged his little curly beard like a lucky charm, and told the presenter that Lady Troutbeck was a classic philistine in an outdated institution who pontificated about what she didn't understand. What students learnt in his establishment was priceless.

'Over to you, Lady Troutbeck.'

'What do you teach them?'

'What do you mean, what do we teach them? They come to learn, not to be taught. And they learn to be the artists they know they can be.'

'So you don't teach them anything?'

'We give them space. We give them the chance to find themselves. We let them think about how to express themselves.'

'Dr Truss,' said the baroness, 'children come to you from school hoping to create. Your job is to give them the skills that enable them to find themselves. Do you teach them to draw?'

'I told you, it's about learning, not teaching.'

'I do beg your pardon. Do you make available to them someone from whom they can learn to draw?'

'We don't do that kind of thing any more. Drawing is a craft. Not an art.'

'Would that apply to painting? Or sculpting?'

'Of course. If people want to be crafts-people, let them go to craft classes in a technical college. If they wish to be artists, let them come to me.'

'So let me get this clear, Dr Truss. Young people arrive at your establishment wanting to be artists and mostly not knowing how to draw or paint because their schools have given up on such old-fashioned accomplishments. They have no skills, are subsidised by the taxpayer who thinks they're there to acquire some, yet you teach them nothing because you despise the basic skills that no decent artist can do without.'

'We give them space, Lady Troutbeck. We give them space to fly with their inner selves.'

'Very well, Dr Truss. Let's look at it from another perspective. Give me an example of how a school like yours produces someone you regard as a great artist.' She paused for a second. 'No. Let me be specific. I know he didn't go to your college, but tell me what Damien Hirst – whom you have described as an artist of the first rank – *learnt* at Goldsmith's College. I know he genuinely wanted to be an artist; despite scoring an E in his A level, he rather amazingly got to art school – he probably wanted to learn to do a bit of drawing and painting, but they were not on offer. What was there for him? Or was he entirely self-made and could have done just as well without art college.'

The baroness would later brag to her friends of how she had set the sap up for this and how, like a low-hung fruit, he fell into her basket.

'Ah, Damien,' he said. 'He has genius, of course, but he would be the first to explain that without Goldsmith's College, which I'm not ashamed to say led the way for the rest of us, he would not be what he is today.'

'And his inspiration was?' asked the presenter.

'Michael Craig-Martin, his tutor.'

'From whom he learnt?'

'The essence of conceptual art,' said Truss, reverentially. 'Michael provided the revelatory moment that released Damien from the constraints that glorified draughtsmen would have imposed on him – through his incomparable articulation of neo-conceptualism.'

'Which is?'

Truss laughed. 'You don't even know that? It's the insight that anything can be a work of art.'

'We're short of time, Dr Truss,' said the presenter. 'Please give us the revelatory moment.'

'Years before Damien became his student, Martin had exhibited what Damien later explained as "the greatest piece of conceptual sculpture that he just couldn't get out of his head".' Truss bent his head for a reverential moment. 'You can't imagine how dramatic it was. High on a wall in an empty gallery, Michael installed a glass half-full of water on a small shelf attached to a wall. He called it *An Oak Tree*. In an accompanying leaflet, he asked himself if it was just a case of the emperor's new clothes, but then explained that this was not a glass of water, but "a full-grown oak tree". He had changed it into an oak tree.'

'But he hadn't,' observed the baroness mildly.

'You understand nothing,' said Truss. 'As Sir Nick Serota himself pointed out, appreciating all art requires an act of faith comparable to believing that in transubstantiation, bread and wine become the body and blood of Christ.'

'But you're an atheist,' said the baroness.

'Yes.'

'So you don't even believe in Jesus, let alone in transubstantiation.'

'That's different,' said Truss. 'That's not art.'

'Nor, apparently,' said the baroness, looking at the producer making a ten-second gesture towards the fascinated presenter, 'is anything we taxpayers would wish to pay you to impart to the young art.' She slowed down her delivery. 'Michael Craig-Martin was a Trustee of the Tate when Tate Britain filled a room with his talentless scribbles and vacuous conceits. You betray your students, Dr Truss. You betray us. And, like Sir Nicholas Serota, who indulges you all, you betray art.'

The baroness woke up, peered into the darkness, put two fingers in her mouth and emitted an ear-splitting whistle. Almost instantly, the neon lights came on. 'Thank you,' she said, with exaggerated politeness. 'Now would breakfast run to coffee and something decent to eat?'

'Coffee, yes. And bread.'

'Eggs?'

'If you promise you won't sing.'

'I promise.'

'Then you can have an egg. One.'

'How were you thinking of cooking it?'

'You wait.'

The baroness allowed herself to fall into a reverie about eggs. She remembered the perfect scrambled eggs she had had on Sarkovsky's yacht, and the excellent Eggs Benedict she had had at the Wolseley with Robert Amiss a few weeks previously, as they prepared themselves for their expedition to Tat Modern. What would Robert be thinking now? Or Mary Lou? Or St Martha's? Or Myles, if he had heard? If she could make no sense of it, how could they? 'Stop it, old girl,' she said to herself. 'That way madness lies. As Kai Lung said, "When struck by a thunderbolt it is unnecessary to consult the Book of Dates as to the precise meaning of the omen." For now, just survive. One day at a time. One foot in front of the other.'

Her custodian spoke, and they went through the bathroom, lights-out, business with the door, and lights-on routine. The coffee was instant, but at least it was strong. The egg was hard-boiled and without salt. And the bread had no butter. But it was food, and the baroness was grateful for it. Having returned her mug and the eggshells, she had to fight off a perverse urge to break into 'Oh, what a beautiful morning', but suppressed it on the grounds that her lifeline was the tenuous deal with her mysterious provider. Telling herself that she might at some juncture have to make a run for it, she forced herself instead to do a few exercises that did not look too ridiculous and lay back on the bed and decided to recite Shakespearean soliloquies. As an intellectual exercise, she tried to take the plays in alphabetical order. She couldn't remember a single line from *All's Well That Ends Well*, *Anthony and Cleopatra* yielded only the dismaying 'All is lost! / This foul Egyptian hath betrayed me', but *As You Like It* was a winner.

Although of a cheerful disposition herself, the baroness had always enjoyed the melancholy Jacques's 'All the world's a stage, / And all the men and women merely players'. On this occasion, though, while she maintained her spirits for most of the six ages of man, she could hardly bear to get through the seventh, and she momentarily feared she might cry as she finished with: 'Last scene of all, / That ends this strange eventful history, / Is second childishness and mere oblivion, / Sans teeth, sans eyes, sans taste, sans everything.' This would be a hell of a way for everything to end. In or out of this room.

Although not much given to worry or

pointless speculation, she couldn't fight off the feeling that whatever Sarkovsky had in mind, it was unlikely to be kind. After all, in Myles's call from Iraq the day before she was kidnapped, hadn't he asked if she'd heard any more from 'that psycho'? He was calling him that, it emerged, because of well-founded rumours he'd heard about the methods he used in settling some personal grudges. She had assured him gaily that Sarkovsky had not reappeared and could be forgotten about and had laughed it off when he told her to be careful.

The baroness allowed her imagination some free rein. Maybe the bastard meant to keep her in this room until she died like the captive in John Fowles's *The Collector*. She then had the even worse memory of the horrible things done to the kidnapped hero in the film of Stephen King's *Misery*.

At this she decided to get a grip, shook her head vigorously and wondered once again what day it was. Clearly she'd been drugged when captured on Wednesday evening; there was no natural light and her watch had been removed, so she had no idea how long she'd been in this room. Would the police by now be taking her disappearance seriously? Would there be any media interest? She recalled uncomfortably that in the past, when involved in *causes célèbres* that had catapulted her temporarily onto front pages, she had merely a walk-on part: other people's corpses had taken centre stage. She hoped that this time any new notoriety she might achieve would not involve her being murdered.

With the help of a small army of police wrenched from other enquiries, Milton was able within twelve hours to piece together the last known movements of all the disappeared. Like the baroness, Hortense Wilde, Gavin Truss, and Anastasia Holliday, had gone missing with their cars; like Fortune and Pringle, Herblock and Marilyn Falucci Lamont had last been seen together hailing taxis. Jake Thorogood, it seemed certain, had been pushed into a car outside his own front door. They had all disappeared within a twenty-four-hour period between Thursday and Friday evenings.

Every few hours Milton had to emerge from the Yard to be snapped by a hundred cameras and give a report to an hysterical mob of reporters demanding to know what he thought had happened, who was responsible, had there been a ransom demand, when he expected to find the missing dignitaries, what was taking so long, and what was being done to protect the other likely victims. Inside were teams of police dealing with equally hysterical enquiries from luminaries of the art establishment who were cowering in their offices and homes demanding police protection.

'We are doing everything we can,' Milton told the media in his best stiff police manner, 'but our resources are limited and our priority must be the missing. We suggest that anyone who fears they might be a target should take obvious precautions. Keep your doors locked and don't open them unless you know who's outside. Travel only in groups. And, yes, I'm sure the general public will be quite safe visiting museums and art galleries. Now, if you'll excuse me, I must go back to work.'

Mary Lou rang Amiss first thing on Friday morning. 'I'm in a state. Are you in a state?'

'Sure am.'

'I know our old girl's been in danger before, but this seems much worse.'

'Certainly does.'

'Can you write?'

'Nope. Can you broadcast?'

'I have to. But it's hard.'

'How do you think Ellis is?'

'Knackered. How's Rachel?'

'Well, obviously she's less upset about Jack than you and I would be, but she's sharing in the general gloom. Plus, school is driving her mad.'

'She told me that dreadful story about wanting to take the kids to see some art. Now I know this isn't important at the moment,

115

but it occurred to me this morning that maybe I could give her some support.'

'Yes, please.'

'Worrying about Jack's got me guilt-ridden about not being enough of a warrior for decent values. Do you think it would help if I offered to do my celeb number and come and talk to her class about art? We could show them pictures and talk about great art being cool and I could do my black role-model bit.'

'I think even her headmaster would have a problem killing off that idea, Mary Lou. You're a star, in more ways than one. Send her an email: it'll be a tiny light in the encircling darkness.'

'Oh, good. Now, as Jack would persist in saying improbably, "I must fly."'

Amiss spent the whole morning reading newspapers and blogs and watching news channels. An alien doing the same would have concluded that on this strange planet nothing mattered but the art world and its denizens, for those who control rolling news seem incapable of focusing on more than one story at a time. The weather was cold and wet, but unfortunate reporters were interviewed outside galleries under dripping umbrellas trying to talk up any evidence of fear or panic they'd uncovered. Photographs of the missing abounded, many showing them socialising with each other in Venice, Vienna, Paris, New York, LA, London and various other playgrounds, which caused the more perceptive viewers to spot that this was indeed an incestuous and opulent world that had little to do with traditional notions of artists starving in garrets.

Of course the media were disappointed that the kidnapper hadn't got hold of a Grade I art celebrity. 'WILL IT BE DAMIEN OR TRACEY NEXT?' wondered one headline hopefully. 'TERROR OF THE MUSEUM BOSSES' trumpeted another, running a photograph of Sir Nicholas Serota looking particularly thin and drawn. 'NIGELLA'S HUSBAND IN HIDING' screamed a third, reporting breathlessly that Charles Saatchi – a man so reclusive he avoided even his own parties – had not been seen for at least a week. Excited by the loss of Herblock and Marilyn Falucci Lamont, and having heard that Jeff Koons was in Europe, the American press were similarly optimistic that he might yet be snatched.

Pooley had had a difficult conversation with Anastasia Holliday's parents in Australia. After the initial shock, there had been an outpouring from her mother about how her lovely girl had fallen into bad company and why it was a tragedy she had abandoned surf for shit – at least, that was what Pooley uncomfortably thought she said. Should they immediately fly to London? Optimism said no, pessimism said yes, cautious policeman said why not give it another day before deciding.

The most recent boyfriend had agreed to come to the Yard, where Pooley had interviewed him briefly. 'Look,' he said, 'we're both from Oz, but I hardly know Annie. But great bird, great body, lol and all that. As for the art, if you ask me, she's been taking the piss and milking those dipsticks for all she could get.'

Closer questioning elicited the information that Anastasia thought Fortune and Pringle wankers and that he'd never heard her speak of any of the other missing people. He added helpfully that she had confided in him that she was running short of another fucking thing to do with anything that emerged from her body, but that she'd said hopefully that while she'd exhausted piss, shit, and everything else that came out of her clacker, maybe there was still some mileage in sweat and chunder if she could work out how to produce them without too much effort.

'Chunder?'

'Vomit.'

Pooley, who despite years as a policeman had never succeeded in sloughing off all inhibitions, hid his revulsion, thanked him profusely, promised to do everything he could to find Anastasia and to report back tomorrow, and rushed back to his office to investigate an intriguing message. It was ten minutes later when he pressed 'Print', waited impatiently, grabbed the pages, and raced to Milton's office. 'There's another. At least I think he's another, even though he's a hedge fund manager.'

Milton looked exhausted. 'What do you mean, "I think he's another, even though he's a hedge fund manager"?'

Pooley was excited. 'I mean other people didn't make the link. He'd been missing a few days but I googled him and saw he'd been buying a lot of very expensive art. Look. There he is: Charlie Briggs. Snapped at a Sotheby's art auction with a model.'

Milton scanned the pages. 'He paid £5 million for what?'

'A Fontana. Lucio Fontana. Look. That's it.'

There was a pause. 'He paid five mill for a plain canvas with a slash in the middle.'

'He did.'

'With cretins like that running our financial affairs,' said Milton heavily, 'it's no wonder we're in the state we're in.'

Pooley was almost dancing with impatience. 'Shouldn't we add him to our investigation? He was also last seen hailing a taxi.'

'When?'

'Thursday evening. The security man at his office said he'd left around half nine.'

'If we do, how many's that? Ten?'

Pooley counted them on his fingers. 'Jack, Sir Henry Fortune, Jason Pringle, Anastasia Holliday, Hortense Wilde, Jake Thorogood, Chester Herblock, Marilyn Falucci Lamont, Gavin Truss and now Charlie Briggs. Yes, ten.'

'I'd better go and tell the AC we've reached a nice round number. That might stop him going on about coincidence. After that we try to find out what connections there are between the missing and Sarkovsky. At this stage, the preliminary interviews are down to you and me. I don't trust anyone else.'

Amiss's afternoon went the way of his morning. Hour by hour, he watched and read every aspect of the lives of the missing being picked over. A sombre tone was adopted by most commentators, who concentrated on what the world owed these people of talent and discernment, with the occasional dissenter opining that they were opportunists who had made fortunes out of endorsing, creat-ing, or buying rubbish. Innumerable celebrities from the art world shared their grief and pain at the fate that had befallen their beloved friends. The social media, on the other hand, were dominated by gossip and rumour and sick jokes and sniggers about sex, drugs, and rock-and-roll.

Late afternoon, the news that Charlie Briggs was thought to be the tenth victim of the same kidnapper cheered everyone up no end, as it enabled them to begin speculating about the safety of every modern-art collector in London. It was a bonus that he was young and good-looking and frenzied attempts were made to link him with Anastasia Holliday, clips of whose frank accounts of what she did with her orifices and her bodily fluids were being held until after the nine o'clock watershed. For now, they were majoring on shots of her falling out of nightclubs.

What confused everyone was where the baroness came into it. In her speech to the House of Lords about contemporary culture, she had trashed the critics and dealers and curators and art schools for being part of a vast liberal conspiracy to destroy everything that made art great and make fortunes along the way. And there were a couple of clips of her being rude on news programmes that made riveting viewing. One tabloid christened her 'Baroness Battle-Axe'. This gave rise to speculation that she was the kidnapper, a suspicion the Assistant Commissioner was beginning to share.

The sane took the view that she was an unlikely possessor of a paramilitary wing, but as stories came out about her involvement in high-profile murder cases in Cambridge and

London, a significant proportion of those following the story on Twitter decided there was no smoke without fire and that she could be some kind of secret agent, except there was no consensus on whom she might be working for.

None of St Martha's staff was prepared to be interviewed, but the desperate hacks roaming its grounds found a few students who couldn't keep their mouths shut. 'The Mistress is, like, cool,' was the quote most of the media ran with. A few dusty peers emerged from the Lords to say pompous things about the baroness being a fine woman known for her integrity and her eloquence. A BBC producer who had discovered Amiss had been a close associate of the baroness in several of her better-known adventures rang to beg him for an interview.

'It would,' he said primly, 'be inappropriate,' and ended the call before the man had the wit to ask him why. The truth was that by now Amiss was so terrified for her that he didn't trust himself to keep his composure in public.

Chapter Six

It was mid-afternoon before Milton was finally put through to Mrs Chester Herblock in her Manhattan home. She sounded hyper. 'Hey, they say you're an English policeman, right?'

'I am.'

'So what do I call you, Mr Policeman? Over here everyone's "Officer".'

'That'll do fine, Mrs Herblock.'

'So what can I do for you, Officer?'

'It's to do with your husband's disappearance.'

'His what?'

'Oh, I do apologise. I assumed you'd been told by the NYPD. It was their job.'

'I haven't been around to be told anything, Officer.' She giggled. 'I've been holed up with a friend and we haven't been taking calls. Only just got home. Chester's hardly ever here anyway, so who'd know he was missing.'

'I'm afraid he hasn't been seen for three days and no one has any idea where he is.'

'Don't you worry, Officer,' she said happily. 'He'll be off with that Lamont bitch. In case you don't know what I'm talking about, my husband is serially unfaithful with bitches of one kind or another, beautiful or sexy or rich. This one's called Mar-il-yn Fal-ucc-i Lamont. I've been expecting him any day now to tell me she's going to be my replacement. Do you know about replacements in my world, Officer?'

'I can't say that I do, Mrs Herblock. Indeed I don't really know what your world is.'

'It's the cosmopolitan art world, Officer, in which people like my husband drift around arty places from Bel Air to Buenos Aires networking and making a fortune in collusion with dealers and curators to persuade ignorant rich people to waste their money on worthless trash. They also trade up in wives according to their beauty or their money or their performance in bed. I'm the sexy third Mrs Herblock and I signed a prenup. Chester's had his fun and now he's thinking of his future.' She laughed again. 'Poor Chester. He finds being only a multi-millionaire a bit constricting. It's time for me to make way for a billionairess.' She paused. 'That's Lamont,' she said helpfully. 'Lucky woman. She was married to an elderly billionaire who croaked while she was still young enough to enjoy the legacy.'

'Oh,' said Milton, lacking anything else to say.

'So what do you wanna know, Officer?'

Milton pulled himself together. 'There is reason to believe that several people con-

124

nected with the art world have been kidnapped, Mrs Herblock, including your husband.'

'What about the rich bitch?'

'She's disappeared ... that is, Mrs Lamont has gone missing too.'

'They were screwing at the Dorchester, right?'

'They were both staying in the Dorchester, Mrs Herblock.'

'In the same suite?'

'No.'

'Next door?'

'I think so.'

'Of course. After all, money's no object.'

'But please, Mrs Herblock, my job is to find them. Is there anything you can tell me that would help?'

'Nope. I haven't heard from him for days, but that's nothing new. Off with the old, on with the new, that's Chester Herblock, whether he's dealing with wives or art. But one way or the other, money will be involved. Plenty of it.'

'Mrs Herblock had met Sir Henry Fortune at some art event,' said Milton to Pooley. 'She described him as an asshole. She'd also heard of Jason Pringle as someone Herblock occasionally did business with and she heard him mention Anastasia Holliday as a hot new talent.

"I looked her up," she said, "and saw that even if she didn't seem to have any talent, she was certainly hot, so it was no surprise Chester was taking an interest."

'When I got her to focus on Oleg Sarkovsky, she remembered him vaguely as the guy Herblock told her was a real sap, that he could shovel any shit off on to him and make a bomb. Then she began to laugh. Apparently he'd been literally successful with shit. Although it was gold-plated. Someone called Terence something-or-other.'

'Rings a bell. But did she have anything useful otherwise?'

'No. But at least we're clear there was a Sarkovsky connection. Herblock's PA was more helpful. She seemed rather more bothered about his disappearance than was his wife and told me he'd made a lot out of Sarkovsky even though Sarkovsky drove a hard bargain. She reckons he'd have earned several million in commissions.'

Pooley gulped. 'Several million? Sarkovsky must have been buying hundreds of millions worth.'

'And some of it he was buying from Herblock's bit on the side.'

'Marilyn?'

'Yes. Apparently Sarkovsky bought about $150 million's worth of conceptual art off her last year on Herblock's recommendation. Herblock got ten per cent.'

'So it's in his interests that prices be high rather than low?'

'It certainly is, Ellis. And no, I don't understand it either. Anything from your end?'

'Nothing, except that Sarkovsky had some slightly fraught dealings with Pringle and Thorogood.'

'In their capacities as dealer and art critic?'

'Yes.'

'This is all ludicrously incestuous.'

'This world is. Apparently although Thorogood was an art critic and innocents like us might think he should be independent, he acted as a kind of authenticator for dealers. Well, for Pringle, anyway.'

'I don't know why we find this kind of thing surprising,' said Milton gloomily. 'I saw a TV programme recently that told me that in the States academic economists were happy to earn a packet from sitting on the boards of companies they wrote about. So what did Thorogood do for Pringle that involved Sarkovsky?'

'According to Allegra from Pringle's gallery, there was some sort of row about graffiti art. Pringle sold Sarkovsky what he thought was a genuine Banksy.'

'Banksy? That graffiti artist who stencils rats and monkeys onto buildings? How can you sell them?'

'It's complicated. Pringle sold Sarkovsky a seaside hut with a stencilled dangling man that was supposed to be a Banksy, but though Thorogood said he agreed with Pringle that it was the genuine article, other critics thought it was a fake and, anyway, it turned out to be a protected hut that couldn't be removed from its location. Sarkovsky wanted his money back, but Pringle was dragging it out and trying to make him take payment in kind. Apparently, he was offering other less well-known graffiti artists, but Sarkovsky was having none of it. It was the big brand names or nothing for him. Allegra said Sarkovsky was very fierce and shouted a lot over the phone.

'Then I talked to Thorogood's girlfriend. She's relatively new, but she remembered he'd been a bit shaken by some Russian threatening to have him shot. Obviously, Thorogood didn't think he meant it, but he was a bit scared.'

'Is that it?' asked Milton.

'No. I talked to Sir Henry Fortune's PA as well. She said rather loftily that while she had never heard of Sarkovsky, Sir Henry was a very famous man who would have been known and respected by everyone in the art world.'

Pooley looked at his watch. 'I need to go. I'm on my way now to see Charlie Briggs's sister and then Gavin Truss's wife.'

'And I've got a number for Marilyn Falucci Lamont's next-of-kin. The AC's out this afternoon but I'm to see him at six. Maybe by then we'll have enough connections made to force the stubborn bastard to take Sarkovsky seriously.'

It was Charlie Briggs's sister Brenda, who'd been staying with him for a few days, who'd reported him missing. Pooley went to the Docklands penthouse to interview her.

'Sorry about this,' she said in a strong Yorkshire accent, as she ushered him towards a sofa. 'It's a bit depressing.'

Pooley looked around curiously. The room had magnificent views across the Thames, but inside was cheerlessly minimalist. 'It needed a woman's touch,' she said. 'All Charlie did was buy whatever 'e were told to buy by whoever were ordering him round. You wouldn't believe the rubbish 'e came home with. Look at that.' She pointed at a canvas leaning against a wall.

'May I look at it?' asked Pooley and went over and turned it round.

'That looks like a vandalised canvas to me,' she said. 'But having seen some of the stuff 'e's paid a fortune for, it's probably worth a bomb so I'd better not throw it out.'

'It's by a famous artist called Lucio Fontana, Ms Briggs, and I think it's worth a few million.'

'Not to me it isn't. Bluddy rubbish.' She sat down on a nearby sofa and he joined her.

'For fuck's sake,' she said, 'what does our Charlie know about art? 'E's only showing off because he thinks 'e has to. 'E don't know nothin' about culture. We never had no money and we wasn't educated neither. 'E's out of his depth, poor lamb.'

'He's been buying a lot of art, Ms Briggs,' said Pooley.

'Stop this Ms Briggs rubbish, will yah? I'm Bren. Brenda Briggs. Known to everyone as Bren. I'm the thick one. Charlie's the brains.'

She stopped and considered that statement. 'Well, the brains when it comes to making money. Charlie's a bit short of brains when it comes to spending it, if you ask me. Krug and girls and now stupid art by people who can't draw or paint.' She looked Pooley in the eyes. ''E'll be OK, Charlie, won't 'e?'

'I very much hope so, Ms Briggs.' He caught her glare. 'Sorry, Bren. But we need all the information we can get. I know nothing about your brother except that he makes a fortune in financial services and that he collects art. And, as I've explained, it's the art that seems to be linking the people who've disappeared. Please tell me anything you know. What, for instance, was ... is ... Charlie like with money?'

'I noticed that "was" turning into "is", Inspector Pooley. Or can I call you something 'uman?'

'Ellis.'

'Ellis? Never 'eard of Ellis. Sounds as posh as your accent.'

Pooley, who had put long hours into trying to modify his Etonian vowels, winced. 'It's a family name from way back. Sort of religious. A bit Welsh.'

'OK. Like Charlie's named after Grand-dad. Now why did you say "was"?'

'No reason. It's just that we're a bit frantic trying to find out what all these people were doing before they disappeared so I put them in the past tense. I think they've been kidnapped. I've no reason to think anything worse.'

She put her head on one side, circled her thumbs around each other and said, 'OK. I hope you mean that.'

'Now you asked about money, and I can see why, because we'd never 'ave thought Charlie would be rich. 'E were crap at everything at school apart from the maths, where 'e were brilliant, so 'e managed to get to uni. A first for our family.'

'He sounds like one of those geniuses who set up Google or Facebook.'

'You've got it. One of those ... what do they call them these days? Sort of autistic lite?'

'Asperger's?'

'That's it. Charlie weren't too good at understanding people, but he certainly understood...'She looked fearfully at Pooley. 'Now you've got *me* talking about him like

131

he were dead.'

'It's OK, Bren. We're talking about his life before now.'

'OK, Ellis. Charlie understood figures and then 'e understood computers and they and 'im were supposed to understand how the world worked. And the world were all about money, and Charlie did things on the computer and 'is firm turned them into money. And 'e got huge money. And 'uge bonuses. And then 'e were given a bit of the company and 'e made even more.'

'What did he do with it?'

''E hadn't no interest in money. 'E'd have given it all away. Our parents wouldn't move, but 'e bought their council 'ouse for them and gave them as much as they'd take. Same with me. Bought me a nice 'ouse and my nail business and I'm doing fine. Me and my 'usband, we don't want nothing more.

'Charlie would have given most of it to charity but 'e had to do the flashy things that made the crazies 'e worked with respect him. Otherwise they'd have bullied 'im even more like they did when 'e was at school. It's all big dick stuff in that world.' She adopted a child's voice: '"Yah, boo, sucks. I wasted more money than you did."'

From further questioning it emerged that Briggs had no steady girlfriend, few friends, and that left to himself his idea of relaxation was to play computer games. But being emotionally reliant on a few of his colleagues who were conspicuous consumers he went out with them for extravagant evenings with expensive girls. Not having any desire for fast cars or yachts or travel, buying art seemed to be the easiest and quickest way to placate his self-appointed advisers.

'Did he know a Russian called Oleg Sarkovsky?'

'Never heard of 'im.'

'Or a favourite art dealer? Or did he go to auctions?'

'There was someone advised him. What was his name? Jason summat.'

'Pringle.'

'That's it. 'E said 'e were very learned. And I know they went to auctions, because Charlie said 'e enjoyed bidding. Said it gave 'im a buzz.'

'Thank you, Bren. I was going to ask if I could send in a team to search the apartment for anything that might be useful, but seeing there's so little here, if it's OK with you I'll do it myself now. Won't take long.'

'Anything that'll help get Charlie back.'

All that Pooley could find that was remotely of interest were a few sale catalogues from major London auction houses with scribbles on them. He said goodbye to Bren Briggs and took them away with him.

Mrs Gavin Truss was pretty, but dishevelled,

weary, and depressed. Her toddlers were getting her down. In her chaotic house in Acton, with two small boys running wildly from room to room in screaming pursuit of each other, she explained that she hadn't got alarmed until Friday morning, since Gavin often stayed out without telling her. 'Why would anyone kidnap him? He's probably gone off with someone for the weekend.'

Then, in response to Pooley's sympathetic but probing questioning, she burst into tears and said Truss was 'a serial shagger', she was his third wife, he was thirty-four years older than her, she'd been his awe-struck student, and she'd been a moron to fall for him.

She'd never heard of Sarkovsky, she'd known Fortune and Pringle vaguely from the days when Truss used to take her out, and she'd had a few dreary incomprehensible lectures from Hortense Wilde. 'Stuck-up bitch,' she said. 'Always trashing everything I liked.'

There were thudding sounds and roars from the next room. She ran out, separated the combatants, calmed them down, and switched on the cartoon channel for them. 'Would you like coffee?' she asked when she came back.

'No thanks. I'm fine.'

He could see her relief.

'What did you think of your husband's college, Mrs Truss?'

'I was a nineteen-year-old from Hartlepool and easily impressed in the beginning. Gavin spotted me and took me to exciting events and I was ever so flattered. But it was all pretty crappy, really, when I think back. They didn't teach you anything except how to sneer at old art and drool over the new stuff. I was secretly relieved to drop out at the end of the first year when I fell pregnant with the twins. I thought it would be romantic to be with Gavin and our babies but it hasn't turned out like that. We bore him, and I'm lonely.'

She waved at the scribbles that defaced the lower section of the walls. 'My boys are conceptual artists,' she said. 'I've named these *Dying Very Very Slowly from a Loveless Marriage*.'

'I haven't fully got to grips with Gavin Truss and Hortense Wilde, Jim, but I've seen Mrs Truss and talked to Gervase Wilde over the phone and neither has heard of Sarkovsky. Neither had Truss's deputy. Truss and Wilde are old pals, though, and Wilde's been a professor at Truss's college for years. I read the lists of the missing out to them and it's clear they knew several of them. I've ticked them off: here's a copy.'

'Thanks, Ellis,' said Milton. 'I didn't do much better with finding out about the Lamont woman. Her daughter was cagey, and said she knew she was friends with Herblock but had no information at all about her London contacts. But then she added that considering Mom spent half her life gadding about Europe at art fairs and auctions, she probably knew anyone worth knowing. "It's like the fashion world," she said. "The same people turn up everywhere deciding what everyone else should think." I don't think she's that fond of her mother.'

He looked at his watch. 'I've got to have another press conference now. You'd better get home. You've had hardly any sleep for days.'

'Neither have you.'

'True. But I can't get away until I've seen the AC and you've got a wife who needs to see you.'

'Mary Lou's working tonight. I've an invitation to eat with Robert and Rachel. Will you call when you've seen the AC?'

'Will do. Tell Robert I'm sure Jack's all right.' He picked up his jacket. 'Why did I say that? I'm not, so don't.'

An hour later, as Milton was pleading with the AC to be allowed to put a surveillance team on to Sarkovsky, the baroness heard his voice: 'You go out room now.'

'Oh, good. I'm going home, am I?'

'You think that you stupid. You meet others.'

The baroness quashed a momentary dread that Sarkovsky might have kidnapped the staff of St Martha's or her close friends, and said nothing. She put on the jacket of her suit of heathery tweed over her grubby purple shirt and followed instructions, first, to wait in the bathroom, and second to leave it, put on the blindfold now waiting for her on her bed, then turn and face the inner wall. She tried to work out why – since she knew Sarkovsky was the kidnapper – it mattered to him that she didn't see where she was going, but there seemed no logical explanation except that he wanted her further disorientated. The door opened, Sarkovsky barked an order, and a rather sweaty hand grasped her arm and the voice of her regular captor said, 'Come with me.'

She followed obediently, irritated that she had failed in her attempt to rig the blindfold so she could see something. She was in the open air, it was cold, and she was on rough ground. A door was opened, she was pushed through it, and the voice said, 'Take it off in two minutes and walk down the stairs. There's no way out here.'

The lights were so bright when she took the blindfold off that she was initially completely disorientated. She blinked steadily until she was able to take in properly the bizarre grandeur that surrounded her. The curved staircase was carpeted in red, the walls were mirrored, and four enormous chandeliers dangled from the gilded ceiling. 'Crikey,' said the baroness, as she put her hand on the gilt balustrade and began the descent. At the bottom of the stairs there was a large, red door, which required so much strength to open that she had to hurl herself at it.

The enormous room that was revealed was lined with large glass tanks and steel, glass-fronted cabinets. There was a noxious smell of rotten meat. To her right, beside the door, was a glass tank about fourteen feet long and six feet high. In one half was a rotting cow's head and an electric insect killer: along with maggots, flies were feeding on the one and dying on the other. The other half contained a large white box from which flies emerged and found their way through holes in the partition.

She walked down the centre of the room and saw that the cabinets lining the walls to the left contained an eclectic and gruesome array of objects that included pliers, an axe, saw, noose, club and spear, crucifixes, bandages and rosaries – some of them spattered with what looked like blood. The same substance was spattered over the outside of the cabinet, and emanated a cloying smell which was only slightly less disgusting than that by the door. To the right were several identical large black canvases. She went over and inspected one of them and saw that the canvas had been blackened by tens of thousands of dead flies: the title was 'Cancer Chronicle (Smallpox)'.

At the end of the room was the *pièce de résistance*, a huge perspex box containing five white plastic chairs surrounding a matching table with the remains of a meal on it. In the corner was a barbecue laden with meat. Everything was covered in live flies which entered via a small hole from the other part of the exhibit, where maggots were hatched, and perished on another fly killer.

'Sweet Jesus,' said the baroness. 'I'm in hell with Damien Hirst.'

She explored further. There were three locked doors – red, black, and violet – and a doorless kitchen scribbled over with graffiti and images mainly of rats. A white door led to a bathroom, on the far wall of which was a sketch of a complex piece of machinery, and a shelf on which were a small irregularly shaped, gold-covered object and a tin. Closer scrutiny revealed that the sketch was called 'Cloaca' and the curved object had a tag saying 'Koh?' The label on the tin was in four languages. The baroness passed on the French, German, and Italian and read the English text:

'Artist's Shit
Contents 30 gr net
Freshly preserved
Produced and tinned

in May 1961'

She groaned and left the bathroom.

Having searched high and low, the baroness had to admit to herself that there was no food, but there was champagne in the refrigerator and she found glasses in a cupboard. She opened a bottle, poured herself a generous amount, and returned to the main room and sat on one of the four large pink sofas shaped like a woman's lips. It was very uncomfortable.

After a few minutes, there was a crashing sound at the door. When it opened, it revealed a plump, dishevelled, middle-aged, bald man in a dinner jacket. The baroness stood up and crossed to him, holding her hand out. 'Jack Troutbeck.'

'What's going on?' He gave her a perfunctory handshake. 'Why am I here?'

'Search me. I don't know why I'm here either. Who are you?'

'I am Sir Henry Fortune, the international curator.'

'Oh, God.' She sat down again. 'So you are!'

He looked around him and blenched. 'Is this a museum?'

'I have no idea. I've been here only a few minutes.'

'Disgusting smell.' His tone implied it was her fault. 'Is there anything to eat? I'm starving.'

''Fraid not. But there's champagne.'

'What good is that? I tell you I'm starving.'

The baroness shrugged. 'There are calories in wine. Do you want some or not?'

'I suppose so.'

The baroness fetched two bottles from the kitchen along with a few glasses and put them on one of the two low tables that sat between the sofas. Both tables consisted of glass tops supported by the form of a woman. Each wore a basque and long black gloves: one was on her hands and knees; the other was on her back but had cunningly bent her body into a shape than supported the table on her bottom. The baroness had already named them Joleen and Trixie.

Fortune poured himself a glass and sat down opposite her. 'So who are you?'

'I'm a member of the House of Lords and Mistress of St Martha's.'

'Oh, my God. I know who you are. You're that dreadful philistine.'

'Do you think we know each other well enough to exchange insults yet, Sir Henry?' she enquired icily. 'I think I'd rather be in solitary, but I don't suppose I have an option. Maybe we should make an effort to be civil.' She got up, refilled her glass, and sat down again. 'Have you been here long?'

'I don't know. Maybe a few days. I've been imprisoned in a nasty cell and I've had nothing to eat.'

'How did you get here?'

'I don't know. Last thing I remember is getting into a taxi with a friend.'

'So presumably he's here too.'

'I don't know. This is a nightmare.'

'Unfortunately not,' said the baroness.

Fortune said nothing.

'What do you think of the décor?' she asked.

'I haven't really looked at it.'

'You're in for a treat if your idea of an interior decorator is Damien Hirst. It's a bit on the gloomy side.'

'Damien Hirst is an artist, madam. It is not his job to cheer anyone up. I have to think about what is here. I don't want to make any rash judgements.' He stalked over to the tank beside the door. 'Is this truly Damien's *A Thousand Years?* I doubt it. He would never sell this audacious yet profound Darwinian masterpiece.'

'Look down the room and you'll see something else by him.'

He strode down the room. '*Let's Eat Outside Today.* It cannot be. It cannot be.'

'Do you recognise what's on the left?'

Fortune's lips went in and out as he ruminated. 'Of course. I've only seen them once. In the White Cube about a decade ago.' He clicked his fingers in frustration. 'What was it called? What *was* it called. Hah! Yes. *Romance in the Age of Uncertainty.*'

'They represent romance?'

'No, no, no. They represent the martyred apostles.'

'Ah, got you. He's showing us the means by which they were martyred. Neat.'

'Yes.'

'And the black canvases?'

'His thirteen *Cancer Chronicles* – smallpox, AIDS, malaria, and so on. But I am sceptical as to their authenticity. Very sceptical.'

'Have you any thoughts on the Mae West sofas?'

'Crude adaptions of Dali's surreal masterpieces.'

'And Trixie and Joleen?'

'What are you talking about?'

The baroness waved at the tables.

'Oh, you mean the Allen Jones sculptures? Which, of course, may or may not be Allen Jones.'

'They're art, are they? I thought they were cast-offs from Hugh Hefner's Playboy Mansion.'

Fortune looked down his nose at her like an Edwardian dowager duchess surveying the shop girl her son wants to marry. He produced a heavy sigh. 'They raise many questions that have been addressed by serious and knowledgeable people: is such forniphilia Freudian, or an ironic comment on sexual objectification and the struggle between the exploited and the exploiting.'

The baroness opened her mouth and closed it again. 'Have a look at the kitchen.'

He came out after a minute. 'The same applies. Of course they look like Banksy, but are they Banksy? That is the question.'

'And our bathroom?'

Fortune disappeared for a couple of minutes. 'How exciting,' he said when he reappeared and threw himself down on the sofa opposite her. 'The same seminal question applies but the Manzoni, at least, would be harder to copy. If all is as it seems, what we have in there are...'

There was a series of thuds at the door. 'If I'm not mistaken, Watson,' said the baroness, 'here is our client now.'

The door crashed open and revealed a skinny, long-haired man in a dinner jacket. 'Jason,' cried Fortune and rushed over to him.

'Oh, Bubbles!' cried Pringle. 'I've had a most ghastly time and they won't give me anything to eat, however I plead. Is there food here?'

He looked around him and screamed. 'Has Damien kidnapped us? Are we an installation?'

'We don't know.'

Pringle looked over at the baroness, who was regarding him with interest. 'Who's she?'

'That bigoted woman who made that dreadful speech in the Lords calling us and

Nick Serota and Charles Saatchi and lots of others terrible names.'

'My name is Jack Troutbeck,' said the baroness. 'And you are?'

'Jason Pringle. I'm an art dealer.'

'Indeed you are, Mr Pringle. Your fame has preceded you.'

'Is there any food?'

'I'm afraid not. But we should remember that hunger strikers have managed to stay alive for more than sixty days, so it's a bit early to make a fuss.'

Fortune and Pringle shot her glances of pure hatred. 'There is champagne, Mr Pringle. I suggest you have a drink. I further suggest that – although you can be assured that I dislike you both just as much as I'm sure you do me – since we're incarcerated together for God knows how long it might be an idea to try to get on if it's at all possible.'

She rose, filled a glass, and handed it to Pringle with exaggerated courtesy. 'Thank you,' he muttered.

However, leaving her with just Joleen for company, Fortune and Pringle withdrew to the sofa furthest away and began what the baroness described contemptuously to herself as canoodling and caterwauling. After a few minutes, there was another assault on the door and a tall, skinny woman in jeans and a big woolly navy sweater appeared. The baroness looked at her in horror. Fortune and Pringle jumped up and rushed over and embraced her. 'Darling,' they cried in unison.

'Oh, Henry and Jason, how wonderful to see you,' said Hortense Wilde, with a sob. 'Is there anything to eat? What's going on here?'

'It seems to be a remake of *Huis Clos*,' said the baroness. 'Would you care for a drink?'

Chapter Seven

'I thought there couldn't be two Ellis Pooleys,' said the elegant man who got up from behind his desk and came forward, holding out his hand.

Pooley shook it. 'And I thought there were unlikely to be two Adam Eichbergs.'

'Do sit down.' Eichberg waved at an upright leather armchair. 'Coffee?'

'Please.'

While Eichberg was talking to his secretary, Pooley assessed the furniture and the pictures and concluded that his old classmate was doing very well indeed. Eichberg put down the phone, sat in a matching chair, and surveyed Pooley. 'You don't look much different from when we were at school, Ellis. I suppose I shouldn't be surprised that you ended up in the police. I seem to remember that you were mad keen

146

on Sherlock Holmes.'

'And I seem to recollect you preferring art to anything, Adam. I remember those Renaissance reproductions in your study.'

Eichberg laughed. 'So in our case, the boys really were the fathers of the men.'

'Though I'd have expected you to go the art historian route rather than the commercial.'

'Couldn't have done it in the present climate, Ellis. I don't fit in with the orthodoxy of the times. As a curator it would have killed me to buy and extol dross. As an auctioneer, I don't care.

'Anyway, you didn't come here to visit an old school acquaintance. What do you want from me? Is it to do with these extraordinary disappearances?'

'It is. I'm trying to establish various links. And I'm told you were the auctioneer at these sales.' Pooley pushed across three of the catalogues he'd taken from Briggs's flat.

Eichberg threw them a cursory look. 'Yes, indeed. They were most successful.'

Pooley handed him a photograph. 'This is one of the missing people: Charlie Briggs. Do you remember him at any of them?'

'I'm not quite sure. I saw this photo in a newspaper this morning, and thought he seemed vaguely familiar. But that's all.'

'He might have been with Jason Pringle.'

Eichberg snapped his fingers. 'Oh, course.

Yes, I remember. He was the one who bought that Fontana.'

'He was indeed. And a few other things.'

There was a tap on the door and a Kate Middleton lookalike came in with a tray. 'Thanks, Jemima. Just leave it.' She smiled a dazzling smile and left in a waft of expensive perfume.

'How do you get Jemimas to lower themselves to make coffee?'

'Come on, Ellis. You must know there's an infinite supply of well-bred young girls with degrees in fine arts who are happy to work for a pittance in places like these.' He pushed a cup of black coffee across the desk. 'Help yourself to milk, sugar, and biscuits.'

'Thanks.'

'Now what do you want to know?'

'If you remember anything of significance about him? Anything that might give a clue as to why he might have an enemy?'

Eichberg frowned. 'In my line of work, discretion is of the essence.'

'As it is in mine, Adam. However, these people are in very real danger. We're desperate for leads.'

'That puts it in perspective. Did you know I'm Jewish? One of the good things about my religion is that it tells me it's OK to break the Sabbath to save a life. So I guess I can break the rules of my ancient auction house for the same reason.'

'I appreciate that, Adam. And I'd be really grateful for anything you could tell me that will help me understand this peculiar world. I'm floundering.'

'I met Briggs with Pringle at a reception where newcomers are fattened up for the market. Briggs seemed a nice bloke but hadn't a clue. Typical ignorant hedgie. Jason Pringle is a shark: Briggs, being ignorant and rich, is typical of his prey. What's more, like so many of these young men who've got rich quick, he's competitive and a gambler. I guess Jason realised early on that he'd do better pointing him at auctions than trying to get him to buy from the gallery.'

'How would Pringle make money that way?'

'By arrangement with the sellers.'

'Can you explain that?'

'Let's suppose I'm an unscrupulous dealer trying to offload an artwork worth, say, a million, on the open market. I'd like to make more, of course, so I tip off my dodgy friends among art advisers and dealers in the hope that they can deliver a mug or two who'll buy or at least drive up the price. If they do so, they'll get a commission. Pringle was good at providing mugs and Briggs was ideal. He'd no idea what he was bidding for, but was happy to go far above any sensible limit on Pringle's say-so and just for the fun of it.'

'As he did for the Fontana?'

'Yes. He paid a bit over the odds for that. But I was more thinking of the way he bid for that substandard Hirst.'

'What's a substandard Hirst?'

Eichberg laughed. 'I can see you're not a fan. Nor am I. When I came into this game it was because I loved great art. I've ended up spending much of my time peddling garbage, but I tell myself everyone involved is a consenting adult – curators, dealers, collectors and, indeed, auctioneers. They all want money or prestige or status.'

'And critics and art historians and teachers?'

'Indeed. They're all caught up in this vast confidence trick.'

'So no one can afford to mention that the artist-emperor is naked?'

'You could argue that the artists are the tailors and the rest are the emperors, Ellis. After all, smart artists have learnt to exploit the parasites. And good luck to them, I say. I live in hope that one day the entire market for this trash will implode and we can get back to selling exquisite tailoring.'

'You were saying about Briggs.'

'We had a lot with an estimated price of nine hundred K. When we reached that, everyone dropped out except for a telephone bidder and Briggs. Briggs finally quit when the price got to just under three million, and the telephone bidder got it for three.'

'If Briggs was that competitive, why didn't he go to three?'

'I saw Pringle whisper to him as I asked if he'd like to raise his bid. And he shook his head.'

'So what do you think was going on?'

'Briggs is rich. Not mega-rich. It would make sense to let him keep his money for the next time round. Assuming Pringle was getting a cut of that deal, which I'm sure he was, he was essentially taking his winnings and keeping Briggs's money in reserve for another punt another time.'

'Who was the telephone bidder?'

'If I ever knew I don't remember. Hang on a minute. I'll get Jemima onto it. I need to go to her. She'll have the catalogues.'

While he was out of the room, Pooley called the office, got an update reporting no news and no progress, and attended to some emails. After five minutes, Eichberg returned. 'Got it,' he said. 'Fiona, our representative who was manning the phone, remembers the guy well. She said she had a horrible time with him because he was furious that he'd paid so much. And yet, he obviously couldn't bear to lose.'

'And he was?'

'You realise how tricky this is, Ellis. We promise client confidentiality. And I know this man and he wouldn't react well if he knew.'

'I understand, Adam. But there are ten

missing people.'

'I know, I know.' Eichberg sighed. 'OK. He was called Oleg Sarkovsky.'

'Yes, I've talked to Sarkovsky, sir,' said Milton. 'It took me ages to get hold of him, but I created merry hell with his people and eventually he called. He says he hasn't seen her since they parted company at the airport weeks ago.'

'Where is he?'

'He claims he's in Moscow, but he could easily be lying. I'm asking M16 to check if he's there. And we should search his London house now. And get that cell phone traced.'

'Hold on, Jim. Hold on. I don't want to ask favours of Six unless we're sure it's necessary. Don't want to be beholden...'

'But, sir...'

The Assistant Commissioner took off his reading glasses, folded them neatly and laid them on the desk. 'Look here, Jim, this is an order. Relations with Six are very delicate at the moment and I don't want any boats rocked. The only reason this bloke's a suspect is that Troutbeck talked about him. If you ask me, she's a more likely suspect. From all I hear she had an obsessive hatred for artists.'

By taking a deep breath, Milton succeeded in keeping his temper. 'I can see why you might think that, sir,' he said, 'but I've known Lady Troutbeck for some years, and although she's eccentric, she's eminently sane.'

'It can be a small step from eccentricity to insanity,' said the Assistant Commissioner, with the faux-wisdom that so grated on his juniors.

'She is also someone who has to live on a salary which would not allow her to employ a team of skilled kidnappers.'

'I suppose you're right. Though they make a lot out of expenses in the Lords.'

Milton kept his voice level. 'Which leaves us with ten people missing and only one suspect, sir. We can't ignore that.'

'But we don't want to make any mistakes. According to this...' he put his glasses back on again and looked at the brief, 'as well as his Kensington mansion, Sarkovsky's got homes in the Hamptons and the Antibes, a Scottish shooting lodge, a helicopter, a private plane and a yacht.' He took off his glasses again, put them on the desk, clasped his hands together and adopted an expression suitable to a primary-school teacher explaining there was no Santa Claus. 'If, Jim, and it's a very big if, Sarkovsky's the perpetrator, the victims could be absolutely anywhere. And, if he'd really had it in for them, they'd be at the bottom of the ocean wearing cement shoes.'

'We can't give up, sir. He's the only lead we've got. There are connections between him and almost everyone on the list.'

'There must be thousands of people in the arty world who innocently know many people on that list, Jim.'

'We know he had rows with some of them. And a really bad one with Lady Troutbeck. We've got absolutely nothing else that makes any sense at all.'

'You call this sense?' The Assistant Commissioner shook his head more in sorrow than anger at Milton's denseness. 'You're seriously suggesting we should bother Six and get a search warrant on the basis that he had a row with that Troutbeck lunatic, who seems to have rows with everyone? Don't think I don't know what she said in the Lords about the Met being full of wimps and appeasers. Anyway, if Sarkovsky hated Troutbeck that much, he could have had her knocked off and dropped down a mine while he was out of the country.'

'But there are the other missing people, sir. And his reputation is terrible.'

'He's got a dodgy reputation and has the occasional business dispute? For fuck's sake, Jim, you know as well as I do that London's full of people with a dodgy reputation. Especially Russians. But they're not mad enough to start mass kidnappings. The odd poisoning, maybe, but not snatching people off the street in broad daylight.'

The Assistant Commissioner picked up his glasses once more, put them on and bent his head again over the briefing papers. 'The first thing the judge is going to ask is why we think Sarkovsky might have had it in for any of the others.'

'There's speculation that he's lost a lot of money on art and he thought Pringle and Thorogood had pulled a fast one. But my hunch is that we're not involved with someone rational. My sources suggest he's in bad financial trouble and it's probably irrecoverable. He seems to have been in close working relationships with a few unsavoury Arab dictators now dead or deposed. If he's losing everything, he could be looking for a dramatic exit. He acquired the money violently. Why not go down gloriously?'

'That sounds like Ellis Pooley is kite-flying again.'

'Ellis's theory is the only one we've got. People do go mad, and this guy – from all we hear – is a paranoid megalomaniac.'

The Assistant Commissioner bent over the file again. 'I'll think about it.'

'We've got to do something, sir. Can't we at least put a team on to investigating what other properties he might own?'

'Surely you realise these people have brilliant accountants and lawyers to keep their business affairs under wraps, Jim. We haven't the manpower for this.'

'We can't do nothing, sir. The press are baying for our blood.'

The Assistant Commissioner adopted his sagacious tone. 'I'm surprised at you, Jim. We can't be jumping to the tune of the reptiles. At least not when we're deciding if we should take on someone of unlimited wealth. I said I'd think about it. And that's what I'll be doing tonight. See you first thing tomorrow.'

Milton could have done with knowing about Martin Conroy, who was sitting at his home computer triumphantly adding another company name to the list he kept in his Oleg Sarkovsky file. As ever, Conroy had worked steadily through the day in his office clearing the urgent files. It was mostly humdrum work, but he never complained. His sequence of bosses in his twenty years in Inland Revenue appreciated him for his competence, reliability, and punctuality. It was a relief to have someone who needed minimal supervision and just got on with things. He was promoted from time to time, but being avowedly uninterested in management, he would never fly as high as his other capabilities could have brought him.

There were two other reasons why he hadn't sought promotion. One was because high office would not have been compatible with his career as an army reservist, the first major outlet for his sense of adventure. Conroy had never wanted to join the army full-time, mainly because, as with the police,

156

there was far too much sitting around being bored. And Jane had made it very clear early on that while she didn't mind him being away for evenings, weekends, and even the odd couple of weeks, she would never agree to being an army wife. She'd become annoyed, though, when he joined the Special Forces Reserve, which required longer and more intensive training.

By the time she stunned him by announcing she had fallen in love with his sister and they had walked off into the sunset, Conroy was set in his ways. He served a few months in Iraq as a member of the clerical support staff and found it both dull and exciting, but he hadn't enjoyed the pain and inconvenience when he took a bullet in his shoulder, and being at the end of his contract, he decided to quit. He kept a few army friendships and attended the odd reunion, but henceforward, he concentrated in his spare time on his second interest, pursuing tax evaders of his choice even when they were none of his business.

His routine was invariable. He arrived at the office at eight and spent precisely seven hours on his allocated work. Since he brought a sandwich with him and ate it at his desk, he was through his work by four, when he turned with eager anticipation to whatever was his current out-of-hours project.

Conroy ran a tight ship and required his

staff to run past him not just the tax returns with which they were struggling, but those they had approved. This process not only provided quality control but also occasionally threw up an unexpected and interesting fact that provided the basis for an informal investigation. Conroy didn't just work at the office: if he felt he was venturing into worlds he didn't want to explore on his computer, he would follow up at home, often with the help of a well-placed phone call to an old comrade. And he also believed in occasional on-the-spot spying.

He had first become interested in Oleg Sarkovsky when the approved tax return of his butler, Joseph Taylor, landed in the in-tray. Conroy's latest project had just come to a satisfactory end when he was able to tip-off the Border Agency that a Clapham restaurant – which claimed to have three employees – was operating mostly on the labour of illegal immigrants.

Conroy noticed that Taylor lived in the most expensive part of Kensington, but had a very modest salary, and he wondered why. A check on the electoral roll showed him living there alone, so Conroy spent some time finding the name of its owner, which proved to be a company registered in the British Virgin Islands which had not disclosed the names of the directors.

It took only a couple of hours to identify

the owner and occasional resident as Oleg Sarkovsky. Conroy didn't like what he learnt from an ex-comrade who was well informed about Russian oligarchs, so he set himself to find out everything he could about him. By now, he thought he almost had him nailed.

Hortense was in animated and distressed conversation with Fortune and Pringle on their sofa when Gavin Truss arrived, wearing jeans and a T-shirt with the legend: 'That which is cannot be true – Herbert Marcuse'. He took one look at the baroness and screeched like a banshee who was having a particularly bad night. Fortune, Pringle, and Hortense wrapped themselves around him and bore him off to their enclave. By now they had glasses and a couple of bottles standing at the ready on Trixie, so there was no reason for the baroness to proffer drinks. She shrugged, fetched herself another bottle, and a hopeful empty glass, and returned to Joleen and tried to think positive thoughts.

When Jake Thorogood arrived, his torn dressing gown failing to cover his bare shins, she was encouraged that she didn't recognise him, but their exchange of names brought neither of them comfort and he was borne off so fast by Fortune and Pringle that there was no time even for a cursory nod. By now the anti-baroness faction had spread over two sofas, so the occupants had to converse across Trixie. She could hear occasional words like 'bitch', 'rude' and 'Neanderthal' which she assumed meant she was under discussion.

She was momentarily cheered when the next entrant was also someone she didn't recognise. He was a dapper man in his fifties, whose expensive haircut, well-fitting tuxedo, and red satin waistcoat seemed to have weathered recent challenges better than the clothes of his fellow captives.

He saw her first, walked over and held out his hand. 'Hey, I'm Chester Herblock.'

'Jack Troutbeck,' she said. But before their handshake was naturally concluded, Fortune and Pringle had swooped once again and hustled him away. Pringle made an attempt to move one of Joleen's sofas, but it proved to be rooted to the floor, so the sofa containing Fortune became full to overflowing.

The next arrival failed to get the door open, and the baroness, being nearest to it, obligingly tugged at the door handle and revealed a stick insect in a sable coat over a long crumpled dirty white silk dress and tot-tering on six-inch gold sandals. Herblock was already there to gather her in his arms, crying, 'Marilyn, darling. We're reunited at last,' and support her back to his group. She was so thin, noted the baroness sourly, that even with her coat on, she made almost no demand on space. Her face was as unlined as that of a fifteen year old: the baroness guessed she was in her sixties.

When no one seemed to recognise the dark young man in a pinstripe suit, pink shirt, matching tie, and fedora when he tumbled through the door, the baroness hoped she might be in luck, but within seconds Pringle had called 'Charlie' loudly, and identified him to the others as 'a dear friend and the purchaser of a darling Fontana'; he had been clasped to their corporate bosom. Herblock gave him his seat and perched elegantly on Trixie's glass top.

By now the baroness was feeling positively lonely in her splendid isolation, but she was not yet ready to do anything about it. She eavesdropped on the whines about food and the smell and the vying for sympathy, but while she snarled to herself about their having the instincts of a herd of sheep, she had some sneaking sympathy for them. She, at least, was not starving: her last secret meal before leaving her cell had been full of carbohydrates. When, occasionally, someone looked over at her with an expression of mingled disbelief and loathing, she raised her glass in a gesture of good fellowship. And when they looked away again, she put a brave face on it and tried not to think about the immediate future. When there was another commotion at the door, she groaned inwardly. All I need now, she thought, to add to the gaiety of nations, is Sir Nicholas Serota himself.

It proved to be instead an attractive rangy blonde, in skintight red jeans, snakeskin boots, and a black top with a neckline that revealed most of her chest. She cast her eye around the room and said: 'Jeez, I don't know about you drongos, but I'm as mad as a cut snake.'

Entranced by the appearance and demeanour of the newcomer, who identified herself as Anastasia Holliday, the baroness decided instantly to make her a friend and ally. After Fortune and Pringle had fallen upon Anastasia with shrieks of joy, and there had been a few minutes for the sharing of recent experiences, the baroness took her by the elbow, detached her from the melee and said, 'I'm Jack, Anastasia. And I like Australians. There is only champagne, but here's a glass of it. Come and sit beside me and tell me about yourself.'

To her relief, Anastasia put up no resistance. 'This is a right crockload of shit and no mistake, Jack. I suppose it's a relief that I'm not alone. I've been like a bandicoot on a burnt ridge.' She lowered her voice. 'But it's not good news to be locked up with those dipsticks? If I have to be in an asylum, I don't want to be with star fuckers.'

'Aren't some of them your friends?'

'Might have said so a few days ago, but I've

had plenty of time to think. Being hungry makes you sharper. One think I thunk was that the arty-farties I've been hanging with – some of them are over there – were pseuds and fuckwits and as dry as a dead dingo's donger.'

The baroness raised an eyebrow. 'Weren't some of them instrumental in making you rich and famous?'

'Oh, sure. But just because you've got a good pimp doesn't make you a happy hooker. I'm over being a show pony.'

Everyone jumped as Sarkovsky's voice announced: 'You all here. Now you listen. I Beeg Brother.'

'You Oleg Sarkovsky,' said the baroness.

'Shuddup you. You talk about me, you die. I Beeg Brother. This Beeg Brother house.'

'What's he talking about?' whimpered Fortune.

'I don't know,' said Herblock.

'Strewth,' said Anastasia. 'Where've you been? Everyone knows about Big Brother. Biggest TV show all over the world.'

'You explain them,' came the instruction.

Crisply, Anastasia explained how people volunteered to shack up together, be spied on around the clock, and win a lot of money.

'You say them eviction consequence of task,' prodded the voice.

'What's the prize?' asked Thorogood hopefully.

'No prize,' said the voice.

'This is illogical,' said the baroness. 'What's our incentive to do these tasks if we all want to be evicted?'

'You evicted, you killed,' said the voice helpfully.

'You cannot be serious,' said Jason Pringle. 'Oh, Bubbles,' he shrieked, throwing himself on Henry Fortune's ample breast.

'I'm sure he's not,' said the baroness gruffly. 'He's just trying to frighten us.'

'It is truth. Now, feeeeerst task. Laidee Troutbeck eat hamburger.'

The baroness's scowl cleared. 'I don't mind that,' she said, 'as long, of course, as it's made of Aberdeen Angus beef. Rump is a possibility, though sirloin is usually preferable. It must have been well hung. And mind you make sure there's enough fat. And that it's coarsely ground. And, of course, rare. Now with it, I want...'

Though oblivious to the incredulous expressions on the faces surrounding her, she registered the menace in the 'Shuddup and follow instruction' that boomed from the speakers. 'The hamburger McDonald's. Surf Turf. Weeth processed cheese.' He laughed merrily. 'From yesterday.'

'It doesn't matter if it's last year's,' said the baroness bitterly. 'Not being food, it doesn't decompose.'

'And with chocolate meeelkshake. Beeg,

beeg, super-size.'

'You cannot be serious, Oleg,' she cried piteously. 'Why would you do that to me?'

'I say you, you name me Oleg, you die. I Beeg Brother. I very serious man. I hear all you say. Anyone talk about Oleg Sarkovsky, Albanians kill him. Hamburger hatch. Kitchen. Eat. Drink.'

'I'm certainly not going to consume such muck,' said the baroness haughtily, grateful that – unlike the others – she wasn't starving. 'I'd rather die.'

'OK. No problem. I happy help.'

'Stuff and nonsense, Ol... Big Brother. You're losing your marbles. You can't bully me.'

'He can kill you,' whispered Pringle, whose normally supercilious expression had long since been replaced by one of abject terror.

'Rubbish,' said the baroness. 'He's having a lark. There's nothing to be worried about.'

'You not eat. No food in house. Never. All very hungry and die.'

'He's bluffing,' said the baroness. She looked at her companions for reassurance and found none.

'Please eat it,' sobbed Pringle.

The baroness looked uncertainly at her companions and saw that Marilyn had begun to cry. Then Anastasia leant over, clapped her on the thigh and said, 'Think bushtucker trial.'

'Think what?'

'It's something people do on reality shows to prove they're tough.' The baroness obviously wavered. 'Look, Jack, if I was you I'd stop grizzling and get on with it. We're in the shit and no mistake. Would you rather eat the Macca's or cark it?'

'Cark it?'

'Like he said. Die.' Anastasia made a cutting motion across her throat.

'I'm not sure.'

'It wouldn't be just you,' said Pringle. 'It'd be all of us. We could end up cannibals.'

The baroness ruminated for a moment, turned her head towards the skeletal Pringle and sighed. 'I suppose if you put it that way, there are worse things than a revolting hamburger. None of you looks edible – except possibly Anastasia.'

She heaved herself up and surveyed her companions. 'I want to do this alone.' And assuming an expression so agonised that Marie Antoinette might have considered it over the top as she mounted the steps to the guillotine, the baroness gazed neither to right nor left as she marched into the kitchen and opened the hatch.

As there was no door to the kitchen, the nine starving people could not but hear the baroness's loud curses as she chomped and slurped her way through her test. There was little sympathy for her when she emerged from the kitchen complaining that she had never had such a disgusting meal in her life. She marched over to the most visible camera and said, 'I've done it. Now what about food for the others?'

'Feerst you go in Diary Room.'

'What?'

'Red door.'

Had the baroness ever seen Big Brother, she would have been less surprised to find a tiny room furnished only with an enormous purple armchair. 'Seet.'

As she sat down, her eyes flickered over to the door opposite the one through which she'd come.

'You crazy if you think escape. Albanians has machine guns.'

'Nothing could have been further from my thoughts.'

'Now. Orders.'

'For food, do you mean?'

'Shuddup. Orders from me. For you. I give food. Drink. Then you start argument.'

'About what?'

'Art. I want argument. Beeg argument. You make them crazy.'

'Is this just for fun, or is there a deeper reason?'

'You discover, maybe. Now you follow instruction. And not say from me. Go in now, say food here in short time.'

'We're all filthy. Any chance of a change of

clothes? And toothbrushes and razors and that kind of thing?'

'Maybe.'

Discretion, concluded the baroness uncharacteristically, was undoubtedly now to be embraced rather than valour. 'OK,' she said. 'Thank you.'

Akim Zeka had been looking at his watch all afternoon, waiting for the moment when he could stop watching those boring people and get away to Edona. The boss had been very reluctant to let him leave even for a short time, but he needed Akim to be ready to direct proceedings later on, and he had known Akim long enough to know that sexual frustration made him erratic. Sarkovsky wished that this operation could be run by someone calm and effortlessly competent like Taylor, but the butler had made it clear that what he did was to run Sarkovsky's UK establishments and that he wanted no involvement in anything that might be less than respectable. 'I realise that with your business interests you need tough people to protect you, sir,' he told his boss. 'But I want nothing to do with those uncouth Albanians.'

Which left Sarkovsky stuck with Akim Zeka and his family to do his dirty work. They were effective enough in their way, and he was pleased with their complete absence of scruples in the way they protected his property and dealt with a few of his troublesome rivals. The preparations and the kidnappings had gone well, even if they had failed with Saatchi and Serota.

'You not forget, Akim. Tonight important.'

'Everything ready. Dritan in charge. I will be back in two hours. All will go very well.'

'No drink?'

'No drink. I go now, Boss. Be back soon.' Akim rushed upstairs and out of the building, jumped into his car and drove as fast as he could to the family brothel in Camden Town.

Chapter Eight

The food was mostly cold meat, cheese, and bread, but it came soon and was plentiful and everyone except the baroness fell on it. Still feeling slightly nauseous, she picked at a few bits of cheese, but concentrated on the accompanying reasonably decent claret. Having remembered uneasily that she had once held forth to Sarkovsky on the evils of Surf 'n' Turf, the baroness decided that since he seemed to have gone mad, in the foreseeable future it might be prudent to keep her mouth shut about what she didn't like. She also resolved to obey instructions with the minimum of fuss.

When they had eaten, they were instructed to look in the hatch, where they found ten sports bags with their names on them. Instructions were to change their clothes quickly and throw what they were wearing in the bath. If their spirits lifted slightly at seeing basic toiletries, they fell when they saw their changes of clothing, but there were no protests.

They reconvened in the living room wearing violently coloured shell suits that made everyone except Anastasia look ridiculous. They were hardly relaxed, but the tension dissipated slightly as the wine bottles emptied. Even the hostility towards the baroness had somewhat abated. She had, after all, succeeded in her task.

By now inmates were dispersed more evenly on the sofas and conversation was general. They were too scared of Big Brother to discuss what might happen, so they engaged in cosy chitchat about the cosmopolitan nature of their world. Anastasia, Charlie Briggs, and the baroness, who had had little to do with this glittering scene, had nothing to contribute to the orgy of reminiscence.

Marilyn Falucci Lamont, it emerged, was a legendary patron of contemporary art who gave mega bucks to famous art galleries and museums and had distinguished collections of her own in her various houses. Her diary was constructed around major art events around the world. She had first met Fortune at a Venice Biennale, Pringle in Madrid and Thorogood in Morocco. Herblock, her long-term adviser, was as peripatetic, flitting around the globe finding new artists for his eager collectors. He had formed relationships with many art colleges, which is how he had come to know and trust Gavin Truss and Hortense Wilde.

The baroness remained silent and listened keenly, but the conversation was too general to give her an opening, so she seized the opportunity of a pause to look at the group with what she hoped was a humble expression and speak to Fortune. 'Henry, when Jason arrived you were just about to tell me about the art in our bathroom.'

Perhaps forgetting that his dignity was undermined by his lime green shell suit, Fortune turned towards her and put the tips of his fingers together. 'Ah, me,' he said. 'The bathroom. Yes, what we have ... or appear to have ... are a Piero Manzoni, a Terence Koh, and Wim Delvoye's sketch of *Cloaca*. Magnificent! And how witty to locate them there!'

'Would you be kind enough to dilate a little on them for me?'

He looked at her pityingly and sighed. 'Where to start?'

'At the beginning. We have plenty of time.'

Fortune picked up his glass, sat back and

looked at her over his glasses. 'It is hard to overestimate the influence of Piero Manzoni. Inspired by Lucio Fontana – of whose work our friend Charlie here recently has been lucky enough to secure a fine example – his ironic questioning of the nature of the art object would prefigure conceptual art and become an inspiration for the *Arte Povera* movement.' He took a sip of champagne. 'I'll explain about that later.'

'How kind,' said the baroness, and reached for the bottle of claret resting on Joleen.

'Manzoni's father was a philistine.' The baroness repressed the desire to say 'like me', and instead put on the fake interested look she had had to acquire many years before for professional purposes. 'He made tin cans. When he told Piero that he thought his art was shit, Piero conceived a magnificent response with an exhibition of ninety signed cans called *Merda d'artista*, priced by weight based on the then value of gold. Since then, of course, their intrinsic value has soared. Nick Serota got hold of one for the Tate for only £23,000 in 2000. He'd have had to pay more than £100,000 only a few years later.'

'Oh, my God,' said Marilyn. 'But that's less than forty thousand dollars. Chester, I've paid much much more for my three tins.'

'Yes, hon, but you didn't buy them until a few years later.'

172

'You bought three tins of shit?' asked Anastasia.

'Sure I did. But two of them were for museums.'

'What a generous woman you are,' said the baroness. 'You were saying, Henry. About Manzoni and ... what do you call it? ... *Arte Povera?*'

The condescension in his voice went up a notch. 'Piero's tragic death in 1963 at only twenty-nine predated a time of economic crisis when in Italy gifted radical young artists rejected the straitjacket of traditional expensive materials like bronze or canvas in favour of openness to, if you like, impoverished alternatives like wood and coal.' The baroness noted that Fortune seemed to be revelling in the sonorousness of his own voice. 'Another seminal moment in the development of conceptual art.' He sighed. 'I look at the Kounellis room in Tate Modern, and again, I envy Nick.'

'Thank you,' said the baroness, noting he seemed to have gone into a jealous reverie. 'And Koh?'

Fortune put his glass down on Joleen, shut his eyes and clasped his hands together. 'What a moment it was! Art Basel 2006! I'm embarrassed to say I had never heard of Terence Koh and then ... aaah! ... I was led to his installation.'

The baroness raised an enquiring eyebrow.

173

'It sounds so simple. Just eighty-eight glass cases, some of which had gold-plated pieces of what he said was his own excrement.'

'Why eighty-eight?'

'A lucky number in Chinese culture: the young man is Chinese-Canadian. So, as you can imagine, I thought of Manzoni; I thought of *Arta Povera*; I embraced the irony that is the combination of the poorest and the richest of materials. Collectors fought to buy the installation. Charles Saatchi lost out, but he gave Terence pride of place at his Royal Academy Show the next year.'

'We were late to Basel,' said Marilyn. 'Otherwise, I'd have got it.'

Herblock patted her hand. 'You got so much else there, sweetie.'

'Nick has one in the series,' said Pringle. '*A New World Order Lies in this Golden Age*, but apparently what looks like excrement is entirely made of bronze.'

'Does that make it worth more or less?' asked Charlie Briggs, who seemed to be finding Fortune's lecture hard to follow.

'A good question, Charlie, but hard to answer. The market can be fickle.'

'What I find touching,' interjected Gavin Truss, 'is that Koh has made many hundreds of thousands of dollars from selling gold-plated shit – from what we call his conceptual bling period – but that he also cares about students, to whom he sells it in its natural state for only $150. As he points out, they're losing nothing, since his shit is worth its weight in gold.'

'Heart-warming,' said the baroness. 'And the sketch?'

'Wim Delvoye's sketch of his *Cloaca*,' said Fortune. 'The digestive machine he designed that turns food into faeces.'

'And its point is?' asked the baroness.

He shook his head at her stupidity. 'Its point is the pointlessness of life, since there is nothing more pointless than an elaborate machine that reduces food to waste. Mind you, I wonder if by selling the output he undermines his existential point.' He sighed. 'Ah, me! These are the unanswerable questions.'

The baroness replaced her glass on Joleen. 'May I make a few observations, Sir Henry?'

He gave a rather superior smirk. 'If you have any worth making.'

'Well, here are a few. Firstly, like Duchamp with his urinal, Manzoni was making a joke, not creating art. It was tough on him that he didn't stay alive long enough to savour it. I'm sure he deliberately spread the rumour that he might have cheated and that the contents might be other than promised, that is, not what it says on the tin.' The baroness never worried that obvious jokes had probably been made thousands of times before, so she snorted at her own wit. She was pleased to see that Fortune was looking furious.

'Manzoni would have loved the very conceptual-art dilemma that a can cannot be opened to see what is inside because if it's opened, the can will apparently no longer be a work of art. In the same way – as I learnt from a recent visit to Tat Modern – Jeff Koons's hoovers will cease to be art if anyone turns one on.

'This is, of course, all bollocks. Tins of shit aren't art. Nor are hoovers and anyone who says they are is either soft in the head, corrupt, or a victim of mass hysteria.'

Fortune was sitting up and expostulating. She gestured at him to be quiet. 'Secondly, Terence Koh discovered, like many artists who preceded him, that the art world is dominated by people who care only for money, and that it can be taken from them in bucketloads if you press the right buttons. Gold-plated shit isn't art: it's a novelty. The only people who could genuinely like it would be coprophiliacs. Like James Joyce.

'Thirdly, *Arte Povera* should be translated as poor art, except it isn't good enough to be poor. Mostly it isn't art at all. What is art in that ridiculous room in Tat Modern dedicated to the wretched Kounellis, the patriarch of that silly movement?'

'Silly? Silly? Oh, my God,' screamed Truss. 'You're talking about the d'Offay bequest that includes Kounellis's magnificent

1969 *Untitled.*'

'The bugger's too lazy to give any of his stuff a title. Are you talking about the sacks of lentils and various other dry goods? How are they art?'

'I bought a few of his Untitleds,' said Marilyn. 'Weren't they scribbles on a piece of paper, Chester?'

'I'm not sure which ones you got, sweetie, but I'm sure they were fine.'

'They'd better be. They cost more than a hundred K.'

'You've been very quiet,' said the baroness to Jake Thorogood. 'How are they art?'

He shrugged. 'Can't say I'm a great fan, but whatever floats your boat.'

'How can you say that?' said Hortense. 'I'm sure you've praised him in the past.'

'Very likely, Hortense. I write for a liberal newspaper, so I have to be right-on. But just at the moment, I'm not in the mood.'

The baroness looked at him with interest. 'You cared about great art once, Jake. I used to read you until you embraced the ugly and talentless. You really lost any scruples you ever had, didn't you?'

He shrugged again. Complete silence descended on the group. The baroness was contemplating how to get them arguing again when the disembodied voice broke in. 'Laidee Troutbeck to Diary Room.'

She threw herself into the chair and gazed

at the camera. 'Was the argument what you wanted?'

'Good argument. You make them angry.'

'I certainly achieved that.'

'Who worst?'

'In what way worst?'

'You think worst.'

'Heavens, that's a big question with such a crew. I'd have to think.'

'I want answer now. Who worst this night?'

'An embarrassment of riches, but if you force me, Jake Thorogood annoyed me most. He knows better and he's not even hiding his corruption from himself.'

'Bedroom black door. Key on table. Say them choose bed. Now. Lights go after fifteen minutes.'

The baroness left him, walked past the group and unlocked the bedroom. Having surveyed it briefly, she turned round. 'We have a bedroom which should be to the liking of anyone who admires Tracey Emin, but I can't say I'm keen.'

The bedroom contained five double beds that looked as if they hadn't been made for weeks. They were all strewn with the same detritus that had made Emin famous. Neon lights around the room said: '*You Had It Coming*', '*Who's Sorry Now?*', '*Here Today, Gone Tomorrow*'. When she spotted the one saying '*Just Deserts*', the baroness winced.

The housemates surveyed the stained

sheets, the bottles, the used condoms and the rest. 'I'm not sleeping in that filth,' cried Marilyn.

'Nor me,' said Hortense. 'We can take sofas.'

The baroness signed. 'I'm sorry to have to tell you that Big Brother says if anyone doesn't sleep in a bed, there'll be no food to-morrow. I'm afraid Miss Emin has designed our beds and we must lie in them.'

Herblock took Marilyn's hand. 'Will you share one with me, hon?'

Jason Pringle was heard to say sotto voce to Fortune that no doubt he'd want to shack up with Charlie Briggs, but the response of 'Sweetie, how could you think that?' seemed sincere.

'Why don't you girls bunk in together?' asked Fortune of the baroness and Hortense, but the look of horror on both their faces put paid to that.

'I'll go with Gavin,' said Hortense.

'And then there were two,' said the baroness brightly. 'So it's me and Jake and Charlie and Anastasia. Or not.'

'It might be good for Charlie and Anastasia,' said Thorogood, 'but I fear nothing would induce me to share a bed with you.'

'I feel rather the same way.'

'Come on, Jack,' said Anastasia. 'We're mates now. I'm going to stick to you like shit to a blanket.'

'An unfortunate image when you think what we'll be sleeping on, Anastasia.'

Anastasia laughed merrily. 'Just call it art, Jack. Now let's go for it.'

In her violet shell suit, the baroness tumbled into her disgusting bed feeling that indeed it was true that even the darkest cloud had a vestige of a silver lining. Not everyone felt that, for in a room containing ten people, five proved to be snorers. Still, they had all had so much to drink, that even the normally light sleepers eventually found oblivion and were so deeply asleep that they failed to notice four men coming softly into the bedroom and removing a comatose Jake Thorogood.

Pooley was shaving when the seven o'clock news told him a body had been found in the early hours hanging in the undercroft on the South Bank, and that foul play was suspected. Within five minutes he had dressed, kissed his sleeping wife, and was out of the door. He couldn't raise anyone at the Yard who seemed to know any more about the corpse, but he had a bad feeling.

By eight Pooley and Milton had informally identified Jake Thorogood's corpse from photographs. The official identification had to await his brother's arrival, but they were in no doubt. He'd been well dead when found at twenty past two in the morning. The pathologist was certain he'd been killed before midnight. 'Garrotted first with wire: hanged later with rope. As you can see, he was bollock naked and had a bunch of black balloons in his hand. Odd business. He'd had a lot to drink, but that hardly explains it.'

With the help of Morrison, palpably indignant at having to be back on duty so early, and of Sarah Byrne, who looked both upset and excited, the story was put together.

'I thought he was wearing an overcoat,' she said, 'but it fell off immediately. Like a loose shroud. Vernon cut the rope he was hanging from and we got him down, but he was cold and dead.'

'Go back to how you found him,' said Milton. 'And don't forget the placard.'

'Yes, well first I thought he was some kind of graffiti,' said Morrison. 'And when the wino said...'

'What wino?'

'The wino that told us he was there.'

'Where is he?'

'Dunno,' said Morrison.

'He disappeared while we were trying to resuscitate the deceased, sir,' said Byrne. 'Maybe he was scared. But I know what he looked like.'

'OK, Sarah. Go on, Vernon.'

'When the wino said there was a body in the corner in the middle of all that graffiti, I thought it was one of Banksy's vandalisms. I'd seen some of his stuff with hangin' men and balloons.' He paused. 'I tell a lie. The balloons were lifting some little girl, weren't they? But they were Banksy anyway. I think the wife bought a postcard of it once.

'Anyway, when we got to the corner, before the shroud fell off, I could see the word Banksy.'

'As you can see from these photos,' said Milton, 'it was attached to the garment.'

Morrison's brow furrowed. 'I didn't see that bit before Banksy,' he said. 'What's it say? Homidge? It's spelt wrong.'

'It's "o-maj",' said Pooley. 'French. That's why it's spelt *"Hommage* to Banksy". And, underneath, "Man with Balloons", which is a reference to Banksy's "Girl with Balloons".'

'That's a bit sick, isn't it, sir?'

'It certainly is, Sarah.'

'So what's with the 'ommidge word?'

'Hommage is close to the same meaning as our homage, Vernon, but where that means paying respect, according to the dictionary, o-maj means something expressive done in honour of someone using elements of their style.'

Morrison looked glazed.

'The murderer is paying *hommage* to Banksy in the manner in which he's killed Thorogood. Or,' added Pooley, who liked to be precise, 'has had him killed.'

Milton's phone rang. 'Thorogood's brother is here, Ellis. Look after him. I'll see you after I've seen the AC.'

He turned to the constables. 'Well done,' he said. 'Well observed and well handled. Congratulations.'

Morrison looked at him, hopeful they might be given extra time off in lieu. 'I know from experience,' said Milton, 'that when you've had a shock like this, the important thing is to go on as if nothing's happened. Go home and get some sleep now. I wish you a peaceful patrol tonight.'

The nine were woken abruptly by the sound of a reveille and the voice saying 'Geddup you now.' In the ensuing melee, with shell-suited people flowing between bedroom and living room and bathroom and kitchen, no one realised for an hour that they were one short. The sheer joy of having showers and baths (free of the clothes that had been removed as they slept) distracted them pleasantly as much as the presence in the kitchen of basic breakfast ingredients.

There was a general attempt at civility so effective that the baroness even insisted on giving Fortune and Pringle the first pieces of toast she had extracted from the toaster. So it was not until breakfast was finished and they went into the living room that Charlie Briggs looked around and asked,

'Where's Jake?'

A quick search confirmed there was no Jake in any of the public rooms: the diary room was locked.

'He can't be gone,' screamed Pringle.

'He must have escaped,' said Briggs.

'How?' asked Anastasia. 'I've examined this shit hole from floor to ceiling and the only way out is that door over there that's locked and barred. It would take a battering ram to get it open.'

At that moment the voice instructed Laidee Troutbeck to go to the diary room, which proved now to be unlocked.

She threw herself into the vast chair. On the table before her was a pile of pads and pencils. 'Where's Jake Thorogood?'

'He is place of dead person.'

'You mean the morgue?'

'Yes.'

'Are you serious, Ol... Big Brother?'

'Oh, yes. I serious man.'

'Why would you want to kill him?'

'He cheat me. He say Banksy real Banksy but not real Banksy.' Sarkovsky sniggered. 'So my men killing him. With balloons. Your idea.'

'My idea?'

'You say you killing Banksy with balloons.'

The baroness's head was spinning. 'Did Thorogood cost you a fortune with the fake Banksy?'

'Not beeg money. Small money, but he make Oleg appeeer stupid man.'

'And that's enough reason to murder him?'

'Nobody make Oleg Sarkovsky appeeer stupid man. I execute.'

'I don't know if I believe you, but if I tell them what you've said there will be mass hysteria and there'll be no arguments.'

'You say them anything. I not interest.'

'So if I say he's just been evicted, you won't contradict me?'

'What means this contradeect?'

'Say I am wrong.'

'Maybe. Maybe not.'

'Presumably you're angry with everyone. Why did you choose him?'

'You say worst.'

She began to expostulate and then stopped. What was the point of arguing with a lunatic? Damage limitation was the order of the day. And dragging things out in the hope that the cavalry would ride over the range before it was too late.

'May I go back to them?'

'Give them paper and pencil and say them drawing.'

'Draw what?'

'Horse. Horse eating. Horse running. Horse fucking. Then lunch and drink. Then argument again. Then game.'

'Game?'

'I say later.'

The baroness got up and began to collect the materials. 'Laidee Troutbeck.'

'Yes, Big Brother.'

'You say me this night who worst.'

'I've never even seen a dead body,' said Max Thorogood. 'It's a shock. Especially when you're not expecting it and it's your kid brother.'

Pooley muttered consolatory phrases. 'May I get you coffee, Mr Thorogood?'

'Yes, please. Are we going to talk about Jake?'

'If you're up to it.'

When they had both been furnished with indifferent liquid, Thorogood had a sip and grimaced. 'So what's happened?'

'We don't really know any more than is in the newspapers, Mr Thorogood, though we do have a line of enquiry that we can't yet discuss.'

'No surprises there.'

'Is there anything you think might help us?'

'Don't think so, Chief Inspector. I haven't really known Jake since we were kids. There were just the two of us and we fought the way boys do, wrestling around the garden, fighting for the honour of our football teams. All that kind of thing. But I looked out for him when we were at school and protected him from the kids who thought he had airs and graces. But we were chalk and cheese. I went off to train as an actuary and I know he despised me for doing something so dull. Then he said he wanted to do a fine arts degree and at first I tried to take an interest. Mum and Dad used to take us to art galleries a bit and I knew my Rembrandt from my Reubens.

'For a while, I loved listening to Jake talking about artists and I was so proud when he became an art critic. I'd read his review every week. We didn't really see each other. No fallings out. But how could you expect us to have anything in common any more? Mum and Dad died early, I was living in Salford with a wife who was a district nurse and two children. Jake was being paid to go to glamorous places with glamorous people and he didn't want to commit, so there was a succession of gorgeous girls of the kind who hang about that world wanting to be famous or rich.

'But then what he wrote stopped seeming real. He seemed to be obsessed with the fashionable. I hate to say it, with my little bro lying dead in that morgue and me terrified that he might have had a really horrible death, but he sold out along the way. I don't know if it was to fashion or to money, but as an actuary, I'd say it might be a bit of both. It takes courage for a critic to hold out against the herd and, if you're hanging out with the mega-rich, it would be really heroic not to want a bit of the action. I mean, you're going to say the Tate Modern is full of rubbish and expect to get good commissions? Pul-ease!'

He had another sip of his coffee, made a face and put it on the table. 'Did he die because he sold out, Chief Inspector?'

Pooley had found a minute to send a text to Amiss and Mary Lou telling them the news, so Amiss was primed and ready for Milton's press conference. He briefly expressed regret at having to announce that Thorogood had been murdered, told them where the body had been found, refused to give any further information for the moment, admitted there were concerns for the well-being of the other nine hostages, assured them the police were working flat out to find them, denied having any idea who was responsible, and then excused himself and went back into the Yard.

Pausing only to text Rachel, Amiss rang Miss Stamp.

'Oh, Mr Amiss, I'm so glad to hear from you. Is there any news? We're frantic here. And those dreadful journalists keep snooping around asking questions about the Mistress. We won't let them in but we can't keep them out of the grounds. They've been hammering on the door and peering through the windows all morning. And I've had to put the phone down on several of them already.'

'I'm afraid there is worrying news, Miss

Stamp. Jake Thorogood, one of those who went missing at the same time as the Mistress, has been found murdered. It's just been announced.'

There was a terrified squawk. 'Oh, Mr Amiss, that's terrible. What happened to him? Is there no possibility it was an accident?'

'I'm afraid he was strangled and then hanged. The police are sure it was murder.'

'The Mistress must be in terrible danger. Why haven't the police found her?'

'I don't know, Miss Stamp. We must remember what an optimist she is and think like her. And we know she's indestructible.'

He heard a sob and felt like joining in. 'Let us do what we can to help her. I need to get hold of the Mistress's friend Myles Cavendish who's abroad and won't know anything about this. Do you have his mobile number?'

'I wouldn't have that, Mr Amiss. You know how secretive the Mistress is about her private life.'

'I do, Miss Stamp. Can you go through any address books she has and maybe old diaries?'

'Oh, Mr Amiss. Won't she be annoyed?'

'I think I can safely say that if she could, Miss Stamp, she would give you *carte blanche*.'

'I'll run up and search her study now, Mr Amiss. But it could take quite a while.'

'And if there's nothing written down, Miss Stamp, you might need to explore her computer. She does have one, doesn't she?'

'Yes and no, Mr Amiss. She hates it, but she learnt to do email. First I'll look for diaries.'

'Is there news of Jake?' asked Pringle.

'I'm told he had a stomach upset during the night and had to be taken to a doctor. It looks like he's got a nasty infection, so he may not be back.'

'Why are you always the go-between with Big Brother?' asked Fortune. 'It seems very suspicious to me.'

'And me,' said Pringle. Most of the others nodded.

'After all, how do we know you're passing on the instructions correctly? And are you an experienced negotiator?'

'I don't know,' said the baroness. 'I wouldn't have chosen the role. Maybe he wants me because I'm the oldest. Anyway, since he's listening in much of the time, presumably he thinks I'm reporting him correctly. Now get cracking,' she said. 'He would like us to draw horses doing anything horses do.'

'Why?' asked Briggs. 'I can't draw.'

'I can't draw either, Charlie, but we are guests of Big Brother and if he wants us to draw, I suggest we should do our best. If we do, I've been promised that we'll have lunch to follow, accompanied by wine. If we don't, there won't be any lunch.' She didn't mention she had had a great deal of difficulty in persuading Sarkovsky to use the carrot of lunch rather than the stick of murder.

The inmates set to with a will. The baroness, who hadn't sketched since school, found to her surprise that she produced something that closely resembled a horse, even if its legs seemed worryingly splayed. After an hour, she surveyed the results. Apart from Marilyn – who admitted to having once had a home art tutor and was competent – the older generation achieved mediocrity. Having been taught to draw at school, they managed to draw animals that were identifiably equine. Briggs was bad and Anastasia was hopeless: no one not on hallucinatory drugs could have seen a horse anywhere in her bold and talentless lines.

The baroness was intensely relieved that there would be a pause for food, drink, and argument before she had to go back to the Diary Room to make a judgement. The gathering had passed that stage of hunger when they would have fallen on gruel with shrieks of gratitude, but they were still rather pathetically grateful for having a choice of several pizzas as well as a decent claret.

Although the baroness's philosophy of life was so *carpe diem* that she always saw the glass as half-full, her appetite was severely blunted by the knowledge of what she would have to do that evening. Besides which, she didn't think much of the pizza.

Chapter Nine

Amiss had spent the rest of the morning at his computer, continuing his obsessive hunt for news, which was broken only by worried conversations with friends. It was just after midday when George, the homeless man who had led the police to the body, turned up at the offices of a national newspaper and offered his story in exchange for help in getting off the streets. And so it was that by early afternoon Milton had to come clean about the balloons and the placard. The '*Hommage* Murder' went viral on the internet.

A certain calm had descended on the group after lunch, which the baroness realised she had to dispel. She poured out some more wine into all the glasses on offer. She was sparing with hers, for she had concluded that if you have the power of life and death, you shouldn't use it when half-cut. 'Just from curiosity,' she asked, 'what do we think of each other's horses? Gavin, perhaps you'd care to tell us why we have in this dungeon a cross-section of those who dominate art, and between us only one of us is better than pathetic.'

'There's photography these days. Why should anyone need to draw a horse?' asked Truss.

Charlie Briggs's brow furrowed. 'You mean that art has nothing to add to a photo?'

'Not a lot,' said Truss. 'Since the camera, there's no point.'

'If photos can replace art,' asked the baroness, 'why is Stubbs's *Whistlejacket* the main draw in the National Gallery?'

'Because tourists know no better,' said Hortense Wilde.

'Stubbs spent a great deal of his life dissecting horses so as to understand how muscle and bone and spirit interacted,' said the baroness. 'He gave us many portraits that have enchanted generations and in *Whistlejacket* he showed us the majesty of the horse and the brilliance of the humble artist. What do you offer instead?'

'We must move on,' said Hortense. 'That's why dreary old-fashioned skills are so unimportant. They might momentarily matter to a generation stuck in the past, but today's technology replaces them.'

'Like what?' asked the baroness politely.

'A drawing app.'

'If I'm not mistaken, Hortense, David Hockney, possibly our best artist of the last fifty years, uses technology as a tool of his art but deplores the fact that the young are no longer imparted any skills.'

Hortense laughed mirthlessly. 'Oh, for heaven's sake, Jack. Hockney! Really! For God's sake, he does landscapes. Since the world was changed by Damien, how is Hockney even shown?'

'So you didn't like his Royal Academy show? I thought it fine and so did tens of thousands of others.'

Hortense looked at her with an expression so patronising it was as much as the baroness could do not to hit her. Then she remembered what she might have to do to her, and the impulse passed.

'Who cares what the public think?' asked Hortense. 'What do they know? Their opinion is worth nothing.'

'Tell me something, Hortense. If this minute you could replace all this Hirst stuff with Stubbs by waving a wand, what would you do?'

Hortense looked around her, caught sight of the cow's head and shuddered.

'Oh, for God's sake, be honest,' said Briggs. 'This whole fucking place is a nightmare. Smelly dead cows and flies and murder weapons. Anything would be better.'

'Yeah,' said Anastasia. 'I'd like something cheerful.'

Fortune assumed his most pompous voice.

'At least we have great art here, Anastasia. Are you suggesting we'd be better off with Jack Vettriano or Beryl Cook?'

Pringle and Truss laughed sycophantically.

'I've seen some Beryl Cook,' said Anastasia. 'All those cheerful fat women having a ball. Yes, I'd trade them in for all the ghoulish stuff any day.'

'And I like Vettriano,' said Briggs. 'Do you remember, Jason? I wanted to buy one of his but you said everyone would laugh at me.'

'And I was right, Charlie. No decent critic or curator would touch either of those pathetic bourgeois throwbacks. The hedge-fundies know that.'

'If I ever get out of here,' said Briggs, 'I will never take anyone's advice about art again.'

A silence descended. Then the dreaded voice sounded. 'Now you play game. Laidee Troutbeck, Diary Room.'

'So, what did the AC say, Jim?' asked Pooley.

'He's finally got it and he's alarmed. Just for now he's OK'd the surveillance, but he hasn't decided yet if we should look for a warrant. He's having another think.'

'And the Commissioner?'

'The AC said he'll be back tomorrow and expressly forbade me from bothering him in the middle of his important discussions at the Interpol conference.' Milton shrugged. 'What can I do?'

'Doesn't he get it?'

'Doesn't he get what?'

'Thorogood is just the first.'

'How can you know that?'

'There are ten of them. As far as we know, the worst Thorogood did to Sarkovsky was to give him a bum steer on something which by his standards cost small change. Allegra thought it was less than a million. Thorogood was a critic, for God's sake, Jim. Not an international swindler of oligarchs.'

'Did his brother know anything helpful?'

'He thought he'd sold out, which is what Jack said. But Sarkovsky is a scoundrel, so why should he get prissy about Thorogood lacking ethics?'

'Because his lack of ethics cost Sarkovsky money, I suppose.'

'In cahoots with Pringle and Fortune. Anyway, what we have to face is that if Thorogood, whose sins were minor, ended up the way he has, why should anyone else be safe?'

'I get that.'

'Worse.'

'There's worse?'

'You know that evening with Jack in ffeatherstonehaugh's that you missed.'

'Well, seeing I missed it, not really.'

'I told you a bit about it. The endless diatribe against contemporary art.'

'So?'

'I didn't tell you about her fantasies.'

'Gimme a break, Ellis. What fantasies?'

'Her fantasies about how to kill conceptual artists in the manner of their art.'

'As in "*Hommage* to Banksy".'

'I'm afraid so.'

'Would you mind getting us some more coffee, Ellis? I need my wits about me.'

'So Jim's worried that when he tells this to the AC, he'll go back to assuming Jack's a serial murderer.'

'But for heaven's sake, Ellis,' said Amiss, 'can't he explain to the cretin that she'll have been describing those fantasies far and wide and she'll certainly have told them to Sarkovsky. To amuse him.'

'He didn't have much of a sense of humour, did he?'

'No. She said custard pies in the face, cripples falling off their zimmers and generally other people's misfortunes were the kind of thing that made him laugh.'

'That's ominous.'

'It sure is.'

'My mind's working overtime, Ellis. Is yours?'

'If he's killed one, he means to kill them all.'

'I'm afraid so.'

'Maybe he's done it already.'

'He's more likely to be stringing it out.'

'He's got to be in London, hasn't he?'

'Looks like it. We've got people checking out his apartment building now and trying to find out if he's been sighted. And we're digging up what info we can.'

'Time isn't on your side.'

'You're telling me.'

'I'm going to try to track down Myles. If you bastards can't find her, it's time to bring in the SAS.'

'I didn't hear that,' said Pooley.

'Sorry. Of course you didn't, since I never said it. What I said was that Jack's close friend Myles needs to know she's disappeared. Is there a number for him among whatever material you took out of their flat?'

'Don't think so. It's very much a *pied-à-terre*. No papers to speak of. Mary Lou might have some idea.'

Miss Stamp was trying to keep calm. 'I've searched high and low but I can't find the Mistress's address book, Mr Amiss. She must have had it with her. And I can't get into her computer because I don't know her password. I've tried variations on Troutbeck and St Martha's, but no luck. But then I wouldn't know what numbers to add. I tried the year of her birth, but that didn't work either.'

'If I had to guess I'd think of British military triumphs, Miss Stamp. Try Waterloo1815 or Trafalgar1805.'

She giggled rather forlornly. 'That would

be like her, Mr Amiss. I'll try them and telephone you back.'

It took five minutes before a disconsolate Miss Stamp reported in the negative. However, Amiss's next suggestion, 'Agincourt 1415', did the trick. It took only a couple of minutes for her to find Myles Cavendish's email address and phone number. Amiss sent an email as well as text and voice messages into the blue and went out to pace around the park, leaving Plutarch draped over his computer, shedding hair all over his keyboard and desk.

The baroness had never watched Big Brother and no one but Anastasia and Charlie Briggs admitted having seen it, but they had told stories that gave everyone a flavour of what was to be expected from a game. By now they were all ready to hear they might be required to dress up in skintight lurex catsuits and perform ungraceful dances, or dress as pastry chefs and throw pies at each other. However, the news that this game was to be conducted in the nude caused a minor sensation.

'I won't do it,' shouted Henry Fortune. 'I will not sacrifice my dignity.'

'Me neither,' said Hortense.

'You play game,' said the voice of Big Brother. 'Or evicted. If evicted, die.'

'He can't really mean that,' wailed Pringle. 'Can he? Is that what happened to Jake?'

Eight heads turned towards the baroness.

'You said he'd been taken ill,' said Pringle.

She thought of trying to keep the fiction going, but realised Sarkovsky's intervention had made it pointless. 'He was evicted. And no, I don't know if that means he's been killed, but I doubt it. However, just in case, I guess it makes sense to do what Big Brother wants.'

'That way we lose our dignity and then we die anyway,' said Fortune.

'Perhaps,' said the baroness. 'But perhaps not. Big Brother may well be joking. Best to keep the options open, I'd say.'

'Oh, Bubbles, you must, you must, you must. It's not as if we're on television. No one will see us.'

There was what sounded like a low snigger.

'Oh, God,' cried Fortune. 'Maybe we are.'

'For heaven's sake, Henry,' said the baroness, 'if we were on television it would be good news. It would make us easier to find. Now if I were you, I'd focus on survival and do what we've been asked to do.

'In the hatch, I'm told, are canvasses and pots of paint. We get a canvas each and we are to paint it using our naked body as the only means of transferring paint to surface. Shall we fetch the materials now and lay them out? Then we can disrobe.'

The baroness regretted that the knot of

dread that would not unravel had stifled her sense of humour, for, at other times, she would have been mightily amused by what went on that afternoon. It was Hortense who had said maybe the thing was to attempt to emulate Jackson Pollock and his drip paintings and with Fortune and Truss produced dollops of pretentious guff on the subject, with a bit of a disagreement about whether he was a genius because of the fractal dimensions of his work or because of his role as a progressive purifier of form.

The baroness, who had been known to throw her newspaper at the wall when she read that yet another Pollock jumble had gone for nine figures, had pointed out rather coldly that they had to go a stage further than the maestro since Big Brother insisted that they couldn't pour paint on the canvas but actually had to apply it with bits of their body. What's more, he had forbidden them to use their digits to apply paint to canvas. Hands were out, and so were toes, though they could be used to put paint on their bodies. And what was even more challenging, no two people were to use the same bit of their body and no one could help anyone else. This information induced a kind of terrified paralysis among several of the gathering.

'We'll have to negotiate who uses what,' said the baroness. 'First come, first served, I think.'

'If I wanted to make a mint out of this in my past life,' observed Anastasia, 'I'd have stuck paint up my fanny and let it drip out.'

'I don't want to act as the health and safety officer, Anastasia, but I'd confine paint to the outside rather than the inside if I were you. Any other suggestions?'

'Isn't there some Russian Sheila who paints with her breasts? I once thought about trying that.'

'Now's your chance,' said the baroness, 'unless Marilyn or Hortense want to counter bid?'

They shook their heads. 'Elbow,' said Marilyn. 'Knee,' said Herblock. 'Shoulder blades,' said Hortense. 'Head,' said Truss.

'Didn't that Riverdance bloke put paint on the soles of his shoes and tap dance on a canvas?' asked Briggs.

'You won't be wearing shoes, Charlie, but there's no reason not to try that if no one objects.'

No one did. 'Bum,' said the baroness. 'As in, I'll paint with it. Now that leaves just Henry and Jason. I'm afraid there aren't many options left for you.'

'I was too shocked to think,' said Fortune. 'What's left?'

'Your stomach?'

'How can I paint with my stomach, you madwoman?'

'Just slap a few colours on and move the

canvas around it.'

'Oh, all right. I suppose I could do that.'

'What about me?' screamed Pringle. 'Am I supposed to use my willie?'

There was a silence until the baroness said, 'Unless you can think of anything else.'

'I can't,' sobbed Pringle.

Anastasia patted him on the back. 'You won't be the first to do it, Jason. There's a drongo back home calls himself "Pricasso". He makes a living out of it and it doesn't seem to do him any harm.'

The baroness stood up and clapped her hands. 'Excellent. That's all settled. Now, shall we make a start? It might be less daunting if we all do it together.'

Apart from Anastasia and Briggs, they were as unappetising a collection as might have been found in any naturist encampment for seniors. At one extreme were the scrawny, like Pringle and Marilyn, and at the other the portly, like Fortune and the baroness. By unspoken agreement, they tried to avoid looking at each other.

Anastasia went to work with a will. After trial and error, her favoured approach was to dip each breast in paint of a different colour and press the canvas against first one, then the other, and then rub it with both. Since he found it difficult to keep within the constraints of the canvas, Briggs seemed more like a dancer on hot coals than another

Michael Flatley, but he became quite interested in the process and kept going back for more paint to smear on his feet.

Marilyn's sharp elbow proved to be a precision instrument. She chose black paint exclusively and aimed for geometric patterns. Herblock's knee was less successful, not least because at the beginning he tried to do it standing on one leg and fell over twice. Hortense obviously hadn't thought her choice through properly. It caused her acute discomfort actually to get enough paint from hand to shoulder blade, and it proved even more difficult to find a way of transferring it to the canvas.

Being shaven, Truss's choice of head had been sensible, though sometimes he miscalculated the density of the paint and ended up with much of it running down his face before he could bend over to apply it to the canvas. The baroness approached her task stoically, smearing different colours onto her buttocks and then rubbing the canvas up down and across them. Watching her technique gave Fortune courage and inspiration, and he completed his picture quickly, which gave him the time and psychic space to urge Pringle on. 'No, Jay. Not the tip. Just smear it along the sides and rub it in sideways. That's it. You've got it. You've got it. That's the way.'

'You can't talk to Ellis about this, Mary Lou.'

'I know I can't. He'd have to turn us in if he knew we were looking to getting a private army on to this. Yet I don't think legal methods are likely to work, do you?'

'Can't say I'm very hopeful, especially at the pace at which they're going. They've only just got started on looking for a property that Sarkovsky might own through a company. And apparently there was a long discussion about whether the wheels should be set in motion to ask the security services to track Sarkovsky's phone. Anyway, there's no harm in talking to Myles about it. He'll make his own decisions.'

'Do you by any chance have an alternative number for Myles? I've heard nothing back.'

'Nope. I barely know him.'

'It's ridiculous, isn't it? They've been an item – well, a sort of an item – for years, but we almost never see him.'

'I think they both like it that way. It's a relationship that allows them to do whatever the hell they like and I fancy he's as secretive and compartmentalised as she is.'

'I just hope he's as resourceful.'

'Me too,' said Mary Lou. 'This sucks. This really really sucks.'

On his way home, Martin Conroy read yet another of those property articles about what the mega-rich went in for. He had seen several about the new fashion for digging deep under big houses to create an enormous basement for one's swimming pool, gym, and spa. Apparently now real opulence had become the name of the game, with Turkish baths, Italianate spas, movie theatres and golf-simulation centres. He wondered if the house in north London that had been bought by the latest Sarkovsky company he had tracked down had been a likely candidate for such improvements. Certainly, enormous sums had been spent until the money suddenly dried up.

Conroy didn't yet know what overall was the state of Sarkovsky's finances, but things looked terrible. The bloke must be getting really desperate. He decided to see what builders he'd been using and if they were legit.

'Max Thorogood's been very helpful,' said Pooley to Milton, who was slumped, ex-hausted, at his desk. 'Turned out he was Jake's only heir, so what with the solicitor, the accountant, the bank, and his newspaper, I've already got an idea of what was going on with him financially. His salary was £80,000, but he had extra income over the past few years in the region of a quarter of a million for consultancy services to Jason Pringle.'

'And consultancy means?'

'Shady authentication for Pringle, I suppose.'

206

'Well, he's certainly paid a heavy price. Sarkovsky, if it's him, is clearly not a forgiving man. And all the information I'm getting about him suggests that even as oligarchs go, he's a ruthless bastard.' He looked at his watch. 'It's ten o'clock, Ellis. We've been here for more than fourteen hours. God knows what horrors tomorrow will bring. Let's go home and get some sleep.'

Bizarrely, the shared ludicrous task had for the first time induced some sense of community spirit. Being naked and covered with paint was a great leveller. The baroness briefly revelled in the absence of hate. It was short-lived, for Sarkovsky had decreed that there must be another argument before bedtime. And before she was required to choose the worst.

When Hortense and Pringle, the stragglers, had finished, the baroness clapped her hands and said, 'Big Brother wants us to decide who has created art.'

'I have,' said Anastasia, displaying her smears. 'If I think it's art, it's art. Isn't that what we've been told to believe?'

'Is it true, Henry?'

'If she thinks it is, it is.'

'That's the kind of fatuous nonsense that has ruined our galleries and art schools,' said the baroness. 'If everything's art, nothing's art.'

Somehow, the mainly middle-aged or elderly paint-spattered people couldn't work up the enthusiasm to argue. Duty called the baroness. 'Is this art?' she asked, presenting her multicoloured bottom to the audience.

'Don't be absurd,' said Hortense. 'Of course it isn't. You're not an artist.'

'If it was Anastasia's bottom – leaving the aesthetic out of it – would it be art?'

'It would have to be selected by a gallery,' said Pringle. 'There has to be a filter operated by people who know.'

'People like you?'

'Indeed.'

'Tell me, Jason, if the Mona Lisa was lying outside your gallery in the gutter, would it be art?'

'Of course. It has been validated and exhibited.'

'If that had never happened, it wouldn't be art?'

'This is puerile,' said Fortune.

'This is totalitarian,' said the baroness. 'You people have set yourselves up as arbiters of taste, and you make arbitrary decisions that suit you professionally. That is why Charlie – in his innocence – spent five million quid on something that when your world comes to its senses, will be a joke. For that amount of money he could have bought a Georgian country house, roomfuls of beautiful furniture, good silver, fine sculpture and paintings his children would have been proud of.'

'Did we really sleep in art last night, Jason?' asked Briggs.

'Of course not, it was counterfeit Tracey, not original.'

'Do we know that?' asked Briggs. 'Maybe Big Brother bought the original.'

'Nonsense,' said Hortense. 'It's not for sale.'

'But suppose it had been, and he'd bought it, and created four identical copies. Would the original have been art and all the others not?' enquired the baroness.

'Of course,' said Hortense.

'Yes,' said Fortune.

'Yes,' said Truss.

'Everyone agree?'

'Not me,' said Anastasia.

'Or me,' said Briggs. 'Now I think about it, it's all a ginormous con trick.'

'Like the Olafur Eliasson nonsense for the Olympics London Festival,' said the baroness.

Pringle produced another signature scream.

'You are unremittingly ignorant, aren't you?' said Fortune. 'The concept is thrilling.'

'Rubbish. The fellow's a fraud.'

Seven shocked faces looked at her, but Anastasia seemed amused. 'A fraud,' cried the baroness. 'A hundred-carat fraud. He's been given a million quid to encourage people around the world to breathe. What bollocks!'

'Oh dear, oh dear,' said Fortune. 'Clearly, you've missed the point of *Take a Deep Breath*.' He shook his head patronisingly. 'Such an astonishing, uplifting end to the Olympics. He will encourage global connectivity.'

'Global connectivity my arse. He will encourage global derision for British culture. Only we could be mad enough to hire a Danish charlatan to produce an invisible piece of art and call it a tribute to British culture.' She slammed her glass down on Trixie. 'It isn't even bloody original. Y'all being experts presumably remember our friend Piero Manzoni's *Artist's Breath* – those balloons filled with his own breath that he used to flog before he opted for the more lucrative shit.

'My God,' she said, warming to her theme, 'don't you realise this is a perfect example of emperor's new clothes? A piece of art that doesn't actually exist? An artistic equivalent of that wally John Cage's piece of silent music.'

Hortense Wilde's face darkened. 'If you wish to describe one of the musical geniuses of the twentieth century as a wally, I suppose I can't stop you. You merely show your ignorance. You are, I suppose, in your crass way, referring to his magnificent *4'33*.'

'His what?' asked Anastasia.

'The master's favourite work,' said Hortense reverentially. 'The high point of his exploration of indeterminacy. A musical counterpoint to Rauschenberg's *White Paintings*.'

'Huh?'

'Rauschenberg was a modernist who exhibited blank canvasses that inspired Cage,' said the baroness. 'Cage's contribution to pretending nothing was something consisted of four minutes and thirty-three seconds when musicians sat there not playing.

'The silence was performed at various times by anything from a solitary pianist to a full symphony orchestra.'

'But that's crazy,' said Anastasia.

'Sounds funny to me,' said Charlie Briggs.

'You don't understand,' broke in Pringle. 'The sounds the audience make become the music. It varies from performance to performance. Genius. As Rauschenberg's white paintings could register lighting.'

'Sounds like this dickhead who's getting the world to breathe so he doesn't have to make anything,' said Anastasia.

'Anyone who doesn't appreciate Cage and Eliasson has no imagination,' said Hortense. 'In art the progressive is all.'

'You're just an old-fashioned cultural Marxist, Hortense, isn't that it?'

'Why is progressive good?' asked Anastasia.

211

'Isn't good good and crap crap?'

'Anastasia,' asked Fortune, 'do you know what you are saying?'

'I'm saying that a lot of modern art is rubbish. And that includes what I do myself.'

'I'm going to ignore that,' said Fortune. 'It's patently untrue. If it were rubbish, Jason would not have exhibited and dealt in it, Jake would not have endorsed it, and I would not have purchased it for public view.'

'Oh, yes you would,' said the baroness and Anastasia together. Fortune ignored the baroness. 'You're upset, Anastasia. It's understandable. We're all under strain. Let's get back to the Olympics.'

'Yes, let's,' said the baroness. 'Leaving this Eliasson creature out of it, the art associated with it is an unmitigated disaster.'

'How can you say that?' asked Marilyn. 'That guy Kapoor's a genius. Don't you get the magnificence of *Orbit?*'

'Genius?' cried the baroness. 'Anish bloody Kapoor has provided the Olympic Park with a four-hundred-foot erection of red squiggles – a helter-skelter – that people can climb up. At a cost of more than twenty million quid! Admittedly, it's paid for by Indian steel billionaires, but we have to put up with the world thinking we think it's art.'

'How can you so fail to appreciate a magnificent monument to instability?' asked Hortense.

'Very very easily,' said the baroness, breathing heavily. 'Kapoor's become the high priest of fairground art. Look what he did mucking up rooms in the Royal Academy by shooting shells of red wax from a cannon. Oh, yes, and giving another over to distorting mirrors. He's a funfair sort of guy. That's why Nicholas Bloody Serota is such a fan.'

Pringle burst into tears. 'I don't care,' he said. 'I just want to be out of here.'

Exhausted, everyone fell silent.

'Laidee Troutbeck to Diary Room. Now.'

As the baroness trudged off, she wondered if she could cope. She was an optimist, so she didn't really believe that she would be sending someone to their death. But she was also a realist, who knew it was possible. And she also knew that while she was a woman of strong opinions and a deep sense of right and wrong, she was unhappy being what now appeared to be a hanging judge. She knew equally that the easy way out would be to refuse to choose. But she knew too that this would be a contemptible route. 'I never expected,' she said to herself, 'to be forced into making Sophie's Choice. But if that's what's going on, that's what I have to do. They may not be children, but I will try to protect the most innocent. And, of course, myself.'

Chapter Ten

It was two a.m., and Morrison and Sarah were on patrol.

'I felt bad about Sarah Byrne,' Milton had said to Pooley earlier that day, 'but I know what a lazy bastard Morrison is and I knew he'd want time off and I wasn't going to pander to him. Anyway, we're overstretched.'

Morrison was indeed aggrieved. 'He's got a nerve, expecting us to patrol by the Thames again,' said Morrison. 'Aren't we allowed any time to get over the shock of findin' a stiff?'

'I guess it's regarded as part of our job, Vernon.'

'I think we should get a special allowance for it.'

'Like a bonus?'

'Well, not like a bonus. More like compo. We sure need some extras now they're slashin' overtime.'

As instructed, they walked all the way around Parliament Square, gingerly avoiding the remaining few protestors' tents. 'Effin' layabouts,' said Morrison. 'Honestly, some people have no work ethic.'

Byrne let that pass. They crossed the street and began to walk by the House of Commons. Morrison jerked his head in the direction of Oliver Cromwell's statue. 'Now there's a bloke who knew what to do with layabouts. Off with their heads. That'd sort them out. He'd have known what to do with all the wankers cheatin' on their expenses too.'

'It's nice when it's crisp like this,' said Byrne.

'Crisp? Bloody cold if you ask me. We shouldn't have to be out poundin' pavements in this weather. All that crap about takin' us out of cars so we could mingle with the public.' He waved crossly at the House of Commons. 'What effin' public? Everyone's gone home.'

'There may be more people on the other side of the river, Vernon.'

'I don't want more people,' he said mutinously. 'And I don't want to walk all the way to that bloody Tate Modern. No one will know if we don't.'

'It's our job to do it, Vernon. We should cross Westminster Bridge now.'

'I dunno what makes you such a glutton for punishment, Sarah. Why do you want to look for trouble?'

'The Sarge said...'

'I don't care what the Sarge said. It's OK for him, nice and snug back at HQ while he orders the likes of us to trudge the streets. Well, I don't know about you, but I'm not a slave.' He puffed up his chest. 'I'm not going any farther without a tea and a sausage sandwich. We'll go to the cabbie shelter at Embankment and I'll cross the river then.'

Not for the first time, Byrne fantasised about kicking Morrison right in the middle of his paunch. 'OK,' she said, 'but we'd better make it quick.'

No one's temper was improved by their being refused service at the cabbie shelter, but Morrison eventually got hold of a sausage in a fast-food joint in Villiers Street, and Byrne was able to steer him towards Waterloo Bridge. 'We've got to walk fast, Vernon, or they'll want to know what's been keeping us.' She accelerated. Knowing himself to be in the wrong, Morrison sulked. Wearily, for she was no more a fan of late-night walking than was he, she drew on the old reliable ploy. 'So did you decide which train to buy, Vernon? You were very conflicted when we talked about it last.'

The monologue went on and on and on, but it allowed Byrne to think about what she had to think about, which was mostly child-care arrangements. The division of labour between her mother and mother-in-law was beginning to show fault lines. She wrestled with her choices, as Morrison wrestled with his, until Tate Modern hove into view.

'You ever been to this, Sarah?'

'No. Have you?'

'No.'

'But I've been to the other Tate. Tate Britain. I used to go there sometimes with my school. I really liked it. Specially the Turners.'

Morrison snorted. 'I've seen them too. Good stuff. But I'll never go again since I went to see the Turner Prize years back.'

'Because?'

'Because it was bloody crap, that's why. Just a bare room with a light goin' on and off. I think the artist even had the bare cheek to call it *Lights Goin' On and Off*. If you ask me, he was having a laugh. When I went home I wrote a letter sayin' that if that was the best they could do they didn't deserve any of my taxes. That modern art. A toddler could do it. And as for this Tate Modern? Did you know they're fillin' it with Damien Hirst's rubbish? The idea is that during the Olympics foreigners will be shown the best of British art. They've even had to reinforce the floors because of all them animals and fish he's had killed for his so-called art. It's not right. I mean I know I eat them, but that's different. It's natural.'

They left the street and walked towards the building. The area was deserted. Even the large grassy area in front of it seemed unoccupied. 'Too chilly there for winos,' said Morrison. 'OK, let's walk round it like the Sarge said and then we can get the hell out of it and go back to base.'

It was then they saw the large, rectangular object that seemed to be obstructing part of the entrance. 'What's that?' exploded Morrison. 'They're leavin' their stupid art outside now where anyone can smash it up. For God's sake, it's made of glass. Any bloody vandal could take a brick to it. No trouble. Not that it'd be any loss.'

Byrne found her torch and switched it on. 'Oh, God, Vernon. Look. It's a naked woman. Floating.'

They surveyed the object. 'It's one of them Damien Hirst things, isn't it,' asked Morrison. 'Didn't he do a dead shark in a tank like this? But this isn't a dead shark.'

'It isn't. It's a dead woman.'

'It'll be a mannequin, won't it?'

Byrne crouched beside the vitrine and shone her torch up and down. 'Don't think so, Vernon. Look. Her mouth's wide open. And you don't get mannequins with bunions.' She shone her torch around the side. 'Vernon! There's a card here.'

'What does it say?'

'"*Hommage* to Hirst". And underneath – "*The Physical Impossibility of Creating Art When You've No Fucking Talent*".'

'It's another one of 'em. Isn't it?'

''Fraid so,' said Byrne, her voice quavering. She ran to the grass. While she was throwing up, she could hear Morrison on the radio explaining to their sergeant that they'd found

218

another 'omidge stiff'.

When the reveille began, the baroness immediately sat upright. Anastasia was stretching beside her. Fearfully, she looked vainly for the person she was afraid would be no longer there. 'Has anyone seen Hortense?'

'She must be in the bathroom,' said Truss, looking at the space beside him.

The baroness jumped out of bed and went outside, checked the bathroom and kitchen, called 'Hortense' and stuck her head back inside the bedroom. 'I can't see her.'

Visibly panicking, everyone tumbled out of bed. It took only a minute before they all stopped looking and collapsed onto the sofas.

'He's killed her,' said Pringle. 'That's two gone. Why didn't we notice?'

'The drinks must be spiked,' said Briggs. 'Or they're piping some kind of soporific gas into the bedroom to put us under.'

'We can't sleep there again,' screamed Marilyn.

'We'll have to, hon,' said Herblock. 'It's that or the Albanians.'

'So we just go into a gas chamber knowing that if we wake up in the morning, another one will be gone.'

'The thing is not to panic,' said the baroness. 'We don't know what happened either to Hortense or to Jake. It's really very unlikely that they came to harm.'

'She's right,' said Anastasia. 'We've got to try to keep cheerful and hope for the best. No point in moping. I'll get washed now and put the kettle on.'

When Pooley rang, Amiss had been reading obituaries of Jake Thorogood and further information about the missing all morning. Although everyone agreed he was a fine writer and very knowledgeable about art, the newspapers were divided on the subject of Thorogood. His own paper, of course, had a whole page of hagiography along with a fine piece he had written on Rembrandt some years before. That he had almost completely changed his tune on conceptual art in the early noughties was explained as a road-to-Damascus experience that demonstrated his intellectual curiosity and his embracing of the new and challenging. More unkind papers hinted that his change of mind might have had to do with his association with the fashionable rich. Suggestions of corruption were only hinted at, for Fleet Street tends not to trash the dead until after what it considers a decent interval – especially if the departed is a journalist – but there were carefully chosen photographs of him with the rich and famous who had money to burn on art.

Max Thorogood had issued a short, formal statement through his solicitors expressing shock and distress at the news, hope that the other missing people would soon be found, and asking for privacy for his family, whom he had taken away to an undisclosed location to avoid the gathering hordes. Thanks to a tip-off from a policeman, a tabloid had got hold of the current girlfriend, who put on a good performance at being grief-stricken. Since his death was such a hot topic, there was a rumour that some newspapers were rummaging around in his affairs with a view to running exposés. The tabloids were in ecstasy.

Pooley found a moment to call Amiss. 'It's grim news, Robert. Hortense Wilde's murdered and it's another *hommage* – this time to Hirst.'

'Oh, God. Not bisected?'

'No. It was the shark. Not the cow. She was suspended in formaldehyde. Naked. Her husband hasn't got here yet to identify her, but there was no mistaking her from the photographs I've seen. But this is off the record for now.'

'And then there were eight!'

'I must rush, Robert. Sorry. I'm going to be interviewing Gervase Wilde shortly. Mary Lou's phone is off so I've left a message just asking her to call you. Can you look after her? She's already very fragile. Please nurture her.'

He left Amiss in what was now his customary dislocated state, pursuing news on the internet, desperately wishing his wife worked in an office rather than a classroom and so was contactable, and checking his iPhone every couple of minutes in the hope of a message from Myles. It was a consolation when Mary Lou called. She was as frightened by the news as he was, but her suggestion of lunch promised trouble shared.

'This one's certainly unusual,' said the pathologist, who arrived shortly after Hortense's formal identification by her husband. 'There are no signs of trauma to the body and she didn't drown, so my guess is she was smothered. Then they wedged her mouth open so it'd stay that way after rigor set in. Then they popped her into the formaldehyde. She looks pretty good really. Even peaceful. Apart from the open mouth. Like one of those animals you'd see in a modern museum.'

'Quite,' said Pooley.

'I've never even heard of Oleg Sarkovsky,' said Gervase Wilde. 'What's he got to do with Hortense? Why would he want to murder her? What harm could she have done to him? She is ... was just a scholar.'

'We were hoping you'd be able to tell us, Dr Wilde. Sarkovsky is a collector and we've reason to believe he'd fallen out with Jake

Thorogood and some of the other missing people.'

'I don't know Hortense's world that well, Inspector. I'd go to art events with her sometimes, but we're both hard-working academics who spend much of our spare time on research into our own specialities.'

'Can we just talk about the people who disappeared at the same time as she did, Dr Wilde? I know this is a terrible time for you, but we need all the information you can give us. We need to stop this maniac.'

Wilde seemed shell-shocked, but he tried to focus. 'Very well. Everything's a bit of a blur, but take me through the names and I'll help if I can.'

'I'll start off alphabetically. Charlie Briggs.'

'Never heard of him until he went missing.'

'Sir Henry Fortune.'

'Oh, yes, I met Henry quite a few times at private views – especially at Jason Pringle's gallery. Hortense really admired Henry and Jason, and she'd have gone to exhibitions Henry curated whenever she could. All those years ago, she thought he'd been hard done by in not being given the Tate to run, but she changed her mind when she saw how Nick embraced the forces of progress. The man's a genius.'

'She wouldn't have had any business dealings with Sir Henry?'

'She gave lectures at some of his events

abroad and she had him a few times to give talks to students about what curating is all about. But that would have been that. Not business in any real sense.'

'Chester Herblock?'

'She got to know him recently. Through Jason, I think.' He frowned. 'I think he asked her to talk to some collector he thought needed advice.'

'You don't know who the collector was?'

'I don't. Though she did say something about his English being bad and that he seemed very ignorant and uncouth.'

'So it could have been Sarkovsky?'

'I suppose it's possible.'

'What kind of advice was she giving?'

'I think Herblock was his art consultant and whoever it was wanted to buy something Herblock thought he shouldn't. He brought in Hortense to point out the limitations of the artist.'

'What artist?'

'I don't know. There were quite a lot of artists of whom Hortense disapproved. She is ... was ... an international expert on post-colonialism and masculism in European art.'

Pooley repressed the urge to say 'There's no answer to that', and instead asked: 'Anastasia Holliday?'

'She knew of her through Jason and she admired what she knew of her innovative art. I think they met when Jason took

224

Holliday to a lecture of Hortense's.'

'Marilyn Falucci Lamont?'

'I never heard her mention that name.'

'You've talked about Jason Pringle. Jake Thorogood?'

'Funny, that. She usen't to think much of Jake as a critic. He was initially terribly stuck in his attitudes, no concept of cultural theory, talked up what he should have moved beyond and was shockingly resistant to the YBAs, so they didn't get on. But he improved a lot in the last few years and they had a rapprochement.'

'Lady Troutbeck?'

'We met her once at our neighbour's. Frightful reactionary. It's a terrible thought that my poor Hortense probably spent her last days on earth in the company of such a ghastly, rude philistine.' His eyes glistened with tears. 'This is very upsetting for me, Inspector. Are we nearly finished?'

'Just Gavin Truss to go, Dr Wilde.'

'Well, of course she and Gavin were great friends and allies at the cutting edge of the avant-garde. Both – like me - were intellectually formed in the crucible of the Frankfurt School.'

'Sorry, sir. Could you elaborate?'

'The Frankfurt School, Inspector. Surely you know about the Frankfurt School? The *fons et origo* of critical theory. That is where Hortense and Gavin and so many others learnt that Western culture is a culture of domination that must be challenged and replaced. When Gavin became Principal, he got rid of the terrible dinosaur who was Professor of Fine Art and gave the job to Hortense. She proved magnificent in making the college a pioneer in popularising postmodern discourse. Good heavens, you know they used to think the importance of art was that it was decorative?' He shook his head and gave a little laugh. 'Hortense taught her students the great truth that what matters is significance.'

'You mentioned that Mr Herblock wanted her to talk to a collector. Would that be unusual? Would she normally have much to do with collectors?'

'No. Hortense was not attracted by the social side of the art world or by rich people. As I said, she was a true scholar.' He smiled proudly. 'Someone once described her as a Robespierre among art historians.'

'And she saw that as a compliment?'

'Of course. Hortense was a woman of great integrity. Once she learnt from masters like Jacques Derrida and Michel Foucault that the imperative was to replace any epistemological foundation for art history by focusing on the processes of cultural transformation, she was on a crusade.'

Pooley felt a devil rise in him. 'A crusade, sir? An interesting choice of word.'

'Oh, my God,' said Wilde. 'How could I have used such an offensive word? I'm horrified. When I think of the seminal work Hortense was doing in exposing Islamophobia in Western art, and then I use such a term!' He buried his face in his hands.

'Don't worry, sir,' said Pooley. 'I understand. Grief can do terrible things to people.'

The baroness had thought long and hard about Sarkovsky. She had no doubt that he was now psychotic, was virtually certain he had had Thorogood and Hortense killed, but was no clearer as to why. The only hope for the survivors, she reasoned, was to keep him interested enough to stagger their deaths rather than just send in thugs with machine guns to mow them down.

Since her natural optimism kept her believing that her friends were smart and resourceful enough to come to the rescue soon, she was intent on staving off disaster. Sarkovsky liked cruelty and had little imagination, and it had taken her idea about nude painting to stop him insisting they have gladiator fights with real swords. Nude dancing was another desperate measure which she successfully traded for his idea of forcing everyone to have intercourse with the people they obviously least fancied. 'Think *Scheherazade*,' she said to herself yet again. 'Keep him sweet.'

She tentatively once more raised the

matter of Marilyn's billions. Surely there was some way that she could buy their safety? But once again, Sarkovsky snorted his disagreement. The thrust of his argument seemed to be that in these days of tyranny by financial regulators, a decent businessman like himself could not expect that a couple of billion could change hands for no apparent reason without anyone noticing. He was ruined in Russia and the West, he was making his arrangements to escape to South America with enough money to live comfortably, but in the meantime, he was settling scores with people who had made a fool of him. One thing Sarkovsky really didn't like, he had made plain on numerous occasions, was to be made a fool of.

'Hortense Wilde! She poisonous art person. I say Chester Herblock I want to buy art same like you and me see in Europe. I get offer good collection, quick sale. Herblock say outmoded rubbish. Not hot contemporary. I say not rubbish. And keep value. He present me that bitch whore, she agree to him, and give me stupid reasons. But everybody say she is great scholar, so I think is truth. I reject collection and that Marilyn bitch whore buys it. I buy more stuff Herblock recommends. It rubbish. Real rubbish. Very rubbish. Fault of bloody Hortense Wilde.'

'I think she probably believed what she

told you.'

'If she believe, she crazy. If not believe, she bad woman. But she make Oleg appeeer stupid. Same Hirst shark,' he sniggered. 'Your idea.'

Memories of other ideas she'd had for killing artists flickered through her memory, and the baroness winced. Not for the first time, she vividly recollected some of the times she had mocked Sarkovsky. Would the time she had laughed at his shirt and he had ranted and raved and finally stormed off in a sulk count as making him 'appeeer stupid'? Mindful of the hoped-for St Martha's bequest, she had apologised the following morning and he had muttered something about how words were a sting more wounding than guns. On this, she hadn't agreed with him then and she definitely didn't agree with him now.

Amiss was in such an anguished state that he'd contemplated the brandy bottle lustfully, but he then concluded that taking to drink at eleven a.m. was something to be done if Jack was murdered. Not when he and her friends were still hoping she might survive. 'We are not all as self-indulgent and self-absorbed as you, Plutarch,' he said. The cat opened one eye and sneered, and Amiss pushed her roughly off the kitchen table. He was still licking the blood off his calf and wondering how such a fat animal could have been so dexterous, when his phone rang.

'I've only got a minute,' said Pooley. 'And I know you'll be going out now to meet Mary Lou. I'm relying on you to steady her.'

'I'll do my best, but tell me one thing. How the hell can you transport something like that tank? It must have weighed a ton.'

'It would have required a truck with a winch, and at every stage the process would have required some very strong men. But gaining access was dead easy. They'd have been able to drive right up to the front of the building to dump her.'

'Security guards?'

'It's like prisons. They're worried about what goes on inside. Not outside.'

'No sightings, I suppose?'

'Not yet. Must go, Robert.'

'Where do you think the next corpse might be deposited?'

'Well, obviously we're thinking about that. Can't stop. 'Bye.'

'After lunch, Big Brother wishes us to dance.'

'Dance?' asked Fortune. 'What do you mean "dance"?'

'Depending on what music he plays us, we will dance appropriately. He has kindly agreed shortly to supply us with champagne to get us in the mood.'

She sat down and surveyed the diminished

group. 'Can everyone dance?'

Marilyn, Herblock, and Fortune, it turned out, attended many balls and regarded themselves as decent performers. Fortune, indeed, fancied himself as a master of the foxtrot. Pringle wasn't keen, but said he could shuffle round the floor if required. Truss was so unhappy and dislocated by the loss of Hortense that he could hardly talk at all, let alone about dancing. And Briggs and Anastasia both said they knew no steps but liked to party.

'And you, Jack?' asked Briggs.

'I have been told I display *élan*, if not precision.'

'What's *élan*?'

'Zeal.'

'I can imagine that,' said Anastasia.

No one had the heart to try any more general conversation, though at various times one or two of them would get up and walk around the room. The baroness noted with some satisfaction that they avoided looking at the rotting cowhead. Indeed, the day before, when Briggs had said how much he hated it, no one had said anything except the baroness, who had quipped that it seemed Hirst was for Christmas, not for life.

When Big Brother said 'Go look hatch', they all busied themselves ferrying its contents to be laid out on Trixie and Joleen. As they finished filling glasses and sat back, the baroness cleared her throat. 'Big Brother has given me Ecstasy tablets and says we're to take one each to help us get into the spirit of dancing.'

'How do we know they're not cyanide?' wailed Truss.

'If they are,' said Briggs, 'why wouldn't we take them? If he wants to kill us, he's going to kill us anyway. If he doesn't, they're probably Ecstasy. Here, shove them over here.'

The baroness passed him the box she had taken from her pocket and he and Anastasia had a look. 'They're Ecstasy,' he said.

'Certainly look that way,' she said. 'Let's take them now. They won't work for a while.'

Anastasia, Brigs, and the baroness washed a tablet down with champagne and passed the box around. With only Fortune expostulating, the others all followed suit. Grumbling, Fortune finally did the same.

'There's just one other thing,' said the baroness. 'When the music starts it's the signal for us to take our clothes off.'

'I thought he might want another nuddy game,' said Anastasia.

'I am expected to dance the foxtrot naked?' asked Fortune.

'That's the deal, I'm afraid,' said the baroness. 'Shall we do it with a good grace?'

'I had to choose here,' said Mary Lou. 'It's the last place I met her. She loved it.'

232

Amiss and Mary Lou were sitting in Covent Garden, in the snug of The Salisbury, a pub favoured by the baroness because of its Victorian fittings, its connection with one of the few British prime ministers of whom she approved, its obdurate refusal to countenance music, television, or gaming machines, its kindly staff and a snug which at many times during the day offered total privacy.

'You're speaking of her in the past tense.'

'Oh, God, so I am. I can't sleep much and when I do I have nightmares. I guess I'm really spooked.'

'Hard not to be. Now what'll you drink?'

'A pint of Tribute.'

It was an unexpected choice from someone who normally drank either wine or Coca-Cola, but Amiss fetched two pints. 'To Jack,' he said. 'May she have a safe landing.'

Mary Lou's face creased up. 'I don't like beer much, but I had to have this. Being here is bringing it all back. She went on about the merits of various brands of real ale for ages, until she settled on Tribute. Then she got upset that I'd only have a half. "What's the matter with you, Mary Lou? You're not becoming anorexic, are you? This noble Cornish beer deserves respect. Not half-measures."'

Amiss laughed. 'I can hear her.'

'So I tried to explain that I have to look

good on television and that means I really can't afford to put on even an ounce. The BBC is even more fattist than ageist. When it comes to women, that is. And she said "Rubbish. No one has such an informed and trenchant interviewing style. You're irreplaceable even if you turn into one of those Red Hot Mamas."'

'She's very loyal to us, isn't she, in her own way. Not that I'm implying her assessment isn't right.'

'I hope it is, but of course they also like me because I'm relatively young, passably good-looking, and black. Which in the Beeb almost makes up for my being American.'

Her face creased up again. 'And that was when I passed on Ellis's latest warning that Sarkovsky was a real bad lot and she must have nothing to do with him. She said she wouldn't be seeing him any more and that we were all fusspots.'

'Well, we've certainly got plenty to fuss about today.' He checked his phone again. 'Still nothing from Myles.'

Mary Lou leant forward and took his hand. 'I've started praying. Dammit, I'm an American. It's what we do. Anyway, I can't think of anything else that might help.'

He put his arms around her and hugged her tightly. A man with a camera came into the snug and took a photograph. 'So who's this you're so friendly with, Mary Lou Dinsmore? It's not your husband, is it? Boy-friend?'

She looked at his triumphant expression and burst into tears.

Chapter Eleven

The Assistant Commissioner was looking shell-shocked. 'Sarkovsky's not in his Knightsbridge apartment, sir,' said Milton, 'nor in any of his other residences, nor on his yacht, and in fact hasn't been seen for even longer than the ten people I believe he kidnapped. We need a warrant. Immediately. I've got the paperwork all ready.'

'What exactly are you looking for?'

'We need initially to search all his pro-perties in case he's imprisoned them in any of them. If we draw a blank, we need to look for information on some place he might own or have rented where he might be keeping them. We need immediate access to his lawyers and accountants too and all his domestic and office employees. And we need to put an army on checking land registers plus title deeds and all the rest of it.'

'Even assuming we can persuade the judge, Jim, this could turn into an international incident. We're not supposed to upset foreigners unnecessarily.'

'We have two dead bodies, sir. At the present rate of attrition, all ten of them will be dead within a few days. I don't think we should worry too much about upsetting foreigners. Collateral damage at worst.'

'Oh, I suppose so, I suppose so. Get on with it, then.'

'Thanks,' said Milton, as he jumped from his chair. As he put his hand on the handle, the Assistant Commissioner called to him.

'Has it occurred to you that you might be barking up the wrong tree, Jim? Maybe Sarkovsky's been kidnapped as well. Now that would put a different complexion on things, wouldn't it?'

'I have only one tree, sir. Until I see another, I'll bark up that.'

Fortunately, Mary Lou had recovered her equilibrium quickly enough to do a deal with the photographer. In exchange for him not using the photo of her crying, she agreed to give him a quote, so the picture of Amiss hugging her was run under the headline 'JUST GOOD FRIENDS', with a few lines about how they were comforting each other over the disappearance of their friend Battling Baroness Troutbeck. The tabloid chucked in for good measure a picture of her on Pooley's arm going into a film premiere, both of them in evening dress, with a caption underneath about her husband, dashing Detective Inspector Pooley of Scotland Yard. With another picture of her interviewing a well-known actor and some guff about her coming top of some poll or other as the sexiest egghead on TV, that was another page of that tabloid happily filled.

'It's Myles, Robert. Sorry I couldn't get back to you until now. Only just got your messages. There was no coverage in the hills. What's up? Is Ida all right?'

Amiss did a double-take before remembering that Myles was one of the very few people in the world who called Jack Troutbeck by her baptismal name. 'No, she's not, Myles. She's gone missing.'

'Tell me.'

When Amiss had finished his brief account, Myles said, 'Shit. This is serious. It's that fucking psycho Sarkovsky, of course. I warned Ida a long time ago, but she had the bit between her teeth then and was galloping ahead. And then when they fell out, she kept saying he was in a sulk and didn't want anything to do with her any more so there was nothing to worry about.'

'The ghastly thing is, Myles, that it looks as if he's been paying far too much attention to her. From what we can infer, he's kidnapped a whole collection of people she's taught him to despise and is knocking them off using methods she suggested when she was being facetious. The guy's a bit literal-minded.'

'What are the cops doing?'

'I think they're just about ready to apply for search warrants, but I doubt if that'll work. We have to assume they're in London. He can't be flying them from a distant location corpse by corpse, can he? But he's hardly going to have them imprisoned in his Knightsbridge penthouse. His butler might object.'

'Of course not. Are the cops looking at his companies to see what properties they own?'

'Yes, but from what Jim says, they're not very speedy.'

'I know a man who'll cut corners, Robert. He'll be in touch with you. We need him to find where they're likely to be. Meanwhile, I'll get someone to start pulling a rescue party together and I'll get out of Iraq as fast as I can. It won't be today, though, and I doubt if it'll be tomorrow. I don't know if you pray, but if you do, pray that she's trying to be a bit more tactful than usual.'

Milton had announced late morning that Hortense Wilde had been murdered, but because of panicking by the Assistant Commissioner he was prevented from describing the circumstances. However, Morrison had done a secret deal with a tabloid contact that would pay him enough to expand his railway and rolling stock to include Eurostar, so the news of a corpse outside the Tate was on the internet by early afternoon. A member of the public who had been passing Tate Modern at three-thirty a.m., and who had surreptitiously taken a photo of police carrying a tank to a police van, saw the news item and called another tabloid. So it was that by mid-afternoon the jigsaw was sufficiently complete for the net to be alive with the second *hommage* murder. After a fraught meeting with the Assistant Commissioner, Milton was allowed to confirm that rumour was fact. The press, who had been frustrated in their attempts to find the always elusive Banksy, were now in hot pursuit of Damien Hirst. The police were putting covert night surveillance on Tate Britain, the Saatchi Gallery, the White Cube, the Gagosian Gallery and any other major locations they could think of that were strongly associated with conceptual art.

'Robert Amiss.'
  'I'm Mike. Myles told me to call you.'
  'Oh, thank God.'
  'We don't talk here. Can you meet me in an hour in central London? I'll text an address.'
  'Done.'
The phone went dead.

By the time Big Brother instructed them to take their clothes off, alcohol and Ecstacy had put everyone in a better mood. There had even been some nostalgic reminiscences of dances of the past. Herblock and Marilyn had had a lovey-dovey interlude recalling their first encounter at a ball raising funds for the New York Museum of Modern Art. They stripped resignedly, the music began and immediately Anastasia and Briggs began to gyrate energetically to the electronic rhythm.

'What is this?' cried Fortune. 'I can't dance to this.'

'It's House music, Henry,' said Briggs. 'You'll get used to it.'

'Dance now or die,' interjected Big Brother.

The baroness joined the dancers, slowly followed by all the others. Still being uncharacteristically more circumspect than anyone else about her intake of alcohol, she was the only person keenly observing the incongruity of the scene, particularly the odd movements of Fortune's stomach. But within a few minutes, like everyone else, she had forgotten about anything except the pulsating beat.

'OK,' said Mike. He and Amiss were sitting in an anonymous room in a hotel on the Strand. Mike was middle-aged, leathery,

240

and his eyes were fixed on Amiss's. 'Now I've got the story. I've got the background. Now what else can you tell me that would help us find the bastard? I don't take kindly to anyone trying to kill Jack Troutbeck. Not just because of Myles. She's our friend too. I won't forget the speech she gave us at that dinner in the Special Forces Club before we went into Iraq.'

'I'm trying,' said Amiss, 'but I wasn't always paying attention to everything Jack said about Sarkovsky.'

'If there's one thing I'm good at, Robert, it's interrogation. Now I want you to go back to the beginning and tell me everything.'

Amiss looked at his watch. 'My wife will be home soon.'

'Tell her to get here as fast as possible. And tell Mary Lou Dinsmore the same. Yes, I know her husband mustn't know about this, so she'll have to lie. Tough. Jack's life is at stake. You may trigger each others' memories.' Amiss reached for his phone. 'And, Robert, tell them they'll be staying late. Possibly very very late.'

'Everything we're finding out about Sarkovsky is appalling,' said Pooley. 'His business seems to be in free fall, not least because he had invested so much in a joint venture with Colonel Gaddafi. Work has stopped on the museum he was building in Russia, his

241

London office has been closed down and his accountant hasn't heard from him in weeks.'

'What have you got out of the accountant? Does he know anything about properties we don't know about?'

'He won't talk. He just won't talk. He's too scared.'

'Get a warrant for his arrest,' said Milton. 'I want him here first thing tomorrow.'

After about half an hour, Fortune stopped dancing and fell on a sofa. 'Geddyouuup,' said Big Brother.

'Can't,' croaked Fortune.

'He really can't,' said the baroness. 'He's got to have a break or he'll have a heart attack. And the same applies to all of us. Whatever you have in mind, that would be a bit of an anticlimax, wouldn't it?'

'You, Diary Room. OK, Fortune stop. All others continue dance.'

As the baroness pulled on her shell suit, for she felt strangely embarrassed at being naked talking to Sarkovsky on her own, she wasn't the only one in the room thinking about *They Shoot Horses, Don't They?*

Aware that she was still under the influence of Ecstasy, the baroness played for time. 'I've got a really good argument planned, Big Brother, but it won't work if everyone's exhausted. What do you think? Will you let us get some sleep?'

Haggling produced the agreement that as people passed out with exhaustion, they could go back to the Emin room and rest. But a few hours later the reveille sounded and within a few minutes they were all back assembled on the sofas. The baroness looked around the crumpled group of depressed people and turned to Truss with a feigned enthusiasm. 'Now, Gavin, I've been thinking about the conversation we had about Kounellis. He had a room at the Tate courtesy of what is laughingly known as the Anthony d'Offay bequest. Now will you or someone else please tell me why the taxpayer got lumbered with paying for this? It wasn't a bequest. It was a sale.'

Outbreaks of incredulity and anger from Pringle and Truss were interrupted by Fortune, who imposed silence with a wave. 'I'll handle this.' He brought as much gravitas to bear as could a plump knight in a dirty lime green shell suit, who had recently been seen naked dancing to acid house. 'Let us be calm. What do you know of Anthony d'Offay?'

'He's a dealer who made a fortune out of all manner of dreadful contemporary artists, collected stuff as he went – especially from his clients – had it valued at a hundred and twenty-five million quid and then out of the goodness of his heart said he'd sell the seven hundred or so items as a job lot to the nation just for what he'd paid for them. A snip at twenty-eight million, we were told by a rejoicing art establishment. But he insists on the exhibits being displayed just as he directs. And that means what are called Artist Rooms just show the d'Offay exhibits of selected artists. And they're mostly full of rubbish.'

'It was incredibly generous,' shouted Pringle. 'Nick said so.'

'Sure was. I'd have paid much more for it than that,' said Marilyn.

'Before you changed course, sweetie,' said Herblock.

'Oh, yeah. Before I changed course.'

'We are familiar,' began Fortune, 'with your closed, ignorant mind...'

'Excuse me,' said Briggs. 'It seems to me that Jack knows quite a bit. She doesn't agree with you, but you can't say she's ignorant. I'd like her to tell me about this transaction.'

'Me too,' said Anastasia.

Fortune glowered, but eventually made to his friends a 'what-can-one-do?' gesture. 'Go ahead. Trash a great man and an incomparable collection.'

The baroness thought of having another drink, exercised iron control, reached instead for water, settled herself more comfortably and began. 'We should have told d'Offay to shove off, but instead, the Tate – or Tate, as we are now required to call it to show we're cool – and the National Gallery of Scotland, who now jointly own the stuff, were abject in their gratitude and sent exhibitions round the country so the population could be elevated by – if you'll excuse the expression that seems to be a constant theme in the genre which you so revere – shit.'

'I can't stand any more of this,' shouted Truss.

'Yes, you can,' said Fortune. 'Allow her to condemn herself out of her own ignorant mouth.'

The baroness made an elaborate gesture. 'Thank you, Henry.

'I will admit that I have not yet made it to Edinburgh to see Mr d'Offay's worthless rubbish in the Modern Art gallery, but I know it includes an entire room devoted to Damien Hirst's *Away from the Flock*, which some of you mightn't know is a pickled lamb. Yep. Damien bought a lamb, he got someone to suspend it in formaldehyde, and, hey presto, the taxpayer is paying for what d'Offay thinks is destined to become a milestone of post-war art. Oh, and it's in Edinburgh rather than London because, apparently, of the ubiquitousness of sheep in Scotland.'

Truss was now so much beside himself that he was rocking to and fro with his head in hands. 'Hey, Gavin,' said Anastasia. 'Cool it. Sometimes we have to hear what we don't like.'

'Would it help if I said something nice

about Hirst?' said the baroness. 'In Tat's Artist Room, I saw a photograph of the artist as a young man posing laughing beside a severed head. He was sixteen and doing something original, even if it was disgusting. I am grateful that he doesn't do scatology and indeed has forborne from forcing any of his excretions on us. Or even, come to think of it, his erections – unlike Terence Koh, who under the mentorship of Charles Saatchi, stuck huge erect phalluses on Jesus and the Virgin Mary, who at the time, if I remember correctly, were in a urinal.

'To give Hirst his due, if he has a penchant for polymorphous perversity, he's keeping it to himself. Unlike other d'Offay artists, like Gilbert and George.'

'I've heard of them,' said Briggs. 'Jason was recommending me to buy some of their stuff.'

'What's in their room?' asked Anastasia.

'Rubbish by two narcissistic weirdos who do photos and montages about themselves. As the great art critic Brian Sewell – who has resisted the barbarians – put it about Gilbert and George, "these names alone are enough to make the heart of the sane man sink". However, Tat disagrees. In its view, they have sacrificed their individual identities to art and thus turned the traditional notion of creativity on its head. So at the expense of the taxpayer we look at their images of fellatio, using improbably large organs of even more improbable colours. Such works, according to Tat, demonstrate their transgression and vulnerability.'

Pringle was becoming hysterical. 'But they do. They do.'

'In my view,' said the baroness, 'the pair should be taken at their own early estimation. As far as I could see, their only worthwhile work in Tat was a photograph of them with cut-out letters pinned to their chests which read "George the Cunt" and "Gilbert the Shit".'

Pringle moaned.

'To move on to the Hirst room. Apart from his rare moment of originality in having that snap taken in a morgue, everything else d'Offay had bought from him was all the old dreary derivative stuff: dead sheep, spots, skulls, pharmaceutical aids. Oh, and butterflies. Another idea pinched from someone else.'

'How can you say that?' said Marilyn. 'I bought plenty of them and I was told they were original.' She shot at Herblock what the baroness thought might be a glare.

He patted her hand. 'Original in the sense that he brought his own genius to bear on the insect, hon.'

'That mountebank – though, I admit, talented mountebank – Salvador Dali was painting butterflies many years ago,' said the baroness. 'Hirst merely produced labour-saving versions by buying job lots of real butterflies and letting them loose in a gallery or sticking them onto painted surfaces. Someone should have set the anti-cruelty people on him. Then an American artist called Precious started using the wings of real butterflies to create the effect of stained-glass windows. Ten years later, Hirst – or rather his assistants – started doing exactly the same. However, death is a big feature of the Hirst brand, and d'Offay wanted a work made specially for him, hence these unfortunate insects randomly stuck on a painting are called *Monument to the Living and the Dead.*'

'You don't get it,' shouted Pringle. 'You just don't get it. These butterflies are a metaphor for mortality. Hirst's work is about life and death: it is relevant to us all.' Then, remembering where he was, he shivered.

'Artists have always been preoccupied with life and death,' the baroness said evenly. 'It is not an original notion. We can meditate on it without having to have this sort of crap all round us to remind us. A few words would do it. May I refer you to the Book of Common Prayer: "In the midst of life we are in death." She looked about her and saw that she had made a tactical error: everyone was now silent and reflective. 'Oh, lord,' she said to herself. 'We're all depressed now. It's the drug wearing off.' Like an old warhorse, she stirred herself. 'But here again,' she cried, 'useless though he is, Hirst is to be preferred to Andy Warhol. Now if there was ever a charlatan who robbed the rich just for the hell of it, it was that preening, narcissistic, self-absorbed old queen who had one good idea and flogged it to death cynically.' She saw Fortune stirring into angry life and settled back to up the ante.

It was after two a.m. when the three friends got back to the flat. 'I know we're exhausted,' said Mary Lou, 'but we've got to get our story straight for Ellis. I've already lied that I had to stay over because Rachel and I had so much work to do on my school presentation. Now let's perfect the next lie.'

Rachel gave her a sympathetic squeeze. 'It's simple enough, isn't it? We've been up late talking about Jack and wondering if there was anything useful we might have forgotten. And Robert just remembered the Albanians.'

'You call him, Mary Lou, and then you can put me on.'

She pulled her phone out of her bag. 'I hate doing this. I absolutely hate it. Ellis and I have never had to lie to each other.'

Amiss gave her a hug. 'I know, but we have to protect him and this is the only way. I'll go on lying about not having heard from Myles. You have to lie about tonight. And at least we're telling him something useful.' He laughed bleakly. 'Late in the day.'

Rachel glared at him. 'Robert, you are not to beat yourself up because you didn't think of the bloody Albanians earlier. It took three hours intense questioning for it to surface.'

'And Ellis couldn't have done what Mike did,' said Mary Lou. 'He's obviously been at this for years. I feel sucked dry.'

Rachel gave Mary Lou another squeeze. 'Robert and I will go to bed now and leave you to ring Ellis. Try not to feel bad. You're doing this for Jack.'

Milton had taken pity on Morrison and Byrne and given them a night off. They wouldn't have found the next *hommage* anyway, since it was much further down the Thames than their beat. Placed outside the O2 arena in Canary Wharf, at a cursory glance, it looked like a statue, so no one noticed it until about four a.m., when a security man having a quick cigarette spotted the notice. 'It's another of those *hommages*,' he told the police. It says "*Hommage* to Koons. Jason and Bubbles". I don't know if it's a novelty statue or they're dead people. The small fat one's sitting on the tall thin one's lap and they're wearing golden suits, golden wigs, and their faces are pasty but their lips are red. The small one's even got a little golden beard. I tell you, I've seen some strange things in my time, but this isn't something you'd want to see before breakfast.'

Having kissed Rachel goodbye and cleared the breakfast dishes, Amiss went out to the newsagents and bought all the papers. 'You interested in these 'omidge murders?' said the newsagent.

Amiss nodded. 'It's because I write crime novels,' he said. 'We have to keep an eye on real-life murders.'

'That was weird, putting that woman in that glass box like that bloke Damien Hirst put that shark. Who do you think's behind it, then?'

'No idea. Some lunatic.'

'If you ask me it's an art-lover,' said the newsagent, guffawing. 'Someone making one of those artistic statements of the obvious. Like that modern art's all baloney.'

'Maybe.'

'Mark my words, there'll be more. You've got a serial killer here. He's going to knock off all those people he kidnapped, one by one.'

'I hope you're wrong.' Amiss smiled wanly and went home.

The security man had always longed for his fifteen minutes of fame, preferably accompanied by riches, and to that end he had melted into the background once the police arrived and had called his favourite tabloid to offer an exclusive. So it was that Amiss knew there were two more *hommage* murders before Pooley had even had time to ring him. Amiss had promised to waken Mary Lou at nine. It was only a quarter past eight, but he roused her anyway, told her there were things to discuss that wouldn't wait, and had coffee and toast ready for when she joined him five minutes later.

Her reaction to the news of the double murder verged briefly on the hysterical. 'Oh, Robert,' she sobbed. 'We're going to be too late. You know we are. There just isn't time to find her. And if he's now killing them in pairs, even if she lasts till the end, there are only two days to go. What are we going to do?'

'There's only one thing we can do, Mary Lou. Or, rather, one thing you can do.'

When she realised that Fortune and Pringle were both missing, the baroness had also had difficulty in staying calm. First up, she retreated into the bathroom. She went over and over what she'd said when required the night before to say who was worst. She'd definitely gone for Fortune, but she might have said something disparaging about Pringle too. 'No, no,' she told herself as she climbed out of the shower. 'It was because they were a couple. And a couple of gays at that, which of course always offended that homophobic shit. So maybe it won't apply to Chester and Marilyn.' She allowed herself to wonder if they'd be better off going on strike and daring him to send in the Albanians. Wouldn't a quick death be for the best? And then she thought of Anastasia gamely trying to be cheerful and suppressed the thought. Maybe even now Milton and Pooley had located the prison and were at the head of a task force of armed cops, all ready to take on Sarkovsky's revolutionary guard.

The image didn't give her much comfort. Whatever way she imagined it, a lot of people were likely to end up dead. And she couldn't see how the six remaining prisoners would be exceptions. Still, her job was to rally them. Before, no doubt, having to pick yet another fight.

She dried herself, put on her soiled pink shell suit, and went out to try to convince five terrified people that their fears were exaggerated.

The Commissioner was back and beside himself with frustration. 'My God,' he screamed at the Assistant Commissioner. 'What took you so long? We should have been in there tearing Sarkovsky's life apart two days ago. I want every member of Murder Squad on this job right now. And I want all our Armed Response Units and Firearms Officers ready to go at a moment's notice.

Where's Milton?'

'Interviewing Sarkovsky's accountant to see if he might know anything about any other properties the guy owns in London. But since he could have bought them through a foreign company, it won't be straightforward. We'll have to give it time.'

The Commissioner, who had always hated and despised the Assistant Commissioner as a lazy, incompetent, buck-passing dipstick who'd only got his promotion because he was a genius box-ticker, thought of beating him to a pulp but then remembered he was a policeman and head of the Met. He clasped his hands very tightly together. 'Just get out and get on with following my instructions, Pilsworth. Now! And tell Milton to get back here as soon as possible and come to see me immediately.'

His phone rang. 'Yes, yes, yes. I'll call the Home Secretary now.'

Chapter Twelve

Pringle and Fortune had neither siblings nor living parents and with the media in full cry, a swift identification was necessary, so rather than put Allegra through it, Pooley sent for Thomas, the porter from Pringle's apartment block. 'It's not that I mind dead bodies,' he said as Pooley escorted him to the morgue. 'What with being in the St John's Ambulance and all that I'm well used to it. But I don't like my routine being disturbed.'

'It won't take long, I promise. We'll have you back at work very soon.'

The sheets were whipped off and Thomas gazed with interest at what was revealed. 'It's Mr Pringle and Sir Henry all right,' he said, 'but I never saw them wearing make-up before. Or wigs. Or gold suits. Or sitting on each other's laps.'

Being a man who liked to follow a thought all the way through, he added, 'Or dead, for that matter.'

'There's no evidence of any prisoners any-where on his properties, Ellis. His domestic staff think he's still abroad. He was always very secretive about his arrangements. The warrant for his arrest has just come through so I've put out a press statement saying we urgently want him to help with our enquiries and that all information on his whereabouts would be welcome. That stupid bastard Pilsworth. We're too damn late with this.' Milton ran his hands through his hair.

'I didn't have time to tell you earlier, Jim, but we've got another lead. Robert and Rachel and Mary Lou were together last night and while talking everything over,

Robert remembered a throwaway line of Jack's about Sarkovsky employing Albanians. Apparently he and Jack were talking about the characteristics of various peoples of the old Soviet Union and Sarkovsky said Ukrainian security guards were so useless he'd replaced his with Albanians. And that reminded Mary Lou that in some recent rant of Jack's she'd speculated on how long it would be before the art establishment would embrace snuff performance art. Her example was an Albanian sticking a screwdriver through his victim's cranium. I've checked this out and apparently it's their signature form of murder.'

'And?'

'And yes, Special Branch are chasing their Albanian contacts as we speak. And they're liaising with the security services too and will have the surveillance underway asap.'

Milton sighed the relieved sigh of a man who never failed to appreciate his luck in having a colleague he could rely on. From bitter experience he had developed the theory that in any institutional hierarchy you were doing well if two out of three in the line of command were competent. Just once in his career both his immediate superior and subordinate had been excellent at their jobs.

It was a halcyon period when no time was wasted on trying to motivate the lazy, clear up after others' mistakes or – as now with AC

Pilsworth – wheedle the blindly stubborn into doing the obvious. Pending trays were cleared and moribund cases reopened. He had time for a life outside work and his marriage flourished. In his self-pitying moments, he could measure the later slow decline in his relationship with Ann by remembering a series of colleagues whose general uselessness caused him to have to work early and late.

'Thanks, Ellis. Call me when the pathologist is ready for us.'

'I rang Mike as per your instructions,' said Mary Lou, 'and I told him everything Ellis has told me about what the Yard are doing.'

'Well done. I know how difficult this is for you.'

'I never thought I'd end up playing Mata-bloody-Hari to my own husband. But I know I've no choice.'

'What did Mike say?'

'That Myles is back, that they're all working flat out and that if they get any kind of decent lead they'll be ready to move. I hope that means what it sounds as if it means.'

'I'd have more faith in the effectiveness of Myles and his superannuated comrades than in the pride of the armed wing of Scotland Yard these days. Between the press and the human rights lawyers, the poor bastards are terrified of making a mistake.'

'I don't know what to think,' said Mary

Lou. 'I've a day of ghastly meetings and the phone will be silent, but it'll be on and I'll keep checking for texts. What are you going to do?'

'For now, I suppose I'll keep reading the fucking papers and hoping for a miracle.'

'This is a weird one,' said the pathologist. 'Not that the others weren't weird too. They were smothered and then put into position on a slab until rigor mortis set in and they could be moved. It must have been hard work to keep them from slumping over during the first few hours.'

'I think our murderer probably isn't short of help,' said Pooley.

'And there's a really peculiar thing about them. There are traces of paint on the thin one's penis and the fat one's stomach. I can't think of a rational explanation for that unless it's a sexual perversion. But from my cursory look, they haven't been having sex.' He paused and thought. 'Well, penetrative sex.' He shook his head. 'Sometimes I think it's time for me to retire, Ellis. It was bad enough when it was ferrets up the bum and then when strangling yourself for kicks became all the rage, but every week there seems to some new sexual perversion. This is a young man's game.' He shook his head gloomily. 'What's been going on here any-way? Who are they supposed to be?'

'It's a pastiche of Jeff Koons's sculpture of Michael Jackson and his chimpanzee Bubbles,' said Pooley. 'The original was made out of porcelain. These two were intimate friends, and the thin one used to call the fat one Bubbles.'

'Blimey, Ellis. You've got a right one there and no mistake. Murderers aren't usually so imaginative. Any guesses as to what he's likely to do next? Or where?'

As Pooley shook his head, the pathologist laughed. 'Do you know what all this reminds me of? Those painted elephants that were all over London a couple of years ago. There were hundreds of those. It's a good thing for you this guy only kidnapped ten.'

News of the Koons *hommage* caused an uproar in the European and American press. While the general public didn't much care about art, they loved imaginative murders and the connection with Michael Jackson was a gift for the chroniclers of celebrity as well as the culture brigade. Amiss tried to keep his brain from exploding by reading obituaries of Hortense Wilde, which mostly listed impenetrable titles of obviously dreadful essays buried in journals no normal person had ever heard of. Almost all had been written by her cultural tribe.

Hortense was agreed to have been a cutting-edge influence in 1973 in achieving acclaim for radical artist Mary Kelly when she displayed her son's dirty nappies in the London Institute of Contemporary Arts. For this, she had been ridiculed by reactionaries. There were those, however, who felt that much more important was the erudition as a cultural analyst that she had brought to the demolition of false gods who had been worshipped just because they could paint. Without theory, as she had explained to generations of students, there could be no understanding of art. Indeed, nothing qualified as a work of art unless it could be interpreted as such by esteemed cultural commentators.

Accused of helping foment hostility towards cultural achievement, Hortense had countered that since art was a cultural construct, no one could measure cultural achievement unless it was firmly rooted in cultural theory and had cognisance of it. Among those wrongly thought to have been persons of some cultural achievement, it turned out, were pretty well every male artist who had ever painted a woman (sexist), or anything foreign (colonialist). Indeed any Western male artist who had ever painted anything was off bounds, owing to being a masculinist, and if they made any money, a capitalist. Hortense Wilde, thought Amiss, was clearly even more of a pill than he had realised, since what was bad she automatically called good and what was good she called bad. But that didn't mean she deserved to be murdered.

Having wrung all they could out of relatives and friends of Thorogood and Hortense, broadcasters were in seventh heaven at having those of Fortune and Pringle to go after. Having concluded quickly that voices from the art establishment lamenting the deaths of luminaries and the wickedness of subverting art to murder were becoming a bit old hat, they went after Thomas, the porter, as well as Allegra and Serafina, who were still doggedly running the Pringle gallery. Having been besieged by the press for some days, the women had become veterans. Together they fashioned a few sound bites mourning the loss to them and to art of their wonderful boss and his inspirational partner and delivered them soulfully on request to microphone and cameras and down telephones.

'Don't you wish we could say what we really thought of them, Ally?' asked Serafina of Allegra.

'It'd get us a global reputation in no time, Fina, but I guess it'd put us in the shit in the job market. Tell you what, let's just get through today, and tonight we'll buy some fizz and go to my place and get completely hammered.'

Fortune's heir was Pringle and Pringle was

Fortune's, which initially made it difficult to get permission to investigate their finances, but they turned out to share an accountant who after Pooley's strong-arming decided to be helpful. 'Fortune's affairs were pretty straightforward,' he said. 'He had a substantial income, generous expenses and earned quite a bit on the side. It was different with Pringle. He made some very lucrative deals in the second half of the noughties, but invested most of his profits in shares that have dropped way down since then. The gallery's ticking over, but only just. Then there was a big sale recently that's ended up with his lawyers. He got the money, spent it, and then couldn't deliver what he'd sold. You'll need to talk to his lawyers to get more information.'

'I don't think it matters for now to find out any more about the victims, sir,' said Milton to the Assistant Commissioner. 'We can, I think, guarantee that they have all annoyed Sarkovsky one way or another. May I suggest that we concentrate resources on finding him?'

'Robert. It's Myles.'

'Thank God you're back.'

'Hope to Christ I'm not too late. Now, there's bad news. Mike's followed up the tip about the Albanians and it's not good, I'm afraid. The cops will get nowhere with the Zekas. They're very very bad people.'

'Who the hell are the Zekas?'

'Albanian über-thugs. They've been providing security for Sarkovsky for some time. If he's keeping these people hostage and killing them, the Zekas are right for the job.'

Amiss despairingly leant his head on his hands and inadvertently his elbow on Plutarch's tail. The result, as he complained later to Rachel, was the transformation of his desk into Armageddon. It was a testimony to his concern for the baroness that he barely noticed the upended desk lamp, the water spewing from the knocked-over glass, and the hundreds of pages of typescript kicked into confusion on the floor. 'Sorry, Myles. I was interrupted. Tell me more.'

'They're a dreadful family, even by Albanian standards. Albanians don't do gangs. If they did, we might get somewhere taking out the main guy and turning over the others. But they do families. They're not like the Mafia. They don't do godfathers. They're more democratic. And they don't talk or betray each other. To neutralise them we'd have to take them all out. Except for the women and children. But frankly, they're such a big family, we wouldn't know where to start.'

Amiss's liberal conscience suggested protesting. He killed it. 'Why are they so dreadful?'

'Robert, in London, the Albanian thugs are the worst. As an Albanian friend remarked to me, it's that the competition is so weak. Well, when you consider that in London we've got Triads, Somalis, Islamists, IRA throwbacks and dozens of others groups of reprobates, that means trouble. Among Albanian gangsters, the Zekas are the tops.'

'And not at market gardening, I assume.'

'No. More at torture and murder to order.'

Amiss tried to keep his voice steady. 'So what's the strategy?'

'We know who they are. We know where some of them live. We're keeping an eye to see who might turn up at their mothers'. But we also know they're randy, drunken, and girl-traffickers, so that gives us another line of enquiry.'

'Why both of them, Big Brother?'

'You say two together. Anyway, I plan execute together.'

'Because...?'

'Because they cheats and liars and homosexualists and frauds and bastards and Pringle dirty Jew.'

'Did they get a lot of money off you?' asked the baroness, trying to sound as if the conversation were normal.

'Not beeg money. It same conspiracy with Thorogood about Banksy. They think they can make Oleg Sarkovsky appeer stupid. But Pringle do bad things with Briggs additionally.'

'Like what?'

'Bidding when I bidding so I pay too beeg money. Dirty crook bastard Pringle secret talking with people and getting commissions.'

'Briggs wasn't trying to cheat you, though.'

'He plot with Pringle. He laugh behind my back. I say you, nobody make Oleg Sarkovsky appeeer stupid man.'

'What about Anastasia?'

'Pringle try trick me about her. He say me she next beeg one, but she crap rubbish con trick.'

'She's just a girl trying to earn a living, surely. She wasn't trying to trick you.'

'Hah! She same all this crap rubbish artists. They all trying cheat rich people. She example, same like Pringle for dealers, Fortune for curators, and stupid bitch whore Wilde for art history person.'

'And Truss?'

'You say me all crap begeeen with teacher. He teach students all crap good enough. He example of big rubbish teacher. All trick people.'

The baroness thought of capitalising on his unusual loquacity by asking what she had done to deserve a sentence of execution, but she knew the answer already. 'So what did you do with Henry and Jason?'

He sniggered the snigger that so grated now on the baroness that she had to exert all her willpower not to flinch. 'Joke execute. Clever. I curate. *Hommage* Jeff Koons Jackson and Bubbles.'

'That wasn't my idea,' said the baroness.

'No. My idea. I clever man. Now, you got idea make me laugh today or maybe I execute all now.'

'For today's game,' said the baroness, 'we are to divide up into three teams and sculpt each other.'

'But we can't sculpt,' said Marilyn.

'This is indeed true,' said the baroness. 'For a group of people with a keen interest in art – and many of whom make a good living out of it – we are singularly short of any ability to produce anything I would call art, even if many of you might say otherwise. However, nonetheless, Big Brother wants us to have a go.'

'Are we to sculpt the head or whole body?' asked Briggs.

'The whole body.' She paused.

'Don't tell me,' said Anastasia. 'In the nuddy.'

'Oh, no. Not again. I won't do it,' said Marilyn. 'Not again.'

'Food?' said the baroness. 'If just one of us doesn't obey, there'll be no food.'

'I don't care,' she said. 'There are worse things than going hungry.'

'Or drink.'

She wilted. 'Oh, all right. In what medium are we to sculpt?'

'Play-Doh.'

'What is Play-Doh?' asked Chester Herblock.

'It's squidgy stuff kids use to make shapes with,' said Anastasia. 'It's good because it's easy to clear up afterwards. I've often helped my little sister make things with it.'

'Indignity piled upon indignity,' said Herblock. 'I need a drink.'

'So do we all,' said the baroness. 'Get a few bottles out, Charlie.'

Naked, they clustered around the vast bucket and each plucked out one of the balls of pastel and began moulding it. 'What size are these sculptures supposed to be?' asked Truss. 'We'd need a few tons of it to do life-size.'

'The idea is to do miniatures,' said the baroness. 'But Big Brother wants us to do the full body.'

'Don't know that that's possible,' said Marilyn. 'The weight of the head will squash the body unless it's fat.'

'So it would work for me,' said the baroness, 'but not for you. Let's think laterally, though. We can make the bits separately and put them together lying on their backs on the floor.'

Anastasia was generous with advice, and the group soon got the knack of squeezing the compound into shape and began to develop a sense of achievement. Watching her work on a likeness of the baroness's head, they managed with their own tasks to make a shot even at eyes, noses, and mouths. From time to time, someone refilled glasses, and, gradually, there was even the occasional drunken giggle. Briggs made a commendable attempt with long yellow slivers of dough to give his bust of Anastasia long blonde locks. The baroness attempted to adorn Truss's face with a halo of black curls. After a couple of hours, they had six reasonably complete small pink corpses stretched out on the floor. Remarking that they might be able to flog the results when they got out, the baroness licensed everyone to wash and dress.

Peace reigned even through lunch, during which the baroness assured them once again that Big Brother was a guy with a great sense of humour who was probably having a laugh with the evictees. Anastasia was equally bullish. Everyone drank a lot except for the baroness, who was awaiting the moment to foment yet another argument.

Amiss was watching a scrum of photographers snapping Anastasia Holliday's parents, who had just come off the plane from Sydney. Having been pursued to the airport by a press posse, they had been greeted at Heathrow by another shrieking the news that two more of the missing had been found dead. Having been given the details, they were asked to describe their feelings.

'How do you think we're feeling, you dip-sticks?' shouted Ben Holliday. 'Our only daughter's missing and your police are as useless as tits on a bull.' As he grabbed his wife's hand and began to plough through the crowd, Mary Lou rang Amiss.

'Ellis just called and I managed to keep him long enough on the phone demanding news of progress to find out that a Special Branch informant in an Albanian-owned brothel reported that some guy called Akim, one of the owners – who is also one of her regulars – was very keyed up on Tuesday night.'

'The night Jake Thorogood was killed?'

'Yep. She was surprised that he was sober, because he almost never is, but he explained that he couldn't drink because he had a very important mission. And she knows he works for a Russian, because when he's drunk he curses Russians. Apparently he didn't stick around long, looked at his watch about ten and rushed off and into his BMW.'

'He didn't say where the brothel was?'

'Just that it was north. And then he had to hang up.'

'Well done. I'll call Mike now.'

'Oh, for God's sake,' shouted Gavin Truss, 'you'll be telling us next that nothing in Tate

Modern is art.'

'Most of what goes on in that repugnant edifice of brutalist architecture too damn right isn't art,' said the baroness. 'Tat Modern is full of tat and is crammed to the gills with the effluence of so-called artists who couldn't draw or paint to save their stupid lives. And any good stuff they've got is doled out grudgingly and rarely.'

'It's the most successful art gallery in Europe. I suppose that counts for nothing?'

'Compare like with like. It's a bloody fairground, not an art gallery. I bet it doesn't have more visitors than the Paris Disney.'

'How can you justify that, you awful person?' shouted Truss. 'What do you mean fairground?'

'Take the Tat's turbine hall. All five stories and forty thousand square feet of it. Now Serota's empire includes vast storehouses full of great art that the public doesn't get to see. You might think he'd be glad to fill this huge space with enormous pictures and grand sculpture. At least occasionally. Henry Moore could cut a dash here. But our friend Sclerota, as I like to call him, commissions installations specifically geared to the hall and otherwise leaves it barren.'

Marilyn was looking worried. 'What do you think, hon?' she asked Herblock. 'Maybe Jack has a point. It's a big space. Maybe it should be filled with something.'

'You might be right, hon. The longer I'm in here looking at flies and dead cows, the more I begin to think we haven't been giving Michelangelo enough respect.'

'You may,' said Truss grudgingly, 'have a point about empty spaces, Jack. I have my differences with Nick. I find him rather un-imaginative. But surely even you can rejoice in the magnificence of Weiwei's majestic installation.'

'I'm lost,' said Anastasia.

'Weiwei's main claim to fame is that the Chinese government persecutes him,' said the baroness. 'Gives him no end of cachet.'

'I think she's actually evil,' whispered Truss to Herblock, who shrugged.

'Oh, I've heard of him,' said Anastasia. 'He did something with sunflower seeds, didn't he?'

The baroness began to laugh. 'That was funny.'

'Him being persecuted by his government was funny?' asked Charlie Briggs, whose brow was furrowed.

'No, no. Him being persecuted by Health and Safety.'

Anastasia was puzzled. 'What? I thought he got banged up in China.'

'Our Health and Safety, Anastasia. They're world class. You see Weiwei produced for the Tat hall an enormous field made of a hun-dred million sunflower seeds. Except they weren't sunflower seeds but porcelain replicas, individually made and hand-painted over a couple of years by sixteen hundred workers in Jingdezhen, which of course you'll undoubtedly know has been the ceramic capital of China for almost two millennia. I think it was supposed to remind us that many poor bastards had nothing else to eat during the Cultural Revolution. No wonder his government isn't pleased with him.

'Having cottoned on to the fact that what visitors to Tat Modern are mostly looking for is a funfair, Weiwei essentially turned a huge part of the hall into a kind of playpen. The visitors played with the seeds as they might with sand, ran them through their fingers, danced on them and rolled in them.'

'Sounds like fun.'

'It was, rather. Whether it was art was another matter, but fun it undoubtedly was. I would quite have liked a bit of a roll among the seeds myself for nostalgic reasons, but I never got the chance. It took only a couple of days for the puritans to strike. Within forty-eight hours, the installation had been roped off and the public ordered to keep outside a barrier lest dust inhalation damage their lungs.'

Anastasia ruminated. 'What happened to the seeds after the exhibition closed?'

'Last I heard they were sold off at Sotheby's about a quarter-ton at a time. The first lot, I seem to remember, went for something like £3.50 a seed. Weiwei won't starve. Mind you, Sclerota's made off with the bulk of it for Tat at God-knows-who's expense. You can look at it, but you still won't be allowed to touch.'

'You are an absolutely appalling woman,' said Truss, his every word dripping loathing. 'What about Louise Bourgeois, if you've heard of her. Would you describe her work as fit for a funfair?'

'Some of it certainly is. Funfairs love freaks.' She turned to Anastasia. 'Bourgeois deserves a bit of respect. She showed an enormous steel-and-marble spider in that hall a few years ago. It was a tribute to her mother, if I remember rightly. I don't know if they got on. Sadly, the public weren't allowed to climb up and down it.

'I admit she has some skill. Amazing that Sclerota let her into the building if you think about it.' She grunted. 'The Belgian who installed huge steel circular tubes for the punters to slide down was more his sort of thing. And someone called Doris from Columbia who beats up furniture and chucks chairs around for a living. Her contribution to the gaiety of nations was to create a five-hundred-foot crack across the hall. Apparently it was about racism and colonialism. It cost about £300K and almost fell victim to the health and safety police because kids tried to jump into it.'

'Why not just turn the hall into a permanent fairground?' asked Anastasia. 'Take away the health and safety people and have daredevil attractions like a speeded-up merry-go-round or dodgems without brakes. Performance art and all that. People like me could do turns.'

She caught sight of Truss's expression. 'Just a thought,' she said, and poured out some more wine.

'Laidee Troutbeck to Diary Room.'

As the baroness reluctantly got to her feet, she tried to summon up a little gratitude that this time, at least, it wouldn't be difficult to choose.

Chapter Thirteen

To Milton's intense frustration, no one had got anywhere in the questioning of any Zekas and no one admitted to knowing anything about the whereabouts of Akim although there were suggestions he might have gone back to Kosovo for a holiday. Worse still, Akim hadn't visited Edona on Tuesday or Wednesday night. She reported on Friday that he'd called to order her to be ready and energetic about four o'clock on Saturday morning, which boded very ill.

The Commissioner chaired the meeting with Special Branch and the Firearms Unit as they all tried to work out what to do. AC Pilsworth's suggestion that Akim Zeka be arrested and held for questioning when he arrived at the brothel was greeted with incredulity. 'You've heard what they're like,' said the head of Special Branch. 'He won't talk. It's a matter of pride. We could hold him for days and get nothing out of him. Our only chance is to follow him back to his HQ, hope the prisoners are there, and try to get them out alive.'

'If any of them are still alive,' said Milton. 'Sarkovsky knows we're after him and he must want to cut his losses and get out of the country. In fact I can't think what's kept him so long.'

There was a long and worried discussion about the difficulty of trailing Zeka from the brothel without being spotted, while having a Firearms Unit ready to roll into wherever he led them. One decision everyone agreed on was that since Fortune and Pringle had been left beside the 02, there was now no point in keeping covert surveillance on the galleries.

Martin Conroy didn't pay much attention to the news, and he didn't care about the art world, but he was sorry that Jack Troutbeck was in trouble. He'd enjoyed the rousing speech she'd given a few years previously at an SAS reunion and had heard vaguely that she was close to Myles Cavendish, under whom he'd served in Iraq. Still, he was a man who concentrated on the work in hand and avoided all distractions, so it wasn't until he got home mid-evening that he looked at the news and saw that the police were looking for Oleg Sarkovsky in connection with the *hommage* murders.

By instinct and by training, Conroy avoided impulsiveness, so rather than immediately ringing the police, he gave himself a couple of minutes to think. Then he looked up his private book of phone numbers and called Cavendish. After their conversation, Cavendish immediately called Mike Rogers and gave him the address. 'I told him not to tell the cops. This is no time to piss about. There's no way the cops could get into that house without Sarkovsky knowing, and if Sarkovsky knows, he'll kill her and the rest of them. We've got to get in there now and without him knowing. I've texted the others with the code.'

'OK. I'll be on my way there in ten.'

Rogers dressed in his discreet combat gear, loaded his boot with a small arsenal and went ahead to suss out the house Conroy had identified. Within a few minutes of locating it, he had parked, put on a balaclava, selected a gun and a sharp knife and had slipped onto the site. He was in his element doing the job that for over thirty years – in the army and working privately – had given him his greatest thrills.

As he circled cautiously around the bank of portacabins, he was almost caught by the lights of the truck that came out of a garage at the back and drew up a couple of feet from him, but he slunk into the shadows just in time behind a half-built wall. And so it was that he had an excellent view of six large men coming out of a doorway carrying between them what looked like a cross and a corpse. When the truck and the van had driven away he made a call to Cavendish.

Followed by a nondescript white van, the brown flatbed truck festooned with the livery of Westminster Council drove from Cockspur Street into Trafalgar Square, took an abrupt left, drove past the fountain and parked beside the empty plinth in front of the National Gallery. It was a cold night with a slight drizzle, so there were no loving couples sitting on the steps or by the fountains. There were taxis going past, the odd bus and a few pedestrians, but, apart from the inebriates who were trying to decide where to go next, people were mostly rushing home.

Two men dressed in oil skins with 'Westminster Council' in large letters got out of the truck and were joined by four more from the van. They hauled grey barriers from the back of the truck and put them all around the plinth, blocking all access. They then took out a ladder and extended it until it reached over twenty feet to the top. Three of them climbed up.

A passer-by became curious enough to come down the stairs and lean over a barrier. 'What are you doing?' he called to the nearest workman.

'We're putting up a sculpture on the plinth for the opening tomorrow.'

'What's it like?'

'Ugly,' said the foreman. 'Black ugly thing.'

The passer-by shook his head. 'Bloody modern art,' he said, and wandered off.

It took them the best part of an hour to hoist the iron structure from the truck on to the plinth and secure it safely. Getting the corpse out of the van and up there was simple by comparison. Although Sarkovsky had protested, it had been decided that a crucifixion was one complication too many, so they just tied the limbs to the cross securely, lowered the winch, retrieved the ladders and barriers and got back in the vehicles. They had just driven out of the square when Vernon Morrison and Sarah Byrne entered it from the Strand.

Morrison was even more fed up than usual. 'I tell you, Sarah, I don't know why we put up with this. What good are we doin' walkin' around and round in the rain only gettin' our death of cold? More and more I begin to think I'll have to pack this job in. It's all right for all those wankers sitting comfy in their offices orderin' us about. And now they're talkin' of fitness tests. Fitness tests? What the fuck? At my age am I supposed to be brawn or brain?'

'I thought we did something useful with those drunks in Charing Cross Station, Vernon. Defused a potentially bad situation, don't you think?'

'You may think so. I still think we should have arrested them.' He looked at his watch. 'We could go back to the station now.'

'Let's just give it another five minutes, Vernon. We're supposed to go round the square. Let's just do that. With everyone in a state at the moment, we don't want to give Sarge any excuse to bawl us out.' Grumbling, he acquiesced. They walked past St Martin's in the Fields with only the briefest of comments from Morrison about how the bloody vicar let down the neighbourhood by running a doss house, then crossed the street to the pedestrianised area. As they walked past the National Gallery, Byrne looked to her left. 'What's that, Vernon. On that plinth?'

'What do you think? Another statue of some military nob. Like on the other plinths.'

'Yes, but there isn't supposed to be anything there. It's the fourth plinth that has different sculptures at different times.

279

Didn't you see they've decided to put something cheerful up for the Olympics? A kid on a rocking horse, I read. This one looks more like the black sculptures on those other plinths that are supposed to be old-fashioned.'

They crossed over. 'This is something horrible, Vernon. I can't see what it is properly, but it looks to me like a man in uniform on a cross.'

'Are you saying it could be another hommidge?'

'I am.'

'Oh, Gawd. What have we done to deserve this?'

Morrison went on grumbling as Bryan pressed the red button on her radio. Inwardly, however, he was thinking that he'd had another bit of luck. Reinforcements would be here in a minute, and once he was sure it was another hommidge and enough cops were on the spot so no one could finger him, he could find a minute to phone that helpful journalist. Hadn't she told him to call her anytime he had any information? He went down the steps to find a suitable place and saw the big white label saying: 'NAZI JESUS – HOMMAGE TO THE CHAPMANS'.

The four Zekas in the van were in high spirits on the way back to north London. None of

280

them had been enjoying this job much because they hated being stuck in the bunker. Akim had told them that the boss had had big plans for it. The room the prisoners spent the day in was to have been a great ballroom. He'd had the staircase down to it decorated the way he liked so as to give the prisoners a good impression before landing them in the horror room. Everyone thought it funny when they saw how shocked they all were when they saw that.

But for weeks now the Zekas had been fed up and uncomfortable in what was no better than a building site and they were overjoyed to think they'd soon be released. They didn't get the point of all the work that had gone into constructing peculiar decorations from pictures, but they didn't care. If the boss wanted them to furnish rooms with disgusting things, or prepare strange deaths for people, that was OK with them. Better than ditch-digging, as Akim constantly reminded them. They had a couple of craftsmen among them who got a kick out of it and fortunately Diran had an artistic streak so painting corpses wasn't a problem.

Having to spend hours listening to and watching the prisoners had bored them senseless except for the good moments when that blonde was skipping around with no clothes on. The optimists among them hoped they might have a chance to screw her before they topped her, and Akim had promised that if there was time they could all have a go. There had been debate as to whether anyone fancied doing it to the old women, and a few had said they wouldn't mind.

They hadn't been allowed out at all – except to strew corpses around London – and they resented it that Akim always got to go to the shop and the takeaways and that he'd even been allowed a visit to the brothel when their needs were just as great. But Akim was Akim, and they did what he told them.

The Zekas didn't like the boss. Apart from a couple of newcomers, the Zekas mostly had excellent English, but the boss was crap. Those who had done a bit of security work for him over a couple of years in London said he was OK most of the time, but that when he got angry he was a maniac and he got angry if you misunderstood an order and said you were stupid even though it was him that couldn't learn the language.

The boss hadn't left the bunker since the kidnappings began. He stayed in his room a lot of the time, he talked to the fat woman sometimes, he spent hours in the room with the screens watching the prisoners – even when they were just talking – but it was the Zekas who had to watch all round the clock in case anyone tried to escape and they had to shoot them.

And then there had been all those strange

killings. The Zekas didn't have a problem with killing: it was part of their stock-in-trade. But all this business with balloons and tanks and funny clothes was not what they were used to. And, indeed, being Muslim, they worried in case their mothers found out about the crucifix and thought touching it haram. The boss was a bit of a pervert, they'd concluded, and while they'd nothing against perverts if they paid for their perversions, what he made them do was hard work. That last carry-on shaving that little guy and blacking him up had been almost as creepy as the business the night before with the two queers. And although they were hazy about their history and weren't quite sure what the Zeka position was on the Second World War, they thought it weird to be dressing up a corpse as a Nazi.

Zekas were proud professionals and none of them would let down the family, so they accepted the risks of the job, but none of them wanted to end up dead or in jail, so they were very happy to have been promised that it would be all over by the middle of the morning and they could go back home with money for all the raki and girls they could consume.

Akim's phone rang as they passed Regent's Park. 'Yes, boss ... yes, yes, all OK. We'll be back soon... What... Why... Straightaway?... Oh, OK... OK... OK.' He hung up, furious that he would not be enjoying Edona this night, and called his brother, who was driving the van. 'OK, Diran, change of plan. Boss wants to leave the country this morning so we've got to kill the others when we get back.' He brushed aside the grumbles about overwork and tiredness. 'It's easy. Won't take us long. First we lock the bedroom, then we open box, collect prisoners from the bedroom, put them in the chairs and slit their throats. Close box again. Put on label saying "*Last Orders*". Easy.'

'Ugh! Flies. Horrible.'

'We have protective headgear. We'll be fine.'

'Will there be time for rape?'

'I'll have to check with the boss about timing. But maybe with a bit of luck.'

'Do we all leave when they're in the case?'

'Boss wants an hour to watch flies get to work. Then we can leave and take him to plane. We must stay with him in case of nosey cops. When he's gone we'll sleep, and then tonight we'll all have a big party with the girls.' Diran grunted unenthusiastically. 'Tell you what. We'll have fireworks too. Tell them.'

The contingent in the van initially reacted as Diran had, but soon he could reassure Akim that the promises had made everyone happy. Akim thought of calling Edona to tell her not to stay up for him, but then he decided not to bother. Waiting and fucking, that's what prostitutes were for. Treat them too well and they might forget their place.

Not only did Amiss know he wouldn't be able to sleep: he knew there wasn't any point in even trying. And anyway he didn't want to. He had persuaded Rachel to go to bed, promising to wake her immediately if there was any news. Mary Lou rang about eleven to report that what sounded like half the Metropolitan police force would be spread around north London in the early hours following an Albanian from a brothel. When she had told Mike Rogers he had thanked her monosyllabically. 'Do you think Myles and his guys have anything up their sleeves, Robert?'

'I can't think what they'd have, Mary Lou, but I won't be surprised if they come up with something.'

'I'm so confused. I think my husband's wonderful, I have great admiration for Jim, but I really haven't got much faith in the police. That asshole Pilsworth just set up obstacle after obstacle after stupid obstacle. Oh, hell. One way or the other, Ellis is going to be out all night, probably chasing shadows.'

It took only a minute to persuade her to pack her toothbrush and come over. For the next few hours they watched news channels, which offered interviews with distraught people from the art world and so-called experts droning on about kidnappings and hostage-releases they had known. From time to time Amiss took stock on his computer and tried to make Mary Lou laugh by reading out particularly ludicrous extracts from appreciations of Fortune and Pringle. Now that he was dead, and was no longer a competitor, European curators had queued up to be interviewed about the breadth and depth of Fortune's cosmopolitanism. He was a curator who refused to be bound by national or cultural barriers. There was, apparently, nothing Little Englandish about Henry Fortune – unlike, they were implying, his London-based equivalents.

'Heaven forfend that at a time when Jack Troutbeck is in mortal danger I should say anything good about Sir Nicholas Serota,' said Mary Lou. 'But when I listen to these patronising tossers implying that what happens on the Continent trumps what happens in London, I want to confront them with the simple fact that even if the contemporary art here is crap, at least people are trying to do something. The French don't even bother any more. They just live off the past. Like the Italians.'

And so, with periodic lapses into invective, nostalgia or frightened speculation, the two friends whiled the hours away.

Now happy about another successful foray

and the promise of celebration to come, and geared up to murder five people who would not pose a problem, the four Zekas were quite cheery as they were deposited at the entrance to the basement. Not until the key had turned in the lock and the burglar alarm been disabled did four men in balaclavas emerge from the shadows, stick knives in the backs of their necks and push them through the door. They were joined in short order by Akim and Diran, both with knives pressing on their necks. Four other men with covered faces stood watching from the sidelines, and a small man stepped forward and asked: 'Who's the leader?'

No one said anything.

'Tell us, or we'll kill one of you at random,' he said. 'And we mean it. We are SAS.'

Five Zekas looked imploringly at Akim, who stepped forward. 'OK. I'm leader.'

'That's good to know. Now, this is what I want you to do.' Cavendish beckoned to Rogers, who showed his machine gun. 'You see, we're not just SAS, Mr Zeka. These people are our family, Mr Zeka. We feel about them as you do about yours. Now listen to me, tell me what I want to know and do what I say, or you'll all be dead. And you won't die slowly.'

Milton and Pooley were so occupied with last-minute details for what was informally known as 'Brothel Watch' that they didn't have time even to take five minutes out to leave the Yard to look at the fourth plinth. What mattered to them but what they didn't admit except to each other – was that the corpse was male. Both of them were tormented by the fear that now Sarkovsky knew the police were after him, he might stop dragging out the killings and see everyone off at once. All they had was the brothel tip, so they were giving it everything they had.

They were furious, though, when it hit the wires that there was another *hommage* murder and that, amazingly, the corpse was displayed right in the centre of London, less than a mile from the mighty Scotland Yard. Even at that time of the morning, there were angry commentators complaining that there should have been surveillance on such an obvious target as the plinth and the National Gallery. The police remained tight-lipped about what they had removed from the plinth, but Morrison's leak got the media going on the Chapman Brothers and their *Fucking Hell* exhibition about Jesus and Nazis.

The Cavendish crew, as they liked to describe themselves, had an unexpectedly easy time. Akim Zeka was no quitter, but he was a realist, and he could see no way out. If these guys were family, they were serious.

They had already shown that they knew what they were doing, and he knew from the way the little guy talked that he wasn't bullshitting.

Akim didn't enjoy the idea of ending up in jail, but he even less wanted to be dead and even less than that did he want his mother cursing him because he'd left her short of a couple of sons and several nephews. The British were mad, so even if they had to go to prison, they'd be out in ten or fifteen years. Edona would be past it then, but there would be others.

'OK,' he said. 'What do you want?'

Half an hour later, a small man opened the door of the Emin bedroom, switched on the light, went over to a snoring, smelly figure, shook her and whispered, 'Ida.' The baroness woke instantly and put her arms around him. 'Ssssh, Ida. Come outside.'

He helped her out and hugged her.

'I knew you'd get here in time, Myles. I didn't know how. But I knew you would.'

'Gavin Truss is gone too, but the rest of you are safe.'

'Are the evictees dead?'

''Fraid so. Now I have to go, Jack.'

'Go? What do you mean, go?'

'I just wanted to tell you you're all safe and the police will be along shortly when we tip them off. But we need to get away. You don't

289

want me to land in jail, do you?'

'Sarkovsky?' asked the baroness.

'You sound nervous.'

'Nervous? Yes, for once, I admit to being nervous.'

'He's dead.'

'The Albanians?'

'Securely locked up. Now you need to go back to bed and stay there until the cops arrive. Then you act surprised. I'll be disappearing again for a while but I'll be in touch when I can. And, of course, you won't mention you've seen me.'

The baroness gave the only real laugh of the week. 'As if I would, Myles. As if I would.'

Mary Lou fell on her phone so enthusiastically that she pressed the red button by mistake, but before she could cry with frustration, Pooley rang again. The call was short and Mary Lou almost collapsed after it. 'She's definitely alive,' she told Amiss, as she began to cry. 'He's seen her. The police got an anonymous tip-off to search the basement of a huge house in Hampstead, they found the door open, five survivors, several Albanians bound, gagged, and locked in, and a dead Sarkovsky.'

'And no superannuated SAS people?'

'Certainly not. Why should there be any?'

'Jack has always instructed me to be an

optimist,' said Amiss. 'That's why I keep champagne in the fridge. Open it and I'll wake Rachel.'

Chapter Fourteen

It was a week after the rescue and Pooley and Mary Lou were at home having their first evening alone since the baroness had first disappeared. 'I'm only just grasping that it's all over,' she said. 'I feel almost normal. And I can't wait to see her tomorrow night. It's a pity you can't be there.'

'I'd love to be at her dinner, darling, but she'll understand why Jim and I should stay away from her for the moment until it's all blown over. She's still being papped wherever she goes and there are a lot of unanswered questions we don't want anyone to ask us.'

'She understands, hon. I'll be going in and out the back door of ffeatherstonehaugh's so it'll only be Robert and Rachel they'll be able to photograph.'

'Myles?'

'Yes. You know Robert wasn't able to reach him until after the whole drama was over but he finally got back from Iraq this morning.'

Pooley leant across the debris of the celebratory dinner Mary Lou had ordered in and took her hand. 'You remember we always agreed to have no secrets from each other?'

'I do.'

'So I should confess that I checked the texts on your phone and found one that was incriminating.'

'What did it say?'

'"She's OK".'

'That was it? Doesn't sound very incriminating to me.'

'It was sent about five minutes before we had the tip-off about where to find them.'

'Did you check the number?'

'No. I deleted it. Besides, I'm sure that number is no longer obtainable.'

'Are you asking any questions?'

'I'm not. I've been able to tell my superiors that I know nothing about who the rescuers were. I'd like to keep it that way. We made a balls of the entire investigation and some mysterious people didn't. I just wanted you and Robert to know that I'm not a mug. And that I understand why and what I don't know. In fact, to misquote Donald Rumsfeld, you might say it's a known unknown.'

'What happened to my correct policeman?'

'Even correct policemen have feelings and understand moral dilemmas.' He leant over and kissed her.

Even by her standards, the baroness was dressed exotically. Her crimson silk robe had a deep purple lining and after she had greeted Amiss and Rachel she turned around and displayed the large yellow dragon climbing up her back. 'After wearing a stinking shell suit for what seemed like years, I had to get something to obliterate the memory,' she told them, as she waved them to seats between Cavendish and Mary Lou, handed them glasses and settled in the empty chair between them.

'To the Marines,' she said. 'And to those who sent for them.'

'Keep it discreet, Ida.'

'That's why I got a private room, Myles. I promise to be careful when the waiters are here.'

'I genuinely have only just arrived here from Iraq,' he said. 'I've been in and out illicitly, so my passport shows I've been there all along. Now what's been happening?'

'The Albanians have all pleaded guilty but presumably their lawyers will come up with mitigating circumstances,' said Mary Lou. 'Anyway, with Sarkovsky dead, it's pretty well all over. No one has a clue who were the mysterious rescuers who got there before the police and never took their balaclavas off. And no one's mentioned you.'

'And Sarkovsky?' asked Cavendish. 'How do they think he died?'

'Looks as if he blew his brains out, Myles,' said the baroness.

'That's the view of the pathologist, Ellis tells me,' said Mary Lou.

'That seems satisfactory, then,' said Cavendish. 'From what I've heard, the chap was in a tight spot. He probably felt he had no option.'

'Though of course there is a school of thought in the liberal press that thinks he was a victim of some rogue paramilitary outfit.'

The baroness snorted. 'You mean the human rights lawyers are looking to get in on the game?'

Mary Lou smiled seraphically. 'Maybe if Sarkovsky had anyone that cared about him there might have been a case to pursue, but no one does. He was effectively bankrupt, his ex-wives hated him and his children are indifferent.'

'Was he really bankrupt?' asked Rachel. 'Wasn't he supposed to be taking off for South America? Presumably he had plenty of money there.'

'I have a friend who works in Inland Revenue,' said Cavendish. 'He tells me that it's fruitless trying to track down money in South America. Now tell me, what's happened to your other companions in tribulation?'

'Anastasia's gone back to Australia with her parents, taking Charlie with her. Since they got out, they've had a torrid week in the Dorchester, since Charlie decided it was time he spent his money in a way he would enjoy. As Anastasia confided to me, even in the depths of the chamber of horrors, she quite fancied the idea of him putting his roaring roger into her laughing tackle.'

She took another draught. 'I do like Anastasia. Anyway, Charlie's resigned from his job, asked his sister to sell his art collection and is going to give some months to thinking what to do with himself. She's doing the same. After all, she explained, when you've come within a bee's todger of death, it changes your outlook. Her parents are ranchers: she thinks maybe that's the way to go. She's decided he needs taking in hand and she should probably marry him though she hasn't told him yet. But I'm proud to say that I'm to be Matron of Honour.'

'So the experience has been good for them,' said Amiss.

'Indeed. Even if it wasn't much good for the rest of us, particularly the dead ones. I doubt if the lives of Marilyn and Chester will be drastically altered. They know only one world. Although I doubt if Marilyn will ever again put money into conceptual art. She is, however, I'm pleased to say, giving a considerable gift to St Martha's.'

'Because?'

'Because a kindly policeman called Ellis Pooley mentioned that an Albanian had said they'd all have been dead three days earlier if it hadn't been that the fat woman made Sarkovsky want to watch them play games and have arguments.'

'You mean you weren't to be knocked off night after night?'

'Apparently not. He had a grand plan for emulating Anthony Gormley by having figures appear all over London on the same day. But then my suggestion of games got the better of him.'

'What do you mean figures all over London? Weren't the last of you to be seen off in that fly box?'

'That was a last-minute substitution. The head Albanian said he had planned some sort of porn Koons death for Anastasia and Charlie. I was to be the *pièce de résistance*. Hirst's golden bull. In a glass tank, on all fours with a gilded head, hands, and feet.'

'And Marilyn and Chester?'

'History doesn't record.'

The door opened, and the head waiter arrived. 'Lady Troutbeck,' he said. 'I just want you to know that the staff of ffeatherstonehaugh's are all delighted that you are safe and well.'

The baroness stood up and bowed. 'Thank you, Vittorio. I appreciate that sentiment. And I'm sure they have outdone themselves to ensure that we have a good dinner tonight.'

'Thank God it's Friday,' said Rachel, as she finished the fifth course and the sixth glass of wine and leant back exhausted in her chair.

'Of course you're the only one among us who keeps regular hours,' said the baroness. 'Good. Now you'll be able to drink some port.'

'First,' said Amiss, 'I want to propose another toast with whatever you have in your glasses. To Rachel and Mary Lou, for triumphing over the forces of educational darkness yesterday!'

Mary Lou's visit to Rachel's school had been an uproarious success. The murders had coincidentally put art so centre stage that the entire school attended her presentation. According to Rachel's account, Mary Lou had excelled herself. She had shown them conceptual art from every angle and persuaded them to laugh at it. She had shown them slides of the Sistine Chapel and told them of Michelangelo's struggles with the sheer physical challenges. She fascinated them with several Rembrandt self-portraits along with stories of some of the tribulations he faced in his private life and enchanted them with his *Lion Resting*. Along with some Van Goghs, she told them of how his mental problems brought about suffering and finally his suicide. She told them simply the story of Icarus, showed them Breugel's *Landscape with the Fall of Icarus* and read them Auden's poem.

Then she spoke about home-grown genius, told them of Stubbs's anatomical dissections and how they had enabled him to produce *Whistlejacket*, and of Turner's life of experimentation with illustrating such intangibles as weather and light. *The Fighting Temeraire* elicited oooohs and aaahs and led her into talking of the Turner Prize with a few choice specimens of winning entries that got them all scoffing.

Finally, she told them the story of the emperor's new clothes and told them that grown-ups and clever people could be very silly and that they should trust their own judgement. 'And the result,' said Rachel, 'was a demand from the kids to be taken to see what they called "real" paintings and a promise from their now very own celeb that she'd go with them. The head and several of the teachers were furious, but they've had to cave in.'

When the acclamation had died down, and to the baroness's delight everyone was drinking port, Rachel asked her question. 'There's something really bugging me, Jack. I looked up the most famous names that have come up in all these discussions, and far too many of them are Jewish for my comfort. I had a look at the *ArtReview* Power 100, and it's laden with Jewish curators and dealers and critics and collectors. It's only the artists who are mostly gentiles.'

'Good grief,' said Amiss. 'You didn't tell me this. It's another international Jewish conspiracy.'

'I know we get blamed for everything from the killing of Jesus to the collapse of the financial markets,' said Rachel. 'And I'm inured to that. But is conceptual art really our fault?'

'Stuff and nonsense,' said the baroness. 'You're being wet, Rachel. You know perfectly well Jews are smart, disputatious, and free-thinkers, and what with being persecuted everywhere they go for those reasons, their skills tend towards the portable. Like ideas and finance and the arts.'

'I know. But then I looked up even more and found the Frankfurt school that started all this cultural relativist nonsense was dominated by them.'

'Look here, Rachel. It's called swings and roundabouts. You buggers are obsessed with education and art, you never stop thinking and arguing and sometimes you get it wrong but mostly you give us great scientists and musicians and thinkers that have a dis-proportionate effect on business and finance because you're so bloody brilliant.

'Although I think the Irish are up there with you when it comes to being good company – and, unlike you, they understand the attraction of alcohol – you are the most entertaining, funniest, warmest and stimulating crew on earth.'

Rachel opened her mouth and the baroness waved at her dismissively.

'There are downsides, of course. You also produce innumerable clever sillies, like Marx and Freud and Trotsky and, indeed, Serota. Israel fights for its life as much with loud-voiced enemies within as with Jew-haters outside. And because most people are less clever, less successful, less perverse and less open to new ideas than you lot are, that gets you hated, especially by poor bastards stuck in the intellectual rigidity of radical Islam.

'There has to be someone to blame for everything. It's your people's burden. Live with it, stamp on your tribal propensity for angst and guilt, however much you might revel in it. And for Christ's sake, lighten up.'

She had another sip of port and looked straight at Rachel.

'Your choice, Rachel. Do you want to follow this perverse tribal trail in a dreary neurotic search for reasons to beat yourself up, or might you just exult in being alive?'

No one said anything.

'Have I made myself clear?' asked the baroness.

Rachel looked back at her and laughed. 'Abundantly clear, Jack. It's good to have you back.'

Acknowledgements

I've been researching this for years and longing to write it, but other projects and life got in the way.

I owe many many thanks to a large number of friends and acquaintances who've variously visited art exhibitions with me, talked and laughed and expostulated with me about conceptual art, listened to my rants and given me helpful suggestions. I have to single out Colm de Barra, Lizzie Bawdon, Rob Bryant, Tony Cahill, Stephen Cang, Mary Devine, Emily Dyer, Barbara Sweetman FitzGerald, Elizabeth Gibbons, Imogen Hartmann, Jo Henderson, Lucinda Hodge, David Martin Jones, Kathryn Kennison, John Lippitt, Jason McCue, James McGuire, Janet McIver, Sean O'Callaghan, Robert Salisbury, Alec Swanson and David Stuart Taylor, but there were several others.

My beloved Carol Scott, who has been my minder for twenty-one years, was as wonderful as ever. Jane Conway-Gordon (who has the misfortune to be my close friend as well as agent) got me going, talked and visited art with me, gave excellent strategic advice on the first draft and performed the delicate calculation of knowing when to kick me and when to empathise. Nina Clarke, as ever, was the great encourager and made valuable comments on the manuscript, as did my brother Owen, generous, as always, with his time and his prodigious knowledge.

I feel real gratitude to those of my readers who kept nagging me to get writing fiction again, particularly the ever-supportive Richard Reynolds of Heffers. At Allison & Busby, Susie Dunlop and Chiara Priorelli embraced a controversial subject with relish.

I read many books and much journalism relating to the madder aspects of the art world. I owe most to Roger Kimball's *The Rape of the Masters* (which also provided the epigraph), Don Thompson's *The $12 Million Stuffed Shark: The Curious Economics of Contemporary Art and Auction Houses*, Sarah Thornton's *Seven Days in the Art World*, to the Stuckist website (*www.stuckism.com*), and to the art criticism of Brian Sewell, who so often seemed to be the only sane person in the lunatic asylum that is the world of contemporary art.

The publishers hope that this book has given you enjoyable reading. Large Print Books are especially designed to be as easy to see and hold as possible. If you wish a complete list of our books please ask at your local library or write directly to:

Magna Large Print Books
Magna House, Long Preston,
Skipton, North Yorkshire.
BD23 4ND

This Large Print Book, for people
who cannot read normal print,
is published under the auspices of

THE ULVERSCROFT FOUNDATION

... we hope you have enjoyed this book.
Please think for a moment about those
who have worse eyesight than you ...
and are unable to even read or enjoy
Large Print without great difficulty.

You can help them by sending a
donation, large or small, to:

**The Ulverscroft Foundation,
1, The Green, Bradgate Road,
Anstey, Leicestershire, LE7 7FU,
England.**
or request a copy of our brochure for
more details.

The Foundation will use all donations
to assist those people who are visually
impaired and need special attention
with medical research, diagnosis
and treatment.

Thank you very much for your help.